scott wellinger

the bestselling author of *Sinn* and **CRASH**

Ebb

a warren dennihan novel

Ebb

A Warren Dennihan Novel

by scott wellinger

For information, address: World Wide Publishing Group.

Printed in the United States of America

10 9 8 7 6 5 4 3 2 1

ISBN: 978-0-9899421-9-5

For SM

The true beauty of Boston

PROLOGUE

RONDO CLEARLY DIDN'T KNOW WHAT to make of his newfound freedom. The early morning walk through Stage Fort Park was normal, but the release from his leash was not. The pull of the collar followed by the release of the clasp was almost too much to wish for. He gave his master a look as if asking if he was dreaming. He wouldn't offer a chance to reconsider. The chocolate lab took off for his adventure, running at full sprint to take full advantage of the many things he had so longed to do every previous day.

The rocks. The ocean. The trees and shrubs that had withstood countless years of saltwater and harsh coastal winds. The smells of late April, the last week of the month in fact. The smells of other dogs that had been to the park before him on their leashes, as per the rules. The scent of the owners that had tethered them. He proudly scouted the state park, smelling and searching. Rondo would mark new territory on this day. His brethren could eat their collective heart out.

Ebb

Ivan Kadishev was feeling good on this particular morning. The tall Eastern European was in rare form. His usual bleak outlook on life, his innate pessimism, had taken the rare day off. He and his companion would do their morning constitutional a bit differently on this morning. Ivan would manage the rocky, sandless beach at his own pace — free of the pulls and tugs from Rondo. Free to think about things other than the possibility of turning an ankle.

The two had lived in Massachusetts together for as long as Rondo had been alive, just over four years. Ivan had lived elsewhere, alone in a new land for two years before their friendship began. Every morning for the past four years they took their walk on the uneven coastal terrain, along the cliffs above the jagged shoreline. Every morning an adherence to the well-posted rules regarding dogs and leashes. Rules shouldn't be broken by those who are not citizens in the strictest sense, for that was an easy way to draw unwanted attention. But that status had now changed. He and his furry friend could now both bask in true freedom.

Nobody was around anyway. The park was always abandoned at that early hour, not even the sun had risen from the wavy horizon at that time some months during the year. But that too was different on this day. While still brisk, the new sun was up and heating both the air and the ocean. The Atlantic never gets warm, rarely above sixty degrees north of Cape Cod, though the local TV weather hottie had said that it was currently the warmest in history. Probably due to global warming or climate change or whatever the media was calling it these days. Another topic that would normally have festered in Ivan's mind, adding to his usual attitude of doom and gloom.

Nobody swam from this shore at any hour, warm or not. The water deep, the current always strong against the high rocks. The undercurrents almost ensured drowning. Never a lifeguard on duty. The danger obvious even to those without the quickest of whits.

A splash could be heard from a distance over the sound of the lapping waves against the rocky shore. Rondo would not only get a rare run, it became apparent to Ivan that his dog was also in the mood for swim. He paddled his way out to sea. Toward what, only the canine knew. Probably a stick, Ivan thought. Maybe toward nothing in particular. Rondo would now need a bath, he also thought. Maybe this was not such a good idea. He also wondered how his furry friend was planning to climb back up onto shore when he was finished with his swim. It was a question the lab had undoubtedly not thought of. That was what masters were for he supposed, to manage such details.

Ebb

Ivan methodically moved toward the water, negotiating rocks while facilitating his balance by grabbing a hold of tree branches and roots. He needed to bring his dog back in, never feeling that too much freedom was possible until that moment. His usual pessimism was inching back into the forefront of his thoughts. Rondo was ruining what could have been a great start to the day.

"Rondo. Come back here," Ivan called. His accent thick. But there was no response. No bark. No whimper. Kadishev followed up with a loud whistle. The dog always responded to his whistles, an almost Pavlovian response. But Rondo was still at sea and all but invisible. "ебать," he cursed to himself.

Ivan moved south along the rocky shore, leash in hand, ready to haul in his normally well-behaved dog. Maybe the dog was looking for an egress, he thought. Or maybe his pet was drowning. Pessimism had fully returned.

He called and whistled several more times, without response.

Worry began to set in, until finally he heard panting off to his left. Ivan looked out toward the horizon, spotting his cheeky lab paddling toward the shore. Rondo was dragging something, huffing and puffing as he tried to breathe around the part of the large object protruding from his mouth.

"What have you found?" Ivan stared out across the waves which pushed his dog toward the shore with swiftness, along with the haul. "Big tree?"

But even as he said it, Ivan knew it wasn't a tree. The object was too pale. Too gray and fleshy. Had his dog killed a large fish? A stronger possibility, though he doubted his lab was quite that good a swimmer. As his wet friend came ever-closer, pessimistic wonder became unbridled certainty. Rondo let the catch go as he came to shore, moving to another area to extricate himself from the drink. Ivan didn't help him as he was frozen, inanimate from shock. Without a proper shore, the catch was pushed by the waves and beaten against the rocks below Ivan's perch. Kadishev's long wingspan was just short of being able to reach down and pull it up, had he had the strength or wherewithal to do so.

Rondo had somehow made it up onto shore further down the coast, panting as he came running back to his master, as if proud of his handiwork. The wet dog shook off as much excess water as he could before looking over the ledge with Ivan.

The milky-white and gray body was floating face down in the wash, slamming against the rocks with each tide like a bag of bones. Each thrust of the water a new assault on the person three feet below. There was no way the person was alive. If the person had been alive prior to Rondo's beach drag, the battering had completed the task of ending life.

Had the macabre discovery taken place earlier in the week, there would have been no choice for Ivan. He would have simply taken his dog out of the park and hoped against all hope that he would escape unnoticed. He would have found a new place for their daily constitutional. But it hadn't. It happened in the last week of April on a monday. A great way to start said week.

Ivan Kadishev had taken an oath, made a commitment to his countrymen. He swore to 'bear true faith and allegiance' to them, even when fallen he presumed. Doing nothing was not an option, so in that way there was also no choice. He had nothing to fear in reporting it; after all, he was innocent. He had not been responsible for the death of this person, surely the authorities would know that. But was his dog responsible? Had Rondo found the body or aided in its destruction?

He decided to reattach the leash before making the call to find out. He removed his phone from his pocket, staring at the touchscreen. How would he explain the dog being off of the leash? How severe was that crime? Would reporting one crime forgive another?

Ebb

He second-guessed his thought.   Maybe he shouldn't make the call.

Part One

The Head and the Heart

April

1

THE 2013 CHEVY IMPALA slowly made its way through the parking area of Stage Fort Park in Gloucester, Massachusetts toward the tumult of vehicles and personnel. The ashen gray-metallic sedan sparkled in the hot sun, the stone and gravel crackled and popped under the tires as they rolled over them, eventually coming to a stop. Though the vehicle was unmarked, anyone with a lick of sense knew it was a Massachusetts State Police car. What was less obvious was that it was from Troop H out of Boston, a major crimes unit.

In Massachusetts, the State Police handle all major crimes along with traffic on the interstate highway system. Although Gloucester was outside of Boston and Suffolk County, Troop H was the closest precinct and therefore assigned to the case.

Two detectives exited the vehicle, the male from the driver side, the female from the passenger as any chauvinist would expect. They made their way over the uneven terrain, over the grass and rock, toward the gaggle of local police and personnel from the Crime Scene Unit. A perimeter had been cordoned off, various workers positioned both in and outside the yellow police tape.

"I'm Detective Sergeant Hobbs, this is Detective Sheed," the male said to the first of the uniformed officers they came upon. They both had their badges exposed in the event that there would be a need for validation. There wasn't one. "Who's in charge here?"

"I guess you are now," the uniform said. "The ME took control of the scene until you guys got here. He's been chomping at the bit for a couple of hours waiting for you." The officer nodded, pointing his chin toward the shore.

"We ran into traffic and we weren't at the House yet. Which examiner?"

"I think he said his name was Bowman. He's down on the ledge, they just hoisted the vic out of the soup."

"Thanks," Hobbs said.   Sheed took in the surroundings, no need to speak as she was not called upon to do so.   They finished the short walk down toward the water in silence; the Medical Examiner, Mark Bowman, spotted them and impatiently awaited their arrival.

"Where the hell have you two been?   I got the call at a little after six," he said.   "It's quarter to nine. Don't tell me you hit *that* much morning traffic."

Again, Hobbs took the lead.   "We were both still in bed when we got the call."

"Together?"

"Go fuck yourself, Bowman," Sheed said.

"No need to get hostile."

"Nobody's laughing.   Even Rick's wife doesn't want to sleep with him," she said.

"Very funny.   Both of you.   So what do we got here, Mark?"

"Floater."   He pointed back up the hill toward the vehicles.   "Guy walking his dog, dog hauls in the body.   Female, probably early to mid-twenties judging by the bone structure."

"Drowned?"   Hobbs hadn't pulled out his notepad, he let his junior female partner take the minutes of the meeting.   Bowman led them over to the body-bag.

Ebb

"Too early to tell. Bruising on the back of the head, but that's normal for drowned victims. Buffeting in the water commonly produces post-mortem head trauma, so it could have happened before, during, or after." Bowman unzipped the bag. "Facial bruising is normal for all corpses also."

The milky-white body was bloated and the skin bubbled like that of lepers. One eye was cloudy while the other was missing. There were holes in the body from where oceanic parasites had hosted on it. Both detectives cringed, despite having each seen an unfortunately high number of dead bodies. Sheed smelled the inside of her right wrist where a bracelet would be, smelling her perfume instead of the aroma of ocean and decomposing corpse. Hobbs was close to retirement, Sheed a seasoned veteran. Both found the scene greatly repugnant.

"Ah, Jesus. How long has it been in the water?"

"It's a she, Hobbs. Not an it. And I can't tell you that yet. This one is going to be tough. As you can see, I don't have much left to work with."

"Hedging your bets already?"

"No, Rick. Crabs and small fish and what-not have been at her. When a dead body is left to decompose in the water, especially salt water, the microbes and bacteria don't break the flesh down as they would on dry land. It's called brining, and if the water temp is under seventy degrees, the body forms a thick, soapy substance which we call 'grave wax'. It preserves the body, but as you can see it still bloats and blisters. Water temp in this area is in the low sixties, which is the warmest since they have been keeping records on such things, but I'll still have to track Atlantic temperature fluctuations to try and determine rate of decomp. That's *if* she was bobbing around this area the entire time. She could have floated here from water that was warmer or colder. That will make T. O. D. a guess at best."

"Lovely."

"I can say that adipocere, which is the process of transforming that fatty layer beneath the skin into grave wax, takes several weeks to two months."

"What about fingerprints or dental records?"

"Are you telling me how to do my job now, Hobbs? Anserina cutis, or goose-skin, loosens and shrivels the skin. Ever been in the water too long and your fingers prune? Her entire body is like that. No fingerprints, no fingernails. If she put up a fight and had DNA under her fingernails, that evidence was taken care of by the ocean. No gums and no teeth. Between washer-woman's skin and — "

" — Hey! Easy on the macho bullshit. I deal with enough of that with Hobbs, " Sheed interjected.

"No offense intended, Lisa.   Washer-woman's skin is just what it's called. Swelling and wrinkling of the skin followed by the shedding of layers. I was just saying that it's going to be nearly impossible to tell you who she is, let alone how she died. Depending on how long she has been in the water and where she was put in, which I told you I probably won't be able to tell you with any certainty, she could have been killed prior to the water and died in the water due to vagal inhibition – "

" – She was raped?"   It was Hobbs's turn to interrupt the examiner.

"No, Rick. Vagal not vaginal. Vagal inhibition is when the heart stops from the shock of immersion in cold water. She could have drowned in the Atlantic for all I know, or hypothermia from prolonged exposure in deeper and colder water.   The one eye I do have is cloudy so I won't be able to see if there is any petechial hemorrhaging.   I will check for froth or foam in the airways or foreign material in her lungs and stomach, but unless she was drowned in the ocean I'm not likely to find anything compelling in the bronchioles and alveoli."

"She was in the water, so it makes sense that she drowned in the ocean," Hobbs said.

"I don't like to presume. She could have been killed then dumped in the ocean. Or drowned in fresh

Ebb

water then dumped in salt water. Or she might have accidentally drowned and floated away from those that were looking for her. That's what I'm saying, folks. I don't know, and from what I have to work with there is a strong possibility that I may never know. I'm just trying to prepare you ahead of time. I've been doing this for fifteen years detectives, bodies from the ocean are always the most difficult. That's why the mob used to give their victims 'concrete sneakers'. Have you ever seen the show *Dexter*? It's effective."

"So you're suggesting that this is a mob hit? She was weighed down with concrete and somehow floated to shore?"

"No, I'm not saying that at all. There are indications of ligature marks but nothing to suggest that a weight was used. What I am saying is that if one wanted to get rid of a body, the ocean has been and continues to be a way to do it with a lesser probability of getting caught because it is exponentially more difficult to run tests. Clear enough?"

Sheed spoke up as if to somehow speak for her species. Insert a ray of optimism. "A twenty-something woman missing sometime in the last two months? Somebody has to be missing her."

Hobbs was less sanguine. "How many twenty-somethings are missing in Boston alone, Sheed?

Ebb

Imagine if she floated here from someplace else? Where
ya wanna start?"

"You're the boss. But we gotta start someplace."

2

THERE ARE OVER 2300 WOMEN REPORTED
missing annually each day in the United States. They
vary in age and circumstance, but the statistical majority
of the missing women are between the ages of 18 and 40.
Larger cities account for a higher proportion for obvious
reasons. For a city like Boston, Massachusetts, a city
with roughly four million people, with sixty or so
colleges and universities, the proportions grow to an
unfortunately high number. The average comes out to
one hundred and four reported Boston area women
missing each month. Each and every year.

The two month window that the Medical
Examiner, Mark Bowman, had given the detectives

might as well have been a garage door. Two hundred and nine females had DPS-159-C forms filled out on them in that time. The Clearinghouse, the state's central repository of information on missing persons, spit out all two hundred of these names to the horror of Detective Lisa Sheed. She shook her head in disbelief as she realized the exponential pain that was caused from these two hundred and nine missing women. How many husbands, girlfriends, children, parents and relatives were hurting? How many families destroyed?

The Clearinghouse holds the name and information of all missing persons as well as those who reported them. Runaways, abductions, and parental abductions are all listed with semi-equal importance. All DPS-159-C's under the age of 15 get an automatic amber alert, receiving the highest level of importance. All under the age of 21 should be reported to the NCIC, or National Crime Information Center. The NCIC avoids the waiting period and enters the missing young adult into an interstate database. Unfortunately this doesn't happen as often as is needed. State and local authorities handle these on a case-by-case basis as adults sometimes go missing on purpose, avoiding the hassles of restraining orders or goodbyes.

More than twelve thousand names go into the Clearinghouse every year in Massachusetts. Of those, more than two thousand get cancelled because the person is found alive, or comes home of their own volition. Nineteen hundred of the remaining ten thousand plus are predominantly females over the age of eighteen. Less than one half of one percent of the nineteen hundred are found either dead or alive by police. This is why private investigators are used in many instances, sometimes consulted by the very police that are tasked to find the lost sheep. To protect and serve. If an investigator is used, the chances of finding the person goes up to twenty-five percent, albeit many are no longer alive when found.

Lisa Sheed knew all of this. She was no rookie. Only she now had to reverse engineer the situation. Normally she would get a name and description which she would use to find the person. But now she had a body, needing to match it to a name and description. It was going to be her and her alone to do this, she knew that as well.

Her partner, Rick Hobbs, was the "thinker not the doer". Only he was no brain-trust. He was overweight and lazy. A self-absorbed, know-it-all, megalomanic that Sheed had inherited in 2004. He had kept his job up to this point because of her work ethic, her close-rate. Hobbs was there to drive the car, most of the time in the wrong direction.

With two hundred nine names to go through, the one thing that she could count on was the lack of help from her partner. It would be Lisa to organize any and all interviews, follow-up on any leads. Hobbs would be in-tow of course, they were attached at the hip during all working hours. He would be virtually useless, yet take the credit for any progress in the case reported to their boss, Lieutenant Manny Titanitaukis.

Massachusetts State Police Detectives are judged on their closure rate. Period. As long as they avoid excessive abuse allegations and keep an average or better closure rate, they fly under the radar. For this reason, many detectives in Troop H would play the odds with their cases. They had no control over which cases they caught, that was done by rotation. But they could control which cases to focus on and devote the majority of their attention to. The layups were always dealt with first. Close it and move on. Get a confession or hand it to the District Attorney's office. The more cases that moved off of a detective's desk, in whatever way possible, the better.

Lisa was always determined to clear the cases she and her partner caught. Every case. But this one had become different. The names and information of over two hundred women stared back at her on her computer screen. Two hundred names, all of whom could have been the bloated and blistered body decaying off the coast of Massachusetts. All of whom demanded justice. All still waiting. Lisa Sheed couldn't solve them all, but she could solve this one. And she was determined to do so.

The call came through to Sheed's desk phone three days later, more than seventy-two hours after the body was found. Mark Bowman was calling to let her know that preliminary findings were completed on the woman floating off the coast of Gloucester. She and, to a lesser extent, her partner's presence was needed at the lab. She and Hobbs would get into the Impala from the motor pool and head across town right away. Lisa tried not to get her hopes up, but try as she might she could not help but pray that something tangible would lead them in the right direction. Any direction for that matter.

Boston autopsies are conducted in the belly of Massachusetts General Hospital, which is located on Fruit Street, across from Lederman Park along the Charles River. If you could fly there in a straight line from the Troop H precinct, the trip would take six minutes. Alas, mere mortals must drive there, fighting traffic on either Washington Street or Storrow Drive. Either was a nightmare, either would take exponentially longer than six minutes.

Mass General is a teaching hospital. Both academic and pathological autopsies are conducted at the facility as well. While the forensic autopsies have the same set-up, they are located on a different and more secure floor. For chain-of-custody reasons alone it was essential to segregate the medico-legal from the medico-academic.

Mark Bowman had expected the two detectives within the hour. An hour was reasonable. He had called Sheed in the afternoon, past the time of day for lunch hours. He was not informed that there would be a delay. In fact the opposite, Sheed had told him that they would be right over. Almost two hours after making the call, the two state police detectives pushed through the basement double doors to the morgue. Bowman was in an irritable mood prior to making the call, the lax stroll through the doors escalated him to nearly irate.

"Take your time ladies," he said. "It's not like I have other things to do today. It's almost five o'clock. I called you two hours ago. What is it with you two? You're always late."

"I'm sorry, Mark." Lisa was embarrassed, her apology contrite.

"I just found out about it, I got over here as soon as I could," Hobbs said. He always passed the buck to his junior partner. He also didn't take shit from Medical Examiners.

"Wait a sec, Rick. Don't blame your bullshit on me. I told you we were needed down here as soon as I got the call. You made every excuse in the book to stall this trip," Lisa said. She turned to the ME "I'm sorry again. I'm not going to stand here and be thrown under the bus. He always does that shit and it's not my fault."

Before Mark could comment, Hobbs spoke which cut him off. The slight further agitated Bowman. "This case is a dud and everyone knows it. We got stuck with it but we don't have to put all of our other cases on the back-burner, cases that are much more likely to get solved."

"That's a great attitude, detective. I'm sure the family of the victim will be very understanding. How do you expect to solve a case that you have given up on from the start?" The ME moved closer to Hobbs, standing almost nose to nose.

"Did you find anything that could point us in the right direction or give us a lead, Mark? Do we even know who the mourning family is?" Hobbs had his arms out, palms up while staring down the examiner. The result was a deafening silence. The tension in the lab was as thick as the smell of cleaning agents. The two men stared each other down, Bowman contemplating using one of the myriad tools at his disposal to saw up another body. The Tuffier retractor was looking like the most promising choice.

Lisa looked around the room as if she had not been there countless times. The tiled walls. The stainless steel tables with the deep utility sink at the foot of them. She had many times witnessed the carnage from the table simply sprayed into the sink and sent through the plumbing via disposal. The instruments. Each tool designed to cut, pry and lever organs out of the corpses. The fluorescent lighting at virtually every level. Beyond the working area where the three people were standing in eerie silence was a three-sided bay of body lockers. On the table in front of them, a baby-blue cloth was draped over the current victim. Sheed knew that under the cloth, the victim's entire body had been further defiled in order to determine who had done so originally. The solemnity of the situation hit her while the two men carried on.

Ebb

"Okay. That's enough boys. Zip-'em up. Measure them later. We need to get down to business, yes? Mark, what do we have? Anything good?"

Mark snapped out of his stare-off and spoke to Lisa. Only Lisa.

"Yes. Right. Detective Sheed, I have still not been able to identify the woman, exactly. I can tell you after examining her various organs that prior to whatever caused her death she was in very good health, caucasian, and in her early twenties."

"Meaning that you don't know what caused her death as of yet."

"I didn't say that, did I? I'm getting there," he said. "Her narrow hips indicate that she had not given birth up to the time of her passing and investigation into her womb confirms that she wasn't pregnant. What few hair samples we could obtain identify her as having blonde hair, naturally not chemically. Under a microscope, I analyzed the one cloudy eye that was intact — structurally I'm ninety percent certain that she had blue eyes."

"I thought eye color was caused by fluid in the eye," Lisa said more like a question.

"Neither light green nor blue pigments are present in the eye. Any eye. Ocular fluid sometimes tells us color, but more often than not it eliminates possible eye colors. If neither light green nor blue pigments are possible structurally, we know that the person had some shade of dark green or brown eyes. We don't often have the type of scenario that we do in this particular instance where we need to scientifically determine eye color. Nevertheless, I'm confident on blue," Bowman explained to Sheed. He was still ignoring Hobbs who listened to the conversation in a quiet fit of his own making.

"Blonde hair and blue eyed young woman. Somebody has to be missing her," Lisa said.

"I should think so, detective. Additionally, while the bloating and body resurfacing from adipocere made my job more difficult, I can say with a high degree of certainty that she was fit. No tattoos for help in identification either."

"Young piece of ass with no tramp stamp? Probably just narrowed the field a bit," Hobbs chimed in.

"Jesus, Rick. Can you give it a rest for a minute? Show some respect if not decency," Lisa said.

Hobbs raised his arms in surrender after making the motion like he was zipping his lip.

Bowman shook his head and continued. "When her body dried and I drained the soap-like substance from the skin that we talked about at the scene, with a process very much like liposuction by the way, I noted that her skin was taught and well cared for. Very good muscle-tone given the circumstances in which we found her. I am putting her weight at between 120 and 130 pounds. For a female of five-foot-eight, that would put her below average weight. I have a ten pound variance because her bowels had been voided, stomach empty."

"Meaning she was held in captivity and starved prior to death."

"That is a strong possibility, detective. Her lungs, specifically her bronchioles, were heavy with fresh water. So was her stomach." Mark let Sheed work through the implications of what he had just said. It took her a few seconds but she understood the meaning quicker than most.

"So she was shoved under fresh water, enough for her to swallow a great deal of it and eventually drown."

"Correct. The voided bowels confirm that she hadn't eaten prior to her torture and the fresh water likely flushed what little masticated food that was in her digestive tract, out of her. What little clothing fibers remained did contain feces. But the ad pestem, was the blow to the back of the head. The hemorrhaging in the brain and the skull fragmenting indicates it was a very hard hit. It was just under the skull so that's why I didn't see it at the scene. Also with the fresh water in her lungs; she was either knocked unconscious from the blow to the back of the head and drown in water other than the Atlantic, or she was tortured by drowning to the verge of death for some reason, then the hit eventually finished the job. In either case her brain was slowly bleeding which would have been excruciatingly painful if she was conscious."

"So the son-of-a-bitch that did this probably took his sweet time. He beat her and dumped the poor girl into the ocean," she said.

"Not necessarily in that order but yes, that is what I am writing in my report. I did find ligature marks. They indicate that she was tied up, but I can't tell you if it was prior to going into the ocean or to hold her below the surface. Either way she never stood a chance."

"So we sort of have an idea of how she died, we just don't have a clue as to who she is or who did it or when."

"And that most likely it was a man or someone who was strong enough to immobilize a healthy woman. I wish I could offer you more, but there is one more thing, Detective Sheed."

"I'm listening."

"Embedded into that soapy material just under the surface of the skin were traces of stained wood and some sort of plastic or hardened resin. From what is anyone's guess. If I h*ad* to guess, I would say it was from whatever hell this poor woman was locked into prior to her death. As always, I'll send all samples over to Maynard for testing. Once my voice recording of the autopsy is transposed I'll send it over to your desk as usual. Maybe something will turn up."

"Thanks Mark. It's a start. Sorry again for jamming you up."

"Clearly not *your* fault," he said loudly while eyeballing Hobbs who had silently taken a chair off in another corner of the lab. "Let's just hope there aren't too many missing five-foot-eight, blonde females in the Clearinghouse," he continued to Sheed.

"Cheers to that."

3

"DO YOU REALLY THINK WE'RE GONNA ID the concrete blonde?" Hobbs was still pissy from the altercation with Bowman and the general disrespect he believed he encountered as the two detectives left Mass General.

Lisa was getting into the passenger seat of the Impala. "Concrete Blonde? What are you talking about?"

"Remember at the scene? Bowman said that people who dump bodies in the ocean tie them down. Concrete sneakers. She was a blonde...."

"You should write headlines for the Globe, Rick."

"It's a gift."

"It wasn't a compliment."

They left the parking structure of the hospital, heading east on Storrow Drive toward the 93 connector. Hobbs was driving as usual.   And as usual he was driving badly.

"Where are we headed?"

"North."

"I get that, Rick. *Why* are we headed north, and specifically where?"

"I wanna have another chat with this Ivan guy. The guy who found the body."

"So you went from being uninterested and content to send this to cold cases in a few months to liking the wit for the crime? How'd you get there?"

"Now that we know a little more about the vic, we can ask better questions."

"To whom? The dog?"

"Very funny, Sheed."

"Seriously?   Who reports finding a body that nobody can identify if they were the one who did the killing? Uh….nobody, that's who."

"I believe that I am still the senior partner here."

"Key word being partner, Rick. You just make decisions for both us and expect that I'll sit by quietly."

"How do you figure?"

"You decided to stall on this. You made us look bad in front of Bowman — "

" — An ME? You're pissed because we rustled the feathers of a medical examiner?"

"It's *ruffled* the feathers, genius. Not rustled. And yes. We work with all the examiners regularly and it would be nice to treat them as colleagues rather than adversaries. Besides, it doesn't end there. What happens when you need a favor from him?"

"It's his job to help us. Those nerds work for us not the other way around," he said.

"Let's see how well that attitude works the next time you need an expedited autopsy."

"I do it all the time. I just get Tits to call over there."

"Whatever. The point is that you just decided that you want to investigate this case, and that you like the poor slob who just got his green card without even discussing it with me. What are we saying to the guy? 'Welcome to the United States. Thanks for signing the guestbook and doing things the right way. You are a good citizen for reporting a body floating in the ocean instead of ignoring it like ninety percent of the people born here would probably do. Most people would probably have kicked the victim back into the water and tried to forget about it, but not you. You did a good thing and we would like to thank you by fucking with you, possibly arresting you as a murder suspect.' Is that the gist? 'Cuz if so, you're a real class-act Rick."

"You don't think he did it?"

"You're not good at reading sarcasm are you?"

"So let's just re-interview him and eliminate him once and for all. Humor me."

"Just go easy," she said. She secretly hoped the dog would eat her partner.

This time the trip to Gloucester took only an hour. During evening rush hour. It is amazing what can be accomplished when an effort is put in, Lisa thought.

Ivan Kadishev and his dog Rondo lived in a small, white, two-story off of Essex Ave. It wasn't much, but it was well-maintained. The backyard was fenced in and Rondo was speaking to the entire world, letting whomever was listening know of the police presence. Ivan was home and expecting the visit as Hobbs had asked a runner from the precinct to call him. His name and address was on file from the initial interview conducted at the scene; but even if it wasn't, it could have been looked up from his driver's license.

Mr. Kadishev was a mechanical engineer who had just come home from his work day. It was still light out and he was likely more interested in grilling a burger and having a beer than speaking to the police.

Ebb

But he was cordial enough despite the horrible cop —
good cop routine that was being played on him.

He didn't know anything more. He had to say it
dozens of times and in dozens of different ways, but the
point finally got across. Sheed could see that Ivan had
had just about enough. They were about two steps from
being thrown out of his house by her estimation. It
probably would have happened sooner if Ivan had
realized that he had the right to. And she wouldn't have
blamed him. The guy tried to do the right thing and he
was being accused and bullied. Ivan knew most of his
rights better than most of the people that were born with
them. He asserted them often. "No, I do not own a gun,
and no you may not search my home for a non-existent
gun …. No, you may not take a DNA sample, of me or
my dog …. No, you may not fingerprint me, not unless
you have a warrant …. " It went on like that for some
time.

The interview was officially over when Rondo
was let back into the house. The chocolate lab was
excited and jumping around. He wanted to play. Have
his belly rubbed. Hobbs wasn't interested. Lisa wasn't
allowed to be.

The trip back to the precinct took forty-six
minutes. The two detectives did little more than check
their messages before calling it quits for the night. They
left the House at 9:40 PM, fortified with no more

40

information than when they left Bowman in the morgue at Mass General earlier that day.

The following day, friday, was dedicated to searching through missing persons. For Lisa that is. She worked on the computer at her desk while Hobbs worked at his, facing her on his computer. Only he was playing Candy Crush. Seniority has its privileges.

While Hobbs was content on waiting for the samples to be sent from the autopsy table in the morgue to the forensics lab in Maynard, Massachusetts; those subsequent findings to be relayed back to him when they were ready, Sheed was actively working the missing persons angle. While the facility in Maynard was incredibly thorough in testing ballistics, DNA, vehicles, and a slew of other types of forensic evidence, they were not timely. Maynard was the only such facility in the state, meaning that they had a backlog of cases. Due to issues in the past, the facility was uber-procedural. Those procedures took time. Sheed wondered at what level her senior partner would be at

Ebb

in Candy Crush by the time the results came back from Maynard.

She had narrowed the search down to 49 missing women. Age hadn't helped much. Once Blacks, Indians, Hispanics and Asians were eliminated, her list was still quite large. She couldn't rely too much on hair color. Women died their hair, usually to blonde. Presumably because they have more fun. Hair color is merely a question to be answered on the Clearinghouse survey. The person reporting the missing woman may not know her true hair color.

Weight could fluctuate as well, and often embellished. So she was left with height, and eye color. She was in the process of printing out the fifty names from their shared printer when her cell phone vibrated in her pocket.

Lisa knew who was calling, it was plain as day on her touchscreen. She also knew she couldn't take the call with her partner facing her. She walked toward the coffee machine and answered.

"Deni. To what do I owe the pleasure?" It was Warren Dennihan, a former Massachusetts State Police Detective who had gone out on his own as a Private Investigator. Lisa had been promoted to his vacant spot, with his former partner in 2004. But there were no hard feelings.

Ebb

"What's up She?" Deni never called anybody by their actual name. It was one of his many 'things'. Another one was his accent. True Boston. True South Boston to be more specific. People from *Southie* almost have their own language.

"Not much. You called me, remember? So what do you need?" She looked around the precinct to see if she was being watched or listened to. She didn't seem to be.

"Wow. Like that?"

"I'm in the middle of a case, and the only time you call is when you need to be hooked up. So what is it? Yellows? Plate number?"

"I can't just call to say hey? I thought we were friends."

"With friends like you, Deni...."

"You're a hard woman." He said 'hard' with a more emphatic *haahd* than the stereotype.

"I'm hanging up now," Lisa said.

"Okay, okay. I called to see if the swimmer is mine." *Swim-mah.*

"The swimmer?"

"Don't play me like that. I read the papers, see the news. Gloucester." *Pay-pahs. Glah-stah.* Lisa was used to it otherwise she might have needed him to repeat himself.

Ebb

"We don't know. I've got it down to fifty possibles. Who's your girl?"

"Lara Myhre. Berklee student. Been missin' a couple months. Was datin' this hockey player that I like for her disappearance but I haven't been able to crack him."

"So who are you working for? Her parents?"

"Yeah. Yuppies from Connecticut."

"Connecticut? Wow, Deni. You really get around."

"We still talkin' about jobs?"

"Very funny."

"She went to school here. Berklee. Big-time music college, you've seen pictures. Parents wanted somebody who knew Boston, so here I am."

"Well like I said, we don't know yet. We're working on it," she said.

"You mean you're working on it. Still with the fat-fuck?"

"You know it. My so-called partner is playing Candy Crush right now and he thinks that I don't know."

"Let you in on a little secret, She? He don't give a shit if you do or not. He's always been a piece of shit and at this point he ain't likely to change."

"Narcissism has a name and it's H-O-B-B-S."

"I don't know that that means but he plays games like we're all dumber than him, but you'd have to be a complete fucktard to be dumber than Ricky."

"I know right? He hates being called Ricky, by the way."

"I know. That's why I do it," Deni said.

"He hates you too. He would kill me if he knew that I talked to you."

"Now or in general."

"Pick one. Anyway, I could bash him with you all day long but I gotta stuff to do. How about you give me the parent's name and number for this Lara and I'll reach out to them."

"Nice try. I get fucked outta my money? I don't think so."

"It's always about the money with you?"

"It's not about the money," Deni said.

"I've seen you get into a cage and fight those UFC animals for money, so don't try to shine me. Or is it because you like beating on people?"

"Pick one."

"Ha-ha. Just do the right thing and give me the parents."

"Nobody does the right thing, She. I just like to get paid for it."

"How very Zen of you."

"Why don't you come give me shit in person?"

"I'm in a relationship, Deni. And you are so not my type."

"I meant meet me at her apartment."

"Who's apartment?"

"His thickness is rubbin' off on ya. Lara Myhre's apartment, who else?"

"Hobbs isn't gonna like working with you again."

"Leave him out of it. If it's not her then it's not her. We can all go back to pretending we don't exist in the same city."

"Do you think that we're gonna be able to figure out if it's her just from going to her apartment?"

"Can't hurt," Deni said.

"Give me an hour. Oh, and text me her address," she said as almost an afterthought before hanging up.

"Can't you look it up from her license?"

"Yes, Deni, of course I can. But you texting it to me will save time. Oh, that's right. You don't text. Or email. Or anything else that is convenient or from this century. Jesus how old are you?"

"It's not the years it's the mileage, doll. I'll meet ya there."

"Yeah fine. I just gotta shake Ricky."

WARREN DENNIHAN IS A COLORFUL MAN. In the literal sense and in the figurative. Literal in that his body is an inked tapestry from his collarbone to his knees with the exception of his man-parts. Figurative in that his past and present were rife with dangerous events and acquaintances. The fabric of the man was weaved together with both physical and emotional scars, not that he let many close enough to see any of them.

He had been burned out of Southie, though he was too stubborn or stupid to leave entirely. To some extent everyone in his neighborhood was being burned out. Gentrification was proving to be a problem for the group he had grown up with. Two income couples, both gay and straight, were buying up all of the three-decker homes. Rents were on the rise, forcing the natives out of South Boston. What was once a community of crooks, gangsters and those that wanted to be, had become an up-and-coming area of Boston. Some thought that was progress. Deni didn't. Those petty criminals now expanded to other neighborhoods. The police used to know where to concentrate their presence. Now, no place was safe.

Warren had rebuilt his three-decker and his reputation in the streets from whence he came. He grew up just blocks from where he was forced to rebuild and now spent some of his time. Had he not made some very important choices many years ago, he would likely still be committing crimes in and around the neighborhood. He had abandoned the thievery, B&E's and so-called friends long ago, just not the neighborhood.

Deni was accepted into the police academy because of those connections, but the agenda backfired. He used those contacts for information instead of busts, which infuriated his supervisors with the state police. The writing was on the wall and he was forced out of Troop H. In 2004, Deni ventured out on his own, initially working part-time for a fellow private investigator.

He now also owned a house in Barstone, New Hampshire, staying there whenever he worked for the attorney he had become friends with in the town of Wayland. Or when he needed the peace and quiet away from the city, which was more often than not.

The small New Hampshire legal firm in Wayland, New Hampshire, had once represented ninety percent of Deni's investigations. Now it only comprised about a third. Deni was doing well in both reputation and finances. What was once a piece-meal existence subsisting on MMA fights and whatever investigations he could get had become a career of doing what he wanted, when he wanted. At forty-one, he was getting too old for Mixed Martial Arts though he was in remarkable shape. Unless it paid well.

He drove his 2013 Range Rover HSE to the Prudential Center parking garage, which took up a square block and multiple levels underneath the skyscraper in Back Bay. Lara Myhre's apartment wasn't located in the Pru, but it was the closest and safest place to park with respect to Berklee College of Music and where the missing woman lived.

He had also had his fair-share of mishaps with street parking and understood the need to spend money for a more secure place to store his vehicles. His Grand Am and both of his former black Escalades had been damaged beyond repair or totaled parking on the streets of Boston. He had upgraded to a Mercedes AMG, given to him for services rendered in 2013. But he had traded the new car for his Rover for reasons that had nothing to do with parking. He told people that he traded it because the small luxury sport sedan was impractical. In truth it was because the car reminded him of the case in which he had earned it. The case that had ended as badly as the would-be relationship that developed during it. His new Loire-blue SUV was worth over $140,000 and street parking was no longer a desired option. Besides, Lara's white BMW 3-series was still in the monthly parking area of the underground garage.

Lara lived on Holyoke Street, near Mass Ave and Columbus. It was a nicer apartment, in a nicer area behind both the Berklee Performing Arts Center and the Prudential Tower. The walk from the garage to the apartment took Deni eleven minutes. As he made the walk he imagined Lara walking to and from her car when she needed to leave the city. Walking to school every day. Detective Lisa Sheed was leaning against a streetlamp post in front of the apartment building, waiting for Deni as he turned the corner from Carleton Street.

Deni's daily uniform consisted of jeans, a t-shirt, and a sport jacket to cover his handgun. That day's version of the uniform as he walked toward Detective Sheed was a well-worn Led Zeppelin t-shirt, his Taurus

PT1911 .45 calibre pistol bulging from a shoulder harness under his black sport-coat. His conceal and carry permit allowed him to keep the weapon on his person unless he was going into such public places like a prison or school. Since he wasn't forbidden to carry one on this particular occasion, it was nestled firmly under his armpit.

"Where have you been? I found a parking spot half a block away," Lisa said as a greeting. "And do you ever change clothes? You look like shit, what's your secret?"

"When you have a cop car, you tend to park wherever you want. I parked at the Pru, that's where her car is still parked by the way," Deni said, ignoring the jabs.

"Your missing girl didn't take her car?"

"No. Which is one of the reasons I fear the worst. She's rich but leaving a new beamer isn't something one would expect."

"She's rich or her parents are?" Lisa's head was cocked like she knew the answer despite asking the question.

"Reserve judgement for when you know what the fuck you're talkin' about, huh?"

"Fair enough. So did she have roommates or do you have a key?" She asked knowing Deni's reputation for tumblers.   There wasn't a lock built that Deni couldn't pick, and fast. Another one of this 'things'.

"It's a studio and I got a key from the parents," he said with a wink. The apartment was three floors up a narrow staircase and the building was old enough to be grandfathered out of requiring an elevator. Moving in and out of these buildings, as college students tend to do with frequency, must be a bitch.

The apartment was listed as a large studio, but nobody that had ever been inside considered it to be one. High ceilings, a large kitchen for Boston standards, an open dining and living space, and a bedroom that was larger than Lisa's.

"This is nice. Nicer than my place. How the hell does a college kid afford this in Back Bay? She really is rich," she said. The furnishings did not scream college student, nothing was past-prime or from IKEA.

"Parents are money. With her talent and looks, she is gonna be money. If we can find her, that is."

"She plays guitar huh?"   Lisa had noticed the five guitars on their stands lining the wall next to the sofa. It was difficult not to notice them. There was a Taylor Builder's Reserve VII acoustic, a white Gretsch electric, a Gibson Les Paul Standard, a Martin 12-string, and a vintage Stratocaster, each polished and gleaming even in the owner's absence. The least expensive axe in the line-up was worth nearly $5,000.

Ebb

"Yeah. Sings too. Did you see her DMV photo?"

"Very pretty. Not many people have a glam license picture."

"I saw a video with her in concert, She. With her looks and talent, she is gonna be huge. She is already makin' a name for herself on the Youtube. Nobody walks away from that."

"'*The* Youtube'? It's just Youtube."

"Whatever. Break someone else's balls."

"So you don't think she just decided to get away? You know, runaway? Get away from the pressure?"

"No. But say you're right. Why not hawk a guitar or five? Why leave the Beamer? Running away with nothing when you could have a pocket full of cash is a stretch. Plus the girl hasn't used her debit or credit cards."

"Fair enough. You said she has a college boyfriend who plays hockey?"

"Plays hockey, yeah. But they don't have NCAA sports at Berklee. Can you imagine how coordinated musicians are? The answer is they typically aren't. You follow the Bruins at all?"

"Who doesn't?"

"Gary Rennick. He gets called up and sent back down to Providence like a yo-yo. He's up right now. Has one goal so far in the playoff run."

"The name sounds familiar. Wait. *That's* your hockey player? Wow. Some girls have it all. I almost wanna find this girl just so I can hate her."

"Why the envy? I didn't even think that you dug men."

"This again, Deni?"

"Whatever. You can save the envy in any case. Rennick is a fuckin' goon. Most penalty minutes in the AHL, most fights, and he's makin' a bid for those records in the NHL even though he spends very little time in the bigs. He's a thug. Six-three, two-twenty-five."

"And you like him for her disappearance, Deni?"

"Absolutely. Just give this sitch a look, will ya. Go to Berklee with Hobbs and check out Lara Myhre. Then have a sit-down with Rennick and let me know what you think."

"Hobbs is never gonna to go for this. Especially if he knows that you turned me on to her. You are persona non grata down at Troop H, my dude. And you know it."

"I do. But you know what your Troop H told Leonard and Sorche Myhre? The parents? 'She's a college student. She missed a check-in, it happens all the time. Give it a few weeks and get back to us.' She isn't even on the Clearinghouse or the NCIC. Your friends just gave them the fuckin' runaround. These poor people have been pullin' their hair out with worry for nine weeks, She. They call every week, and every week they basically tell these poor people to fuck themselves. Just look into it, will ya?"

"I'll see what I can do."

"One more thing. Give me a ride back to the Pru."

"You're in good shape, you can walk," she said.

"Correction. I'm in excellent shape, but that's besides the point. I want you to check out her car."

"Sign of a struggle?"

"Come with me and see for yourself."

The drive two blocks up and over to the Pru took longer than if they had walked. Then as long to find the correct color code for the monthly parking area. It took a visit to the parking office on the first level to get directions to the yellow level. While in the office, Detective Sheed inquired as to the monthly rate to park in Boston's largest parking structure. $500 a month. And yes, it was paid in full and on time each month. Her hunch was confirmed. Sort of. As they reached the white Beamer, she ran the hunch by Deni.

"Her parking space is paid every month and on time. She hasn't gotten evicted from her apartment more than two months after she disappears …. someone is still paying the bills. Rennick or her parents?"

Deni had already thought about it and done the checking. "Parents. I thought the same thing. Parents are convinced that she is comin' back. And breakin' a lease in this city is expensive. Rennick pays for nothing. The same friend that I had look into her finances, looked into his. No expensive gifts that I can tell. A girl like this could have any guy she wants but she goes for a cheapskate goon."

"It's a girl thing, Deni. Eventually they outgrow it and learn to appreciate a nice guy, hopefully before a beating or a divorce."

"*They?* Are you speaking from experience?"

"You know my deal. Most men are assholes that's why I steer clear …. hey did you just break into her car?" Deni had the driver door to the BMW open, his arm open like a valet inviting her to enter the vehicle.

"Relax. Her parents gave me the key. The lease is in their name."

"What am I looking for?" Sheed made her way to the car but paused as she waited for Deni to give her some space.

"I don't want to taint your impression. Give it a once-over and tell me what you see." Deni backed away, giving her the space he sensed she needed.

Sheed knelt down just outside the car, first looking under the driver seat then at the pedals. Once she determined that those were clear, she put her knee on the driver seat and scanned the interior in its entirety.

"I assume the car is as she left it, or at least how you found it," she said out to Deni.

"Yep."

Sheed turned around and noticed a keyless fob in Deni's hand. "There's still a fob in the ignition." Another fob was in the console ready to start the car.

"Right."

"But there's no sign of a struggle, Deni. No blood. She opens the car door, puts the fob in place, maybe she starts it, maybe she doesn't but she leaves it in for some reason."

"If it's a car-jacking, she could just drive away if it's already started. Which leads me to believe that she knew whoever approached the car," Deni said.

"Mmmmm. Maybe," Lisa said. "Okay, I'll bite. She knows the person enough to have a conversation, then what? He takes her in the middle of the parking structure? With all these people around? Did you look at the CCTV footage?" She pointed toward the ceiling.

"Blind spot. Can't see a damn thing. Her parents should have gotten a reduced rate. The car wasn't secure, and it damn sure wasn't being watched. I figure if she knew the guy, she left willingly."

"But left the key in the ignition? Do BMWs even lock when it's still in the ignition? Expensive cars tend to have idiot-proofing," she said. She was shaking her head like something didn't add up.

"That's what makes it weird." *Wee-yahd.* Deni let the information sink in for a few seconds. The detective worked it through before coming to a decision. Lisa went from shaking her head to nodding.

"You've peaked my curiosity," she finally said. "Blonde, blue-eyed, and the height and weight match. Missing about the same window as our vic and her disappearance is wonky. Technically she isn't a missing person because she's not in the Clearinghouse, but I'll run it by Hobbs."

"And you'll keep me posted?"

"On the D-L, yes. But information needs to go both ways. You forget I know you."

"Yeah, yeah."

"Where are you parked?"

"In this place? Who knows?" Deni hit a button on his own keyless fob. The horn echoed from nearby, the hazards flashed and reflected off of the concrete on the ramp just fifteen yards ahead of them. "Hey, how is that for luck?"

"Irish. You have the best …. no fucking way, Deni. *That's* your ride? What did you steal it?" The

Ebb

Land Rover was still flashing. The shiny blue SUV looked almost black in the garage lighting, accented with silver gills and alloy wheels.

"Of course not. It's kinda flashy and way too many bells and whistles, but I fell in love with it as soon as I test-drove it."

"You're a big fish now, huh?"

"I work hard for it."

"Work hard you say. Seems like a man's version of working hard is having a woman do all the work."

"Easy with the feminist shit. I'm not Hobbs. I'm askin' for help, not askin' for you to do all the work."

"We'll see."

5

THAT NIGHT, BETWEEN HIS FIRST AND SECOND glass of Redbreast 12 year Irish Whiskey, Deni called Leonard and Sorche Myhre at their home in Fairfield, Connecticut. They were home, which was usual for the last nine weeks. They had rarely left home since learning of their daughter's disappearance. It was a friday night and Deni had a drink in his hand, which was also usual though he wasn't normally at home. Definitely not in South Boston.

He sat on his high-backed barstool at his bar. The bar was built between his kitchen and parlor on the first floor of his three-decker. Deni was watching his flatscreen behind the bar, which was playing the Bruins highlights on NESN. And he was getting angrier by the minute.

The Bruins were playing and losing to the rival Canadians in a best-of-seven playoff series, but that wasn't why he was upset. Gary Rennick flashed on the screen several times; a hit, then a fight, another dirty hit followed by more time in the penalty box. Finally a celebratory fist-pump and a group hug as they showed several different angles of him scoring a much-needed goal from the blue-line. He wore a smug grin with a full set of teeth as his teammates congratulated him. Fans were in the background pounding on the glass. Deni wanted to pound on Rennick.

Three fingers of the amber liquor over rocks is what it took to acquire the courage to call his clients. The phone rang, picked up after just the second ring.

"Hello?" The male voice was inquisitive yet hopeful. Deni pictured him on the other end, somewhere in his large and beautiful, ocean-front home on the Connecticut coast. His missing daughter was taking a toll on the man. The once kind eyes and gentle features were becoming hardened. He was aging in years by the day. Deni was watching the degradation occur with every meeting.

"Mr. Myhre? This is Warren Dennihan. Deni."

"Yes I see that. Your name appears on the caller ID. Do you have some news?"

"Possibly."

"What does that mean? Possibly? Deni it has been nine weeks. My wife read a statistic online that stated that if missing persons are not found within the first seventy-two hours — "

" — I'm sorry to interrupt Mr. Myhre but — "

" — Call me Leonard."

"I'm sorry to interrupt you, Leonard, but getting hung up on statistics isn't very often helpful. Especially when you get those statistics off of the damned internet. I told you when we initially spoke in your home that this could be a mercifully short process or an indefinitely long one. I know it's taken a while, and I thank you for bearing with me but I assure you that I'm doin' all I can. I'm callin' because I would like to set up a time to meet. I have some news, which may mean nothing. But it could mean something. I'm leaning toward that it could."

"Well? What is it?"

"I'd rather not say over the phone. I'd much rather do it in person. As I said, I'd like to set up a time to meet with you. I would come to you, but you should probably come to Boston."

"What is it, Deni? Just come out with it."

"There is really no good way to say it, and it might not even be accurate or applicable. So you might want to come to Boston. How is monday?"

Ebb

"*Monday?* Do you realize that it's friday night? How are we supposed to wait until monday for news about our missing daughter? Let me put you on speaker." The noise changed in Deni's ear. There was no way that the phone call was going to go smoothly, he knew that going in. That is why he needed the whiskey. At least that is what he told himself. But this was tougher in real life. Much more so than when he played it out in his head while watching the asshole who was responsible for it on the television.

"I'm here Deni. Please tell us what is going on with Lara." It was Sorche. Sorche is the Gaelic-Irish name for Sarah. Sarah means 'Pure Lady' or 'Happy' depending on the dialect and religion. Hebrew or Catholic, she did seem pure and elegant in the times that Deni had met her. Always pleasant. Always optimistic. Although she didn't sound very happy to Deni at the moment, not that he could blame her.

"There is no easy way to say this, and keep in mind that it isn't definite. I really wanted to speak to you in person — "

" — Oh my God, is she dead? Deni is she dead?" Sorche was in near hysterics. Through the tiny speaker on his phone, Deni could hear Leonard trying to console his wife. He imagined him embracing his beautiful wife in their parlor. The last nine weeks had taken a toll on her as well, as one would imagine. Their daughter was missing for more than two months and intelligent people realize the probable outcome. The Myhres were intelligent people. But the head and the heart are two very different things.

"I honestly don't know for sure. But the body of a young woman was found in the ocean up Gloucester," he said. The discovery was all over the news, whether that news had reached southern, affluent Connecticut he didn't know.

"Gloucester? That's north of Boston. Why would she be in Gloucester?" Sorche was trying to work through the denials, reasons why it couldn't be her daughter. Reasons for hope. "It might not be her. Her car is still parked in the garage, so it couldn't be her. You're just calling to let us know that it's not her, right?"

The emotion and vulnerability coming through the phone was getting to Deni. He had been called a heartless prick too many times to count. In truth, most times he had been. He tried to stay removed from emotion. He tried to just do his job and get paid, which often came off as heartless. But the middle-aged couple on the other end of the phone had pulled a chord. Deni wasn't a parent, nor could he completely understand what his clients were going through. But he felt for them just the same, even when his head told him not to. The head and the heart are two very different things.

"You're right Mrs. Myhre. It's probably not her. But just the same, maybe you will want to come to Boston? We should rule it out. I promised to keep you posted and that is what I'm doin'. We will know more by monday.   Could you meet me in the city on monday?"

"We'll be there tomorrow morning," Leonard said.   He stated it as fact.   An inarguable statement. Though Deni did try to negotiate.

"Tomorrow is saturday, so the — "

Deni realized that the phone was now dead. Negotiation over. They had hung up.

"Shit."

He immediately dialed Detective Sheed.   This was also going to be a tough conversation but for different reasons. Very different emotions.

"Deni you just left me like two hours ago," she said when she picked up the phone.   "I have nothing more to say to you at the moment."

"Did I catch you at a bad time?"

"It's friday night and I'm not on-shift, do the math."

"I'm sorry but this is kinda urgent."

"Make it quick," she said.

"I called the parents. They're kinda freakin' out and they'll be in Boston tomorrow. My guess is early morning."

"Jesus Christmas, Deni. Why would you do that?"

"I wanted to prepare them. There are more leaks in Troop H than …. uh, things that leak. I didn't want them to learn that their daughter was dead on the six o'clock news."

"You don't know that their daughter *is* dead for one hundred percent certain, you idiot. Now they're going to be all over us first thing. Hobbs isn't even on board yet."

"Well, he better get on board."

"Godammit Deni. How do I let you get me into these messes? This is going to create a shit-storm of the highest order."

"I'll call you as soon as I hear from them tomorrow."

"Yeah fine, whatever. Thanks for fucking me big-time."

"Sorry, She. I owe you one."

"I lost count at one hundred, asshole."

6

THE FIRST THING ON THE TO-DO LIST FOR Hobbs and Sheed on saturday morning was to visit Berklee. Hobbs double-parked on Boylston Street across from the Hynes Convention Center, trying to get into the Berklee College of Music Administrative Building. Since it was saturday, the building was locked and nobody opened the doors. Most calloused citizens of Boston would just as soon step on your neck as look at you; however a kind twenty-something directed them to try the building on the corner of Boylston and Mass Ave, the performing arts building.

Boston is filled with one-way streets, Boylston is one of them. They couldn't take the first left, Gloucester

Avenue, for the same reason. They took the next left on Fairfield near the marathon finish line, then the following left onto the very chic Newbury Street in order to reverse direction. The street names which alternated directions off of Boylston were in reverse alphabetical order, all the way down to the public garden and Arlington Street, though they wouldn't need to travel that far. Three blocks back and left onto Massachusetts Avenue brought them back to the Berklee Performance Center. The trip took nearly fifteen minutes even at almost nine in the morning, though they could have walked it in less than four.

Hobbs parked the unmarked Impala in the alley behind the building, where large tractor trailer trucks were being unloaded. The flashing of badges ceremony occurred; explanations from the Teamsters from the moving company informed them that they were unloading stage lighting, special effects, and sound equipment for a performance. The detectives followed the movers into the back of the building, which was backstage of the large theatre. A hipster female stage manager was barking orders to people and checking things off on her clipboard. The mover in charge pointed her out and left without introducing her.

Hobbs took the lead in approaching the young woman, again flashing his badge and again introducing himself. Sheed showed her badge as well, but kept quiet. She was currently in the doghouse, her presence more insignificant than usual.

"Detective Sergeant Rick Hobbs. I was told that you're in charge?"

"Yes, and I don't have time for this. Dress rehearsal is tonight. What do you need?" The woman with short blue hair, matching royal blue eyeglasses, and dressed in Urban Outfitter clothing was annoyed and impatient.

"What's your name miss?" Hobbs didn't take shit from women. Period.

"My name is none of your business until you tell me why you're here? Do you have a reason for being here? If not, you can show yourselves out the same way you came in. The building is closed to the public." Blue-hair was speaking to Hobbs but gave Sheed the look from head to toe to head again.

Sheed read what she needed to from the situation and interjected despite already being in deep shit with her senior partner.

"I'm sorry, maybe we got off on the wrong foot. We're major crime detectives with the state police. We are here about Lara Myhre. We understand that she goes to school here."

The fight seeped out of blue-hair. She turned away from Hobbs and spoke directly with Sheed. Hobbs realized that his partner was going to get further

Ebb

than he was.   That realization in and of itself was a minor miracle.

"Oh geez. Yeah. Yes. Well, she used to go here. She was supposed to be performing in this show as a matter of fact. Showcase. The best that the school has to offer perform, and she was definitely the best."

"So she dropped out?   I'm sorry, I didn't catch your name."

"Julie.   Julie Spaulding.   I'm a music business senior here. This is my final Showcase, Lara performing would have made it so much better. All the greats drop out."

"What do you mean 'all the greats drop out', Julie?"

"All the super-talented drop out. You can only learn so much music theory or harmony or whatever. Performing is performing. Recording is recording. If you can write music you can write music. You don't need people who are no longer famous teaching you things that you already know," she said.   She continually took brief looks away from Lisa to take note of what was happening with her troops.

"So Lara decided to leave? You know that for a fact?"

"No, but it seems reasonable. Why else would she not show up for classes again?"

"Maybe something happened to her. Is that possible?"

"Yeah. Talent happened to her," Julie said. "She got confidence in her three years here. She's a gorgeous and talented woman who finally realized that she didn't need Berklee anymore. Charlie Colin from the band *Train*, Diana Krall, Ben McKee from *Imagine Dragons*, Susan Tedeschi, Natalie Maines from the *Dixie Chicks*, John Mayer .... all Grammy winners, all went here, and none of them actually graduated. And those are just off the top of my head. There are probably a hundred more. Lara was the female John Mayer and she was convinced that they were related."

"*Was*?"

"Is. She will be the next big thing. 'Was' because she isn't here anymore. What is this about? You said 'Major Crimes'. Did something happen to her?"

"We're not sure. We're just trying to find her. Her parents haven't heard from her, so we would like to talk with her. Do you know where we could find her?"

"Talk to her boyfriend," Julie said with a roll of her eyes.

"I take it you didn't approve? We heard that he was a famous hockey player. A girl could do worse," Lisa said.

"Listen we weren't close, okay? But it's a small school. He showed up here from time to time. His name is Gary Rennick, you might have heard of him. If you are into the tall muscle-man type, then I guess she did well for herself. But I thought she could do better."

"You liked her, didn't you Julie?"

"Who didn't?" Julie had forgotten about the movement around her, she was concentrating on her purple shoes.

"I get it, believe me I do," Lisa said. We just need to find her. So can you think of anything that might help? We'll go see Rennick, but is there anything else? Her apartment looks like she is ready to come home at any minute, all her guitars are still on the stands and her car is still in her monthly spot."

Julie looked up into Sheed's eyes, trying to see if what she had just heard was true. The detective could see that she was surprised by the new information.

"I don't know anything else. Not really. She wouldn't just leave her guitars, though. She always had one on her or within reach." Julie paused. Nobody spoke to fill the void. Workers moved around them seemingly on mute.

"You should really look at the tapes," she said after some time.

"Tapes? I don't follow."

"She's amazing. She didn't have a lot of friends here because of the jealousy. She has been in multiple performances, multiple Showcases. The school was riding her for all they could get out of her in order to recruit new students. They knew what everyone knew, that she was going to be huge. Berklee wanted to be part of that. Things can get kinda cutthroat. 'Why does she get this, or why does she get that?' I can't imagine that anybody would do anything beyond gossip and backstab, but you should really see what I'm talking about."

"Backstabbing?"

"*Verbal* backstabbing," Julie said.

"Do you have them handy? The tapes?"

"Yeah, of course. Gimme a sec to get things in order and I'll meet you up in the booth." Julie pointed toward the front of the theatre, where the sound and effects booth was dark. She ran off to deal with some things that she needed to fix with her team. Yelling and pointing ensued.

Hobbs moved back to Sheed after blue-hair went back to work. "This is bullshit. Lesbo-smurf is wastin' our time. We don't need to see her MTV videos. I'm gonna fuckin' kill Dennihan when I see him. He's got us runnin' around all over Boston on a saturday morning for nothin'. And you .... you fell for it hook, line, and sinker. You don't remember what a shit-bag he is? I was never happier than when he got fired."

"He didn't get fired and you know it. Deni may be a pain in the ass but he's a bloodhound when it comes to these things. You didn't like him when he was your partner, and you're still a little butt-hurt that he left you. Look at it this way, Rick - it's a lead. We need to figure out who the woman is, why not exhaust all leads? We never would have gotten here without Deni, she wasn't in the Clearinghouse or the NCIC. If this turns out to be her, we're way ahead of the game. We would still be scratching our heads years from now without him." Sheed let the lesbian comment slide.

Julie met them in the control booth after a short time. She had used the term 'tape', but the videos were digitized. She pulled up several performances, queueing them up on the computer. All of the videos vertically lined the right side of the screen. She told them to run down as many as the detectives cared to view. She stayed for the first minute or so of the first video, then left to return to her duties onstage.

The first video was of a gorgeous female with a blue Stratocaster and long-haired drummer far behind her. The two were alone, almost lost on the enormous stage. As the camera panned in, virtually getting closer to Lara Myhre, she began to play her guitar. It was difficult to determine which was most haunting; the sound of her guitar, her voice, or her beauty. And she was model-beautiful. She could have been twin sisters with Kate Upton, though less voluptuous and her eyes more blue. Lara's blue eyes were as bright as the lights which lit the stage, performing to the filled seats in the audience. The blue guitar accented just how piercing her eyes were. Lara's long, blonde hair spiraled down to her small chest, framing her slightly freckled face. The high definition struggled to find a flaw.

The guitar had an indescribable sound. Lara's left fingers moved about the frets, her right picking at the strings just behind the pickups. It looked effortless. She began singing a cover of the London Grammar song *Stay Awake*. If the guitar and drums didn't do the job of transporting the audience, Lara's voice did. Nothing more was needed. The theatre was as full as the attention she received. Lisa found her captivating. Lisa was far from alone in that way.

"....*Stay awake with me*," Lara sang. "*.... Take your hand and come and find me*."

"I'm trying sweetie," Sheed said under her breath. "I'm trying."

DENI MET LEONARD AND SORCHE MYHRE at Mass General at 8:00 AM on saturday. Though he knew Mark Bowman, the Medical Examiner assigned to the autopsy, he wasn't allowed anywhere near the body. The ME spoke to Deni privately, telling him that there were chain of custody issues, not to mention felonies like interfering with an ongoing investigation that would get them both in serious trouble. The ME would not speak with the parents, nor allow anyone access on or off the record without tacit or stated approval from the detectives assigned.

Bowman called both of the detectives at Troop H and on their respective cell phones, but neither Hobbs nor Sheed answered. He went back to work while the trio sat in a waiting room.

And so they waited. And waited longer. Leonard had called his attorney, who said that he would see what he could do to allow access and get back to him. But the Myhres were still waiting at 10:00 AM Deni called Sheed who didn't answer. He then called his friend and New Hampshire attorney that he worked for on occasion. There was nothing legally that he could do either.

At five minutes to eleven, the two detectives walked into the waiting area in the basement of the hospital. Deni met Hobbs halfway down the hall as the detective looked fit to be tied and he wanted to keep any and all fisticuffs away from the overwrought parents. Hobbs didn't wait until they were in close proximity, he yelled across the corridor.

"You've got some set of balls on you, asshole!" Hobbs pointed at Deni, still moving toward him from the waiting area. Lisa continued walking past them toward the Myhres.

"Lower your voice, Ricky. The last thing in the world I want is to work with you again, so this an unfortunate thing for both of us."

"I should kick your ass and send you upstairs to the ICU. Getting involved behind my back? Have you lost your fuckin' mind?"

"You're upset, so I'm gonna let that slide. You and I both know that I would beat you inside out. Just calm down. Those are the parents over there, Ricky. Just try to have some class will ya?"

Hobbs looked over Deni's shoulder. The two men were almost the same height, Hobbs at six feet was much wider, however. "This isn't over, Deni. You and I are gonna have words."

"Can't wait. Can we get on with it now?"

The two walked over to where Lisa had already made acquaintance with the parents, and was in the process of letting them know that she had officially registered Lara as a missing person.

"…. and I apologize on behalf of my colleagues who have given you the runaround. We are going to do the very best that we can to find her and bring justice to whomever was involved."

"Better late than never," Leonard said.

"I can't even imagine your frustration," Lisa said. "And this is my partner, Rick Hobbs. We were just over at Berklee, which is why you were waiting so long."

"Senior Partner," Hobbs corrected. "I'm sorry that you have come all of this way for nothing — "

" — For nothing?" Sorche was taken aback to say the least. "We came here because this is where the woman who was found is said to be. We came here to disconfirm that the woman is Lara. I would hardly call that for nothing."

"Yes, well I don't know what your PI told you, but the body is beyond identification. Daughter or not, you won't be able to tell who she is," Hobbs said. He seemed to be the only one not interested in the feelings of the parents.

"I think what my partner is trying to say is that the best way for us to move forward with identification is with a DNA sample. Would either or both of you be willing to volunteer an exemplar? We would expedite the testing so we can eliminate your daughter as being the deceased, in the probable event that the results come back negative," Lisa said.

Both the Myhres looked to Deni with a look of both confusion and concern. It was obvious to Deni that something was wrong, so he pulled them aside after asking for a minute with his clients. Hobbs and Sheed took a few steps in another direction, adding space for their own private discussion.

"We would like to avoid any DNA sampling if at all possible," Sorche whispered once they were out of earshot.

"I don't understand. The test will just be saliva, not blood. A quick test will tell us what we need to know," Deni said.

"There are some very good reasons for not wanting to submit to these tests," Leonard added.

"Neither of you are considered suspects in her disappearance or worse. Are either of you wanted fugitives? I'm at a loss here." Deni looked back and forth to both Leonard and Sorche, neither face divulging any information.

"Confidentially?"

"Of course. I signed a confidentiality agreement when you hired me."

"A DNA test won't match the body that was found," Sorche finally said.

"Isn't that what we are hoping for, guys?"

"If it is Lara, it would still not be a match."

"Of course it would …. wait. Neither of you are her biological parents," Deni said. "And you don't want anyone to know that fact."

"Because nobody needs to know." Sorche was staring into Deni's eyes. It was a stern look to make him appreciate her and her husband's desires.

"All due respect, I needed to know. Does Lara know?"

"She was a bright child. Can we speak about this later Mr. Dennihan?"

"My father was Mr. Dennihan and we are definitely gonna talk about this later. Let me handle this." He turned toward the two detectives who were finished with their conversation, the five of them reconvened.

"Okay. The DNA thing is out. It's an invasion of their rights to have such personal information in the hands of out-of-state police. We're gonna approach this a different way."

"You're not in charge here, Deni." Hobbs was going to make this difficult if not embarrassing for his former partner.

"Pursuant to Commonwealth general law, chapter 152-section 21-part 1, parties retaining the use of a Private Investigator or other licensed agent shall also retain the cooperation of police with said agent," Deni recited. It was easy to remember because he had to remind police regularly that they were forced legally to cooperate with him.

"As long as the investigator isn't interfering with the investigation," Hobbs added.

"Well, that's for a judge to decide. In the meantime, I'm proposing that we allow these people to view the deceased."

"I hate to get between you two, but Deni — what good will it do for them so see the .... uh .... body? I've seen it and it isn't something that they will want to see," Lisa said. She looked at the Myhres and almost pleadingly shook her head. "There isn't anything that is identifying, let's put it that way."

"She has a birthmark on her hip," Sorche said to the group.

"Excuse me?" Hobbs was getting more than irritated. "There's not much more than a skeleton left, Mrs. Myhre. Just do the DNA sample and stop playin' games."

Leonard took umbrage and was about to defend the honor of his wife, but Deni stepped in.

"Let me spell this out for you chapter and verse, Ricky. The mother of a missing woman has just told you of an identifying birthmark. You can like it or lump it, but we're gonna get Bowman involved. If there is a birthmark, or if there is a possible way of identifying the departed, we're gonna do that. Any of this gettin' through?"

Hobbs didn't respond.

"I believe you owe the lady an apology," Deni said to him.

He remained silent.

Sheed gently touched Sorche's hand. "I'll go speak with the Medical Examiner. I'll be a few minutes but I will be back as soon as I can. There is a bank of

Ebb

vending machines one floor up, maybe you could use a cup of coffee?"

"I'll bring them up," Deni said. He looked at Hobbs. "Don't follow us."

Sheed entered the lounge with the vending machines twenty minutes later. She informed Deni and the Myhres that they would be able to view the body from an observation window. The deceased would be pulled out of a locker and loaded onto a gurney, then wheeled close enough to the window for them to see.

The news made Sorche weep almost immediately. Her bottom lip quivered and she was losing the battle for grace. The fact that a birthmark was indeed on the person laying on a gurney, that it must have been on her hip, was enough to confirm her worst fears. She knew before seeing it that it was her daughter.

The trip to the observation window took some time. They stopped regularly for Sorche's crying jags. Sorche needed a moment to compose herself seemingly every few feet. Once they were standing in front of the window, Lisa knocked on the outside of the glass to give the go-ahead. The curtains parted.

The body lay there before them. The five were outside the room, Bowman was inside. The ME pulled the light blue cloth covering the top portion of the corpse down below what was left of the face, the bottom up to the waist. Bowman was careful to keep the torso and genitals covered for the sake of feigned dignity.

The gray body was little more than skin and bone. Nobody but a mother would be able to identify it. Sorche looked from left to right, foot to head. There in the middle, on the left hip of the departed, was the birthmark. The dark patch on gray skin was the size of a silver dollar but with the rough shape of California. It was once a cute, freckle-colored blemish on an otherwise perfect body. What lay before them was not cute. It was something out of a horror film, made more horrific to Sorche because it was her daughter.

Deni made the motion for the curtains to be closed when the wailing began. Sorche's knees gave out and would have collapsed to the floor had it not been for her husband. Leonard tried to remain strong for his wife, holding her to his chest. Lisa began to tear-up as well, blinking erratically to fight them off.

Lisa put a hand on Deni's forearm, whispering into his ear. "This is heart-wrenching. Nobody should have to see their dead child. Especially not like this."

Hobbs approached the couple.

"I'm very sorry," he said.

Ebb

Leonard stared at the detective through his watery eyes, responding to him through the lump in his throat. His bottom lip quivering.

"You should be."

8

THE MYHRES MADE THE TRIP BACK TO THEIR home in Connecticut from the Mass General parking structure, but not before being questioned by Detective Sergeant Rick Hobbs. Now that the body had a name, he wanted to start working on her murder. The unsolvable case in which he was originally content to pass off onto cold cases was now one working against his closure rate. Within ten minutes of confirming that their daughter had been murdered; Hobbs asked details about what was going on in their daughter's life.

'When was the last time that you saw her alive? Who do you think is responsible? Did she have any

Ebb

enemies? I need to know each of your whereabouts for the entire week of her disappearance,' were all questions fired off at the grieving.

Mr. Sensitive.

They had no sooner driven off when Deni grabbed Hobbs by the lapels of his sport coat. "What the fuck is wrong with you? I swear to everything that is holy that I would give you the beat'n of your life if you weren't a cop."

"Assaulting a state police officer is mandatory jail time, Deni."

"And that is the only reason you still have teeth, Ricky."

"Boys. None of this is constructive," Lisa said. "Rick, you could have been more tactful. You know that it wasn't them. You said, 'I'm just doin' my job' like fifty times, when we both know that this was something else."

"Are we pulling our punches on investigations now? We have to look at every lead," he said.

"This isn't about you and me, Ricky," Deni said. "This is about a dead woman. Jesus she was still a kid. Put your personal shit aside for a second and focus on the fact that she was murdered. It was barely ten minutes before you started punchin' the parents in face, speakin' of punches." Deni finally let go of his former partner with a little shove.

"Like I said, I was just doing my job."

"While you were adding insult to injury, you could have been thinkin' about who actually did it."

"And who is that, Deni? It's only officially been a homicide for a few minutes and you already have it solved? You should still be a cop, superman."

Deni took a step back toward Hobbs, who bravely backed away.

"You're not smart enough to know where your own dick is."

"So solve this for me superman so we can all go home," Hobbs said.

"It's the boyfriend. Gary Rennick," Deni said.

"Gary Rennick? As in the Bruins defenseman?"

Deni looked at Sheed. "Don't you two talk?" He turned back to Hobbs. "Yeah. She was datin' him. He's a fuckin' thug. And I wanna be there when you question him."

"No way. Absolutely no way. We will let you know what happens, after it happens."

"Look, I've already got a history with this guy. I was onto him right off rip. Don't make me call Tits, Ricky."

"Stop callin' me Ricky. You think going over my head is gonna help you?"

'Tits' was the nickname of Manny Titanitaukis, though people only used it behind his back. He had been in charge of Troop H and Deni's Lieutenant back when he was on the force. Deni knew where the bodies were buried, so to speak, and Tits therefore owed him in order to let them rest in peace. Deni generally got what he wanted when he called upon his former boss, and nobody but the two of them quite knew why. Hobbs knew that the phone call would favor Deni, but he was calling his bluff just the same .

"Fine. Have it your way," Deni said he retrieved his phone from his pocket. "She, keep me posted. Set up the interview and let me know where to be and when. Please." He then turned toward his Range Rover and dialed.

"You got it," she said as he walked away. Hobbs eyed her down. If looks could kill, she would have been a chalk outline in the parking structure.

The next game of the Bruins series with Montreal was held in Canada on sunday, meaning that Rennick and the rest of the team were out of town. The interview had to wait until monday, decided after going through the player's agent and attorney. Official police procedures and courtesy towards Boston sports gods were very different from the way Deni conducted investigations. In the four 'meetings' that Deni had with Gary, he had not once contacted his agent or lawyer. Ambush was a more accurate term. Appointments were a convenience for the innocent.

Tits had commanded that Deni be allowed to be present for the interview in an observing capacity. The Lieutenant was reluctant at first, an up and coming sports celebrity under investigation tends to make politicians squeamish. And Tits was most definitely politically minded. It took a call from the Myhre attorney, informing him that a civil suit against Troop H was forthcoming due to the handling of the missing persons case up to date, but allowing Deni to be apart of the investigation would eliminate such a proceeding. The lieutenant's hand was forced, and if anybody involved thought that Deni was going to be merely an inactive participant, they were kidding themselves.

Deni met with Sheed for lunch so they could go over how the interview would go. She had somehow ditched her partner. How Lisa had accomplished this feat, Deni didn't know but he was glad for Rick's absence.

They ate at Durgin-Park because Deni said that he wanted to go there, and because he was paying. Cops don't eat there unless it is a special occasion, and they definitely don't eat there for a monday lunch. Not on their salaries. The sign said, 'established before you were born' and the interior was designed to make it seem old-world. Deni was already at a corner table by a window when Sheed arrived. He pulled the chair out for her like it was a date, she tucked herself under the white tablecloth in a cushy brown chair.

"I don't have a lot of time. Hobbs wants to do the same thing when I get back from lunch. He knows you're gonna wanna take charge of the interview and he is still pissed that you are even gonna be in the box with us," she said.

"I figured. I already ordered a chilled seafood platter for us to start on. Do you know what you want to eat?"

"You *are* buying right?"

"Yeah. I told you I would. Get what you want."

The waiter came over in his super-starched, white shirt to attain orders. No alcohol, though Deni wanted some. Lisa got the Durgin-cut prime rib, no dainty salad for her. Though where she put it was anybody's guess. A high metabolism was Deni's attempt at one. Sheed obviously burned her fuel instead of stored it. Deni ordered the lamb chop.

"So he's probably gonna have agents and attorneys and shit there," Deni said after the waiter left them.

"He might. How many times have you taken a run at him?"

"Four."

"And you came up empty each time? Why do you think it's him Deni?"

The platter of seafood over ice had arrived. Oysters on the half shell, shrimp cocktail, crabmeat cocktail, chilled mussels, and a small Maine lobster which they called a 'chicken lobster' for some reason. It was no sooner set on the table and the two went at it like vikings without missing a beat in the conversation.

"Oh just the fact that he was her boyfriend, nobody really likes him with the exception of his teammates, and he is one brutal motherfucker. He hit someone into the boards so hard one time when he was down in Providence, that he pulverized the poor prick's face."

"Hockey is a brutal sport," Lisa said. "I'd have thought you'd love it."

"I do. But she was too good for him. The girl was super-hot and super-talented. Did you see her video on the Youtube?"

"For the tenth time, it's just Youtube. Not *the* Youtube. You sound like a senile old man. Yes, I saw a few from Berklee. So talented. Her voice and her guitar still haunt me."

"Me too. Everyone loved her. Maybe some were jealous, but you glom onto somebody like that — you don't kill them. Maybe she was gonna dump him, maybe she cheated. Who knows? But this guy is good for it. Mark my words."

"Not to burst your bubble, but you may have your sights on the wrong guy."

"Yeah, okay. Is this you talkin' or is it the fat-fuck?"

"Do you know a guy named Cole Renner?"

"Yeah. I used to work for him a little bit on the side as an investigator before he got out of the business. He helped me get my start. Why?"

"I know you know him, Deni. You're not the only one who does his homework." She tossed an emptied lobster claw onto the tray of ice, her hands in need of a cloth. The server seemed to have been waiting in the wings as he showed up with a warm linen scented with lemon for her. "Thank you," she said before he fled again. "This is nice, huh?"

"Yeah it's okay. So what is this about Renner?"

"We had her apartment dusted," she said.

"Yeah so?"

"So his fingerprints were in the apartment."

"Again, so what?"

"You don't seem surprised."

"I'm intrigued, I'll give ya that. But kill her? When did you do all this?"

"What? You think we just sit on our hands and wait for you to come up with all of our suspects? We had it dusted on saturday after she was officially dead. I got the list of all known prints by email yesterday. The Myhres have some kinda clout by the way, Tits blanket-approved all overtime. Could Renner have been having an affair with her?"

"Cole? Naw. He has a demanding trophy wife already. Can you see Lara Myhre, about to be a huge musical sensation, going out with Cole Renner? I think he's a security guard for some pharmaceutical company now. We don't really keep in touch that much but I don't see it. Kinda two different leagues, not to mention the age difference."

The main dishes arrived, the large hubcap of ice and shellfish detritus was carted away.

"We subpoenaed her phone records. Luds confirm several calls to and from him. There was some sort of relationship there, Deni. Jesus this steak is good."

"I'm glad you like it." Deni was no longer hungry.

9

DENI SPENT ONE HUNDRED FIFTY DOLLARS on lunch and he didn't get what he wanted out of it. Suddenly there was a focus on Cole Renner, a former boss. He couldn't go so far as to call him a friend, Deni didn't have many of those. But Deni was definitely friend-ly with him and his wife Christina. He was one of the guys in a tux in their wedding in fact. He was not on board the Cole train, he was still locked-in on the Gary Rennick train. Still, there were some questions that needed to be asked and answered.

Those questions would have to wait until after he was through with Rennick, however. He headed over to his old workplace, the precinct near Downtown

Crossing which everyone at Troop H called 'the House'. He blasted Gary Clark Jr.'s *When My Train Pulls In* through the 29 speakers of his Meridian 3D surround sound system in his Range Rover. He needed pump-up music, and he was getting it. Odd that the blues could feel so good to his soul. Deni listened to the young blues master shred chords on a Epiphone Blak and Blue Casino through the 1700 watt audio system that would make George Lucas cream. The music got his juices flowing, forgetting about Renner and helped him get game-focused on Rennick.

"*Whoa I'll be ready now,*" Gary Clark, Jr. sang. "*…. I'll be ready when my train pulls in.*"

And so was Deni.

Interview room two was already full when Deni arrived. He saw that Rennick and several suits were present, which Deni concluded were his agent and lawyers. The two detectives were inside as well, all having a chat. Deni looked at his Sinn watch, confirming that he was on time. He stopped a runner that was moving down the hall and asked her what was going on?

"Interviews. What do you think is going on?" She tried to move around him, but he wouldn't let her pass.

"Yeah." She flipped the top sheet over. "Let's see …. box 2 was booked for one-thirty."

Deni looked at his watch again, as if he didn't know what time it was. 2:00 PM. The runner snuck off, Deni too preoccupied to notice. "Those mutherfuckers changed the time," he said to the empty hallway.

Deni charged into box two and went right for Hobbs. Had he been allowed to have his weapon in the police station, he may have gone into the interview room literally with guns blazing. "You think you're pretty slick ya fat fuck?"

"Oh, Deni. Yeah glad you could make it. There was a scheduling thing. We had to bump it up, didn't you get the email?" Hobbs knew Deni's aversion to electronic media and also knew that a missed email would be the best plausible excuse.

"You!" Gary Rennick realized who had just come stampeding through the door. "Perfect."

"I'll be with you in a minute," Deni said to him.

"No, you won't. Officers, I want to file a restraining order against this guy," Rennick said.

"It's detectives not officers, and that is not an option to you at the moment," Sheed said. She stood and tried to coax Deni into a seat. "Deni, I had no idea that the time got bumped up, I'm really sorry."

"You say that with prime rib still stuck in your teeth."

She was embarrassed and took another seat as her chair was now occupied by Deni.

"I'll be needing a copy of this interrogation," he said to the room. "But I'm here now, so catch me up Gare."

"It's Gary," he said.

"Whatever."

One of the two lawyers spoke up. "We are not here for a confrontation or an interrogation. "We are having a discussion about the unfortunate demise of one of my client's past acquaintances."

"As long as you keep rackin' up your fees, huh guy? I might be late, but I'm gonna get my questions answered. With any luck you won't be walkin' outta here, Gare."

Hobbs tried to interject but Deni stopped him in his tracks. "You had your turn. Sit there and shut up or I'll give ya a beat'n in your own house." Hobbs knew the look he was getting and he didn't want to push further.

"Who are you?" The lawyer looked around the room, keen to accept an answer from anyone.

"I'm the investigator for the family of the deceased. I've been working on the assumption that Lara Myhre was missing until now. Now we know different, and *your client* was the last person to see her alive."

"With the exception of the person who killed her, Mr….," the lawyer replied.

Deni ignored the response and the search for his name. "Where'd you take her after you left the Pru parking garage, Gare?"

"It's Gary. Are you trying to get a rise out of me?"

"Maybe. Is it working?"

The lawyer spoke up again. "Look whoever you are, I'll have no truck with — "

" — be quiet. You said this isn't an interrogation, so I can ask whatever I want however many times I want," Deni said.

The lawyer looked to Sheed. "You don't have a problem with this?"

"It's not my problem to have," she said.

"Fine. We can leave whenever we want, which is now." The lawyer stood, urging everyone else on his side of the interview table to do the same. All remained seated.

Gary put his large hand on the shoulder of his standing attorney, pulling him back to his seat. "It's okay. Let's just get this over-with, once and for all." He turned to Deni. "I've told you before and I'll tell you again. I have no idea what you are talking about. I hadn't been to her car in the Pru, I heard it was there but I had never been to it. Whenever we went out, we went in a chauffeured car. I always use a service." Rennick turned to Detective Sheed who was seated toward the corner of the room. "You can check. I'm sure he already has."

"We will," Lisa said.

"Good. We met back when I went to BC. I went out one night to Wally's, she was playing. You know the place on Mass Ave?"

"Yeah, dive joint," Hobbs said. Rick is a jazz fan, Wally's features many nights with live jazz bands.

"Right. Well, it turns out that she plays there a lot, like most musicians at Berklee. They pay the performers shit and the place is always jammed with student patrons so they make bank. Different kinds of music on different nights, sometimes different types of acts on the same night. Anyway, we hit it off and started seeing each other regularly."

"So what happened, Gare?"

"What do you mean 'what happened'? I got drafted, sent down to Providence. The AHL. I didn't see her that much anymore."

"Until you got called up. What? She move on and you got pissed?"

"What is it with you? Why do you think that I hurt her?"

"Let's see …. she's dead for starters. She didn't die of old age, so I'm guessin' you had somethin' to do with it. Maybe it was an accident. You're a big guy, she's small ...."

"You got it all wrong."

"Do I? Nobody seemed to like you, not anybody she hung out with anyway. Her parents never even met you, so she was probably ashamed of you. Ya never bought her any gifts. Girl like that, you gotta give gifts." Deni was pushing. He had no good cop to work with. Sheed had received the non-verbal cue from her senior partner to stay seated in the corner and quiet after the 'we will' comment.

"She is .... *was* rich," Gary said. "Do you know how hard it is to impress a girl who can have anything that she wants? Tiffany's isn't gonna cut it. We never seemed to have time to meet her folks. I travel a lot," Gary said.

"You cryin' poverty now?"

"No. Just stating facts. Everyone thinks athletes make all this money. Agents are expensive. Lawyers. Do you know how much insurance costs for someone who gets hurt for a living?"

"Stop. You're breakin' my heart, Gare. You get paid hundreds of thousands of dollars to play a game. And your stock is on the rise. What happened? She want more from you now that you're gonna make big bucks? And you wanna play the field, right? She was hot, but you could be dating supermodels now that you're a big deal. Why not right? Fuck, Brady's got one — why not you?"

"Again, why do you think I would hurt her? She was a nice girl. A good, decent girl with a ton of talent."

"And she is dead and you are a brutal son-of-a-bitch. I ain't no math whiz but it seems to add up. Talk to me. Was it an accident?"

"So that's it? Because I play hockey? Do you watch hockey? Do you know the sport at all? I'm guessing not."

"Enlighten me." Deni sat back in his chair.

"I'm a defenseman. A defensive defenseman. Meaning I'm an enforcer. Someone fucks with my scorers, I rattle 'em. Get them off of their game. Sometimes it takes a good hit. Sometimes it takes a fight. I gotta do whatever I gotta do to make sure that our scoring lines get chances."

"You like your job, huh? You have the top hits, penalty minutes, and fights in the entire AHL. You hospitalized a guy. You get very angry which means you have a temper. I looked you up."

"Like I said, you know nothing about hockey. Do you know how aggravating it is when you get shoved, poked, hit, hooked and constantly fucked with while you are trying move the puck or score a goal? It's frustrating to say the least. It would be like the catcher in baseball being able to poke at you and fuck with you while you are at bat trying to get a hit. It's hard enough without the other guy."

"So you fight."

"So we fight. It keeps the other team honest.

"And you bring that frustration home? She get mouthy one too many times?"

Sheed looked uncomfortable with the comment but begrudgingly let it go.

"I leave it all out on the ice. Look, investigate me all you want. I didn't hurt her. I'm just asking that you do it discretely. If the league finds out that I'm being investigated for a murder, my career is shot."

"At which time we will not only sue the Massachusetts State Police, but we will sue each of you individually as well," the lead lawyer added. "Slander and liable have consequences. Now we have cooperated beyond what I think is reasonable. It's time for us to go. If you have anything further for my client, you will contact me directly. He has a playoff run to focus on."

Deni had nothing more to throw at the hockey player and his staff. He looked to Sheed who shook her head. The signal was clear. There was nothing concrete in order to arrest him or keep him.

"We'll be in touch, Gare."

10

DENI STAYED AT THE PRECINCT just long enough to get a tape of the first half-hour of the Gary Rennick interview, and to have words with Hobbs. By the time he was headed out of the lobby, his blood was boiling. It had turned into a bad day and a bad time for Sheed to want to speak with him. She had been waiting for him in the reception area of Troop H.

"I've got nothin' to say to you, She."

"I'm sorry. That's all I wanted to say. I had no idea. I was told to be back from lunch by one-thirty so we could go over how to approach Rennick."

"And you couldn't call me when you knew different?"

"How was I supposed to do that with Hobbs in my hip pocket? I do still have to work with him, ya know."

"I'll get over it. But I ain't yet. We'll talk when I've calmed down."

"Yeah I know that look when your Irish is up. Probably a bad time to tell you that I still don't think he did it," she confessed.

"Rennick? That fooled you? She .... he fuckin' did it."

"You don't like the guy, I get that. But we had the Beamer dusted. No prints from Rennick."

"So he wiped the car down," Deni said.

"Then we wouldn't have found other prints." She handed him a fingerprint analysis report.

"Cole Renner? Again?"

"Looks like it. Why does a forty-five year old security guard trade phone calls and have fingerprints all over the twenty-two year old victim's apartment and car?"

Deni just shook his head. Whatever logical explanation, and to him there must be one, he couldn't find it at the moment.   The pause was filled with the commotion of the lobby.

"I know the guy, She.   He wouldn't do this. There's an explanation."

"And we are going to need to know what that explanation is. From him."

"Let me talk to him first?"

"Deni, that is the very definition of interfering with a police investigation.   You can't sanitize the evidence by getting first crack at it.   I get it, he's your friend.   But all roads right now lead to Renner. Clearly there was opportunity and means, if I had a motive I'd apply for an arrest warrant right now."

"When are you two planning on going to see him?"

"It's getting late," she said as she looked at her oversized man's wristwatch. "I've got to write up the interview and do some fives. I can hold off Hobbs until tomorrow morning."

"Good. Let me go talk to him. If he did it, I'll be the first one on board. But I'm tellin' ya he didn't."

"So we are clear - I'm telling you *not* to talk to him. For the record."

"Fine.   For the record.   If this goes sideways you've got your out."

"Keep me posted, Deni."

Ebb

"Like you did me?"

Cole and Christina Renner reside in North Billerica, Massachusetts. There are some good parts of the town, which is where the couple lived along the Concord River. Most of the town was seedy, however. There is a prison in Billerica a few miles away from a country club. Cole and his then girlfriend had once been proud citizens of Boston, but the prospect of marriage and children had necessitated the need to move to the suburbs. That necessity mandated by Christina.

Deni drove north on Interstate 93 in silence. He needed to wrap his head around the how and the why the investigation had come to this. He hated the overused term 'surreal' but that is how he felt. The usual luxurious ride of his SUV didn't seem so wonderful. He got off of 93 and finished the trip north on Route 3 consumed in deep thought.

He had called Cole to ask if they could get together prior to making the trip. Renner sounded

Ebb

happy to hear from Deni, it had been a long time. If he wondered what had brought about the need for a monday evening chat, he didn't let on. Cole said that it would be good to see him, that his wife would like to see him as well, and to meet at his house. He would go home directly from work, as if that was unusual.

Deni had hit commuter traffic, so he didn't make it to the Renner's until a little after seven. Both Cole and Christina were waiting at their open front door as Deni walked up their driveway. Christina looked the same as she did the day Deni had met her. Nary a wrinkle around her green eyes or a hint of gray in her long raven hair. High maintenance has its perks. Cole on the other hand had aged a bit. Some people think that age on men make them looked more distinguished. To Deni, the man just looked like a tired forty-five.

"Deni. What a nice surprise. How long has it been?" Christina met him at the bottom of her front steps. A kiss to each cheek, a new custom.

"Too long. You look great. Pilates? Yoga?"

"A girl has her secrets. Come in. Dinner will be ready shortly."

"Cole," Deni said as he ascended the steps. Hand out for a firm handshake, an old custom. "How are you?"

"Busy these days." They went inside. The evening was bringing about a slight chill, as late April does in Massachusetts.

"Yeah? Are you still with …. uh, where is it you work again?"

"Muro Pharmaceuticals in Lowell. Yeah, still there."

"They must pay good. Big house in a nice neighborhood."

"Big house equals big mortgage. We moved here for the school system, only we still don't have any kids." The two men walked into the immaculate home.

"Are you guys tryin'?"

"Chris is adamant about it. At first we were 'not preventing it', then it went to 'actively trying', and now she is studying cycles and timing. We are about one step away from going to a fertility guy. At forty-one she knows her time has just about run out. We've been tryin' for six years. My take on it is — if it happens, it happens. You wanna drink?"

Christina had either heard her husband or had the usual woman's intuition. "We don't have your favorite, but we have some kind of Irish Whiskey," she called from the kitchen.

"I'm okay but thanks."

Ebb

Cole immediately knew something was wrong. Deni never refused a drink. It was another one of his 'things'.

"Hey Cole, make any new additions to the man-cave?" Cole's 'man-cave' was actually just the garage, only they didn't put cars in it. Last Deni knew, it had a bar, a large flatscreen, darts, and a pool table. It was the only room Cole was allowed to decorate, which meant it looked like a frat house.

"I'm not sure. When was the last time you saw it? Come on out and take a look." Cole was staring at Deni, trying to find the true purpose of the visit in the eyes of his friend. He truly considered Deni a friend.

"Don't go too far boys. Dinner is almost ready and I want to catch up with you Deni. You must have a new girl," she said as she popped her head around the corner. "You always seem to have a new girl."

"Yeah — not at the moment, Chris."

"You still see that Althea woman?"

"When she'll see me," Deni said as he was being ushered down the hallway toward the man-cave.

Cole made a bee-line to the refrigerator behind the bar once they entered the converted garage. He popped the top off a Harpoon UFO. "Okay. What gives?"

"Is it that obvious?"

"Deni, you show up on a monday night out of the blue and have been uncomfortable since you walked in the door. It's been a while, so I just figured you were embarrassed that so much time has passed. Then you decline a whiskey. I'm an investigator, Deni. I taught you a thing or two as I recall. We go way back. What's goin' on?"

"You *used* to be an investigator. Now you're a security guard and Chris has never worked for a paycheck a day in her life."

"I'm a security analyst not a security guard, fuck-o. You came to insult me?"

"No. I'm sorry, maybe I am confused. So what, you run background checks and shit?"

"In part, yes. It's a decent living. What is this about? You need a job? Things not going well for you? What happened with Ryan up in New Hampshire? I hear his firm is doin' really well. You drove here in a Land Rover, so things can't be that bad."

"It's not that, I'm doin' fine."

"Deni, you're scaring me. What's up?"

"Lara Myhre."

Cole's face went white. He was still standing behind the bar. He looked down and began to pick at the bar-top before slugging back the rest of his beer. Deni gave him a few seconds.

"You can't tell Chris." Cole tossed the first bottle into recycling, then opened the frig for another.

"Don't tell her what? That you were bangin' her?"

"What? Jesus, NO. I'm back to doing for-hire investigations," he said.

"So why do you look like a ghost?"

"I figured you were here because you know I am back to doing PI work on the side. Taking some of the food off of your plate."

"And Chris doesn't know?"

"After that mob thing ten years ago, she is very set against it. She's really not into the 'possibility of being a widow' — thing."

"So you don't work for Muro anymore?"

"No, I still do. She thinks I work a ton of overtime and go on business trips. I love Chris with all my being but she doesn't understand that all of her pretty things cost money. Fendi fuckin' bags and Jimmy Choos don't fall from the sky. Now she's talkin' fertility specialists? I can't keep up."

"So Lara Myhre. What were you doin' for her?"

"Finding her biological parents. Wait. What do you mean *were*? You aren't gonna muscle me off the case are you?"

"There is no case," Deni said.

"I know. Whoever her biological parents were, they are dead-set on keeping it a secret."

"Bad choice of words, Cole. There's no case because she *is* dead."

"Shut the fuck up. Seriously?"

"As a heart attack. It gets worse."

"Worse than the girl is dead and that I have no case?"

"Oh fuck yeah. The police have a hard-on for you. Your prints are all over her apartment and car. They have her phone records, it's just a matter of time before they show up on your doorstep with a search warrant. Tomorrow morning actually."

Cole guzzled the rest of his second beer. "Fuck me."

"Yep. Fuck you. Do you still have an investigator's license?"

"Yeah but through Muro. I can do investigations for them, I kinda skirted the system by takin' side jobs."

As an employee of Muro, the pharmaceutical company paid for his investigator's license. He was only allowed to execute background checks and such through them and for them. There are privacy and harassment laws, his extracurricular moon-lighting was not-so-technically illegal.

"Do you have any paperwork on Lara? Did she sign a contract with you or a confidentiality waiver?"

"Yes, of course."

"That's a start, but you and I both know that an illegal contract is not a contract. It explains the phone calls and fingerprints, but operating without a license carries a mandatory prison sentence, Cole"

"I would rather fight that than a murder charge."

"Except that if she figured out that you weren't legit and exposed you, you'd be fucked. It's called motive. You officially have opportunity, means, and motive."

"Deni you gotta believe me, I didn't touch her. I didn't even know she was dead. I haven't been in contact with her for weeks because I had nothing to report. As a matter of fact, the last actual conversation she said how disappointed she was that things were going so slowly. I mean I was working it on the side. I didn't have the kinda time to spend on it as I wanted. I told her that I would just charge her a flat-rate instead of my usual hourly fee. It appeased her and she said to call her when I had something because she was tired of calls with no news. Other than that we played phone-tag. I've left her some messages since then but she never got back to me. I just figured that she was pissed."

"I believe you. I just found out from her parents that she was adopted. I don't think that they knew she was looking into her real parents," Deni said.

"You're right. And she wanted to keep it that way. She said that her parents were her real parents, but she just had to know who her birth parents were. She had a big imagination, Deni. She had all kinds of ideas who they were. She had all kinds of reasons for wanting to know. Medical. Heritage. It was eating her up, but she didn't want to hurt the people who raised her." The third beer had been removed from the fridge and nearly finished. "What do I do now, Deni?"

The door to the house opened. Christina smiled and invited them inside. "Dinner is ready. I hope you're hungry." She noticed how somber the room was. She looked at the large flatscreen that was turned off. "I'm surprised you're not watching the hockey game. Isn't the Bruins playoff game about to start?"

"Not tonight, hun. Tomorrow night," Cole said. "Probably a Sox game though."

"Well, get in here and get it while it's hot." She turned and went back into the house.

Deni turned back to Cole. "Do you wanna tell her or should I?"

11

DINNER AT THE RENNERS DIDN'T GO WELL. It didn't go well primarily because there was no dinner at the Renners. Christina had a melt-down and Cole spent the evening begging for forgiveness after telling her the news of his impending arrest. Food was thrown, doors were slammed. Deni got out of there as soon as he could, but not without getting all of the information Cole had collected on behalf of Lara Myhre. He drove north to his house in Barstone, New Hampshire fortified with copies of her birth certificate and social security card.

He was home in Barstone within the same hour of leaving North Billerica; his gun and keys on the small table just inside the front door, and a Redbreast poured within a minute of entering that front door. He needed to relax. He needed to think and get his mind right. Alcohol would help, music would also. He decided to turn on his stereo, turning the music up louder than he would be able to in Southie. In Boston, his three-decker had tenants above him on both the second and third floors. The houses were juxtaposed very close to one another, all three-deckers lined up in a gentrified row. In Barstone, there was more room between the homes, not acres but enough. In Barstone, there were no other tenants in his home. People are more tolerant in the 'Live Free or Die State' even if there were.

Kings of Leon echoed out of his Bose Environmental speakers. *Tonight* happened to be the song shuffled from his 100-disc Yamaha CD changer. His stereo had the ability to play MP3s but Deni was still embracing Compact Disc technology. In truth he preferred vinyl, only nobody sold records anymore. He tried to relax as the music played, though the song was unsettling.

"…. *Everybody knows it's strange …. There's somethin' on the way…., There's somethin' on the way …. "* Caleb Followill sang. Deni turned the stereo off.

He took the documents given to him by Cole out of the manilla envelope, studying them in silence. Lara's birth certificate was the first document, the embossed New Hampshire State seal on the top left corner.

Hm.   Thought you were from Connecticut, he thought.

Her full name was the first item listed on the left under the seal. Lara Victoria Myhre. Followed by her date of birth.   June 4, 1992.   Born Nashua, New Hampshire at Dartmouth-Hitchcock Hospital.   Born to both Leonard and Sorche Myhre, maiden name Beurn.

How do you have a birth certificate with the Myhres on it?

The next document was a photocopy of her Social Security Card. In 1992, Social Security Cards were printed with 'Social Security Administration' in a red circle in the center of it.   Other generations may have read 'Department of Health and Human Services' or 'Department of Homeland Security' or others. The first three numbers for Lara's social were 002, which is a designation for New Hampshire.

The final documents were discharge paperwork from Dartmouth-Hitchcock Hospital dated June 6, 1992. According to all the paperwork given to him in the legal-sized manilla envelope, Sorche Myhre gave birth to a healthy baby girl on June 4, 1992 and walked out of the hospital with her two days later.   There was no indication of an adoption, no indication that Lara was not the biological product of the love between Leonard and Sorche Myhre. If Deni didn't know better, he would have thought that the Myhres had Lara in New Hampshire and moved to Connecticut at some point in her childhood.

Deni decided to call Leonard and Sorche at home. It was 9:30 PM on monday night. It had been a long day for them. It had been a long day for him, but he felt that his questions couldn't wait. The hour was probably past a socially acceptable time, but two whiskeys and the dozen or so questions rattling around his sluggish brain necessitated the immediate conversation.

"Hello?" It was Leonard.

"It's Deni. I'm sorry if I woke you, but I have some questions for you."

"I know it's you Deni, we have caller ID. Your call is fine, we weren't sleeping. It's been a very long and terrible day."

"I can't imagine, but it hasn't been roses for me either."

"If you are calling about your fee; I've sent you a check for your current fees, and I would also like to retain you to augment the investigation of her murder. We were still in such shock when we left the morgue that we didn't really have a chance to discuss things."

"I kind of already inserted myself into the investigation. I was going to see this thing through one way or the other, Leonard. But that's not why I'm callin'."

"Oh? Do you have some news on that front?"

"Did you know that Lara was looking into her birth parents?"

"I believe my wife told you that she has been inquisitive about it for some time."

"Inquisitive turned into hiring another investigator to find them. She didn't want you to know apparently, but with you paying her bills I wasn't sure if you figured it out."

"No. Hold on please," Leonard said. There were muffled voices in the background, Deni assumed he was speaking with his wife. Thirty-seconds later, Leonard returned on the line. "Deni, would you be willing to come down to Fairfield tomorrow?"

"Of course. I was hoping to kind of go over this tonight, I need to get to the bottom of this," Deni said.

"Do you think that this had something to do with her death?" Leonard ignored Deni's whiskey-infused need for immediate answers, instead inquiring to receive his own. Deni played along to get along.

"I honestly have no idea. I still feel in my gut that Gary Rennick is involved, but there are a lot of moving parts to this. In the interest of full disclosure, the police are gonna probably make an arrest tomorrow. They have a suspect."

Ebb

"Gary Rennick?"

"No. The investigator that Lara had hired to look into this. I know the guy, I used to work with him a long time ago. I'm tellin' you here and now that he didn't do it, but there is enough circumstantial evidence where they aren't gonna let him slide. It might be on the news, but please don't get sucked into it. I think that the adoption angle is key, and my interest in it at this point is two-fold; I want to disprove the investigator's guilt, and by doing so hopefully prove that Rennick did it. I know that Sorche said that she wanted to keep wraps on the fact that Lara was adopted but I think the cat is out of the bag on this."

"I understand. And frankly at this point it doesn't matter."

"We're gonna have to go through this point-by-point," Deni said.

"I'm not sure how much we can add, but we will see you in the morning," Leonard said, again avoiding answering any forthcoming questions that night. Deni read the writing on the wall.

"Will it be both of you, or do you have to work tomorrow?"

"I have taken indefinite bereavement leave, so I will be here," Leonard said.

"I'll be in Connecticut first thing."

Ebb

The four hour trip would mean that he wasn't going to get much sleep. Not that he would get any regardless.

12

THE ROUTE TO FAIRFIELD, CONNECTICUT from Barstone, New Hampshire skirted the city of Boston, affording Deni the ability to make excellent time. Interstate 93 south broke off onto Interstate 84 South in Lowell, Massachusetts, which was just north of the morning gridlock. The three stops for as many turbo'd Dunkin' Donuts had fortified him with enough pep to arrive at the Myhre home at precisely 8:30 AM on tuesday, less than four hours after he had left his home.

The Myhres had an assortment of warm pastries and hot coffee waiting for Deni when he arrived. Neither of them looked like they had slept, though they were neatly groomed and dressed to receive. Deni wondered if they were up all night making pastries.

They invited him in, getting settled in a large parlor with floor-to-ceiling windows along one wall which provided a view of the ocean. He sat on a sofa across from them, the coffee table with refreshments between them. The wall behind the sofa where the two mourning parents sat was covered with pictures of Lara. Her wall of shame. Every event from toddler to high school graduation was accounted for. Deni sat with his back to the very body of water where Lara was found, looking over the photos behind her parents without staring to spare them any more anguish. There wasn't a bad photo to be found. Even at very young ages, it seemed that Lara knew where the cameras were focused. Photogenic doesn't say it. Cameras were meant for beauty like Lara Myhre. Deni was glad that he had chosen the sofa where he sat, though the wall would still be there for the parents to agonize over after he was gone.

Deni produced the manilla envelope with the documents in it after pleasantries were exchanged. He rested it on the table. "Shall we get down to business?"

The couple held each other's hands and nodded in the affirmative.

"So let's start from New Hampshire. Were you living up there in 1992?"

"No."

"Okay, so why were you up there?"

"Because that is where our baby was," Sorche said.

"I realize that this is uncomfortable for you, but this is gonna go a lot easier if your answers are a little more free-flowin'. This yes-no thing isn't gonna get us very far."

"You asked us a question, and we answered it," Leonard said.

"Have it your way. So you were up in New Hampshire to get a baby because, what? There aren't any babies in Connecticut that need adopting?"

Sorche looked a bit hurt by the sarcasm but continued on. "We went through what was the leading adoption agency in New England at the time. It may still be. The agency paired us with a baby that was being born from parents who insisted on a closed adoption."

"Closed adoption meaning that the birth parents wanted nothing to do with the baby and wanted to remain anonymous."

"Correct. Which suited us fine. We couldn't get pregnant but wanted a child. It was our hope that Lara would never know that she didn't come from my womb," Sorche said.

"But she did find out."

Sorche stared down into her hands which were still enveloped by Leonard's. More tears fell. "She was so bright. She noticed that she didn't look like either of us, or any of our family members. Leonard is math and science minded, Lara was so creative. I was athletic and until a few years ago ran marathons. Lara tried all sorts of sports but they never took. Music was her forte, which of course we supported. We were a very happy and loving family, but as she grew up she realized that she was very different from us.

Volleyball. That was when she knew for sure. She needed her birth certificate to play in the thirteen to fifteen year old league. She developed early and some of the parents thought she was older. She saw on her certificate that she was born in New Hampshire and knew from our stories that neither of us had ever lived there. She figured it out and asked us outright. All that grief and she never played a single game. She warmed the bench."

"So you never denied it."

"No. We have never lied to her. We always told her the truth about everything, though we didn't tell her that she was adopted until she asked. She was fifteen. It became almost an obsession with her. She would dream about who her biological parents could be, why they had given her up. She would talk about it all the time. One time she accused us of not telling her who they were because we feared that we would lose her."

"And you never told her who they were?"

"We didn't know. The process was completely closed."

Deni took a sip of his coffee, trying to collect his thoughts. It also gave them a chance to catch a breath, though Sorche was doing all of the talking. And the crying.

"Did Lara ever ask about this adoption agency? I don't have any indication of who that was, which means that the investigator that Lara hired might not know." Deni pointed to the manilla envelope but didn't open it.

"She never asked and we never told her. We hoped that it was just a phase, that she would grow out of it. We were her parents. We took her home from the hospital," Sorche's face was like an overfilled sponge, puffy and leaking fluids. Deni wanted to give her another minute to regroup but he felt that it would take a while and he had a train of thought that he didn't want to lose.

"We will get to that in a minute. I can tell you that she did feel that you both were her real parents. Her only parents. That is why she told the investigator that she wanted to keep it from you. She told him that she wanted to know for personal and medical reasons. There may have been a history of breast cancer or heart disease or something that might be relevant."

"Thank you for saying that, Deni. We were very close to her, and we know that she loved us. But she did have this fascination that she came from an aristocratic heritage or something. Which may or may not be true, who knows? The agency that we went through only place offspring from the best-of-the-best with suitable parents of the same caliber. Those are their words not mine. The process cost us over $50,000 I think." She looked to her husband who confirmed the figure without a word.

"But how do you know?"

"Excuse me? How do I know what?"

"This may be insensitive, but kids don't come with pedigrees like dogs right?"

"I don't follow." Sorche's face became less sad and more stern.

"I mean no offense, but it's like bottled water. People could be filling up glass bottles from the water out of their bathtubs, but they put a fancy name on it and charge you eight bucks. You think you're gettin' some fancy water from the Alps but it's tub water at the end of the day."

"Are you insinuating that Lara was tub water? How dare you?"

"I'm not insinuatin' anything.   I'm just askin' how ya know."

"The agency is one of the best in the country and very highly recommended.   They do both open and closed adoptions. Everyone who has ever gone through them has always been happy. We were. And frankly it is very insulting that you would think otherwise."

"Mrs. Myhre, I don't think otherwise.   I'm just askin' questions.   Your daughter was gorgeous and talented. Everyone that I have talked to loved her, even those she competed with at her school.   Good or bad genes, you both did a great job.   Now …. what's the name of the agency?"

She seemed satisfied with the explanation but still unsettled. "Regis and Chapman.   They have an office in Nashua, New Hampshire that we went to.   I forget the address."

"That's okay. I can call information," Deni said as he wrote the name of the agency on the back of the manilla envelope. "I'm sorry to have to rehash this and take up so much time, but I do have a few more questions."

Leonard looked at his Alpha Omega watch and Deni could see that the Q&A was taking a toll on Sorche. Deni didn't waste any time getting into his next line of questioning.

"I'm gathering that neither of you knew that she had hired Cole Renner to investigate this?"

"No," Leonard said.

"She was paying him and you pay her bills."

"She has had credit cards and bank accounts since she was thirteen. We fill the tank and she spends it how she sees fit. There has never been a problem with her being overly extravagant or seemed like she was taking advantage, so I've never itemized each expenditure," Leonard explained.

"So she could have been paying the investigator and you would never know?"

"Precisely. It is all done through a money manager. He notifies me when and if money is moved into her accounts but that is about it."

"Never-ending supply of money is nice, huh?"

"I don't think I like your tone, Deni."

"I meant no offense. If it wasn't an issue, then it wasn't an issue. Let's move on. So the birth certificate has both of your names on it. It was like her biological parents never existed. How is that possible?"

"As my wife said, it was a closed adoption. There was nobody else to put on the record. Legally, Lara was born to both my wife and I. We were in the hospital the moment she was born, though not in the room. Lara stayed in the hospital for a couple of days to make sure that she was okay. She was a bit jaundice, but it went away. We were allowed to visit her but only during certain times and we had to be completely sterilized. She came home with us. We are the only parents she has ever known."

"And that was at Dartmouth-Hitchcock?"

Both nodded.

"And neither of you ever saw the mother or father? You must have been up in the same section of the hospital."

Sorche again took charge, though it was obvious that she wanted to be through with the conversation. "There were many deliveries and many people in the hospital and in the waiting room. We didn't leave for two days. We kept to ourselves, we didn't want to know. Don't you understand, Deni? We *still* don't want to know."

"I do understand that. And I again apologize that I have to go through this with you. But this is the only way that I can see that we are going to find Lara's killer. I've learned from working for attorneys that in order to find out what happened, you sometimes have to prove what didn't happen." Deni looked at his watch because Leonard continually looked at his. It was a little after ten. He wondered if Cole was being arrested, or if he already had been. "I've taken up enough of your valuable time and dug up stuff that you would just as soon leave buried. But I'll get him."

Everyone stood. Deni was tempted to take half of the basket of pastries but thought better of it. Leonard walked him to the door, looking around to make sure that the two men were alone.

"Deni, a private word?"

"Sure."   They stepped outside onto the front lawn. There was light traffic on Fairfield Beach Road, but not loud enough to drown out the waves crashing on the beach behind the house. The late morning sun was warming the day, the coastal breeze was warm and easy.

"You're a very passionate yet calloused man, aren't you?"

Leonard, I meant no disresp — "

" — You're just doing your job, which is what I'm paying for. Which is why I wanted to speak with you privately."

"I'm listening."

"I'm paying you for a result," Leonard said. "I don't have anything to leave anyone anymore, so money isn't an issue. I want you to promise me that you will find who did this." Leonard had a firm grip on Deni's elbow. "Look me in the eye and promise me."

"I promise. I think I know who did it. I just need to prove it to the cops."

"The result, Deni. Focus on the result and don't bother."

Ebb

"Pardon?"

Leonard shook his head and looked out at the road. He fought back tears. "Don't bother proving it to the police. Just kill him."

Part Two

The Hard Way

May

13

DENI REPEATEDLY CALLED SHEED once he was
back on the road, bearing north out of Connecticut. She
didn't answer the first time, nor the fifth. *She's probably
arresting Cole,* he thought. He was tempted to get off of
Interstate 93 as he eventually approached the Route 3
exit in Massachusetts. He wanted to see what help he
could lend Cole Renner. Possibly be there for Christina.
But what could he do besides get himself arrested?
Hobbs and Sheed liked Renner for Lara's murder. At
the very least they had some questions for him. Deni
interfering with the detectives cuffing and stuffing Cole
into the back of an unmarked car would only get

himself stuffed into the seat next to him. That wouldn't help prove his innocence.

He stomped on the accelerator, continuing north on 93. He dialed his phone again though the number was listed in his contacts and his Range Rover had voice command capability and Bluetooth.

Again there was no answer. Deni didn't leave a message.

He manually dialed another number. A female answered the phone announcing that he had reached the law office of Ryan Wells and Associates. Deni was one of the 'Associates' with an office at the firm, though he had never spent any time in it.

"Ang, it's Deni."

"Hey Deni. Long time no see. We've got some work lined up for you."

"I'm good, thanks for asking. Can I yell at Ry?"

"Very funny. He's in his office with a client. Can I help you with something?"

"Yeah, maybe. What does his schedule look like for the rest of the day? I really need him to carve out some time for me."

"Ooh. I don't know. He's super-busy today."

"Let me put it another way, Ang. I've got a five-alarm fire. It's gonna happen one way or the other, but I would rather not embarrass him in front of clients or whatever."

"Oh no. Have you been arrested? I can send one of the — "

" — I haven't been arrested. Yet."

"Wow. Okay, okay. Let me see what I can do. What time do need to see him?"

"I'm on my way there now."

"Oh shit."

Deni hung up and cranked the stereo. *Underdog* by Imagine Dragons was playing on one of the Rdio satellite stations the dealer had preprogrammed into his Rover. The drum beats, electronic chords, and singing came to him from seemingly every angle. Each of the SUV's speakers doing their part. He had never heard the song before, but he liked it and it was marginally lifting his spirits.

Within twenty minutes of the phone call, Deni was walking under the sign and through the front door of Ryan Wells & Associates. The sign had once read 'Grantes, Wells & Associates' but the founding partner had left to start another firm and another life in South Carolina. Angie Wells, formerly Angela Grummond when she had interviewed for the reception job, was in her usual position behind her desk. Ryan Wells, now the fountainhead of the firm, was standing in the doorway to his office as Deni entered.

"So what did you do now?" Ryan had the beginning of a smile, one corner of his mouth was raised. He remained in the doorway donning his hippie linen suit.

"Funny. Where should we talk?" Deni looked at his watch. "We could go across the street to Sully's." Sully's tavern was the Wayland hot-spot down and across the main thoroughfare.

"Why don't we all go into the conference room," Angie alternatively suggested. She was going to be a part of the conversation which Deni was more than fine with. Her new role in the firm was one of paralegal. Whether she was going to be in the conference room for the sake of curiosity or as part of her duties, Deni didn't know. Nor did he care. Angie was as good a friend to him as Ryan. Plus they were married so there wouldn't be any secrets anyway.

An intern took over at the reception desk. Angie didn't offer an introduction, and Deni wasn't interested in one. Interns seemed to come and go, Deni wasn't at the Wayland, New Hampshire firm enough to get to know any of them. Instead, Angie led the way into the new conference room.

The firm had started from humble beginnings, and while they were not currently the hub of New England legal representation, they were a household name and were doing better than most. The conference room had once served as the kitchenette and coffee area as well. Now they had a dedicated conference room, which was once Jacob Grantes' office.

"So what happened?" Ryan was the last to take a seat, as he was the last one to enter the room and close the door behind them.

"Do you keep tabs on Boston news?"

"I try to, yes," Ryan said.

"I do," Angie said. "You never know where the next big case will come from. We run late-night ads in that market and have had some bites."

"Well, there was a woman found in the ocean up Gloucester. She had been missing for nine weeks. I was hired by the family to look into her whereabouts because the police couldn't have given two shits."

"I think I might have seen something about that," Angie said. "I didn't know you were trying to find her."

Ryan was nodding his head, jotting things down on a yellow legal pad.

"Do you remember Cole Renner?"

"Cole Renner as in our former Lead Investigator?" Ryan was no longer looking at his legal pad, his attention was fully on Deni.

"Yeah, that Cole Renner. He was arrested for it today."

"Oh my gosh," Angie added.

"Only he didn't do it."

"And he needs legal representation? I can — "

" — No, Ry. Well, maybe. But just listen, Okay?"

Ryan and Angie were quiet, not offended by Deni's curtness. They knew him, they had been friends for a long time. That was just his way. They listened while Deni told the name of the murdered victim found in the ocean at Stage Fort Park. They listened while he told them that the affluent parents of the victim had been concerned when they hadn't heard from her and hired him to look into their missing daughter.

Deni told them that Lara was a talented guitarist and vocalist going to Berklee, and how he felt her disappearance and now discovered body was the handiwork of Gary Rennick. He then told them who Gary Rennick is.

He next explained how Cole Renner had been hired by Lara Myhre a few weeks prior to her disappearance to find her biological parents. How the closed adoption by the Myhres through a premier firm had made that investigation fruitless and frustrating for both the victim and Cole. How Deni had known nothing about this at the time of his investigation. The evidence that tied Renner to the victim was going to be used by Deni's former partner, Rick Hobbs, to hang him.

Ebb

Ryan and Angie listened without interruption as Deni laid out the entire sequence of events as he knew them. All of the events that had led him to that moment. When it seemed that all of the available facts had been told, Ryan spoke.

"You know that you're taking a huge bite out of a big steak on this one, Deni. A Boston sports god?"

"I know in my gut that he did it. It shouldn't matter that he plays for the Bruins."

"Boston sports fans are very forgiving. The only thing that you could do to lose their love is to leave and play for the Yankees or something. Take Aaron Hernandez. I wonder how many Patriots fans would accept him back with open arms right now? I would bet that you would be surprised by the outcome of that anonymous survey," Ryan said.

"That would never happen, Ry, and you know it. The team wouldn't have him back even if he didn't do it."

"And that is not the point I'm making. If you are a good player, in a huge sports town like Boston, the fans are willing to overlook some pretty big character flaws. I can keep going, Schilling stealing millions. Manny being Manny. Celtics' Jared Sullinger more recently."

"So what, he gets away with murder? Ry, I'm not gonna let that happen," Deni said.

"Maybe I'm confused," Angie said. "Ryan is a defense attorney, Deni. You aren't a statie anymore. What is it that you think we're going to be able to do?" She reached across the conference table, grabbing Deni's hand.

"I want the detectives to look at Rennick instead of Cole. The only way to do that is to prove Cole's innocence so they can look at another suspect. *The* suspect. We have to solve this adoption thing."

"Now I'm confused," Ryan admitted. "How does looking into a closed adoption, which is nearly impossible by the way, get us to proving that Rennick is the person who killed this Lara Myhre? Besides, from what you've said, all they have is a circumstantial case."

"People have been convicted on circumstantial cases. And the theory bein' that if Cole was about to solve the case and tell Lara who her birth parents were, then she probably wouldn't expose to the police the fact that he was operating without an investigator's license. But Cole wasn't close, and Lara was gettin' frustrated. The cops are gonna use that as motive for shutting her up, since that's a B felony with mandatory prison time," Deni said.

"But you just said that he wasn't close to solving it," Angie said.

"No, he wasn't. But the cops don't know that. I solve the adoption sayin' that he and I were working together on it, I have a legit investigator's license so he can work for me on it, that takes the motive away. It also makes Hobbs and Sheed look into who really did it, instead of him."

"I'm all for helping Cole out, but what you are preposing is dangerously close to misconduct and interfering with a criminal investigation," Ryan warned.

"You're the lawyer, but as long as I don't have to lie in court I think we are good. Lying to a police officer is only a misdemeanor, lying on the stand is perjury. Perjury means bye-bye Deni."

Ryan nodded. "And if you don't play this right, it will be bye-bye PI license."

"So let's do this right, Ry."

Ryan left the conference room and came back with a thick book that looked like an old Encyclopedia Britannica. It was a Westlaw book. He flipped to a section, put the book down on the conference room table, then sat himself.

"New Hampshire RSA 5-C:14. Legal closed-adoption records are sealed and confidential. Falsely obtaining those records is a Class B felony, which carries a mandatory sentence. Deni, I think this is over before it began. This crème-de-la-crème adoption agency of yours, I would have to assume, is a legitimate operation."

"So that's it?" Deni rubbed his head. "I can't believe that that's it."

"We could file a motion in probate court to have the records opened, if they are still operating out of New Hampshire. That would force the adoption agency to unseal the file. We could argue that the process was not legal, in the strictest sense, and therefore should not benefit from the protection of C:14."

Angie was making notes on what her husband had just said. The motion meant that she would have work to do.

"Okay. Now we're talkin', Ry."

"Before you get your hopes up, you need to know that this the flyer of all flyers. You know me, the 'hippie lawyer that takes the long-shots', but this is going to be a tough one. Courts don't like to open sealed files for just any reason. And we are fishing. We don't have a legitimate reason that any of what transpired was illegal," Ryan explained.

"They basically brokered a baby for fifty-grand," Deni said.

"And it's not illegal to sell your baby. Period. It's not illegal to give away your baby. If you neglect your child, the state can come and take your kid away. Then the child becomes a ward of the state. None of that happened here.   From what you described, this Regis & Chapman set up an adoption and as soon as the doc cut the umbilical cord, the Myhres took their baby home."

"Then I'll go through the hospital," Deni said.

"Medical records are sealed as well, with even less wiggle-room. And I know that you know that."

"It's no wonder why people fuckin' hate lawyers, Ry."

"Don't take your frustrations out on me or Ang. This is your gig, we're just trying to help."

"Maybe I'll just go and ask nicely."

Angie chuckled. "Then you might want to work on your delivery."

14

RYAN AND DENI DID GO TO SULLY'S TAVERN after the meeting in the conference room. It was tuesday night and the place was packed. It had once been a true dive bar, but the owner had decided to give it a makeover. It now had modern furniture and fixtures, replacing the pool table and dartboards because they commandeered valuable table space, and the new mandatory uniform for the female servers was a foray in minimalism.

The two men were able to get a corner booth, the previous occupants were not subtly asked to move out by the massive bouncer. He and Deni had a history, one where the bouncer not only admired Deni but was also fearful of him.

The need for bouncers at Sully's was not to examine identification or eject underage drinkers, although those tasks were sometimes needed. The need for muscle was due to the all-female staff wearing almost nothing and being encouraged to flirt with every male guest. Alcohol has a way of making men think that the flirtation is real, that they actually have a chance of hooking up with the female who is serving them food and drink. The muscle was to remind patrons that they could 'look but don't touch boys'.

The buxom server with red hair sashayed over to the booth once Deni and Ryan had sat. Deni ordered his usual Redbreast 12 year Irish Whiskey. Ryan ordered a Gin Lane, which was a handcrafted signature cocktail. The server flirted a bit and made sure that the two gents were well aware that she would be taking great care of them. Deni had no doubt that she would be keeping her eyes on them. At $30 a round before tip, she stood to make a good chunk of change on their table alone.

Deni turned to Ryan after the server left to fetch the libations. "What the hell are you drinkin'?"

Ryan gave Deni a long tablet-style menu with signature cocktails listed on it from the other side of the table. "Gin Lane," he said as he pointed to it.

Deni read the menu aloud. "'Hendrick's Gin, mint, cucumber, lemon-lime and soda.'" He turned back to Ryan. "Fourteen bucks. Did you lose your balls and grow a vag or what?"

"Why do you care what I drink? It's good."

"I'll take your word for it. Gin is nasty anyway you 'craft' it. Tastes like pine-needles."

"Not Hendrick's. It's made with cucumber. You should try it, Deni."

"Yeah I think I'll keep my sack thanks. So you don't think the motion is gonna fly?"

The server brought the drinks, handing the tree-hugger in the linen suit his drink first. "My boss says I need to hold a credit card if you're gonna run a tab. No offense, it's just really busy and you are getting top-shelf stuff. I like top-shelf men."

Deni rolled his eyes and gave her his credit card before Ryan could produce his.

"Deni, I got this."

"You're workin' for me for a change. Least I can do is buy you a couple of foufy drinks."

The server accepted the credit card, storing it in her ample cleavage and left with another wink. Deni wondered if she had a nervous tick or if she winked at people so often she didn't even realize she was doing it anymore.

"So to answer your question, no. I don't think we are going to win the motion," Ryan said after a sip of his drink.

"Why not? Adopted kids find their long lost parents all the time. If it's such a process, how are all these other idiots gettin' it done?"

"There are several types of adoptions," Ryan said. Then he went on to explain them.

He explained the domestic agency adoption, the kind done by the Myhres, first. This is when prospective adoptive parents submit information about themselves to an agency or agencies, who then pass the information on to the birth parent or parents. If the birth mother (and to a much lesser extent the birth father) is interested, the agency facilitates in the adoption process for a fee. Open adoptions are the most popular form of domestic adoption, the birth parents and adoptive parents will meet several times prior to adopting and will keep in touch after the adoption is finalized.

Some agencies still execute closed adoptions, which is when none of the birth or adoptive parents ever meet. Because of litigation after-the-fact, less agencies are still brokering closed domestic adoptions. Because of these lawsuits, the courts have made it nearly impossible to unseal closed adoption records.

Ebb

For context, Ryan explained other forms of adoption as the second round of drinks arrived. International adoptions go through agencies as well, and are almost always open. The birth mother outside of the United States often gives up her child for the chance at a better life. These are statistically always open adoptions because the mother always want to remain part of her child's life.

Independent adoptions work through a lawyer rather than an agency. Ryan had worked on two in his career. These are generally less expensive as lawyers only charge their normal legal fees, and ensure that the contract is legal. Birth parents can sell or give their baby away without the use of a lawyer, but often times will get sticky in subsequent years because there wasn't a written contract clarifying rights.

Finally, Ryan explained the foster care system of adoption. The child in these cases has been deemed a 'ward of the state', meaning the child was abandoned or taken away from the birth mother. The foster care system uses temporary homes to house the waiting child, the state pays a stipend to care for the child. Sometimes temporary houses take on multiple children as way to make money, the awaiting children can often end up in very bad situations because of it.

The third round of drinks arrived, Ryan had fallen behind because he was doing all of the talking.

Ebb

" …. Anyway, that is probably more than you wanted to know but I just wanted you to understand how it all works. These people are able to find their biological parents because there is usually a long trail of documents, all open, for an investigator such as yourself to find. You've never looked into an adoption before?"

"Once for JG. But he dealt with most of it. All I had to do was go and find the new residence of the parents. I didn't have to deal with all of this bullshit."

"For whatever reason, these people gave up Lara. There isn't going to be a paper trail. If they went through that kind of money and effort to stay anonymous, there probably isn't anything we are going to be able to do to find them."

"So what do you suggest my next move is? The parents want justice, and Cole going to jail for the rest of his life ain't sittin' right with me. The fuckin' father wants me to kill him."

"I must be drunk already. Myhre wants you to kill who? Cole?"

"No, Rennick. He is convinced that he did it, because I'm convinced he did it. I told him that I was gonna try to solve the adoption mystery so I could clear Cole. He told me not to bother and just kill Rennick."

"Yeah well I would advise that that not be your next move."

"DUH. Ya think? What is?"

Ryan thought for a second, took a sip of his gin. "What I would suggest I'm not legally allowed to suggest."

"I know. So we'll play it straight. We'll try it your way, Ry. When do you think this court thing is gonna happen?"

"Couple of days, max."

"Fine. You've got a couple of days."

Ryan nodded, understanding the implication. "So what are you going to do in the meantime?"

"I'm gonna make Gary Rennick really uncomfortable. Maybe pick a fight."

15

RISTUCCIA MEMORIAL ARENA in Wilmington, Massachusetts, is closed to the public during Bruin's practices. Only the press and those allowed by either Owner Jeremy Jacobs or General Manager Peter Chiarelli are allowed access to the team. Especially during a playoff run. The Bruins often used the Wilmington facility for practices when The Boston Garden wasn't available, which was often. The Celtics played at the Garden as well, though not that May because they hadn't made the playoffs and their season was over. Concerts were held there. Cirque Du Soleil. There were all sorts of events which made the Garden crew put up the boards and uncover the ice, then tear it down again, making the arena unavailable.

Deni knew a lot of people in and around Boston. Some were from his neighborhood. Some were from when he used to run with crooks. Some from being a police officer, while others he had met through Mixed Martial Arts. Boston may have millions of inhabitants in the city itself, but it is still a small world. Wilmington was thirty minutes north-west of the city, and Deni knew the Zamboni driver for 'The Rist'.

The Zamboni driver told Deni that the Bruins had two skates scheduled for wednesday. Deni opted for the afternoon practice because he was mildly hungover from Sully's. He had put a dent in his head and his credit card from the experience.

He was allowed in through the service entrance and led to the stands as prearranged. The large men skating on the ice had their playoff beards and were virtually flying around the ice. Coach Julien and his assistants were on the ice as well, blowing whistles that pierced Deni's ears and sluggish brain.

The offensive lines were at one end of the ice running drills with Chad Johnson, the backup goaltender in net. The defensive lines were on the opposite end running drills with Tuukka Rask. Deni made his way around the rink to the end where the big defensemen were skating. All the names were there.

Ebb

Tory Krug. Corey Potter. Zdeno Chára, at six foot nine before he put on his skates. And Gary Rennick who was getting razzed by the veterans.

Deni watched for a little while from high in the stands. He didn't want Rennick to see him just yet. Watching the men skate live was very different from seeing it on TV. The men moved fast, attaining top speeds of nearly twenty miles per hour. Getting hit by someone who is roughly two hundred pounds at that rate of speed and has razor sharp blades on his feet is dangerous. Slammed into the boards, down onto the ice, shoulder to shoulder, all of it punishing the bodies of the players. Deni wondered how much harder the hits were outside of practice, when they were checking skaters on the opposing team. It was brutal and he loved it.

He was a bit disappointed when he sensed that things were wrapping up, but duty called. He needed to set up his ambush, so he went toward the walkway to the locker room.

The defensemen were let off the ice first. The door to the bench opened and the men began walking with their skates on the rubber matting toward the dressing room. Deni was there waiting.

"Hey guys. Did you know that your new defenseman is a fucking murderer?"

Rennick went white. "Who let this guy in? No autographs now man," he said nervously. He was quite obviously trying to pretend that Deni was a crazed fan.

"I've already got your signature on the Rights Waiver form when you talked to the state cops. Did you boys know that he was pulled in for questioning? He murdered a twenty-two year old college girl. Big fuckin' man huh? How many of you boys have daughters?"

The line of men had stopped. Nobody was making their way toward the dressing room anymore. They were all turning to look at Rennick.

"Go ahead, tell'em Gare."

"I'm gonna fuckin' kill you," Rennick yelled.

"Say it louder, Gare. First the girl, now me."

It was a train-wreck and nobody could take their eyes off of it.

"Did she beg before you drowned her? How long did you have to hold her under the water? Tiny girl like that, you must have felt so strong."

The coaching staff had finally taken notice of the commotion. Coach Julien made a motion for security to remove the unwanted visitor.

The embarrassed defenseman was being stared at by his teammates. "The guy is fucked. I'm gonna sue him," he said to them.

"You are my personal project, Rennick. Everywhere you turn, I'm gonna be there." Deni was now being dragged toward an exit by security. Deni could have easily fended them off, done bodily harm to both of the security guards. But he didn't. Or brandished his weapon, but he wisely left it in the Rover.

"If she doesn't haunt you every night, I'm gonna," Deni continued to yell as he was dragged further away. "Don't close your eyes, 'cuz I'll be there."

The guards didn't ask how he had gotten in. They didn't take down his name. They simply deposited him outside of the arena toward the parking lot.

In the parking lot, there were a few sports reporters loitering about. ESPN. Hockey Digest. Hockey News. Some local news teams. They were all looking to acquire a sound bite from one Bruin or another, something to give the fans during their playoff run. 'Is there a goaltending controversy?' 'What is the plan to stop Montreal's top line?' The team would be accosted on the way to their vehicles.

Deni couldn't leave well enough alone. The sight of the reporters gave him an idea.

He decided that it was time to out Gary Rennick. The bastard was getting away with murder, and he needed to pay. The detectives weren't interested in pursuing him, they had decided that an innocent man was good for Lara's murder. The police were wrong and he was determined to expose it to the press. The press would make the police do their job. The police would have to look into Gary Rennick for the murder.

Deni spoke to the reporters, holding his own impromptu press conference. Instead of getting a scoop on how the Bruins were going to get through the current round of the playoffs, they learned that new kid that just got called up, the hot hand from Providence, was a suspected murderer. He was one of Boston's adopted sons. Boston College's top defenseman; earning the best defensive defenseman both his junior and senior years there, the first to ever receive the award more than once. He was drafted by Boston. He played for Boston's AHL affiliate, which made him one of their own. And now he was tearing it up in the bigs. He was called up because of injuries, but he belonged in the NHL. He belonged to Boston. And now he would stab the hearts of those who made him, those who loved him. The city's adopted son was a murderer.

The press was going to have a field day.

16

THE WEDNESDAY EVENING SUN was low on the horizon, dying until its rebirth. The light blinded Deni through his driver-side window despite the tint. He drove north as his house in Barstone was much closer from Wilmington than his place in South Boston. The traffic was as light as his mood since Deni was quite pleased with himself. He had rattled the cage of the bear. Gary Rennick's days as a Bruin were numbered. Betman, the NHL commissioner, would demand sanctions if the Bruin front office didn't react. And react they would. They would have no choice once the news of Rennick's alleged murder involvement was plastered on the front page of every paper, the lead on every local television sportscast. It was probably big enough to make ESPN take notice, though little time was devoted to hockey on Sportscenter. Barry Melrose might have a quip.

Deni's cell rang as he was crossing the border into New Hampshire. The Rover's bluetooth tried to accept the call through the stereo/navigation system but he didn't let it. He accepted the call manually.

"Deni, it's Cole."

"I'm workin' on gettin' you out. I've got Ryan Wells workin' on it too. You probably shouldn't have wasted your one call on me, guy. You shoulda called Christina, she's probably worried sick."

The right to a single phone call from jail is a myth. There is no, "You have the right to remain silent …. " yada yada and a single phone call. The myth originated because of a suspect's right to an attorney and the need for that suspect to contact said attorney. But it is a myth just the same. The police can contact legal representation on behalf of the accused. The phone call is a courtesy. It is also not uncommon for a cooperative suspect to be granted more than one call. The entire situation is arbitrary, dependent on the whims of the arresting officers.

"Deni, I'm not in jail. I wasn't arrested thanks to you."

"Really? That's great. What a relief. Glad I could help. What happened?"

"You giving me the heads up gave me time to get my ducks in a row. The two detectives, Hobbs and Sheed, came by yesterday morning. They wanted to conduct an interview, so I gave it to them straight. I showed them the paperwork that I was working on Lara's case, the confidentiality agreement and stuff. Everything they had was circumstantial and explained. They were outta here in less than two hours. Other than the fact that Christina kept interrupting to come to my defense, the whole thing went smooth as silk."

"Quick and dirty. So it was painful but it's over," Deni said.

"I don't know about over. They said I would be getting a summons to appear for conducting investigations without a license. We will see what happens there. But yeah, quick and dirty. I never even had to leave my house. Thanks for the heads up."

"No problem. I'm glad it worked out. Give wifey a hug for me. You keep outta trouble. Oh, and let me know when that court date is. I can say that you were working for me. It might help."

"Will do. On the hug that is. Don't worry about the appearance, I'll deal with it. But keep in touch huh? It shouldn't take a homicide for us to see each other," Cole said.

"I hear ya."

The day was getting better by the minute for Deni. He hung up with Cole, making a mental note that he needed to make up for the dinner that never happened. He also wanted to thank Sheed. He had told her that Cole was innocent, and she had obviously taken it to heart. Hobbs would have wanted to conduct the interview in Boston, which means that if he had his way they would have dragged Cole from his home in North Billerica to do so. Sheed must have pushed to conduct the interview at the suspect's house. He also knew that it was very likely Sheed who had pushed for the decision not to make an arrest. He dialed her number as he pulled into his garage in Barstone.

"Hey Deni." He was surprised she picked up, as she had been ignoring his last few phone calls.

"Hey, I heard that you didn't arrest Cole Renner. I wanted to thank you. Can you talk or is your shadow right there?"

"I'm at my desk, but he is off doing something meaningless I'm sure. Listen, it had nothing to do with me. There was nothing there. He had been in touch with her and access was explainable. His motive was shaky at best."

Deni had arrived at his home. He threw his keys in the basket that was on a small stand by the door.

"Yeah well, I have seen people get arrested on less. So you're gonna look at Gary Rennick now?"

"No. Deni, I hate to be the one to break it to you, but this case is probably not going to get solved."

"You've been workin' with Hobbs too long, She. The fuck kinda attitude is that?"

"Hey watch it. I want this bastard as much as you do. Probably more. I look at the long list of names on the Clearinghouse every day and it makes me sick. Some sick fuck tortured this girl. Nobody is better than anybody else, Deni, they all deserve justice. They all mean something. But this girl had talent. She was rich and beautiful and talented and smart and loved. If we can't solve this one, then what the hell are we doin' here?"

"So go break Rennick's balls," he said as he took a sip of the whiskey he had poured.

"No wonder you're still single, Deni. You don't listen. Let's say you're right. Let's say that Rennick did it. How are we going to prove it? We don't have a tight window for an alibi, even. We don't know if he was the last person to see her alive, because we don't know what exact day she went missing. We even shelled out some serious coin to the National Oceanic and Atmospheric Administration to look at tidal currents and predictions data."

"What the hell is that?"

"The NOAA looks at tidal ebb and flow, weather patterns and stuff. We wanted to see if they could figure out where exactly she was put in the water and when, based on where she was found and when. Top dollar to expedite it. They laughed at us."

"So all we know is that she was hit on the back of the head and drowned in clear water, then dumped at some point roughly nine weeks ago in salt water," Deni said like he was stating a question.

"That about sums it up. The guy who did this was smart. The decomp from the ocean left no DNA and messed with our time of death. We've got the stuff that was pulled from under her skin still on queue over in Maynard but unless that has the name and social of our doer stamped on it, this is going to end up in cold cases. Sorry Deni."

"Well, I don't give up that easy. There has to be another way to go about this."

"Good luck finding it and keep me posted. Hobbs is officially moving on, we have to focus on our other cases."

"Meaning *you* have to focus on your other cases," Deni corrected.

"You got it."

"I guess Leonard was right," Deni said.

"Leonard Myhre? How so?"

"He said that I shouldn't waste my time with the police and that he wants me to kill him."

"He hired you to kill him?"

"No. He was upset. He just meant to go around the police. Do you think that I would admit to a detective that I was hired to kill someone? He wants me to stay on the case until the killer is called onto the carpet. He had a moment of weakness. Told me to basically save the police from having to bring him to trial."

Lisa let Deni's last comment hang on the air for a moment, both phones were silent for a few moments.

"Huh. I guess I would want whomever did it to be dead also. But you need to keep us in the loop, Deni. You can't go rogue."

17

THURSDAY MORNING, after his second cup of coffee, Deni decided to go to Regis & Chapman, the prestigious adoption agency that handled Lara Myhre. He knew it was a shot in the dark but he wanted to acquire as much information as he could to complete the file. If he had to close the book on the case like the police were preparing to do, he wanted to be able to at least hand the Myhres every known detail. He would tell them who had given birth to their daughter, what they wanted to do with that information was their business. If they even wanted to read the report since they said that they didn't want to know.

Cole was officially off the hook but there was still Gary Rennick on the loose. A fact that Deni could not abide.

The drive to Nashua, New Hampshire from the Barstone/Wayland area took thirty minutes and virtually all of it was on Route 111 west. Nashua was Wayland's twin city in New Hampshire. The two cities were the biggest of the state, and the only classified as such. Cities are not elevated from town or township based on population alone; they are designated such based on a number of other factors such as governmental hierarchy, public transportation, and others. Nashua and Wayland are identical in almost every category.

Regis & Chapman had a storefront location in a building built in the late 1800s on the corner of Main and Canal Street in downtown Nashua. There were boutiques, eateries, an art gallery and an adoption agency all lined up in a row in that building. The local chapter of the Better Business Bureau was likely very proud. Metered angle-parking faced the building and the Nashua River beyond it. Deni thought it very swanky if not a bit pretentious.

He imagined that there would be a little bell as he walked through the door with lace curtains, but there wasn't one. The receptionist behind the open desk inside Regis & Chapman was attractive and bored.

There was nobody in the waiting room which was set up like a luxurious living room. The receptionist's posture changed from slumped boredom to erect perkiness as Deni crossed the colonial style room and through the various furnishings.

The receptionist gave him a long look from top to bottom as he made his way across the room toward her. Her face didn't give away if she liked what she was seeing or if she was offended by it. He wore his usual uniform, the only variation was the grey t-shirt with a *Boston Scally Co.* logo on the front.

"Hello. Welcome to Regis & Chapman. How can I help you?" She looked up at Deni from her chair.

"I'm looking to get some information about an adoption that was arranged by you guys," he said.

"Do you have an appointment, Mr. …..?"

"Dennihan. And no." He removed his New Hampshire Investigator's License from his wallet, showing it to her." As he was making the transaction she noticed the handle of his pistol in the holster under his jacket.

Her demeanor changed again but this time to serious concern. The chameleon handed back his license, told him to take a seat in the spotless living room as she picked up the phone receiver on her desk. Deni did as he was instructed but listened intently to the short conversation taking place at the reception desk. He could only hear one side of the chat of course, but it didn't sound like the receptionist was bored anymore. She sounded like she was being scolded. For what, Deni didn't know. She was just doing her job.

Within one minute of the termination of the phone conversation, a tall and anorexically thin blonde woman opened an office door and elegantly made her way toward Deni. Apparently she was as busy on the other side of the office door as the receptionist was on his side of it. He thought that at $50,000 a kid, they didn't need to be very busy. That was a 1992 dollar amount, he imagined it had gone up since. Inflation.

The tall, middle-aged blonde stuck her hand out like Deni should kiss it, he gave it a firm handshake instead.

"Nora Chapman," she said. "Mr. Dennihan is it?" She retracted her hand like Deni had spit in it.

"It is. Everybody calls me Deni."

"My receptionist informed me that you are an investigator looking into a past adoption?"

"Yeah. You guys arranged one back in 1992. I know the adopting parents and the adopted kid's current name, social security number, and the hospital she was delivered at. I need you to fill in the rest of the blanks," Deni said.

"I'm sorry, but we don't handle adoption inquiries. Information is available on past adoptions through the city clerk or the courts. For various reasons, our policy is to refer all inquiries to them."

"Nora Chapman, you said your name is?"

"Correct," she said.

"As in the other half of Regis & Chapman?"

"Yes."

"Seems to me you could make an exception to your own policy," Deni said forcing an uncomfortable smile.

Nora stared at him. Her eyes had the expression as though he had just taken a shit on her Persian rug, while her mouth also made an effort to smile.

"Be that as it may, it *is* my policy. It's a policy that is non-negotiable," she insisted.

"Everything is negotiable, lady. What's your price?" Friendly wasn't working.

"I beg your pardon? The insinuation is vulgar," Chapman said.

"Fifty grand to arrange an adoption is vulgar. You're money hungry, clearly. So what's the price. I need to know who you arranged the adoption for. We can do this the easy way or the hard way, but make no mistake I'm gonna get what I want."

Ebb

"I think that I would like you to leave." Nora's arm extended toward the door, as if Deni forgot where it was.

The receptionist was trying not to watch the commotion in the center of the living room in front of her, but the urge to watch was irresistible.

"I'll be outta your hair as soon as you tell me what I want to know. Listen, lady. I know that you don't know me so I'm gonna give you a little information. I get what I want. Period. I've been hired to find out who the birth parents are of a female born at Dartmouth-Hitchcock Hospital here in Nashua. Lara Myhre. Your agency arranged the adoption. So again, we can do this the easy way or the hard way, but make no mistake I'm gonna get the information. Save yourself the grief. Think of me like a rapist. You can kick and scream all ya want but this is gonna happen. Why not just give me the information I want?"

The receptionist giggled from behind her desk, ducking behind her computer monitor.

"Charming. You have ten-seconds to leave the premises or I am going to call the police, Mr. Rapist."

"Have it your way. I'll be back." Deni made his way toward the front door. Before closing it behind himself he called back.

"Try not to miss me."

18

WHILE DENI WAS MAKING FRIENDS in Nashua, Ryan Wells was in Wayland County Probate Court. He was able to get a thursday morning docket in front of the Honorable Steven Kimble. Ryan's motion to unseal the records of the closed 1992 adoption had been filed and a hearing had been expedited as Ryan knew the judge's clerk from the country club.

The hearing was not a formal one. The judge wasn't presiding in a courtroom or wearing a robe or even holding a gavel. He was behind his desk in his chambers. The court stenographer was present to make a legal record of the hearing. The judge's clerk and Ryan's club friend was also in attendance if the need

Ebb

arose to look up a legal precedent or to get the exact wording of a statute. Both the stenographer and the clerk were off to opposing sides in the chamber, Ryan and Judge Kimble were on opposite sides of his large oak desk in the center of the room.

The motion to unseal the documents would either be granted or quashed. If granted, a notice would be sent to Regis & Chapman. The agency would then either send the records over to Ryan Wells & Associates via courier, or they would fight the ruling. Ignoring the writ would earn Regis, Chapman, or both a contempt charge and jail time. If that occurred, an attorney could fight the judge's ruling on their behalf. That would require a much more formal hearing under a superior court.

"Ryan Wells. How are you?" The judge held up his finger to the stenographer, letting her know that she needn't start recording the proceeding as of yet.

"Very good, Your Honor. How are you?"

"Very well, thank you. Are you going to attend the Gala at the Wayland Country Club? You are a member, yes?"

"Yes. Well, no. Yes I am a member, but no I won't be there. My wife and I have a conflict unfortunately," Ryan said.

"Pity. So we have a motion to unseal the documents of a closed adoption."

"Yes, Sir."

"This should be a short hearing," he said to his clerk. He nodded to the stenographer, stating the date and the business at hand for the transcript. "I've read your brief counselor and I see no reason to open the files," he continued for the record.

"Before you quash, Judge, I would like to point out that the adopted child is deceased. In Preacher v. Harris the higher court ruled in favor of the greater good. The only issue that could possibly arise from opening the records would be from the birth parent or parents," Ryan argued.

"I see that citing in your motion." The judge looked to his clerk who was behind a smaller desk in the corner on a computer. The clerk slash friend was researching the finding.

"Your Honor," the clerk said. "In that case it was the biological father who was dead, waiving his right to anonymity in his last will and testament. He bequeathed all of his possessions to the last living heir. The adopted child was that last heir. The records were unsealed in order to find that heir and carry out those final wishes."

"I concede that the case isn't exactly on point, Judge," Ryan said. "But the spirit of the finding is the same. Because of the death of one of the parties the documents are said to protect, there is far more good than harm in opening the sealed records."

"Are the birth parent or parents still among the living, Mr. Wells?"

"I don't know that. I won't know that unless the motion is granted."

"Then I don't see how we can determine how much harm can come from this," the judge said. "You've put the horse before the cart has even been built."

"Pardon me Your Honor, but with all due respect, this legal conundrum of chicken and egg frustrates the legal proceeding. You won't grant the documents unsealed without knowledge of who the birth parent or parents are, yet we cannot know that unless the records are opened."

"Welcome to probate court, counselor. Sealed records are such to protect all affected parties. I am loathe to create a precedent which opens legally confidential documents to fish for evidence that would support or deny a claim to attain said documents."

"Your Honor - "

" — Motion to unseal the adoption record is quashed," the judge said.

"Your Honor - "

" — GOOD DAY, Mr. Wells."

"Hey Deni. Where are you?" Ryan had called Warren from the confines of his Audi after the unproductive hearing with Judge Kimble.

"On my way to Dartmouth-Hitchcock, where are you?"

"I just got my ass handed to me in Kimble's chambers. The motion was quashed. A big no-go on the adoption records. I'm not the kind of guy to say, 'I told you so' Deni. But if I were that kind of guy, I would be saying, 'I told you so.' Judges don't like to do anything that can embarrass themselves. Having their ruling overturned in a higher court is embarrassing. We might have gotten the information if the motion was granted, but more likely it would have been overturned in superior court anyway."

"I just left the adoption agency, they definitely would have fought it. That woman has an enormous stick up her skinny ass."

"So you're having the same kind of day I'm having so far?"

Ebb

"Sounds like it," Deni agreed.

"So why are you going to the hospital?"

"See if I can find anything out from them."

"Deni, you had a better chance at the agency. Medical records are sacrosanct."

"Yeah, well …. If they say no, they say no. But they can't say yes to something if I never ask."

"How very philosophical of you. Did you trade Brazilian Jiu-Jitsu for Yoga?"

"No. I'm just tryin' to stay positive for once. I've matured."

"Funny."

"Besides, I'm not askin' for anybody's medical records. I'm just askin' for names out of those records."

"It's a slippery slope with hospitals. They don't want to get sued. First they give you their name, then an insurance company …. If you backdoor the information that you want because of information that they gave you, the hospital will have a new owner. My advice is don't ask for a list. See if someone can tell you verbally who was giving birth in June 1992. Plausible deniability. They need to be able to deny ever telling you anything. But if they want to keep their job, likely nobody is going to tell you anything."

"Let's hope that I get someone dumb or disgruntled," Deni said.

"Happy hunting."

19

DARTMOUTH-HITCHCOCK MEDICAL CENTER is an enormous level-one trauma hospital. They have many satellite facilities, the Nashua location is by far the largest. In fact, it is the largest hospital in the state. The Dartmouth University School of Medicine is housed in one of the buildings as well, instead of with the rest of the campus in Hanover, Hew Hampshire.

The maps and directories didn't help Deni find where he was going. It was like being dropped onto the green of a massive university campus. There were many buildings, all conducting various medical business. Research, medical students, cancer, emergency trauma, mental healthcare, rehabilitation, and neuroscience were but a few of the divisions within the various buildings within the gigantic complex. He drove in through the north entrance and parked in the visitor garage.

He left his gun and holster in the glove box for legal reasons and explored the campus. Twenty minutes of wandering led Deni to wonder if he was ever going to find the birthing pavilion, and if so, would he ever find his SUV again.

He eventually admitted that he was lost to the woman who had already made that determination at her first glance at the lost puppy. She introduced herself as a concierge, which confused Deni as he had thought that he was in a hospital not a hotel. He said that he was looking for the place where babies are born, which the accommodating woman took to mean that he was father to a child that was being born in their pavilion.

With healthcare being on the minds and tongues of the entire country, medical facilities were doing everything they could to draw consumers into their profit centers. All wanted to be the best and brightest in the field of medicine, all wanted to provide the best in medical care. To be the first choice in care for someone who is ill and give the best service to both those seeking medical help and the loved ones who would visit them. Dartmouth-Hitchcock was no different. In fact, they wanted to compete with the Boston facilities which had a long history of being the best in east.

To that end, the concierge procured a golf-cart type conveyance to personally drive the father-to-be to the birthing pavilion which was on the opposite side of the complex. Deni never corrected her on the trip over. In fact, he decided to feed the misconception. By the time he had arrived on the correct wing, his non-existent wife and unborn son had backstories. Between lies, Deni found out that the pavilion was built in 1990 and is an exclusive facility as price often eliminates or reduces insurance coverage.

When he and his tour guide had arrived at the front desk of the pavilion, Deni immediately took note of the high level of security. Sphincter tight. Because he was being escorted by the concierge, he was allowed to pass through the entrance to the wing without question, but that seemed impossible had he not had the fortune of running into her.

He made a joke about the high level of security and it was explained that they take it very seriously. Each child has a coded medallion fastened to him or her, if the medallion gets within twenty yards of an exit, alarms will sound. Deni wondered if that type of security and technology was available in 1992. He never received an answer.

Ebb

Down the hall, various rooms had handwritten tags with names on the outside of the doors. Deni noticed that each room had one name, meaning that each of the rooms were single mother/patient. He quickly took note of one of the names as he was brought to the reception desk.

The concierge made introduction to the receptionist, Carol, who inquired Deni's name.

"Cormier," he said.

"Ah yes. She has already been brought over to the spa. You can join her if you wish or you can wait here Mr. Cormier."

"Spa? I'm confused. Isn't she here to deliver a baby?"

"Of course. But when contractions start, the water and bubbles relax her. You may see for yourself if you like."

"No, no. That's fine. I'm old-school. I'll wait here until it's all over."

Both of the woman were very put-off by the fact that Deni wanted to remain outside of the delivery process and deemed him as unsupportive. With that, the concierge left to find another lost puppy. Carol tried to go back to work, but Deni didn't let her.

"So how long have you worked here?"

"Almost ten years," Carol replied.

"Oh. So you must have a ton of seniority. No holidays or night shifts for you, huh?"

"Not even close. This is a really nice hospital and a super-nice maternity unit. Nobody leaves this job."

"Nice work if you can get it. So which one of these girls do you have to bump off?" Deni looked around at the various women in colorful scrubs milling about.

"What are you talking about, Mr. Cormier?"

"Which one has the most seniority? Who's gotta go before you get bumped up?"

Carol looked thoroughly confused. "I have a lot of work to do. You can have a seat in the lounge if you like."

"No thanks. It's stuffy in there. Plus nobody is probably watching what I want to watch on the TV. I'm just curious who has the most seniority because my friends had their kid here. It was a while back, so I wanted to see if someone would remember them."

She didn't seem satisfied with the explanation. "Even if there was someone here now that was here when your friends gave birth, we can't really talk about it. You understand, I'm sure. Patient confidentiality? You wouldn't want us to speak about you, I'm sure."

"Oh …. We both know that you'll be talking about me after I'm gone."

Carol didn't hide the roll of her eyes as she went back to work on her computer.

Deni was getting nowhere and he was getting there slowly. Time to put his foot on the gas.

"Listen, maybe you could just tell me if any one of the pajama girls was here in 1992. I can talk to them and they can either tell me stuff or not. That way I can get out of your hair and into someone else's."

He was attracting attention, and not in a good way. One of the other females in a scrub uniform approached the area from behind the counter, behind Carol.

"What's happening over here? Are you harassing her? Flirting with the receptionist while your partner is giving birth is pretty sick. You should be ashamed."

Time to come clean, Deni thought. *Mostly.* He took out his wallet, producing his investigator's license for New Hampshire.

"My name isn't Cormier. It's Dennihan. You can call me Deni. I am trying to find information about the birth of a child here in 1992. It was an adoption and there has been a death in the family. I have been hired to track down the birth parents. I am hoping that someone here was working on any or all of the days of

June 4th through 6th, 1992. That's when the child was born in this very hospital."

There was silence between the two women, who didn't look at each other, only at Deni. One or both of them must have pushed a silent alarm because within ten-seconds of completing his plea, he was being dragged out of the hospital by security. Again, he could have fought back. Neither of the men were particularly strong or adept at holds or restraints. Deni was a coral belt, or master in Brazilian Jiu-Jitsu, meaning that he could have run a clinic on the two lads. But to what end? So he took his lumps and was thrown out.

He shouted from the parking structure at the two guards who were going back into the medical center. "I've been thrown outta better hospitals than this!"

Everybody has to do things the hard way, he thought.

20

THURSDAY EVENING, ROUGHLY ONE WEEK INTO the Lara Myhre murder case, and Deni was nowhere with it. After leaving the hospital on thursday he went home to Barstone. Once there, he put on a pot of coffee and contemplated his next move. Nothing came to mind. Caffeinated as much as irritated, he decided to blow off some steam with a run. He wanted to beat the shit out of someone at the gym, but he liked his MMA gym in Brookline, Massachusetts better than the one he had found in New Hampshire. Beating the crap out of someone who doesn't have the faintest idea of how to fight back isn't fun, and it certainly isn't therapeutic. So he ran.

He ran ten miles in the eighty-degree, early-evening, early May sun. He sweat and he ran and he thought as he pounded the pavement. Still he came up with no legitimate way of attaining the names of Lara Myhre's birth parents.

It was no longer a way to finalize a case or to tie up all lose ends. It was now a mission. Deni didn't give a rat's ass about much of anything in life. Not until you said that he *couldn't* do something did he make what was forbad his number one goal. It was yet another one of his 'things'.

He took a shower and made a trip to Margarita's Mexican Restaurant in Wayland, just on the other side of the Boston commuter rail. The restaurant was packed with people either celebrating Cinco de Mayo early or were getting their livers ready for the holiday.

Deni started off with the Mayan Shrimp, which are normally fried but he had them grilled as was his normal request. The grilled shrimp were then tossed in chipotle aioli and put on top of corn salsa and extra avocado. His shit day was getting better. Next he had the Ahi Tuna Street Tacos, which were his favorite. The rare tuna with orange slaw he thought was the perfect combination. He washed it all down with a few La Chica margaritas. He normally hated margaritas, but he was forced to try one on a date once and became hooked. He hated the name because it was designed to be low calorie and made for 'chicks'. But they tasted great. The establishment had a policy of allowing a maximum of two because of the potency, but Deni was always allowed more. He was neither a chick nor a lightweight.

Somewhere between margarita two and three he decided that he was going to have to get dirty on this case. He was going to have to get his information the illegal way. The hard way.

The lights for Regis & Chapman were extinguished, as one would expect at 2:00 AM friday morning. Deni wanted to break into the establishment earlier on thursday night but there was an eatery slash bar that was located two doors down in the same building as the adoption agency, and people were milling about in front of it smoking cigarettes. Thirsty thursday was still in full swing.

The building shared a back alley which faced the Nashua River. Deni had reconnoitered the rear entrance only to come to the realization that the alley was busier than the front of the building. Dishwashers and bartenders and servers would go back there for their own cigarette breaks; gossiping about coworkers, going over details about what they were going to do after their horrible shift, and the horrible people who were not only paying the bills in their sections but adding to the tips needed to pay their own bills.

By law, the alcohol cutoff in Nashua is 2:00 AM on thursday nights/friday mornings; however, this particular establishment for whatever reason decided to close for business every night at 1:00 AM. Deni thought, *smart — nothing good ever happens after 1:00 AM anyway.* By two, the eatery was finally dark, the disgruntled staff had gone to one home or another, and Deni could do his handiwork.

Deni grew up in South Boston stealing his daily bread. Bread being car stereos. The occasional car. He started as an apprentice at ten years old, his mentor a mere fifteen. At forty-one, there was not a lock built that he couldn't pick. In and of itself this is an impressive skill. Arguably not an admirable one, but impressive nevertheless. Made more so by the fact that he can do it in seconds. Deni can break into your house while you are still looking for your keys. It is yet another one of his 'things'.

Security systems, however, can be tricky. They can be tricky if you don't know exactly how to circumvent the elaborate set up. Deni was not good at technology. Cameras and infrared scanners. Lasers and motion detectors. All a major headache and to Deni a state-of-the-art that he could not wrap his brain around. As an investigator, he would sometimes get consulted on how to set up these elaborate systems. In every consultation he advised to stay away from the big corporations like TYCO, Honeywell, or Vector. Major security companies have 24 hour remote surveillance, which is an attractive component, but that also means that the system can be remotely shut-off 24 hours per day. Deni was chuckling to himself when he saw the ADT sticker proudly displayed on both the front window and the door to the alley.

Deni dialed the cell phone number of an acquaintance that worked at the ADT emergency switchboard. The two had a long history, as they knew people who knew each other. They had met long ago and Deni would occasionally call and pay him a small fee through a third party, their mutual acquaintance. You are only as secure as the one watching your back.

"It's Deni. I need a safe word."

Ebb

"Usual charge."

"And you'll get it."

"What's the address?"

Deni gave him the address on the corner of Main and Canal. Deni heard the clicking of computer keys in the background. After a few seconds, the acquaintance told him the safe word.

"Papoose."

"What? What was that again?" Deni had never heard the word before, and needed to hear it again."

"Jesus, Deni. Papoose. I could spell it for you, but you won't need to spell it."

"I got it. Fuckin' pretentious people."

"Good luck."

Deni removed the two titanium pins from his wallet. He had four tucked away there, but the other two were backups. The two pins he removed were to pick the lock to the back door from the alley. One pin would be pushed into the keyhole and then eventually turned to disengage the bolt when the lock allowed the bolt to recoil. The second was for the tumblers. Locks can have as few as five or as many as fifteen tumblers. This is what the high-points of a key hit to lift them, allowing the lock to turn. For anyone who has locked themselves out of something, they know how infuriating it can be to lift all of the tumblers

190

Ebb

simultaneously. This is the tricky part. And the easy part for Deni.

The back door had a lock and a deadbolt. The deadbolt was tricker. It had fifteen tumblers and took the most time unlock. He was inside the back door in less than twenty-five seconds. Deni closed the back door, locking himself inside. He then made his way around the inside of the agency by the light of his cell phone. He didn't have a flashlight app, he just kept touching the surface of his iPhone to keep the screen illuminated.

The agency phone rang within seconds of being inside. Deni picked up, knowing who was on the other end of the line.

"This is ADT, we are showing an alarm going off. We see on the cameras that someone is inside, however all of the lights are off. They are using a small flashlight I believe." The person on the other end of the line was not his contact, which was Deni's expectation.

"It's okay. It's just me. I think we have a tripped breaker or something, none of the lights work. Safe word is papoose," Deni said hoping that he pronounced it correctly.

"Very well then. Would you like us to send help?"

Ebb

"That won't be necessary. I'm sure the police have better things to do than help me find a tripped breaker."

"Have a nice night then."

"You too," Deni said and hung up.

Deni had assumed that there were cameras, but the caller had confirmed it. He would need to ensure that he kept his cell phone away from his face for fear of it providing enough light to get an image of him. He moved away from the reception desk, where he had answered the phone, toward the door that Nora Chapman had come out of when they had met. Locked.

Less than ten-seconds later he was on the other side of that door inside her office. Most of the time in gaining entrance was consumed in reacquiring the pins that he had slipped back into his wallet while speaking to the ADT representative.

He was about to insert the pins back into his wallet when he saw the bank of tall filing cabinets along one of the walls in the large office.

Fuckin' Fort Knox.

There was no indication from the outside of the cabinets what Nora's system of filing was. Alphabetical? By year? Dewey Decimal System? Deni decided to work from left to right, the cabinet closest to the door first. He popped the lock and opened the top drawer of the first cabinet. Alphabetical by year. He closed the top drawer and moved to the second. Regis & Chapman had been doing business since 1989.

How old was Chapman when she got into this business? She looks good. Stick up her skinny ass, but she looks good all things considered.

He moved on to the next filing cabinet to the right. No file for Myhre. Deni now realized that the information he was looking for would be under 1992 but by the birth parents last name. Information which he didn't know. He also realized by looking at the files that the agency was rolling in money. There were over forty files under 1992. Deni wondered if whomever Regis was had as many or more for the same year. At $50,000 a pop, he decided he was in the wrong business.

The phone rang out at the reception desk. Deni listened while the voicemail picked up on the third ring. The system was silent for both the outgoing message and the message from whomever had called. Only he determined that whomever had called hadn't left a message, because within a few seconds the phone was ringing again.

Shit.

Quickly he scanned through as many files as he could, looking for the name Myhre on any of the paperwork in the files. He didn't have much time. He didn't know how much time it would take for the local police to be on the scene, but he knew he was going to find out.

Abrahams, nothing.

Bertrand, again no.

He went as fast as he could, moving from the files closest to him toward the back of the filing cabinet. The light was dim and his window for gaining information was closing. Past the C's and D's. There weren't any E's. The first document inside all of the files, attached to the inside of the front cover, seemed to be the quick reference sheet for the files. Supporting data took up the meat of each file. Once he had ascertained where to focus his attention, he moved much more quickly.

Red and blue lights began to reflect off of the walls. Nora Chapman's office didn't have any windows, but Deni had left her office door open and the windows facing the street allowed the flashing lights into the agency. The strobing reflected off the walls and into the office. It was past the time to get out of there.

Ebb

Nora Chapman had received a phone call, raising her from her slumber next to her husband. It was ADT. She was informed that though the safe word was correctly used, the operator suspected that her business had been breached. ADT was recording the suspected intruder, though the lights were out and the light being used wasn't enough to determine who it was. After a few questions and answers it was determined that it wasn't anyone authorized to be there, and that she did want the police to be notified. Nora would meet them at the agency.

She lived only three miles away. Nora had arrived almost simultaneously with the NPD. She wore a long, thin overcoat over her pajamas, a ball cap on her head with her blonde pony-tail pulled through the hole in the back.

Nora unlocked the front door and the police were inside within minutes. The lights were turned on, the four policemen from two patrol cars went in. Nora was told to wait outside while they did their job. She heard "Clear" repeated several times.

She was allowed inside by one of the policeman who ran back out the front door, saying something into the radio receiver on his shoulder. She quickly moved inside, directly to her office. Nothing appeared to be out of order as she took a cursory inventory.

Ebb

Then she noticed it. The lock on the second filing cabinet was popped out. Someone had been in her office and in her files. Her mind raced to determine who it might be. The filing cabinet contained her 1992 files. Then she knew.

21

DENI DIDN'T GET MUCH SLEEP for the remainder of friday morning. He spent the rest of the morning trying to figure out the coded file that he took from Nora's office at Regis & Chapman at his dining room table in Barstone. The file was indecipherable as far as he was concerned. Unlike the others that he had searched through, there was no meat to this file. There was just the crib sheet that was attached to the inside front cover. Other than the name Myhre, there was almost nothing to indicate that he indeed held the file of interest. Just the dates, the name Myhre, and a slew of codes. And he was lucky to get out with that before the police came in. He studied the single document that constituted the file but his focus was intermittently interrupted by thoughts about Cole Renner.

Christina had called both his cell and his home phone in Barstone about her husband late thursday night. He could only assume that there would be a message regarding the same topic at his place in South Boston. Deni hadn't heard the message until he went home after the close call at the agency as he had set his cell to go directly to voicemail. Hearing the concern on Christina's voice from his voicemail, he called her right away despite the early hour friday morning. Given the tenor of the message, he knew she wouldn't be sleeping. He was correct.

Her husband was missing. They had dealt with the Mass State Police on tuesday morning, she explained when he called, and they had spent the rest of the day together. Cole had taken personal time for the rest of the week because Deni had warned them on monday night that tuesday was going to be an interesting day. He wanted to ensure that his job wouldn't be affected by his arrest.

Since Cole hadn't been arrested, the couple decided to pseudo-celebrate by spending the rest of the week together. Possibly make up for the massive fight with makeup sex. She said that it was a fun time and that he received a call early thursday evening after they had tried yet again to make a baby. Once he hung up

Ebb

the phone, Cole said that he had to run a quick errand. No further explanation, just that he had to run out. He would be right back. Only he never returned.

After hanging up with Christina, Deni tried Cole's cell phone. As if his wife hadn't already tried that. No answer, straight to voicemail. Thinking that maybe the police had called him in to answer a few more questions, he called Sheed. Again, straight to voicemail. He left a message for her to call him as soon as she got the message. *It's very early in the morning,* Deni thought. *She'll call back in a few hours.*

He called Christina again. He told her that the police probably had wanted to chat with him further. That Cole likely didn't want her to worry so he didn't tell her where he was going. He told her that she shouldn't worry and that he would call her the moment he confirmed that that is what happened. Christina was having none of it and said that she was going to go down to Boston personally to find out for herself.

Deni had gone back to studying the file at his dining room table in Barstone, though his thoughts returned to Cole often. Friday morning continued on slowly as he oscillated from concentrating on the file to Cole. The codes meant nothing to him. Cole leaving his wife to run an errand bothered him. Then back to unsuccessful decryption. Wash rinse repeat.

His phone rang at 7:22 AM. Deni had dozed off for a few minutes. More like he was lost in thought. His head popped out of his hand, elbow resting on his dining room table. A red hand-print was emblazoned on his forehead as he scrambled for his phone. He recognized the number. It was Sheed.

"Hey She," Deni said when he picked up the call.

"Sorry to wake you."

"I wasn't sleeping, it's okay. I called you first."

"Yeah well, we were kinda busy down here."

"You two are makin' moves leavin' me in the dark? What's going on?"

"As usual you don't have the entire story and don't know what you are talking about, Deni."

"Why did you pull Cole in for more questioning? He didn't do it, She."

"Where are you right now?"

"New Hampshire. Why? What's up?"

"Can you come down to the House?"

"Sure, but why?"

"Renner's wife is down here and she needs some support. She needs a friend right now."

"I don't know that we're friends. I was in their wedding. I know them. Why do you guys keep hasslin' him? Just let him go. You want the wife outta your hair? She'll follow him outta there."

"Jesus Deni, why can't you just do things the easy way? You make things so hard sometimes. He's dead, okay? Your friend is dead and not naturally."

"What?" Deni stood up and started pacing his house. "Say that again, slowly."

"You heard me. It's not pretty. She doesn't know yet. Just come down, will you?"

"I'm on my way."

Deni raced his Rover south on 93. The SUV wasn't fuel efficient when he drove it normally, pushing the accelerator to the floor he could almost watch the needle on the fuel gauge moving toward empty. At times like these he missed the Mercedes AMG or at least something faster than the SUV. The normal hour and ten minute drive took thirty-two minutes. He was lucky not to have been picked up by patrol, double the posted speed limit gets you locked up.

Christina spotted him entering Troop H from her sentry in the reception area. She immediately ran to Deni and hugged him.

"Thank God you're here. Can you talk some sense into these people? Why are they giving him such a hard time? So he was picking up a few extra bucks on the side, he had nothing to do with that girl's death. You know that, right?"

"Yeah, Chris. I know that."

Ebb

"Then tell them," she said. She pointed down the hall to where Hobbs and Sheed were standing beside their desks.

Deni wasn't sure what to do. He wanted to tell her what was going on, but he was also hoping that it was a mistake. That maybe he wouldn't have to tell her anything at all. He decided to hug her again to conceal his obvious unease.

"Let me go see what I can do," he finally said to her. He left her in the reception area where they keep suspects and those that are waiting for them. The two detectives spotted him coming toward them. Hobbs wasn't happy about it.

"Not this fucking guy again," Hobbs said as Deni approached.

"Talk to your partner. She's the one who called me down here," he said to Hobbs. He turned to Sheed. "Tell me this is a mistake. You wanted to fuck with me, so you dragged me all the way down here for nothin'."

"How much of a dick do you think I am?" Hobbs gave Deni a little shove as he asked the question. Deni was looking at Sheed so he didn't see the shove coming.

"I wouldn't need to ask you the question except that I know the lengths you would stoop, Ricky."

"And I think you know I wouldn't do that to you," Sheed said. "We're confident. The chems did a number on the body, but between the car being less than half a mile away and what we're sure the dental records are going to confirm .... it's him."

"Chems? What the fuck happened?"

"Somebody did a number on him. Cape Ann RV Park up Gloucester. A camper goes to dump his Winnebago waste tank to get an early start, maybe beat traffic, finds Renner floating in the chemicals. Do you know what those chemicals do?"

"Breaks down the waste," Deni said with a cringe.

"Exactly. Eats through anything. We know he wasn't in there long based on what was left to find. Also we just saw him the other morning," Sheed said.

"Have you talked with Chris yet? About anything?"

Both detectives shook their head. Deni knew from experience that Hobbs would avoid that type of conversation at all costs. Sheed had called him to help her with that part.

"Christina thinks that you called Cole down here for more questions. Because that was my guess. She called me late last night sayin' that Cole got a call in the evening at some point. So you might wanna check his luds. She thought he left to go run a quick errand, but he never came back. So obviously whoever called him drew him out to kill him and dump him. You said his car was parked near the campground?"

"Yeah. Truck stop just off 128. We had troopers canvass the place, nobody saw anything. Not much traffic in and out of the place that late at night. Only reason we knew about it is because Gloucester PD got a call about an abandoned vehicle at the pump. Card swiped at the pump is Cole's. The vehicle is obviously Cole's," Hobbs said.

"Any camera footage? Those gas stations usually have CCTV," Deni asked.

"Guy knew all the camera angles. Renner goes off camera and never comes back on. Nozzle still in the tank," Sheed said.

"So he gets called way out to Gloucester of all fuckin' places, decides to stop for some gas. Or that was the meet spot and he was the first to show. Either way the guy shows up while he's fillin' up, then what? Cole goes quietly with him and leaves his car like that? No way. Cole ain't no prize fighter but he can handle himself. There would have been a struggle, which people had to have seen, or it was somebody big enough to make it a non-fight. Gary Rennick."

"Jesus Christ, Deni. Not this again," Hobbs said.

"Makes sense. Think about it. Gloucester. AGAIN. Cole was lookin' into Lara Myhre's adoption.

Lara Myhre was the woman dumped in the ocean in the first place. Both of these deaths are outta Gloucester. I don't believe in coincidence. Do you? Or you?"

Both were again shaking their head. There isn't a cop alive that believes in coincidence. Not a good one anyway.

"Just one problem with your theory," Sheed said after a few seconds. "Gary Rennick was at the Garden last night in front of about 20,000 fans. I thought you were a hockey fan."

"I was busy." Deni was searching through his brain, trying to find an answer. "Fuck!"

"Exactly. Fuck."

"Are you gonna leave Rennick alone now? My advice is that you leave him alone," Sheed said. "He's gonna sue your ass after the stunt you pulled. He probably played his last playoff game until this is sorted out. Have you seen the papers today?"

"You know I haven't. You called me, I came straight here."

Sheed turned to her desk behind her. She grabbed the Globe and handed it to Deni. "Made quite the scene. They're gonna want his head on a plate and for no reason."

"No reason? He deserves it. He's a fuckin' murderer," Deni said as he glanced at the photos and headlines.

Sheed shook her head, Hobbs cursed as he walked away from the conversation.

"Are you plugged in, Deni? You just made the case that the two murders are linked, which I can't even believe that I actually agree with you. He couldn't have killed Cole Renner, and I don't like him for Lara Myhre either. But you have a hard-on for him. You can't see past the fact that he didn't do it. You're gonna ruin his life and yours for a murder that he didn't commit."

"He fuckin' did it. Who else could have?"

"You can't have it both ways. You're gonna have to face the fact that whoever did Lara, also killed Cole."

"But why?"

"You said it yourself. This adoption thing. She was looking into it. Cole was looking into it for her," Sheed said.

"Nine weeks later? Pretty thin."

"Didn't you start looking into it?"

"What the adoption? Yeah. Why?"

"Are you making any progress?" Sheeds hands were on her hips until Deni passed the paper back to her. She returned it to her desk and sat on it.

"No. I'm not sure. What are you gettin' at, She?"

"Because if we run with the assumption that the two murders are linked, and why; that means that whomever was monitoring the adoption angle thought that Cole was still looking into it, not you."

Deni nodded like he understood her train of thought. The weight of it hit him like a punch to the face.

"Deni, why would Gary Rennick care if Lara was adopted or not?"

"But it would take someone large to move these bodies around. To take down Cole without making a scene. He fits."

"Do you know how many big guys there are? And you of all people should know that strength doesn't always come in large packages. You're not the biggest guy in the world. What are you, six feet? 170?"

"Yeah. Give or take."

"Pretty damn thin and pretty damn strong," Lisa said.

"So where do we go from here? And don't gimme that shit about 'probably not getting solved'. Two murders. The motherfucker has to pay."

"*You* don't go anywhere, Deni. Especially nowhere near Gary Rennick. *We* move forward without you. You were allowed access as a courtesy to the Myhres, that ship has sailed. Take Christina over to the morgue, we'll meet you over there."

"You're gonna lock me out and make me tell her? Nice."

Ebb

"You owe me. And it will be much easier coming from you."

"Oh yeah. I'm sure this is gonna go nice and easy."

22

THE WEEKEND WAS LONG AND AGONIZING for
Deni. It was exponentially worse for Christina Renner.
The trip to the morgue was heart-wrenching, even
Hobbs was choked up. The widow couldn't contain her
emotion when the body was exposed to her for viewing.

Bowman or one of the other Medical Examiners
hadn't yet examined the body. The cover was pulled
back for an identification, but the exercise was cruel.
The look through the glass was more for the
psychological closure than for an identification, as it was
impossible to tell who the person was. Most of the blue
waste chemicals had been rinsed off to stop further
degradation, ceasing the enzymes from eating away any

more flesh or possible evidence. The chemicals had steeped into muscle and tissue and bone, staining what had remained a light blue. The remaining carcass was a cross between Blue Man Group and Freddie Krueger.

Deni stayed by her side at her house in North Billerica for the majority of the weekend. He did as much as he could to keep her comfortable, but he was failing. He wanted to sedate her with medication, but she refused. Instead, she would go on long crying jags between the repeated playing of the song *Salvation* by Gabrielle Aplin. The song was more tormenting than healing, he thought, but people find solace however they can. People grieve differently, there isn't a right way because it always feels wrong.

She pulled Deni close for emotional support each time she replayed the song. He was not good at these moments, never had been. He normally would have called upon someone else to take his place, but the truth was he felt guilty.

Sheed had inferred that he was responsible for Cole's death. He had taken up an investigation that had stalled. Deni had done something to get close, and Renner had paid the ultimate price for it. Christina was paying for it. What he had done he didn't know, but it seemed a logical inference. And the guilt was eating at him from the inside. He felt the punishment appropriate, adding further veriscolor on his soul.

Ebb

He would normally have crawled into a bottle. Redbreast had been his psychiatrist for years, the Irish Whiskey soothed and numbed and sterilized. But he was needed. He stayed with Christina until it seemed he was no longer needed.

The family hovered around her on sunday. Cousins two and three times removed came to aide. Both sides of the family had crowded to commiserate. Deni was feeling more and more like a third wheel. Or a hundred and first wheel. Nobody overtly made him feel that way, they all thanked him for his friendship and concern. But it seemed a family affair, and he gladly retreated to his three-decker in South Boston sunday night. It was a minor miracle that he didn't drink away what was left of the night. Or monday.

His desire for justice was stronger than his desire for whiskey, which is saying a lot. He called the Myhres to keep them apprised of what was happening. He had a file that he couldn't read, and the investigator that was originally looking into it was murdered. They seemed numb to the news. *Maybe they're drinking whiskey*, he thought.

Deni's next call was to an old friend. An old girlfriend to be exact. Althea Milonas and Deni had an on-and-off relationship which had gone on for years. The 'off' times were Deni's doing, much to the chagrin of Althea. She went on pining for him, waiting for him to need her.   Which he often did, but not for the emotional and physical wantonness which was her desire. He would come back for her computer skills.

The two were opposites in almost every way. Althea being reserved, Greek, voluptuous, and a computer genius. Deni being brazen, Irish, athletic, and technologically retarded.   The overlap was that they were both a little crazy. Together they made each other fit for a straitjacket.

Their sexual escapades were another area in which there was some common ground. Deni would often need help with an investigation, and it would always lead to sex. Both of them enjoyed the animalistic love-making that inevitably ensued once they were together. It was everything outside of sex that mucked up the would-be relationship.

Althea works in the IT department of NEESI, New England Emergency Services Information. In fact, she *is* the IT department. Every call to 9-1-1 in New England goes to a centralized location and then dispatched locally.   That location is in Natick, Massachusetts.   Althea was the resident computer genius and Deni thought her talents were wasted there.

Deni's call soliciting her help resulted in her taking the day off from work at NEESI. She had been there for years and had more accrued time to use than she would ever actually take. Althea loves her job and is extremely good at it. NEESI needs her. But she needs and loves Deni more.

Her apartment complex, also located in Natick, is just like any other in Metro-west. Hotel-style buildings with large parking lots and an outdoor pool. The size of the residences were larger and less expensive than the city that was but two boroughs east. Natick is a large commuter district known for shopping malls and Doug Flutie.

Deni had driven west on the Mass Pike and was at Althea's apartment by ten in the morning on monday.

"You said it was urgent. What is it that you need this time," she said without greeting. The door closed itself behind Deni as he walked in to her apartment living room.

"Sorry to put you out."

"I don't know if I can keep doing this, Deni. I must be like a half-dead mule to you. You just kick me and see if you can get another mile out of me," she said, still standing.

"You know it's not like that. You can bill me for your time if ya want."

"What like a whore? Real nice."

"People get hired to do stuff all the time, wacko."

"And if they do it for sex, it's called being a whore," she yelled.

"Who said anything about sex?"

"Have you ever come here for help and it *not* end with the two of us in the sack?"

Deni shook his head and ignored the jab. He wanted out of the argument. The same argument every time. One that he could never win because he needed her. An angry Althea was an uncooperative one.

"Do you remember Cole Renner?"

"Of course," she said as she tried to compose herself.

"Well, he was illegally investigating a closed adoption on the side," Deni explained. "The young woman that hired him was the adopted kid and she was murdered. He was coming up blank. I was looking into her disappearance for her family, then picked up with the adoption investigation from where Cole was struggling, which was basically at the beginning. Cole was killed thursday night."

"Oh my God. His wife .... Oh what's her name? .... Christina! She must be going mental."

"You could say that," Deni said.

"So what do you need from me?"

Deni produced the file from the adoption agency, handing it to Althea. She opened it, revealing the only piece of paper that it contained.

"Filing codes. You need me to decipher the filing codes?"

"Is that what they are? What is that?"

"I forgot that you think a computer is an expensive paperweight."

"I'm not that bad, Al."

"Yeah. You are. Where did you get this file?"

"From the adoption agency. Regis & Chapman. Up Nashua."

She threw the file onto her coffee table, her hands up like she was being held at gunpoint.

"Whoa. I'm not touching this," she said. "You're into something illegal and I want no part of it."

"Al, two people are dead. That file probably contains the reason. You are what stands between the bastard that did this payin' for it, or go on continuing to do bad shit."

"You're not a cop anymore. Let it go."

"I can't and you know it. I was hired to do a job, and I'm not gonna stop until it's done. I gave the parents my word. You should see this girl, Al. She had an amazing life in front of her. Musician going to Berklee." He opened another file with pictures of Lara Myhre, handing it to Althea. "And Cole got tangled up in somethin' he didn't even know about, and I can't let the sonofabitch get away with it."

Althea stood in her living room, staring at the twenty-two year old beauty.

"She's stunning. Did you fuck her?"

Ebb

"Al."

"If any of this comes back to me, I will drop a dime on you as quick as lightning. I'm not going to jail," she said after some thought.

"Deal."

Althea's spare bedroom was her office. She had an elaborate computing station set up. She explained to Deni that she was completely firewalled, as if he would know what that meant. She further explained that she had double-spoofed IP addresses so nobody could track her searches, nor get into her computer to see what she was doing. She, on the other hand, could do just that. She was able to look into virtually anyone's computer that she wanted to completely undetected, firewalled or not.

"…. Just because I can do it, doesn't mean that I like to. Or that I should," Althea was saying.

"You're doin' a good thing here. Trust me."

"It isn't ethical."

"Ethical is doin' the right thing. These people at the adoption agency ain't doin' the right thing by keepin' this a secret. Who are they protecting?" Deni was pacing the space behind Althea in her office.

"Themselves, idiot. How would you like it if you had gotten someone pregnant, you both agreed to give up the baby only to have them knock on your door twenty-two years later? They probably want to put it all behind them," she said as she typed code into her computer.

"I have nightmares about that very thing all the time, but that's not the point. Listen, I'm all for keepin' their secret but we gotta look at the big picture here. Lara was the one who wanted to know, and she isn't here anymore. If her murder and Cole's turn out to be separate, then there is no harm. But it's suspicious that the only connection between Lara and Cole is this adoption, and they're both dead."

"Okay, so the codes on the file sheet are encryption codes for the files that they have on the hard drive.   That much I've figured out," Althea said, changing the subject. "I'm inside this Nora Chapman woman's computer, as you can see."

"I'll take your word for it."

"What I can't figure out is the correlation between the codes and the files on the hard drive."

"So what now?"

"The trick here is to figure out which files these codes belong to in order to unlock them. She has three-quarters of a terabyte of information on her drive. Each file has yet another code buried in the drive. I need to determine how the codes on the crib sheet lead to specific files on the drive."

"I don't know what that means."

"It means that she has a shitload of files and I need to know which ones to look into in order to unlock them with these codes. Think of it like the show *Jeopardy!*. I have the answer but I need to figure out the question."

"Why didn't you just say that in the beginning?"

"I did. This could take a while. If you're thirsty go get a drink. I think I still have some of your stuff in the liquor cabinet in the kitchen," she said.

"I'm good."

"Deni, I can't concentrate with you breathing down my neck. It's sexy and distracting. Go do something that's not in here."

He left the room for the kitchen. He opened the frig, found a bottled water and went to the couch. He found a rerun of the show *Modern Family* in syndication on one of the networks. He had just finished an episode when he heard Althea call him from the next room.

Deni entered the office, Althea grinning from ear to ear. He moved behind her, standing over her shoulder looking at the computer screens.

"Got it. Lovering. The birth mother's name is Lovering. Lovering gave birth and her child up for adoption. The child was named Lara Myhre two days later by her new parents Leonard and Sorche Myhre.

Ebb

Here is Lovering's social. I've got the doctor's name ....
the works."

"You did good, Al. You did really good." Deni
looked at the birth mother's social security number,
which started with 010. "That's a Massachusetts
number. Why would she go all the way up to New
Hampshire to have the baby? It must have been another
way to keep it a secret."

Althea shrugged her shoulders. "People move
all the time." She began to print out all of the files that
she had uncovered. She knew better than to email them
to Deni.

"We will see. I'll have Sheed look into the
number so I can track her down. Nice work."

"I would like my reward now," Althea said.

"What? You really are gonna charge me? How
much?"

She grabbed his groin, squeezing and releasing
repeatedly. She rubbed and stroked him from outside
his pants.

"We'll work something out."

23

THE PHONE WOKE DENI UP TUESDAY morning. He was still at Althea's, still paying off his debt. He rarely if ever made it out of her apartment without sex. This time was no exception. They had used each other. He needed something. She needed him. Deni heard his phone ring, his arm was under Althea's pillow. He needed to remove it to get to the dresser. He padded naked across the room to his phone once he did.

It was Ryan Wells.

"Deni where are you?"

"In Natick. What's up?"

"You're having sex at a time like this?" The on-and-off relationship was well known to those that knew

Ebb

Deni. Ryan had met her a few times and thought highly
of her. He also knew she lived in Natick, and was the
only reason that Deni would go into the town.

"What business is it of yours, Ry?" Deni had
slurred the question, still trying to wake up.

"It's my business as your attorney. The Nashua
police want you for questioning. There was an incident
at an adoption agency?"

"Oh Fuck."

"You've got that right. You're looking at two
Class-A felonies. Breaking and Entering, and Larceny
Over."

"How do you know the police want to talk to
me?"

"You showed the agency your New Hampshire
Investigator's License. That license is tied to me because
you do work for me from time to time. They called here
looking for you. They went to your house and you're
not there. I told them that I would get ahold of you and
that we would go to the police barracks together."

"I showed them my license when I went there —
big deal," Deni said.

"How stupid do you think these people are? You
show up out of the blue looking for information and the
very same file that you were asking about is gone."

"That's some coincidence."

221

"Cops don't believe in coincidences. You should know that."

Althea was now up and had gone to him by the dresser. She was seducing him while he spoke with Ryan. Deni wondered if she would still be as amorous if she knew what the call was about.

"I'll be there shortly," Deni said to Ryan. "Let me get showered and dressed." Then he hung up.

"One for the road before you go?" Althea was on her knees in front of him. Before Deni could utter a word of protest, he was in her mouth and he no longer had the ability.

Deni didn't rush to get north to speak with the Nashua PD. In fact, he took his sweet time. Nobody rushes to face their doom. Some things can wait, while others are more dire. Another round of sex after being fellated, Deni deemed the latter. The blowjob led to more elaborate positions after he reciprocated with oral techniques of his own.

Ebb

A shower, coffee, and breakfast was more important as well. When having to face a battery of questions from the police, a routine colonoscopy would likely take precedence. Figuratively they were about the same thing.

It was after 1:00 on tuesday afternoon when he finally arrived at the police station. Ryan had been there and waiting for some time and he didn't look happy about it. The two detectives who curtly introduced themselves as Hastings and Landon didn't appear happy to him either. So nobody was in a good mood. A perfect way to start.

He was led into an interrogation room. The room looked like every other on the planet. Hollywood gets the stereotype from somewhere. Or everywhere. Ryan was there beside him, ensuring that whatever was going to happen was done by the book. Deni's Miranda rights were read, he signed the form confirming it, and then the questions began. They were innocuous at first. Then they weren't.

" …. So you're trying to tell us that this is all just a coincidence? That you visited the agency, spoke with one of the proprietors and were asked to leave, which you did having not received the very file that was stolen thursday night?" The one that called himself Hastings was the 'bad cop'. Deni had been in these types of rooms more times than he could count. He was almost always on the other side of the interrogation, in his adult life at least. And he preferred it that way.

"I'm not sayin' it's a coincidence, chief. You are. I'm just tellin' you that I went there. She basically told me to fuck off and I left."

"And you have no other explanation? What if I told you that we have you on camera breaking into Regis & Chapman and going through Nora Chapman's files? That you somehow obtained the password to try to circumvent the security system? Would you care to revise your statement?"

"I believe my client has already answered that. Several times. He doesn't need to answer it again," Ryan said.

"You can listen to your attorney if you want. But now is the time to get your side of the story on the record," the one who called himself Landon said.

"If you told me that you have me on camera breaking into that business, I would tell you that you are full of shit." He knew they were lying. If they had any actual evidence that he had committed the crimes they wanted to charge him with, the crimes that he actually did commit, he would already be arrested instead of being interrogated. The hour-and-ten-minute interrogation was to try and trip him up. They should have known better.

"And your fingerprints are all over the place. We've already matched them to your license on file. Save yourself here. Just own it so we can all move on," Landon said.

"*If* you've matched my fingerprints, which I highly doubt, it wouldn't be unreasonable. I told you that I was there," Deni said. He was grinning which was pissing bad cop off.

"You smug bastard. I don't know why we're trying to help you Dennihan. We've got you dead to rights," Hastings said.

"Then why aren't I in cuffs. Are you gonna arrest me?"

"Deni. Maybe we shouldn't antagonize them," Ryan whispered.

"They're full of shit and they're tryin' to railroad me," Deni replied, not whispering. "They have an unfortunate set of circumstances, and the rich lady wants justice. So they're gonna try and pin it on me."

"Because that is the only logical conclusion. The establishment was broken into and the only thing that was missing was the file you requested." It was now the all-Hastings show.

"That's not the only logical conclusion," Deni said. "But you need someone to arrest and you need it quick, so I 'm the path of least resistance for you."

"If you have another explanation, I'm all ears. Should I get some popcorn?" Hastings turned to Landon. "This is gonna be good."

"The file I requested is from a closed adoption, it's her job to make sure that the file stays sealed. She wants to protect her clients, her image, as well as uphold the law. Ryan filed a motion to unseal those records."

Ryan nodded his head in agreement. He was eating it up.

Deni continued, "We were going about this legally. If we were to win that motion, then she would be forced to produce the file. If she staged a break-in and the file was stolen, she would no longer have it to hand over."

"Ha! You're actually sitting there with a straight face trying to tell us that she staged this herself?"

"No. I'm sayin' that it's a logical conclusion. You said there was only one. Since that's wrong, I'm givin' you another one to ponder. You said that whoever broke in knew the password. So that means it had to be an inside job." Deni was still smiling. Nobody seemed to have anything else to say.

"Well," Ryan said as he stood up. Deni did likewise. "If that is all, we are going to leave now." The two detectives looked at each other in disgust, letting the suspect and his attorney walk out of the interrogation room.

Once they were outside of the station, Ryan spoke first.

"Don't do that again, Deni. You're lucky. So far. I hope they have other cases and aren't going to focus on this too much. And let's hope that this Nora Chapman isn't going to make you her personal cause."

"I had to do what I had to do. I've got a lead now. Wait. Hold on my phone is vibrating," Deni said.

Ryan stood there as Deni took a few steps away and answered his phone. He was joking with whomever it was at first. Then he got pale. Deni's hand went to his head, then he squatted in the police station parking lot without moving another step.

"What is it?"

Ryan was given the international sign to hold on, the pointer finger in the air.

When he hung up, Deni stayed in the squatting position.

"Fuck me."

Part Three

From the Heat to the Flame

May

24

DETECTIVE LISA SHEED FOUND A CORNER inside the Troop H precinct to dial her cell phone. The call was off-the-books and she wanted the call to go undetected. She liked Deni, but not because she had any attraction to him. She felt for him because he had been done wrong in her eyes. He had been run out of the Massachusetts State Police Department because of the games that people play. Politics was a game that Deni didn't play, it simply wasn't part of his DNA. He was forced out because his focus was on the job, which was to bring people who committed crimes to justice. No judgements. If you did a crime and were caught, you had to pay for it. If life were only that simple.

She was also jealous of him in a way, because he was able to attain justice without the red tape. She had gotten to know a little bit about the man behind the huge myth. He was complicated yet focused. He did bad things but for the greater good. And she couldn't believe what was coming at him next.

"Hey She. What's up? I'm kinda in the middle of somethin' at the moment," Deni said.

"Where are you?"

"Did we start dating and I not get the memo? Every time I talk to you, you wanna know where I am."

"I need to know because it's important. I shouldn't even be calling you, Deni. You are in a world of shit."

"What now?"

"Have you seen the news today? Watched TV at all?"

"No. I've been busy. What's goin' on? I don't have time for Trivial Pursuit."

"You better make time. Gary Rennick's body was found outside his apartment building early this morning. It's been a mob scene. Tits has the go-ahead to make this priority one. Rennick is already on the slab down at the morgue."

"Holy shit."

"Oh it gets better. Who was the last person that was publicly seen in an altercation with him?"

Deni was silent.

"I take it by your silence that you know how fucked you are. You are the prime suspect in a high-profile murder and they've got a BOLO out on you. Whatever road you are on, there is about to be a cop on your ass. Everybody knows what a hard-on you had for Rennick, and now he's dead. You didn't just kill someone, Deni. You killed a fucking Boston Bruin, which in this town is like a god. It's not just the police who want to make mince meat out of you."

Deni was whispering into his phone. Lisa didn't know if it was because he was in a public place where he couldn't speak privately, or if he was so shocked that he no longer had the ability to project any volume from his voice.

"But …. I didn't. I mean, She …. I …. I didn't kill him."

"Just get down here. And if I were you I'd get a ride. Bring your lawyer."

click.

"Fuck me."

Ebb

The second interrogation of the day was much like the first, only Deni didn't find any fun or humor in it. This time he wasn't being accused of breaking into someone's business and wreaking a little havoc. This time he was being charged with the murder of an up and coming Boston sports star. No rapier whit or double-talk was going to extricate him from the chest-deep sea of shit that he was in. And without any waders.

Ryan had driven the two of them down to Boston in his Audi A6 for two reasons. The first being that Deni was shaken up, and his driving would likely have been more erratic than usual. The second was that Deni's SUV was a dark blue cop magnet. Deni was going to get a ride into Downtown Crossing one way or another. It would be in the comfortable passenger seat of a luxury sports sedan, or handcuffed in the back of a cruiser. Ryan thought his car was the more obvious choice.

Ryan and his associate-now-client were immediately led into the largest interrogation room. Again, Deni had been in the stereotypical room called 'the box' more times than he could count; though never on this side of the large table with microphones in the center of it. Not for the crimes that he was suspected of committing.

As a defense attorney, Ryan was familiar with the box as well. Miranda rights were again read, the card signed, and a formal proclamation of why Deni was wanted for questioning.

Hobbs was present in the interrogation room. Sheed was also, but Hobbs took the lead and played the role of the bad cop. He was relishing every minute of it.

"You have no idea how long I have waited for this moment, Deni. I mean I've dreamt about it. You have been walking a thin line for so long, I figured one of these days .... " Hobbs made a gesture with his hands, one hand falling off of the other hand which was supposed to represent a cliff.

"You wanted my client to come in for questioning. Is there a question coming? Neither of us are going to sit here and listen to your verbal abuse, Mr. Hobbs."

"Detective Sergeant Hobbs," he corrected.

"Was that your question?"   Ryan was being sarcastic and antagonizing. He was trying to bring Deni back to being himself. The suspect remained silent as was his right and necessity at the moment.   Deni appeared to be in another world, lost deep in thought.

"When was the last time that you were at or near his apartment building?"

Ryan nodded for Deni to answer.

"That depends on where *his* apartment is," he said.

"C'mon Deni. You know where Gary Rennick lives. Lived. You've made no secret that you've been stalking him."

"Yeah at the rink and out on the street, not at his place. I kept track of Lara Myhre's apartment, figuring he would go back there."

"So you're saying that you've never been down to the Seaport District. Park Lane?"

"Park Lane as in Park Lane Apartments?   The luxury skyscraper?"

"Yes. Stop playing stupid," Hobbs said.

"I wouldn't say never.   I went to Legal Harborside across the street a few weeks ago. I can't recall ever being in the Park building. Is that where he was killed?"

"I'll ask the questions, Deni. You know how this works."

"Have it your way Hobbs. You can pile it on as much as you want but I didn't kill Rennick. Just give me a T. O. D. and I'll give you my alibi."

"We're working on that, don't you worry. In the meantime we have more questions."

"This sounds like a fishing expedition," Ryan said. "Deni came down here as a courtesy."

"Deni came down here because there was going to be a manhunt if he didn't."

"Be that as it may, you don't have enough facts to interrogate my client. You just want to get him to say something to incriminate himself, which isn't going to happen," Ryan said.

There was a rapid knock on the door. A runner entered the box and handed Sheed a folder sharing a few whispers. Sheed took the folder and had the brief conversation because she was the detective standing closest to the door. Hobbs moved across the room toward her; both he and Sheed huddled reviewing the contents of the file after the runner had departed, and before moving forward with more questioning.

Hobbs moved back to his position as interrogator slash bad cop on the opposite side of the table. Ryan and Deni remained seated waiting for the short conference to be over so the interview could resume.

"You've never been into the luxury apartments at Park Lane? You're sure, Deni?"

"Not that I can recall. I've definitely not been to Rennick's apartment in that building. Was that where he was killed? In his apartment?"

"Where were you late thursday night into early friday morning?" Hobbs sat down. He had been standing or pacing the room up to that point. Deni knew Hobbs and knew that this meant that he was settling in for a long interrogation. He also assumed that the file that the runner had dropped off was the Medical Examiner's report. She had run it over to the box as was likely instructed from the morgue at Mass General. Lastly, he knew that he could not tell the police where he was on thursday night. He was breaking into Regis & Chapman in New Hampshire that night. He would need to admit to one set of crimes to prove his innocence in another, albeit a more severe set of crimes. He looked to Ryan to bail him out.

"My client does not need to answer that at this time. At such a time as you have more evidence linking my client to your victim, he will gladly render an alibi."

"He just said that he wanted to give us his alibi," Hobbs said.

"Hobbs cut the bullshit, will you? I don't like you and you don't like me — those are the cold, hard facts. But let's not make this personal. I liked him for

Lara Myhre's murder. I wanted to get him wound up. Make him make a mistake. I wanted to shake him up and make his life difficult. Maybe he would be banned from the league until I could prove it. I wanted him to pay, but I didn't want him dead."

"Didn't Leonard Myhre ask you to kill him?" Hobbs had a smirk on his face as he looked Deni in eye. Deni looked over to Sheed. Lisa was the only way that Hobbs could know about Leonard Myhre's request. She shrugged and stared at her shoe laces.

"Murder for hire? That's what you think this is?" Deni was incredulous.

"Are you asking for my client's financials?"

"Not at this time. But we may," Hobbs said.

"What you have is an unfortunate set of circumstances. Deni doesn't like you and you're still alive. Clearly he doesn't kill everyone that he doesn't like. My client didn't like Gary Rennick. He admits that. But beyond his distaste for the man, you cannot place him in the victim's apartment because he has never been there. While he might have motive, he doesn't have access or opportunity," Ryan said.

Sheed spoke up from her corner by the door. "What about the back alley?"

"Back alley? What back alley? At Park Lane?" Deni was confused.

"Yes. Have you ever been back there?" Sheed moved from her corner by the door, joining them in a seat next to her partner.

"Uh, I don't think so. Definitely not on thursday night," Deni said.

"We have dusted the equipment for prints, Deni. We already know that you're jerking us around," Hobbs said.

"Look, I was in New Hampshire thursday night." Ryan firmly grabbed Deni's forearm. He did not want Deni to bury himself. "I got this Ry." Deni pulled his arm away and turned back to the detectives. "Check my phone records. You people can track where my cell phone was located, right? I must have made a call or two. I wasn't in Boston."

"He was with me," Ryan said. It was a lie. It was also a felony to intentionally mislead the police during an investigation, and as a lawyer it could get him disbarred. "He would prefer not to tell you exactly where unless absolutely necessary because he was working for me on a case. Since he was working for me, and therefore my client, the information is privileged." Nobody reacted.

The statement was left for all occupants in the interrogation room to ruminate. The silence was thick and palpable.

"So what happened? Level with me," Deni said after a time.

"Garbage and recycle guy came to pick up the cardboard," Sheed started.

"Sheed!" Hobbs clearly didn't want his partner to divulge too much information. Any information for that matter. Lisa ignored him which she would pay for later. She felt bad for betraying Deni, for telling Hobbs things that weren't meant for him to know. It was the second such betrayal; first when the interview time was bumped up for the victim, and then with the conversation about Leonard Myhre in confidence. She knew by looking at Deni that he wasn't the killer, as if it was a question prior. She knew without having to look at him. Everyone had a role to play, she had played hers but it was time to stop pretending.

"Relax Rick. Deni, LTK is the restaurant in the lobby of the building, they go through a lot of cardboard boxes. The people moving in and out of the apartments in the rest of the building also have a ton of boxes. They all get put through the building's cardboard baler in the back alley. A Teamster normally unloads the bale from the machine and loads it onto his truck for recycling. Only the cardboard was soaked in blood. And according to his statement," she said as she consulted her notebook. " It, 'stunk to high heaven and was loaded with flies and maggots.' He's not supposed to take the bale if it has plastic or any other material in it. Cardboard or paper products only. He thinks that maybe because of the restaurant there was meat or something in one of the boxes and that he needed to take it out. So he cuts the wire ties and the cardboard opens up like an accordion to reveal Gary Rennick's body crushed like a pancake in the bale."

She looked at another page in her notes. "PTR 7200 HD Baler/Compactor. Spec on it says almost 3000 PSI. More than enough pressure to do the job."

Deni knew from past experience in homicide cases that the skull is the most dense and difficult body part to crush on a human body. An adult skull is crushed at roughly 1400 Pounds per Square Inch. This baler's hydraulic compactor compresses the cardboard at more than double that. He imagined the compression plate of the baler coming down on Rennick.

How anybody had gotten the victim into the baler was an important question. Deni continued to picture the result of pulverized bone and flesh and organs. Imagined the sound of the pops and snaps as the compactor pressed down on the body. Rennick had been squished like a bug into an enormous cardboard sandwich. The room was silent while Deni put all of the pieces together.

"Were there any fingerprints on the baler?"

Ebb

"Deni, it's in a back alley in the seaport district of Boston. Of course there are fingerprints on the baler. Dozens," Sheed said.

"Mine?"

"No. At least not yet," Rick said.

Well, whoever did this had to be strong. Rennick was in top physical condition. Big Boy. To get him into a baler would be a problem. Were Rennick's prints there?"

"So how'd you do it, Deni? How'd you muscle him in there?" Hobbs was not letting it go and avoided the question about the hockey-star victim.

"Funny guy, Ricky. No witnesses? Who was the last person to see him alive and when?"

Sheed asked, "Why do you want to know if Rennick's prints were on the baler?"

"If you were being shoved into a compactor, wouldn't you grab onto the edge or try to stop yourself from being thrown in? If his prints aren't on it, then that means that he didn't put up a fight, which means that he was knocked out or drugged out or already dead before going in. Unconscious people can't fight back."

"This isn't your case, Deni. And as far as I'm concerned you're the last one to see him alive and you're still a suspect. The prime suspect," Hobbs said.

"You're the only one, Rick," Sheed said. "He has an alibi and the circumstances are too convenient. Deni, he was a 'healthy scratch' for game 6 according to Bruins officials.   He was actually a no-show for the game.   So he was missing much earlier in the night. Whomever killed him had him on lock-down for a good long while before killing him and he could have drugged him up during that time.   Examiner puts time of death at between midnight and three in the morning."

"And I have confirmed his alibi for that time span and you have just confirmed that you cannot place him at the scene.   So Deni is officially not your murderer," Ryan said.

"We now have a serial killer in Boston," Deni said.   "I think we have to tie the victims together at this point.   That makes the most sense, right?   Lara has Cole look into her birth parents.   Cole uncovers something that he doesn't even know he uncovered, or more likely I did when I took over the case.   Whatever got uncovered was bad enough where action was necessary. Lara and Cole are killed to keep all the bodies buried. But the question remains, why go after a public figure? He wasn't a household name yet but he was gettin' there.   Why expose yourself to that degree?   Why kill him?" Deni said it out loud to the room as the thoughts entered his brain.

Hobbs stood, Sheed followed his lead.   "We will let you know when we figure it out.   Stay available but away from this case, Deni."

There wasn't enough evidence to arrest Deni and everyone in the room knew it. Whether the two detectives believed his story was another question. It certainly appeared to all involved that Sheed did. In any event, an alibi means that there wasn't opportunity. There was motive in spades but motive isn't enough to arrest.

When the party broke up, Hobbs went in one direction while Sheed, Deni and Ryan headed in the other down the hall.

"Got a minute, She?" Deni gently tugged on her elbow, pulling her aside. Ryan read the look on Deni's face and kept walking.

"Hey, I'm sorry I threw you under the bus with Rick. I didn't know what to think when Rennick was found. I mean, I knew but I didn't."

"Fuck it, She. You can make it up to me. I need you to look up a name and social for me. Please."

"Ah, what are you doing? You just heard him, Deni. He wants nothing more than to arrest you. He's been fantasizing about it for years."

"This has nothin' to do with that. It will take you two-seconds."

"It would take you two-seconds if you knew how to google someone. Shit. What's the name?"

Ebb

He handed her a piece of paper with the name 'Lovering' and her social security number on it.

They both walked to her desk where Lisa moved her mouse to awaken her computer. She looked around and confirmed that her partner was not in the immediate area.

"I really gotta stop doing this kinda stuff for you," she said.

She typed in the information, the data appeared on her screen in all of an instant.

"Chamille Lovering. Lovering is her maiden name though. It's Destrier now."

"Say that again, slowly. Destrier?"

"You know her? Chamille Destrier?"

"Yeah. Just about everyone knows her. Ho — lee — shit."

"Good news?"

"I don't know if it's good or bad, She. But I could kiss you."

"Yeah, please don't."

25

ROMAN DESTRIER IS AN INTERNATIONAL finance magnate. He had become what he is today in part because of his talent but also on the backs of those that had built him.

He grew up in an upper middle-class home where he was told as a child that his parents were well-off. Affluent. By the standard in which he lived today, he grew up poor and virtually homeless. He did well in school and went off to attend Duke University, studying economics, business, language, and international finance.

Roman Destrier fell in love with Duke and Duke history. When he wasn't studying for either of his double-majors or double-minors, he was studying the nouveau-riche history of American Royalty. The money and means in which the United States was built. He decided then that he would make such an empire for himself. Destrier would be another name to add to the list of entrepreneurs that had built America. Astors, Wideners, Guggenheims, Carnegies, and soon Destrier would be added to the list. He too would be a virtual king.

His ambition caught the attention of many who sought to groom him. Some of the largest firms in the world tried to obtain his services, to mold him, make him theirs. They were all too large for his taste. Schwab, Morgan, and Chase were just some of the established domestic firms looking to take Roman into the fold.

Another such wooer was Norman Craig. Norman Craig was a self-made millionaire. He formed CIG, Craig Investment Group, some fifteen years prior. Craig hadn't taken hand-me-downs, scraps from the enormous table. He had made his own name, very much the way Roman desired to. Norman Craig had a daughter roughly the same age as Roman, which he would have matched with the young talent had she not been so taken with her college beau.

Norman Craig's daughter, Anna, was a Boston University socialite studying business. Anna had attended a Women in Business conference at BU in her sophomore year where she had met another beauty from a neighboring school, Wellesley College. Anna and the Wellesley student, Chamille Lovering became fast friends. The two were practically inseparable from first meeting.

Anna's father was looking to sweeten the job offer by showing young Roman a good time while he visited the area. Norman described the man he was pursuing for his international division to his daughter and Anna could think of only one match. Roman and Chamille began seeing each other exclusively immediately after that trip.

Everything was falling into place for Roman and Chamille. Roman had a new job in Boston, in a new skyscraper in the financial district. A new home that they were having built as a replica of *Rough Point;* the Guilded Age mansion and estate in Newport, Rhode Island that was once owned by the Vanderbilts and later sold to James Buchanan Duke in the early 1900s. Roman had fallen in love with it, the idea of what it represented. The mansion was being built in an up and coming bedroom community in southern New Hampshire. Roman and Chamille were also making plans to be married. The power couple had helped build the town of Wayland with the Craigs.

Ebb

The honeymoon didn't last long for the young couple. Roman worked incessantly and he traveled a great deal for his work. Chamille rarely saw him. If her time with her husband was sparse when he was a Vice President at CIG, her time with him was nonexistent when he formed his own conglomerate, Monarch. Within a few short years of being married, the two had built an empire, homes and flats all over the world, but were rarely in the same zip code. Roman had made millions for his clients, and was worth hundreds of millions personally.

Chamille was young and beautiful and bored out of her mind. She had millions of dollars in her discretionary accounts. She had a staff at her beck and call. She could buy anything that her heart desired. She traveled wherever she wanted whenever she wanted. And she could count the number of times she saw her husband annually on one hand.

She knew he played around. No man with that amount of power and money could go so long without sex. If he was having sex with his wife with such infrequency, he must be getting it from somewhere else. So she played the field as well.

Mrs. Destrier spent most of her time in Wayland, New Hampshire by choice. A woman of her means could go anywhere in the world and live like a queen. And she sometimes did. The Destriers had estates and penthouses all over the globe. When someone receives no attention; however, they seek it out wherever they can. She was royalty in New England, definitely in Wayland. Why would she permanently move anywhere else? Chamille could not go anyplace in New England without being fawned over. Everything was a game. A game where she was queen of the land. The country club. The envy of every female who met her.

If they only knew.

26

IT WAS TIME FOR DENI TO VISIT Chamille Destrier.
He and 'Cammy', as he called her, had their dealings in
the past and it was always a fiasco. She had a staff that
protected her and when Deni did break through for
some face-time, she had her own agenda. Her own
game. Occasionally sex. He was not looking forward to
the forthcoming visit but she had some explaining to do.

   In one of the several times he and Chamille
spoke, she had explained that she had not been blessed
with children, nor that she wanted any. Her husband
was not often around, which made having a child a bit
difficult. Unless the child wasn't Roman's. If that was

the case, she would definitely have some explaining to do.

By the time Ryan had driven him back to Nashua to get his Range Rover, it was getting to be late afternoon into early evening. Some called it happy hour. Deni usually called it prevening. After the day that Deni had, he needed a drink — happy hour or not.

He drove to the replicated Rough Point in Wayland, New Hampshire and pressed the button at the gate. Behind that gate was a long drive with tall trees lining both sides, a home that ten or more families could easily live in, a guest house, a house for all of the staff, a house for all of the cars, even a house for the boats on the man-made body of water that lead to the Nashua River.

The all-too-familiar British-sounding voice answered from somewhere inside the massive estate. Deni believed him to be Indian as his skin was dark. He thought that because sometimes Indians sound like Jude Law instead of Rajesh Koothrappali from *The Big Bang Theory*.

"Hello. How may I help." The Indian was Nigel, Chamille's personal assistant.

"Hey Nige. It's Deni, Warren Dennihan. I need to speak with Cammy."

"It is Nigel. You know this yet you insist upon calling me some basterdised, Neolithic, version of my actual name. Just as Mrs. Destrier's name is Chamille, not whatever vulgar obscenity you've expelled. To what do we owe this particular unannounced visit?"

"That's between me and Cammy. I need to see her. It's important."

"Your calls are always urgent and important. I'm afraid with history being precedent, I will need to be apprised of your reason prior to providing access."

"The classics are always nice, Nige, but how about some new stuff? Just open the fuckin' gate so I can talk with her."

"And I believe that I have informed you that your request will be impossible. Shall I say it in different terms Mr. Dennihan?"

"Let's try somethin' different. How about I be the problem and you be the solution? You know me, Nige. When I want somethin' I won't stop until I get it. I want in. If you're not gonna help me than I'll make you a promise. The promise is that when I do get in there, I'm gonna beat the tan off ya. You're gonna need more than that snooty accent and big vocabulary to save you're sorry ass then. So how about that gate?"

"You may do what you like, and consequences will be as they may. Should you breach security, you will see that Mrs. Destrier is not on the grounds prior to the proper authorities removing you. You will then have gone through the trouble for nothing."

Ebb

"She's not here?"

"As I've said — "

" — Then why didn't you just say that in the first place? I wouldn't still be sittin' out here with my dick in my hand talkin' to the help."

"Yes. Charming."

"Where is she? And don't tell me that it's none of my business. I just want to talk to her."

"You may wish to try the Wayland Country Club. I believe she is hosting a rather posh soirée this evening. They have their own security that you can threaten."

The drive from the Destrier estate to the Wayland Country Club wasn't a long one. Getting inside is what took the majority of the time. The valets wouldn't park his Range Rover though the vehicle fit in with the other types that were seeking service. Deni wasn't dressed for the occasion, his *Soundgarden* t-shirt and jeans prompted the request for his invitation prior to parking his vehicle. An invitation he obviously didn't have. Plan b. He proceeded further down Wayland Country Club Road to the service entrance. Caterers and such were parked in the back, Deni did likewise. He parked next to a red Passat with Massachusetts vanity tags reading 'RedCR 1'.

Deni walked through the rear entrance like he belonged there. The immediate room was a large receiving warehouse. Cases of wine and glassware and carbon dioxide tanks and other supplies lined the walls under the appropriate labels. To his right was a production kitchen. The workers were diligently performing their duties. To his left was a doorway which took Deni to a bank of doors juxtaposed down a long corridor. He tried door after door. Some were closets of various purpose. A bathroom. Finally a gym-sized dressing room like one would see backstage of a large theatrical performance.

Chairs with women sitting in them were set in front of counters with well-lit mirrors. The women in the chairs were getting their hair and makeup manipulated by other women who were fortified with tools for the purpose. None were Chamille Destrier, in a chair or otherwise.

Deni moved through the line of chairs making his way to the back of the room where he peeled back a thick, heavy curtain. Behind the curtain was the subject of his search. She too was getting her hair serviced though in a private setting. She sat in a chair in front of a large mirror, tools for hair and makeup scattered about the counter. An attractive blonde woman looked to be applying a gross of pins to Chamille's hair, pinning at the nape of the neck.

Chamille Destrier, for as long as Deni had known her, had always looked like Angelina Jolie. Whether she had undergone surgeries to make that happen or not, he didn't know. She normally wore her long, flowing, chestnut hair in loose waves. Her skin had always been, and still was as she sat in the chair, tanned and porcelain.

"Cammy!" Deni shouted after he peeled the curtain back to reveal her. He made his way to her on the other side of it.

"Deni. What a surprise. I didn't realize that you were sent an invitation. You're clearly not dressed for it," Chamille said. A large, cut man wearing a tuxedo and a similar tan to Chamille's moved from a hidden corner toward Deni. "It's all right Ludo. Deni's not here to hurt me. You're not here to cause a scene are you? We can do those things to each other after the event if you'd like." She gave him a wink, her large lashes waved at him. The man named Ludo took obvious umbrage and was just as clearly unimpressed.

"I need to talk to you, Cammy."

"Don't call me Cammy here. Only privately."

The blonde with hair tools in her hands tried to make a run for it. Most likely wanting to let the rich woman and the intruder have their private moment.

"Oh Sarah, don't go. He looks threatening, but he's just a teddy bear. Aren't you, Deni? He's an investigator, though I'm not sure how good he is — he often needs my help." Chamille was motioning for the blonde to come back to the chair.

Before Deni could say anything, she made introductions.

"Deni this is Ludo Rossi. Ludo, Warren Dennihan," Chamille said. He made no attempt to shake Deni's hand. As Ludo receded back into his corner, Chamille silently mouthed the words, "New boy-toy" to Deni.

"This is Sarah," she continued. "She owns Red Carpet Ready in Boston. All the people being serviced out there work for her. Completely transforms the beautiful into gorgeous. She's the best there is."

"Yeah nice to meet ya," Deni said to her. He turned back to Chamille. "Can we speak privately?"

"Not now Deni. I'm getting Chignon-ed right now. Maybe when Sarah's finished. It's a busy night.

Ludo, take Deni out to the gala and get him fixed for a drink while he waits. No promises Deni, but maybe you and I can arrange that alone time later.   I do like our *intimate* chats."

Deni rolled his eyes and walked with Ludo out of the dressing room and into the dimly lit ballroom. There was a big chandelier which didn't have a want for more crystal hanging from the ceiling. Several bars and bartenders were set up along the perimeter of the room. Small cocktail tables with candles were set around an oak dance floor. A band was playing on one end of the room, elevated just above the few couples dancing to a jazz arrangement of John Legend's *All of Me.*   Most attendees were mingling with cocktails in hand.   All were dressed like they had been nominated for an Oscar.

The tuxedos were basically interchangeable while the elegant dresses were strapless, shoulderless, backless, and shameless.   It was difficult to say with certainty what was more eye-catching, the sequins on the gowns or the exposed breasts protruding from them. Deni thought that they might be equally as expensive. He didn't fit in as he was sans-jacket since he wasn't carrying a gun which needed to be concealed.

Ludo led him to a closet in the front of the ballroom where a slew of suit jackets were lined up on hangers.

"Forty regular?"   Ludo's accent was a thick Italian.

"I'm good on the jacket there Giovanni. I don't know where that jacket's been."

"You will need to wear a jacket if you wish to stay.   We have an open bar," he said as a means of persuasion.

Ludo held the jacket open for Deni to slide his arms through like the good servant he was. The label on the inside of the jacket said *Jones New York.*

"New York? I fuckin' hate New York. What else you got? What are you wearin' slick?"

"Ike Behar.   We will not exchange," Ludo said with a forceful pat on Deni's back after putting the jacket on him.   His Italian accent was as thick as if he had just arrived in America that day.

They then made their way over to the nearest satellite bar where Deni ordered a Redbreast Irish Whiskey, neat.   He was handed a whiskey which was excellent but it wasn't Redbreast.   He could have a hundred whiskies lined up in a blind taste test and he would be able to pick out his favorite.   But he didn't complain. Ludo had a glass of Champagne.

"I can tell that you like her.   Let me give you a piece of advice, kid.   Cammy will use you up and spit

Ebb

you out. Trust me. She doesn't respect you so you'll be out on your ass in about a minute — "

" — I think I will not take advice from a man like you," Ludo interrupted.

"A man like me, huh? She's married, rich as fuck, and she ain't about to give it all up for the cock-of-the-month. But if you think you got a shot? *My advice* is to play a little hard to get. Attractive women are thrown off by rejection. Tell them 'no' once in a while. They lead men to believe that they crave attention, to hang on their every word. But the fact is that gorgeous women like Cammy respect bein' ignored. They respect you bein' indifferent about their beauty."

"I can never be indifferent to a beautiful woman, as you say."

"Then you'll just be the cock-of-the-month, guy."

Just then, royalty entered the room. Chamille Destrier entered the ballroom in her *Lady in Waiting* gown by Nicole Miller. The music stopped and light applause took the place of it. Strings of sparkling diamonds fell from her earlobes toward her lace covered shoulders. Grace and elegance was being surrounded by those with invitations, Deni wasn't going to get anywhere near her in the immediate future.

He turned around to the bartender and asked for another whiskey and glass of Champagne. He slung the remains of his first back, accepted the new round and

259

hurried back to the dressing room. Empty. An egress from the private room led to the service parking lot. The pretty blonde was packing the red Passat.

"Sarah, was it?" Deni handed her the glass of Champagne when he bridged the gap from the back door to her vehicle. She didn't take it.

"Yes. What did Mrs. Destrier call you, Deni?"

"Yeah."

"Well, Deni, I'm tired. I've been doing makeovers all day and I just want to get back to Boston."

"I'm from Boston too. Southie. I have to come up here all the time, just like you I'm sure. You do this kinda stuff for Cammy regularly?"

"I can tell where you're from by your accent. I don't mean to be rude, but I really do want to leave. I'm paid to show up and make people look glamorous. Wedding, gala event like this one, whatever. Cammy is just another client."

"Oh I'm sure. She pays you enough to make your year I'd guess. All that staff in there? And all those women must chat you up while they're sittin' there in the chair. You must know all the dirt. Here. It's just a drink." He pushed the wine flute toward her again. She took it, slung it back, and handed the empty glass back to Deni.

"Drinks over. Thanks. And now I gotta go."
Flirting was getting Deni nowhere. He changed to the
hard-line.

"There's no such thing as hairdresser-client
privilege. You can tell me whatever dirt you know
about Cammy. I can have a lawyer subpoena you."

"And I wouldn't be in business for very long if I
told tales out of school. My clients want their privacy as
much as they want to know 'who are you wearing?'.
Sometimes they gossip and tell me things that are best
suited for a shrink, and sometimes they don't. Look,
you obviously want to dig up something on Mrs.
Destrier, I get that. I'm sure you have very good
reasons, but please leave me out of it. Have a lawyer do
whatever you want, but I don't tease and tell." Sarah
got into her car.

"You're a tease all right," Deni said.

"Funny." She closed the door, started, and
backed her Passat out of the parking space. She pushed
the button which rolled down her window. "Hey, do
you have a girlfriend?"

"No why?"

"I guessed as much. Never-mind. I was gonna
give you my card."

She rolled up the window and Deni watched her
drive out of the parking lot.

"That went well."

27

TUESDAY BECAME STILL LONGER and more frustrating for Deni. As his vexation grew, his patience proportionally diminished. The gala event seemed to go on ad infinitum. Chamille, the elegant host, made her rounds and graced the members of the club and invitees with her presence throughout night. Deni couldn't get a word with her until only those who were too gauche to understand that the party was over remained in the ballroom.

Deni approached her and Ludo who was still by her side at the end of the event. Her trophy was as dutiful as ever.

"Hey Cammy. Can we have that chat now?"

Ebb

"You're still here, Deni?" She asked like she didn't know. Women like Chamille Destrier always know who is in the room just as they always know where a camera is pointed. They don't have a surprised look on their face unless they've just had Botox. "I'm quite tired just now. My needs will be met by Ludo tonight. Maybe we can schedule something where we have much more time to …. talk."

"I've been waiting here all night and you know it. Everything is a game with you, Cammy. I have questions for you."

"And she told you that she is tired." Ludo wasn't just a pretty face, he was strong. He put his hand on Deni's shoulder, gripping it to make his point. If he continued to be hostile, Deni was going to have to make him bleed. Deni removed Ludo's grip with one of his own, twisting the Italian's arm until Ludo was forced to kneel on the floor.

"If it's so urgent, ask me anything you like. So long as you make it quick," she said. "Let poor Ludo go please."

Deni looked at Ludo after freeing him. Stared him down actually. He then turned his gaze over to Chamille who understood his non-verbal point.

"Ludo, if you have any thoughts of trying that again, Deni is probably going to hospitalize you. I want you in one piece tonight, so just stand there and look pretty. Deni, you can ask me any question you like in front of Ludo."

"Were you tracking your daughter, Lara Myhre, or did she find you and threaten you?"

"Ludo, why don't you go have the car brought around," she said. Deni must have just given her a Botox injection. The stunner was stunned.

The Italian looked at her more wounded than anything that Deni could do. He left her to do as he was asked.

"How long are you gonna keep this one around? 'Til Roman comes home?"

"Roman is in Dubai last I checked. He probably has a harem and not likely to leave anytime soon. Ludo's good looking and will do for now. He doesn't do what you do to me, but a girl has to make-do." Elegance was back in her voice. It was forced but she was making an attempt at grace.

"With your skin it's nearly impossible to tell your age. You and Anna Grantes are about the same age, so I'm guessin' you must have had Lara at what, twenty?"

"What are you talking about, Deni?"

"Your baby that you carried to term and delivered at Dartmouth-Hitchcock in Nashua on June 4, 1992."

"I've never had any children and you know that. Haven't we had this discussion before? I don't want to ruin my body by forcing another living thing out of it," she said.

"Is that you talkin' or is that what the father said?"

Tears began to form in Chamille's eyes. She was fighting them off and winning, but the droplets were present.

"You're obviously mistaken. And I really do have to go. Had you said that you wanted to hurl accusations at me instead of ask me questions, I wouldn't have given you two-seconds of my time."

"What I can't figure out is if it was Roman's idea to give her up or yours?"

"Deni, for the last time, I have no idea what you are talking about and I want you to let this go. Please. Just let this go."

"Why, what are you afraid of? She's dead. She can't harm you. Not anymore. You saw to that. Did you have the boy-toy do it? He'd do just about anything for you."

"What you are saying is slanderous. I have a reputation. I am a public figure. A pillar. If you make things difficult for me, Deni, I will have no choice but to cease our friendship."

"We ain't friends lady. I banged your ovaries around just like all the other …. aaaaaah. So that's it? Lara wasn't Roman's? You two weren't married yet, that's why you used Lovering on the closed adoption paperwork. Was he off on one of his long trips and you had the kid under his nose without him knowin'. Why not just abort? Why risk getting caught? Why risk a leak at Regis & Chapman? Why go all they way up to Nashua? Plenty of good hospitals in Boston. Couldn't do it could ya? All that talk about passin' a baby was just a front, huh? Were you still at Wellesley?"

"I never cheated on Roman before we were married. I didn't wander for the first few years after we were married."

"So she was Roman's."

"I'm warning you, Deni. I will sue you for everything that you own and everything that you will ever own. You can't go around making unfounded accusations. I am a public figure. A pillar."

"You're not gonna try and kill me are ya? Like you had Lara killed? Like Cole? Like Gary Rennick? How many people have you killed to keep your little secret? And why? She just wanted to find out who gave birth to her. Her parents are Leonard and Sorche Myhre, not Chamille Lovering and Roman Destrier. You can't make this go away, Cammy. Your high maintenance ass is in a sling."

Ebb

"Don't say that I didn't warn you, Deni," she said as she brushed by him to the front door where her chauffeured Bentley Flying Spur was waiting.

Ludo opened the rear door for her to slide in. The two men stared at one another for the time it took Chamille to do just that. The Italian then followed her into the back of the vehicle, closing the door behind him. The 'Fire on Ice' white Bentley drove away.

28

THE WAYLAND COUNTY WOMEN'S Correctional Facility wasn't open for visitation on wednesdays. There are certain days and times when someone without any outstanding warrants can visit an acquaintance or loved one who is a guest of the state, but wednesdays aren't one of them. Deni had called ahead to determine if he could visit and was told that the soonest visitation time for women in maximum security was saturday. He felt it was too long to wait.

Deni called Ryan Wells. He asked the attorney to go with him to the prison, which would tie him up for yet another day. At least a large portion of it. Lawyers can visit clients who are incarcerated on any day and most times therein. Ryan Wells was not the legal representative of record for Anna Grantes, but he is an attorney. He could make up a story as to why he was the lawyer visiting instead of her actual lawyer if the question was raised.

Ryan agreed, though reluctantly. His caseload was getting backed up and he was forced to delegate his work to his interns, which he didn't like to do. He was paid for services rendered. His clients paid those large sums for his work, not for work that he passed off to an intern. The hippie lawyer had a conscience for more than just the environment. He would need to follow-up on the delegated work to ensure that his clients were getting what they had paid for. Sometimes the follow-up and correction to that work was more time consuming than if he had just done it himself. Added to the queue was his wife and assistant who highlighted the fact that the pile on his desk was no longer acceptable.

Wells picked Deni up at his home in Barstone, driving his Audi A6 over to the prison. Ryan took the opportunity to discuss another case on the drive.

Ebb

"Since you are eating up another day of important work, it's only fair that I get a free consultation," Ryan said to his passenger. "I'm getting very behind in my cases."

"Ok. Shoot."

"There is a heroine dealer that was killed in his own home about six months ago. The police arrested my client and the trial is coming soon. They have witnesses who will testify that they saw my client in the area many times in the past, but not necessarily on the day of the murder. They did, however, find my client's DNA at the scene and — "

" — Ha. DNA," Deni said.

"Yeah. DNA. What's so funny about DNA?"

"It's useless, Ry."

"DNA evidence isn't useless Deni. It has been used to imprison and exonerate countless suspects over the past few decades. It's used so often because it is widely recognized as the most accurate science for — "

" — And that's why it's bullshit. Everybody relies too heavily on it now. DNA has become the end-all be-all form of evidence. Makes the police lazy."

"Because it's so reliable? I'm failing to see your point," Ryan said.

"If I wanted to get away with murder? I would hit up every barbershop, whorehouse, and Dunkin' Donuts in the area."

"Brothels, barber and coffee shops? Deni, have you been drinking? We can't go inside the prison if you've been drinking."

"Relax. Too much DNA is like no DNA. If you tear apart a scene and you've got hundreds of different people's DNA, it makes the actual killer's DNA useless. Just another strand in the meltin' pot. The cops have to investigate every single one of those suspect's motives, means, opportunities. Not to mention verify alibis. If I was gonna kill someone, I'd litter the scene with hair, spit, and jizz. So what if they found my DNA? How many other strands did you find? It would be thrown out as evidence, and there probably wouldn't be much more. Because cops are lazy. They stop investigating once they match DNA so they can clear their caseload."

"It's a good thing that you don't kill people, though you get accused of it often enough."

"Very funny. So find out if they found any other forms of DNA at this drug dealer's murder scene. I can look into the case if ya want. How soon do you need it?"

"Soon. We go to trial in two weeks," Ryan said.

"Let me tie up Cammy and her boy-toy in a neat little bow for the police and then I'll get on it."

"You think she did it?"

"Who else?"

"You were so sure Gary Rennick did it until not so long ago, if I remember correctly," Ryan said.

"Until he wound up dead, smart-ass. Cammy couldn't do it by herself, she wouldn't want to break a nail even if she was strong enough. She had her boy-toy, Ludo, do the heavy lifting. He would do anything for her. He's convinced that she loves him. And I could see that he loves her. Anyway, now I gotta prove it."

"You should let the cops handle this," Ryan said.

"I don't have a whole lotta equity with cops right now, as you well know. The guy I liked for it is dead, and they probably still think that I did it. You shouldn't have lied for me by the way. You could get into a lotta trouble.

"You would have done the same for me. Once they find the real killer it will be a moot point."

"Another reason to see Anna. She knows all about this I'm sure," Deni said.

"And I'm sure she can't wait to tell us."

Ryan and Deni were put into a conference room where they waited for Anna Craig. They were told that they didn't have a record of an Anna Grantes in the prison. After Anna's divorce, she had gone back to using her maiden name. Twenty minutes after being escorted into the prison conference room, the door opened. A butchy, female Correctional Officer led a woman with dirty-blonde hair into the conference room.

At the sight of Ryan and Deni, the inmate began to shout.

"Oh fuck this! No fuckin' way! CO! Bring me back to my cell." She turned, trying to force her way back out the door that she was led through.

"It's ok, officer. We have some bad news that she doesn't want to hear. You can leave her here please," Ryan said.

"She's all wound-up. Do you want us to keep someone in here with you?" The CO was yelling over the inmate's shouting. The tantrum was loud but otherwise not going anywhere.

"That won't be necessary. You may want to lock her down in the seat just to be safe."

She pulled the inmate over to the conference table by her cuffs. Anna's ankle shackles were then locked into the eyelet that was embedded into the concrete floor, after being forced to sit. Her hands were locked to the eyelet in the heavy conference table which was also bolted to the floor.

"This is what happens when you don't act like a lady," the CO said. "I'll be just outside the door if you need me," she said to the two visitors.

Anna stopped shouting once she realized that her tantrum was futile.

The inmate that was sitting in front of Deni and Ryan was not the same Anna that they had known for years. Two years had undone a lifetime of privilege and beauty. She had once had more vibrant blonde hair with strawberry highlights. It was now a matted mess. Her slate-blue eyes were once beautiful. They looked tired and aged as she stared them down. Her once athletic build was now thicker and her posture slumped. Elegant and proper had turned vicious and vulgar.

She spat at them.

"Classy," Deni said.

"Fuck you, cocksucker. I'm in here because of you."

"No, Anna. You're in here because of you," he responded.

"What the fuck do you want anyway?"

"We need your help," Ryan said.

"You came to the right place," she said. "Go fuck yourself."

"Chamille sold you out a ways back. You have the chance to return the favor," Deni said.

"Oh Yeah? What's the queen up to these days? Too busy for a visit obviously."

"You don't think that Chamille Destrier would ever show her face in a place like this, do you Anna? You were friends since college. An un-needy one. You're of no use to her now."

"So what'd she do?"

"She had a child way back when she went to Wellesley. You were there for support, I'm sure."

"So fuckin' what? That ain't illegal."

Ryan interjected, "No, but are you confirming that she did have a baby back then?"

"I'm not confirming shit. I'm just saying that you don't need my help to find out something that isn't illegal. What does it get me? Why the fuck would I help you if it doesn't help me?"

"Maybe I could get Brady up here to see you," Deni said.

Her eyes began to tear up. She stared at her dirty hands. "I don't want my son to see me like this. Even if Jacob would let him."

"He wouldn't have to know. I can schedule a trip up here to see me, his 'Uncle Deni.' He's growing up fast. You should see him, Anna."

Ebb

"Kid doesn't even know who I am. It took JG about four-seconds for the divorce papers. He and that slut of his are probably married by now," she said through tears.

"There was nothing …. Forget it. This is getting us nowhere. He's married to someone different, ok? Do you want to see your son or not? What do you want, pictures? I'm tryin' to help you so you will help us. You and Cammy were inseparable. Best of friends. I know you know that she had that baby girl. And when it comes down to it, you may need to testify to it."

"Or just sign an affidavit if you don't want to face her in court," Ryan interjected.

"You want me to help? Tell me what this is really all about."

The two men looked at each other. Ryan shrugged to Deni as if to say that it was his call. Deni figured that he had to go for broke as he was not going to get her to tell him anything without feeding her the information she wanted.

"The girl that Cammy had at Dartmouth-Hitchcock in Nashua grew up and hired an investigator to find her birth parents."

"You? She hired you, Deni? Poor thing."

"No. She hired someone that I know. He wasn't really getting anywhere because Cammy has put up some serious road-blocks. She must have found out about the investigation because she had both Lara and this investigator killed. I started looking into Lara's murder and was looking at someone else for it," Deni said. He looked at Ryan who was just nodding. "The man that I thought was good for the murder was also killed."

"If you were pointing fingers at this other guy, why would she have him killed? He could have taken the wrap for the entire thing. Once again, you are out of your league Deni."

"I found you didn't I?"

"I don't think that I want to help you, asshole."

"You said that you would help if we told you the truth about why we wanted you to tell us what happened back then?"

"I was just curious. You're both wasting your time. Just leave her alone. You'll never make anything stick to queen bee anyway."

"So you won't help us?"

"You can't give me anything, and I fucking hate you with every ounce of my being. I'm not saying or writing a goddamn thing. So no. I guess you're pretty fucked now, aren't ya?"

"Anna — "

" — CO!"

The Correctional Officer unlocked the door and entered the conference room.

Ebb

"*My lawyer* and his pet are done with me."

29

THINGS WERE NOT PROGRESSING as Deni had hoped, quite obviously. He spent the ride back from the prison venting, pontificating about conspiracies and coverups. Cursing about how the pieces to the puzzle didn't fit and weren't likely to unless he could find a smoking gun, some shred of evidence to tame Chamille Destrier once and for all. Ryan drove in silence, letting the pot simmer and steam else it boil over. Nobody wanted to be in the vicinity of Warren Dennihan when he had reached his boiling point, Ryan had seen it first-hand one too many times.

The definition of Irish temper is Warren Dennihan.

When the short jaunt was over and the venom-spouting had subsided, at least for a brief moment, Ryan inquired what Deni was going to do next. Warren told him that he was going to go someplace that could give him information without breaching confidentiality. He was going to Wellesley.

Deni had worked out in his mind while he was spitting and sputtering that when Chamille Destrier was pregnant, she couldn't have hidden it from everyone. Somebody other than her protective inner circle had to have known about the pregnancy. In 1992, Chamille Lovering would have been in her final year at Wellesley College. Somebody who went to school with her had to have known about her predicament, and going there would point him the right direction.

Once he found someone who would verify the pregnancy from the college, he would then get the story on the record. What he had at present was a file and evidence that were poison from forbidden fruit. The file was stolen and the secure information that was hacked from Regis & Chapman were both inadmissible pieces of evidence. He couldn't just hand them over to the police. The theory that Lara and Cole were killed in an effort to keep Chamille's identity a secret was one that the police would not act upon unless he had all of his ducks in a row. Deni very much needed to connect the dots with as much legitimate evidence as possible since he was skating on thin ice himself. He was Hobbs's suspect in the piece that didn't fit. Why Gary Rennick needed to be killed was that piece.

The trip from Barstone to Wellesley, Massachusetts was two hours of fighting traffic on 93 and Route 9. Fighting traffic and juggling phone calls.

He called the Myhres to let them know what he had found out but couldn't yet prove. Only they didn't answer the phone. He was forced to leave a vague message about finding out the identity of Lara's birth parents and to call him back.

Next he called Sheed to keep her apprised of where the investigation was leading. She didn't accept his call either and he was forced to leave another vague message requesting that she return his call.

Finally, he called Althea to thank her again for her help and to let her know that New Hampshire authorities knew but couldn't prove that he had broken into Regis & Chapman. He wanted to make sure that she was secure and that nobody would ever be able to prove that she hacked into their computer. Of course that was the call that was picked up. Althea ripped him a new one.

Wellesley College is a private college for women in the small affluent town of Wellesley, Massachusetts. Located between Natick and Newton, if one were to drive in either direction on Route 9 and blinked, they may miss it. Which is more than fine with the locals. There is very little parking because this community doesn't want tourists.

The college is as picky about who attends the school as the township is about those who live there. Less than a quarter of the women who apply to the school are accepted; exorbitantly high property values, and astronomical taxes on those properties, make an even smaller percentage of home-buyers move into the town. There are even rumors that neighborhoods have purchased houses for sale to ensure that only the most suitable buyer be able to move into it.

The administrative offices at Wellesley College are located at 106 Central Street. Deni was forced to find metered parking on Washington Street, an eight minute walk away.

The brunette behind the counter in the registrar's office was a portrait of prim and proper. Her off-white business suit was crisp; the violet silk blouse beneath it was buttoned up to cover what would have shown ample cleavage, not a hair out of place, her nails painted to match her blouse. Deni wondered how much time it took to put herself together every morning. It was a nondescript wednesday afternoon in May after all, not a cotillion.

Deni was in his usual jeans and t-shirt. He had worn a sport jacket but it was warm and had taken it off, leaving it in his SUV with his weapon rather than carry the jacket on his walk. His faded *Pennywise* t-shirt didn't brighten the room. She looked at him as though her cat had just left her a dead token of affection at her front door. Deni doubted that she knew that his t-shirt promoted the name of a band, and not a statement of support for the frugally poor.

"You seem lost," prim and proper said. "May I help you find your way?"

"Hopefully. I need to look up somebody that graduated from your fine school in 1992."

"And you are?"

"Curious," Deni said. "Who are you?" There wasn't a placard indicating a name on the high counter between them, just the one saying 'Office of the Registrar'.

"I'm unable to help you," she said.

"Oh? School records are public information, lady."

"Not at a private college, *sir*."

"If an employer wants to verify a degree, they would have to go through you. Right?"

"That would be correct."

Ebb

Deni flashed his investigator's license for Massachusetts. "Then I suggest you start typin' into your computer."

"And your manners leave much to be desired."

"Maybe we got off on the wrong foot. Hello. I need to verify a student who claims to have graduated from Wellesley in 1992."

"Are you a prospective employer? I highly doubt that. I think that I am going to call security now."

"Go ahead. I was hired to do background checks on prospective employees. I need to know if Chamille Lovering graduated in 1992? Security or not, I'm not leavin' here without that information."

Prim and Proper visibly struggled with what to do for a time before she typed into her computer. "I don't have a Chamille Lovering matriculating or graduating that year. Now can you please leave?"

"1992. You're sure?"

"I know how to do my job. Yes I'm sure."

"I wasn't sayin' that you're incompetent. Rude, but not incompetent. What about 1991?"

She typed the updated year into her computer with a huff. "She attended in 1991, spring and fall semesters. Hmm."

"What hmm?"

"This is interesting. She initially received all 'Incompletes' for the fall 1991, but they were reviewed and updated."

Deni pretended to be stupid regularly as a means of trickery. People underestimate those that they feel are less intelligent.

"Let's say for the sake of argument that I didn't go to college, what does that mean?"

"I'm stunned that you don't have a higher education."

"Are ya happy now? You got your jab in, can we move on?"

"It means that she didn't complete the coursework for whatever reason in her second-to-last semester here. Either she or someone on her behalf took the issue up with the Board of Trustees and the grades were adjusted to 'Pass'."

"What does 'Pass' mean? I thought you got like and 'A' or 'B' or somethin'."

"Normally yes. But there are circumstances where credit is granted for the course or courses based on a 'Pass' or 'Fail'. They counted toward her degree but not her GPA."

"And this is done all the time?"

"No. It's done on occasion, as I just said. Somebody had to pull some very large strings to get an entire semester changed. Are we finished now? Can I go back to work?"

"I'll be outta your over-sprayed hair in a sec. So she dropped out her senior year? Never came back for her spring semester her senior year? Does it list a reason? Medical?"

"It doesn't say. But I can tell you that she never completed her coursework for her Bachelor's Degree. She received an Honorary Business Degree in 1993."

Deni must have looked confused or the woman assumed he didn't know what an honorary degree was. After the brief pause, she explained it.

"An Honorary Degree is given to people who donate large sums of money, or who are speakers at commencements, or some other dignitary that the school would like to honor. Thus the name."

"So a person can buy a degree from the school?"

"As I said, sir, it is honorary. Some people have buildings named after them, some get a piece of paper. It's just how things are done."

"I should have just bought a degree," he said under his breath.

"Pardon me? I didn't hear you."

"Nothin'. So who were her friends? Who did she hang out with when she did go to classes?"

"I would have no idea. It was in 1991. In case you're unaware, that was a long time ago. You could look at a yearbook or the college newspapers for the time she was here."

"Colleges have yearbooks?"

"Small ones do. Wellesley does."

"Yeah ok. Where can I get those?"

"At a place that I'm sure you are very unfamiliar with. The library."

30

THE WELLESLEY COLLEGE LIBRARY HOLDS PAST yearbooks and newspapers for alumni as well as current students interested in said alums. They don't give them away or lend them out for free, however. The library keeps all of the unsold yearbooks on hand to be purchased, copies of the student weekly newspapers are reproduced and sold by the page. Deni left the library with the bulky research material after doing considerable damage to his credit card. He would have stayed at the library to look everything over; but it was stuffy, silent and at an all-women's school he stuck out like a rhinoceros on a chicken farm.

Ebb

The eight minute walk back to his Range Rover culminated with a $50 parking ticket. He looked at his watch. Four minutes over the expired meter time. The meter maid must have been lying in wait. Deni noticed the restaurant Blue Ginger just down the street and on the opposite side. A valet out in front was just setting up his stand for the night. Deni was hungry and had heard about the celebrity chef/owner, Ming Tsai, for some time.

Deni pulled out of his expensive metered spot, drove down the street, pulled 'a bitch', and opened his door for the valet. He grabbed the research material from the passenger seat and accepted the token from the valet. "Enjoy your dinner," the valet said.

The restaurant was nearly empty as it had just re-opened for dinner. A few people were kibitzing at the bar and lounge which didn't hold a table large enough for Deni to spread out his research material.

The attractive Asian host said, "Welcome. How many are in your party?"

"Just me. I'd go into the bar but I need room," he said as he lifted the bundle under his arm. "You got a quiet spot in corner with a decent size table?"

"Of course. Do you have a reservation?"

Deni looked around the dining room, which was candle lit and empty. "Do I need one? When is your rush, like seven? I'll be gone by then."

Ebb

"We can put you at a six-top in the back. It's a large table, are you going to be comfortable at a table that size by yourself? Also you don't have a jacket, your tattoos ...."

The short sleeves of his shirt had risen up to expose the tapestry that was normally covered by larger t-shirts. The sleeves of this particular shirt were just a bit shorter than his others.

"I don't give a shit what people think about me. I didn't realize it was a jacket and tie kinda place. I gotta jacket in my car if need be," he said.

The host giggled and motioned for him to follow her back to his oversized table. On the way she said, "I just need it back by seven-thirty. I've got a reservation and people around here don't like waiting."

"No sweat. How's the food?"

"You've never been here before?"

"No. Wellesley is a little out of my way," he said.

"Oh it's amazing."

He was led to the back of the restaurant, the open kitchen was to the right. The mirror above the kitchen staff allowed for an interested spectator to watch the dishes being prepared. It was like a live version of The Food Network.

Deni was no sooner settled when another young female approached to serve him. She let him know that she would be his server. He always wondered why servers always notify him that they would be his server in every restaurant that he had been in. Why else would they be over to his table speaking to him unless they were the ones that were going to be 'taking care of him'?

He ordered a whiskey that wasn't Redbreast because they didn't have it. The beverage menu had all sorts of handcrafted concoctions, but none had whiskey and all seemed sweet.

"I'm going to be taking my time," he said to the efficient server. "I've got a lot of stuff to look over. The nice lady that walked me back here told me that your next party to be seated here is at seven-thirty, so I'll be here until then. No offense but the less you keep interrupting me, the quicker I'll be outta here and the bigger your tip."

"Absolutely no problem. I just didn't want you waiting for me. Just signal to me when you need me. Are you a picky eater?"

"No. Why?"

"Each month Chef Ming features a different winemaker and creates a five-course meal to pair with it. You can just get that and I will leave you be."

He liked her already.

Deni's experience with wine amounted to whatever wine the girlfriend du jour was into. But the wines that showed up and cleared; along with the various courses of Shumai, Lamb Belly, Sashimi,

Sweetbreads, and Sablefish, were superlative. Deni wasn't paying attention to what he was eating and drinking, he just knew that he was enjoying every bit of it.

He looked over the various Wellesley student newspapers first. His thought process was that if Chamille Destrier was the same socialite back when she attended college as she is today, she would be in many pictures and articles. But she wasn't.

Food and drink were silently placed in front of him and taken away. The service was felt but not seen or heard. It was exactly what he needed to concentrate. If any of the other patrons were staring or giving him odd looks, he didn't know it. The restaurant was most definitely filling up, every table anxiously anticipating their own culinary delights. The murmur grew louder as did the music level. None of it took Deni's focus off of the task at hand.

Next, he turned to the yearbooks. Chamille Lovering was in more pictures than Deni could count. In each picture, he would look for familiar faces. Or the same faces. He looked through every picture, circled the female faces of each reoccurring student. He believed that if Chamille was photographed repeatedly with the same women, those women had to be familiar if not friends with her. Someone would know about her predicament back then. He just needed to find her. The

Ebb

names of each subject in the various photographs were listed beneath. He had just shy of a dozen women to track down. He wrote them down on a separate piece of paper.

Eleven women. Any of whom could be anywhere in the country by now. Anywhere in the world. He hoped for a falling out. That one of the eleven would want to speak to him. Want to dish the dirt. But he needed to find them first. Eleven would have been a daunting number had he not been completely enamored with his dinner experience. Instead he was filled with food and optimism.

At 7:15 PM the server brought over the bill. Sticker-shock kicked in. The server failed to mention the price of the aforementioned five courses of 'amazing'. Premier food and service had a premier price. Once his heart started to pump a normal amount of blood back into his brain, he decided that it was worth it. He paid the car payment sized bill with a twenty-five percent tip thinking that the server likely made more per day than he did.

He gave the valet his token and waited for the car to come from wherever it had been stashed. While waiting, Deni gave the attractive host a wink and she excitedly came over to him from behind her podium.

"How was it?"

"It was worth my kid's inheritance," he said. She laughed and gave his bicep a squeeze.

"Hey, while you're here. I know your busy, but can you tell me if any of these ladies come in here? Or if you've seen them around town?" He had dog-eared several photos from the yearbooks. He didn't need to show her all of them, as most of them contained the same women.

She shook her head for a few of the pictures, then looked around the lounge and dining room to ensure that her duties weren't being neglected. Then she put her hand on one of the pages, stopping Deni from turning to another page. "This lady. I see her fairly regularly. Hmm. The name under the photo says 'Dawson' but her reservations are always under Dawson-Prim. That's definitely her though. She's very particular."

"Yeah that's definitely the crowd. Thanks, doll."

She gave him a business card. It had Ming and his wife's name on it with the phone number to the restaurant. She flipped the card over for him which had the name *Ani* and a phone number hand-written on the back.

"Annie," Deni said.

"It's pronounced Ah-knee," she said. "But you can call me anything you want as long as you call me.

He handed her his card. "Call me when that lady comes in again, will you? I'll make it worth your effort."

"Deal," she said with a wink as she went back to her podium.

Deni turned to the front window to see his SUV out in front.

The valet brought him his Rover and Deni shelled out another $40. *I almost should have just taken another parking ticket*, he thought. He decided to spend the night in Southie since he had been drinking and was already just outside of Boston. A trip back to his house in New Hampshire would have been a much longer drive. He noticed the sign on Route 9 stating that he had entered Newton.

See ya Wellesley. See ya real soon.

31

MERIDETH DAWSON-PRIM BEGAN HER thursday as she did virtually every other weekday. She woke up with her husband who immediately took nourishment in the form of coffee via a Keurig. She made herself a cup before motivating her two pre-teen children to get out of bed. Merideth would then make a healthy breakfast for her brood which her husband refused to eat despite her begging. He would make some argument as to why granola wasn't really food, give his wife a peck on the lips, and leave for his office job in Boston. She would see her kids off to school and then get ready for work herself, where she was Executive Director for a non-profit fundraising company.

Ebb

At her position, Merideth was not required to keep exact work hours, which suited her rigorous working-mom schedule. Her husband was the only facet of her life where she didn't have complete control. Her children were well-behaved else suffer her wrath. The Dawson-Prim home in Wellesley was neat and orderly, everything had an exact place and situated as only someone with OCD could appreciate. Her subordinates did as told or consequences would be swift and harsh.

She went in to her office at ten, as she did every workday unless a pressing matter at home dictated otherwise. Merideth's assistant immediately filled her in on any messages or appointments that needed to be addressed that day. Merideth had been through countless assistants in her time as Executive Director due in large part to her untenable needs and inevitable human error. The non-profit put up with the various complaints about her because she raised more funds than anyone in the history of the organization. And they paid her well for it. The non-profit was very profitable for some.

One of her many commands to her assistants was that Merideth's lunch-meetings always be scheduled after the typical noon-to-one lunch rush. She wanted to be doted on when dining out, especially if she was with a client or donor, not just another table in a sea of guests in a dining room. Her assistants were always clear on this point, or they were no longer her assistant.

A 1:30 PM lunch-meeting was scheduled at Blue Ginger that thursday. Merideth was slated to woo a potential donator with deep pockets. He had given before, she was confident that he would give again. This time she was seeking a $100,000 donation for autism research. This type of donation required the perfect pitch and the perfect meal.

She arrived at the restaurant precisely on-time, as always. It was an indignation in a long list of annoyances to be late, a characteristic that many of her clients and donors didn't share. When asking for large sums of money, however, one cannot point out the character flaws of those potentially writing a check. So Merideth waited with quiet pique.

The potential benefactor had arrived, the lunch well under way, the $100,000 check all but written when a new annoyance inserted itself.

"Mary. Funny I should run into you here. How are you?"

"You must have me confused with someone else, my name is not Mary, " Merideth said as she tried to return to her conversation at the table.

Ebb

"Merideth Dawson-Prim right? You hyphenate now but I know you from one of the sorority reunions that my wife brought me to. Wellesley College."

"Again, there is a mistake. Wellesley doesn't have, nor has it ever had, *sororities*. We have societies and I am in the middle of an important meeting, so if you don't mind …."

"This won't take long," the intruder said in a softer voice as he sat in one of the two empty chairs at the dining room table for four.

"I beg your pardon, sir. I have politely asked you to leave. I don't believe that I know you and I don't know how you know me, Mr. ….?"

"Dennihan. You can call me Deni. I'm an investigator," he said in a soft voice as he showed his license to the table. "Sorry about the ruse and interruption to your little lunch here, but I've been dyin' to get in touch with you."

"Be that as it may Mr. Dennihan, I am in the middle of a business lunch. Can I set up a later time or date where we can meet?"

"No. You'll just avoid me and my calls. This won't take long. You remember Chamille Lovering? Destrier now."

Merideth was looking around the room for help. The server thought that her guest was seeking assistance and promptly approached the table.

"I see you have another guest, can I get you something, sir?"

"I'll take a whiskey. I'd love to eat but I won't be here that long."

"No he won't. He'll have nothing. He is bothering us and we would like him to leave," Merideth said.

The sever stood frozen, uncertain of how to proceed. Awkward took on a new meaning.

"Maybe I should give you two a minute," the benefactor said as he made a move to get up from the table.

Merideth put her hand on his forearm. "No. Please don't go — "

" — Maybe you should give us just a minute, guy." Deni gave him a nod.

"Sure thing." The gentleman dabbed his mouth with the cloth napkin from his lap and walked away from the table.

"Soooo ….," the server said, her eyes as big as silver dollars.

"So please go get me my whiskey. Thank you."

The server happily left to do just that.

"Do you realize what you have just done? I have never met anyone so rude in my entire life. You are causing a scene, now please go before I call the police to remove you."

"It's a public place, lady. It wouldn't have been a scene if you had just gone with it. Just a guy meeting up with an old acquaintance as far as the restaurant is concerned, but you blew it. Just answer a few short questions and I'll be outta your hair before the cops can even get here. Now - I know that you know Chamille Destrier."

Another look around the dining room for help, and further confirmation for Merideth that none was coming. Her previous dining companion was leaving the restaurant.

"I knew her, yes. We are in touch on occasion when I need a donation or she needs support from the foundation where I work. Why is this important enough to cost a very needy charity $100,000?"

"Huh? What are you talkin' about?"

"Nothing. Please move on so I can get this over with."

"You were friends with her back at Wellesley College, right?"

"We were friendly. What is this about?"

"So you knew that she was pregnant in 1992?"

Stunned silence. Again she looked around the restaurant for an egress. She would have gladly accepted an 'eject' button to launch herself skyward if one was offered.

"Mary? Look at me. Nobody is going to come save you. You're not in any danger unless you lie to me. Just tell me. You knew right?"

"My name is not Mary. I have no idea what you are up to, but — "

" — No buts. Yes, or no."

"Yes. Are you happy? Yes, I knew she was pregnant. And she wanted to keep it a secret. She gave the child up for adoption. Why are you doing this?"

"Because her child was looking for her, and her child is now dead. Dead trumps charity, lady."

Another bout of silence. She looked into Deni's eyes to see if this was some hoax, some trick. Merideth realized that trickery had left the building along with her $100,000.

"Oh my. That is terrible. And you're looking for Chamille? She is very well-known, she has a palace in New Hampshire. Wayland I think."

The server arrived with Deni's drink. The server was about to ask another question but Merideth waved the back of her hand, the international sign for go away. Deni took a sip of his drink and continued.

"Wayland you *know*. And I know all that too. What I need is proof that she was pregnant and that she gave birth to a girl in 1992."

"We weren't that close. I know she was pregnant, and I know that I helped her with her classes when she started to show."

"What does that mean, help with her classes? I went to the registrar's office and they said that her grades were changed to passing."

"I went to her professors and told them that she was taking a medical leave for the rest of her third year. Usually in college that means Mono, so that's what they probably thought. I got lecture notes and things, turned in her papers for her. She was very vain. Once she started to show, she stopped going to classes. Stopped going to society meetings. She fell off the planet. Chamille had the baby in New Hampshire to the best of my knowledge and she begged me not to tell anyone, not that anybody ever asked. And I haven't betrayed her confidence for over twenty years."

"Who was the father?"

"I assumed Roman Destrier. They were married the next year," Merideth said.

"But you don't know for sure?"

"Chamille wasn't a party girl like that. She was the glamorous party girl, and still is. She wanted to be seen and talked about but in a good way. Her reputation was everything to her. She wouldn't sleep around. While most girls were sneaking off to BU or BC or something to sow their oats, Chamille was building her brand. Besides, she was already dating Roman in her sophomore year I think. She knew that she had a catch and not to let him get away."

"Well, the two rarely see each other anymore and she has a revolving door to her bed."

"Not then. She was devoted to Roman. They were going to build a world together. As far as the public is concerned, they have. I'm sure the baby was Roman's."

"And I'm going to bring it down."

"To what end, Mr. Dennihan? You sound like you're from Boston, so you must know that the Destriers are royalty. You'll need an army to even put a chink their armor."

"She had the poor woman who was searchin' for her birth parents killed. She needs to pay for it."

"Are you suggesting that she killed her own child?"

"She gave it away only to have it return. In her eyes she was a threat. You said yourself that image was everything to Cammy. Her kingdom has only gotten bigger," Deni said.

"I don't see Chamille killing someone, anyone. Her own child? I've known her a long time, she wouldn't — "

" — Not herself no. I'm way ahead of ya. She had a minion do it. You're gonna be contacted by a detective to take your statement. A lawyer down the line probably."

"No. I absolutely won't be disloyal to Chamille. She has been good to me over the years, I like to think that I've done well by her."

"Today not withstanding? She had three people killed to cover this up. You're loyalties are admirable, lady, but they're best suited for someone else."

"*Three?* What happened to one? You said she had her daughter killed."

"And an investigator and the daughter's boyfriend to point suspicion at someone else. Listen, I used to be a cop. If you give them the runaround they are gonna sick the District Attorney on you. Three murders that they are gonna demand justice for. Royalty or not, she and everyone involved are gonna pay. The DA will compel your statement. You can face jail time if you refuse. Do yourself a favor, lady. Do the right thing."

Ebb

As Deni was leaving Blue Ginger, he gave Ani a wink. She left the podium after a quick word with her colleague and followed Deni out the front door.

The two met a half-block down Washington Street, out of immediate sight of the restaurant.

"You're lucky I was here today. I almost never work lunches," she said.

"I appreciate the phone call."

"I saw the reservation and you said it would be worth my effort. I'm very curious as to my payment."

"The least I can do is take you out for a nice dinner. Do you have someplace you like other than the restaurant you work at?"

"There are so many. Do you live in the city?"

"Southie."

"Toro is on the South End," Ani said.

"The South End isn't Southie but Toro sounds good. What are ya doin' later?"

"Hopefully you."

32

DENI WOKE UP TO HIS RINGING CELL PHONE
early friday morning. His disorientation from the
sudden sound initially made him think that it was his
alarm clock. He didn't yet know if he was still sleeping,
hungover, or still drunk from the night out to Toro with
Ani. By the third ring he was conscious enough to free
himself from entanglement with his bed companion and
scramble for his jeans pocket instead of the snooze
button.

It was Sheed.

"Jesus Sheed. I called you yesterday. If you
were avoiding callin' me back, couldn't you have
avoided it for another hour?"

Ebb

"Where are you?"

"Here we go. This again?'

"Fine, don't tell me. But you are in another fix and I don't know if I can stop this one."

"What are you talkin' about now?" He was wide awake.

"I was looking at the Clearinghouse again this morning. Guess who's name is on it?"

"Are we playin' games now? Spill it."

"Chamille Destrier."

"Fuck you. Seriously?"

"A Nigel Singh reported her missing. Apparently she never returned from an event that she was hosting. Normally it takes a few days of being unaccounted for in order for the police to take this seriously, especially an adult, but we're talking Chamille goddamned Destrier here. I called the New Hampshire State Police who told us that this Nigel reported that you were threatening and looking for her."

"This is bullshit, She. She's makin' a run for it."

"You've lost me."

"If you would return my calls once in a while, you would know what's up. She did it. She and her boyfriend Ludo Rossi. Now that I'm onto her bein' the birth mother of Lara Myhre, she's gettin' outta town."

"And you can prove this, Deni? 'Cuz last I checked, you thought Gary Rennick was good for it. And we know how that turned out."

"I can prove that Lara was Cammy's kid. I can prove that Cole Renner was investigating it. They're both dead." He ignored Sheed's jab. There was no defending it anyway. He had a gut feeling and it had turned out to be wrong.

"And why haven't you given me this information on Chamille Destrier?"

"Because it might not be proof that can be used in court. It definitely can't be used in court. Plus you never answer your phone."

"Uh huh. And what about Gary Rennick? How does he tie in? Right now things are stacking against you like you can't even imagine, my dude. Look at it from my point of view. From Hobbs's point of view. You dig your nose into a murder and Cole Renner gets killed. According to the New Hamp Statie I spoke with, you were accused of breaking into the very adoption agency that handled Myhre's closed adoption to get information that you just said that you have. You make a huge scene at the rink and are a suspect in Gary Rennick's murder, a guy that you liked for Lara's death from the beginning. This is also a guy that the man that's paying your fees wanted you to kill, lest we forget," Sheed said.

Ebb

"Lisa I - "

" - Oh I'm not finished yet. Nor are you apparently. You then go and harass the woman that you believe to be Lara Myhre's biological mother. A woman who is rich as all fuck and could buy the police department if it matched her shoes. She is now missing and you are AGAIN the last person who saw her."

"Gimme a break. You know this is a set-up. You do know that don't you? She's probably with her cabana boy on a private beach drinkin' a piña colada made of gold. You said it yourself. She's rich as fuck and can take a trip whenever and wherever she wants."

"All of this shit is adding up, Deni. If she's on a beach, prove it."

"Have you looked into her passport, She? Even on a private jet her passport gets registered."

"No, I haven't. Cuz it's not my job. I'm just letting you know that you've gone from the heat to the flame."

310

Ebb

Ryan's morning shower after his almost daily session of making love to his wife was interrupted by a phone call. Had the call been five minutes earlier, he would have been inside Angie and neither one them would have answered. Angie preferred sex in the morning. Ryan was like clockwork physically and ready for the task. He was listening to Phish jam out on *Waiting All Night,* hippie-dancing in the shower while soaping himself when the phone was handed to him through the open shower door.

"Your friend," Angie said. He took the phone and she walked away after closing the shower door.

"He's your friend too," Ryan called after her. "What is it now, Deni?"

"How'd you know it was me?"

"Only you can piss my wife off like that. She loves you and hates you at the same time. How many days this week have been consumed with your bullshit?"

"Too many. Sorry, Ry. But I gotta talk to ya."

"Right this second? I'm in the shower. No jokes about me being naked and wet please."

"Don't worry. I'm not in the mood for jokes," Deni said.

"It's that serious?"

"Cammy took off with her flavor of the month. Nige filed a missing persons on her after she didn't come home from the event at the country club tuesday night. I was there and people saw. Sheed called to warn me that shit is comin' my way."

"Hold on a sec, will ya?" Ryan rinsed off the soap and turned the water off in the shower.

As he was drying himself he got back on the phone. "Okay slow it down for me. Did you lose your cool at the club?"

"No, not really."

"What does 'not really' mean? Did you or did you not cause a big scene?"

"No, Ry. What do you take me for?"

"You're you. Past experience leads me to believe that you probably hurt someone or hit someone or made a threat to do one of those things."

"Well, I didn't. I may have twisted an arm, but nobody got hurt. I did that at her house."

"You followed her back to her house?"

"No. I went there first. Nige was there as always and was bein' a typical douche as always. He was pissin' me off so I told him I was gonna beat him or hurt him or somethin'. I forget my exact words."

"And Nigel was the person who filed the missing persons report on his employer, a wealthy and influential woman who was last seen with you."

"Correct."

"Aaaaahhhh, Deni.

"Don't 'aaaaahhhh, Deni' me. What do I do? Should we go see the cops? Tell them that she is probably under a palm tree somewhere gettin' the tannin' oil licked out of her?"

"No. Just keep calm and let me make a few calls. I'll call the Wayland County DA, Tim Cromwell. If he wants your ass on a plate, he'll tell me and then we can figure out what to do. He won't go for an arrest unless there is evidence of foul play. But this is Chamille Destrier we're talking about. When the queen goes missing, heads will roll."

"All right. Thanks, Ry." It sounded like Deni was going to hang up.

"Hey Deni!"

"Yeah?"

"Keep a low profile if you can, will you? Please? For me?"

"You know me," Deni said and hung up.

"I do. And that's what I'm afraid of," Ryan said to no one.

33

ANI WAS NOT HAPPY ABOUT BEING EJECTED out of Deni's bed. She wasn't happy about the early hour, nor about the manner in which she was raised from a sound sleep next to her newfound lover. A phone call started a tempest of clothes being tossed to her and chatter about where she needed to be dropped off.

She didn't do one night stands. Ani had made an exception with Deni. She had gone to bed with him quickly but not with the intention of it being a one night stand. There was something about him that she was immediately attracted to. Something about the way he carried himself turned her on, the fire within her grew over dinner the previous night.

The discussion at Toro was mostly about her, which was an unusual occurrence on her dates. The conversation usually centered around the man she was out with, but not so with Deni. He answered questions when asked, but mostly inquired about her. At 28, she was somewhat younger than him but she didn't initially know by how much. She thought he was in his early to-mid-thirties. He was very fit and he drove a nice car so he had to be somewhat successful.

Deni had remarked that it was always difficult to determine age with respect to people of Asian decent, which led her to believe that he was surprised by her age as well. As a grad student, her hosting career was coming to an end in the near future.

She had decided in the restaurant earlier in the day that she was going to sleep with him. He was sexy and mysterious. Until that point it had only been a flirtation. Her wantonness grew during dinner and when she went back to this three-decker in Southie afterwards. His place was nice, much more posh than she expected from the surrounding area as they drove up.

His naked body was nicer. His hairless skin rippled over lean muscle covered with a tapestry of tattoos. The 'V' shape from his hips pointing below his washboard abs down toward his pelvis made her wet.

Ebb

She didn't do bad-boy, but she did Deni. Over and over again. It was a magical night for her. Until morning.

She had only been resting for a couple of hours when she was roused from bed, her skirt, blouse, and lacy A-list undergarments were tossed to her. He apologized about it, said that there was an emergency, but he needed to go. Which meant that she needed to go. Deni had put a cup of coffee in the hand that wasn't carrying heels as he ushered her out the door and into his SUV.

He apologized one more time when he dropped her off at her apartment. He promised her that he would call before pulling away from the curb. She stood on the sidewalk watching him drive off, deciding then and there that she would sleep with him again if given the chance.

Ebb

New England Emergency Services Information, NEESI, is a quick trip west on the Mass Pike from Boston and was the next town along Route 9 from Wellesley. Deni had been to the building many times before and knew that Althea would already be busy at work. The facility is somewhat secure as one would imagine. The hub for incoming 9-1-1 phone calls and dispatch to various local authorities would require a protected environment. Deni's face was very recognizable after years of visits and was allowed to stroll through the nondescript Natick building at quarter 'til eight friday morning.

Althea Milonas was diligently working behind her desk inside her chilled and glass-encased terrarium. The tiny multi-colored LED lights on several computer towers behind her were blinking away mightily, indicating that they were also busily taking care of business. Had someone not known that she was in her office, they might have missed her behind her two abnormally large side-by-side computer flat-screens. She was very much like the shy animal at the zoo who the spectators know is in the vivarium but cannot see.

Deni didn't knock prior to walking into the cold room, another one of his 'things'. Althea moved her head to her right, looking from behind one of her screens to see which intruder had been rude enough to enter without announcing themselves.

"Deni. What are you doing here?"

"You don't sound happy to see me."

"Always. But you normally get your fix and I don't see you for a while. I can't take another day off. I have things I need to take care of."

"You probably have more time comin' to you than you know what to do with, Al."

"Be that as it may, emergency calls come in 24-7, 365. The system has to work or people can die. It's important work," she defended.

"I get it. Can you take a break?"

Althea jiggled her watch and moved it to an observable spot on her wrist. "I've only been here for an hour or so."

"I was thinkin' you could maybe look somethin' up for me here," he said still standing by the now closed office door.

"You're such an asshole. I have work to do which doesn't include errands for you."

"C'mon, Al. I need your help."

"No 'good morning'. No 'I brought you some coffee'. You're not even pretending to want to see me, you just need my help. I must be some kind of sucker, huh?"

"You're right. I'm sorry. Your tits look as big and beautiful as ever and I'm a shit-bag. Can we move on? You can tell me how much of an asshole I am once

I'm behind bars, which could be any minute if you don't help me."

"What happened?"

"I think I'm bein' set up for a fall. That lady that you found for me, she's done a Houdini."

"Lovering was it?"

"Lovering, yeah.   Only now she's Destrier, Remember? Chamille Destrier," Deni said.

"*THE* Chamille Destrier?   As in Chamille and Roman Destrier?   The adopted girl was the biological daughter of the Destriers? *WOW.*"

"Adopted woman, yeah. And she was murdered along with Cole Renner. I couldn't figure out why they would kill her boyfriend too, the hockey star — until now. It was to put me down. Now Cammy has taken an unannounced vacation and everyone is pointin' fingers at me again. I need to find her, Al."

"And you think that I can help?"

"Yeah.   You can dig into her financials. Bank, credit cards, whatever.   She isn't the 'gonna go someplace and rough it' kinda chick, so she needs money. The kind of money she needs isn't likely to fit in a pocket book."

"It's called a purse or bag, Deni. Nobody says pocket book anymore. What are you sixty?"

"I think you're gettin' focused on the wrong thing here."

"And I think you're forgetting that I can't do what you need me to do *hee-yah*," she said making fun of his thick accent.

"Why not?"

"It's illegal. As a former cop, you should know that."

"It's borderline. You're not takin' any of their money, your just trackin' it," he said.

"We both know it's a cybercrime — *another* cybercrime — and you want me to commit a felony where I work. I don't shit where I eat."

"You've done it for me before, Al. 'Sides, it's a white-collar crime. You'd really fill out a prison jumpsuit. Better than I'd look, don't ya think? I need your help. How long are you gonna make me beg?"

"I really need to say 'no' to you. Just once. Once, so you know that you can't always get what you want from me. Do you have any information at all on your Cammy?"

"She's not *my* Cammy," Deni said.

"I've heard the rumors. What am I, stupid?"

"Apparently not."

"And you keep coming back to me, so there you go Mr. Man. I have her social from the ID search, what else do you have?"

"That about covers it."

"You never make things easy."

Ebb

"Easy is boring," he said.

Althea again needed her privacy as well as the absence of attention from her colleagues in her glass case. More nine-to-fivers would be arriving imminently, more operators and such would make extra trips by Althea's office to peer in. Small workspaces engender more access into personal lives. Everyone in the building knew about Deni from his visits, they knew more from Althea, and yet more from the gossip around the water-cooler. His appearance friday morning added yet another chapter to his story and a welcome distraction to their dreary work day. Getting rid of Deni while she worked was essential in getting rid of the looky-loos.

She first began by getting Chamille Destrier's date of birth from her name and social security number.

Once she obtained this from a simple google search, she began looking through all of Chamille's UCC filings using her name, date of birth, and social security number. Uniform Commercial Code filings with the office of the Secretary of State are recorded for every deposit into a bank, or loan from one, for more than $10,000 per transaction per day. Most people don't have large amounts of money to move into their bank accounts on a daily basis, meaning that they deposit

$9,999 or less at a time. For wealthy people, $10,000 can be pocket change.   For the Destriers, they made substantially more than that on accrued interest in just one of their accounts, per day. Each time such sums of money were moved from account to account, the bank doing this would file a form. Althea was able to obtain a long list of bank accounts and numbers along with the transactions from those filings.

Many, but not all of the accounts listed Roman Destrier on them. Althea was then able to get his date of birth and social security number.   The dam opened at that point and she was able to deeply delve into the various accounts, printing all the documents and organizing them by bank and account therein. It would have been much easier to email them to Deni, but that would leave an electronic footprint in addition to her lover's aversion to electronic mail.

Once it was all compiled and put into a cardboard file-box, she called Deni to come back to NEESI. Althea had this all accomplished by the time she was ready to leave for her lunch hour.

She told him not to come in, she would meet him in the parking lot. She walked out of the front door of the NEESI building with the file-box in her arms. Only she didn't see Deni.   Left to right, she searched the parking lot.

Ebb

A dark blue Land Rover SUV with gray gills pulled up in front of her. The glass was tinted so she couldn't see the driver who had cut her off. Deni got out of the vehicle, opened the rear door, took the box out of her hands, and loaded it into the back. Althea slowly made her way around the front of the vehicle and got into the passenger side.

"Where did you steal this? It's gorgeous," she said when both of them were inside. Deni drove to a remote part of the parking lot.

"I've had it for a while. You like it?"

"I love it. Did you win the lottery or something?"

"No. I traded in the Mercedes for it. It has more room," Deni said.

"You had a Mercedes? Where have I been? I thought you had that Escalade that was beaten to shit."

"I got rid of the Caddie a while ago. Maybe you just forgot."

"Deni, I would remember a fucking Mercedes. Or a Land Rover. But who am I kidding? It's not like you take me anywhere, how would I have seen what you drive? You just come around and fuck my brains out and then your off on your merry way — wait .... you smell like sex."

"Are we really gonna do this again? Broken fuckin' record. What'd you find?"

"Of course. What can I do for you, right?"

"Al?"

"Fine. I printed out all of the information for you and it's in the box. Between the two of them they have roughly eighty different accounts. Eighty."

"Eighty accounts? Who has eighty fuckin' bank accounts?" Deni's head hit his hands which were resting at the eleven and one positions on the steering wheel.

"Rich people. Insanely rich people. Do you know that they are self-financed and self-insured?"

"I don't even know what that means."

"It means that they loan themselves and their employees money, making money on themselves and the people they pay. Health and life insurance are the same thing. All backed by one of Roman's financial divisions under the Monarch umbrella."

"So instead of payin' bills, they pay themselves? They make money on their bills?"

"Sort of," she said shaking and nodding her head like a bobblehead doll.

"So where is she?"

"I don't know, Deni."

"All that paper and you don't know? Why am I here?"

"Take it easy tiger. Nobody can trace where she's spending money. All of her money is funneled through prepaid credit cards."

"Huh?"

"I would think that a guy with a Land Rover would know a little more about money. They are self-financed. No MasterCard or American Express. No Visa or Discover. The cards are *backed* by Amex and Visa, but only because most establishments don't take Destrier. Or Monarch as the case may be. They have built up so much wealth that they have a blanket backing by major credit card companies who don't track their purchases. The Destriers deposit money into an account that these prepaid credit cards draw from. No records are kept, at least none that I can find. It's ingenious actually."

"Yeah …. Really great. I love the forward-thinkin'. So any suggestions on what the fuck I do from here? I got a box full of useless paper."

"There is one oddity that you could look at. You're welcome by the way."

"Thanks. You're right. I'm just under the gun, you know I appreciate it. Now what am I thanking you for?"

"Roman used to be a big shot for your friend's father-in-law right?"

"Norman Craig was JG's father-in-law at one time, yes. Anna Craig played matchmaker for Cammy and Roman, who used to work for Craig Investment Group. CIG," Deni explained.

"So why would Roman Destrier deposit $25 million into a CIG account?"

"They're both finance moguls," Deni said with a shrug. "They probably transfer money back and forth all the time."

"It was from one of Roman's personal accounts. He is the only one authorized to touch money in that account, which was then transferred to yet another account yesterday. It's the first time money has been moved from that account since it was opened roughly three months ago. That account is now closed. I'm no financial genius but it looks to me like the money was laundered.

"Three months ago?"

"About that, yes," she said. "What? You've got that look again. That sexy look like you know something nobody else knows."

"Cole started lookin' into Lara's birth parents about that time."

"Coincidence?"

"I don't believe in coincidence, Al, and you know it. Chamille Destrier wants to keep her kid a secret for whatever reason, and at the same time that

Cole starts looking into her parents a huge amount of money is moved into a CIG account. Then transferred out and closed. Yesterday. The day after Chamille Destrier disappears," Deni said.

"These people are worth billions, Deni. They have hundreds of millions of dollars at their disposal. *Cammy*, as you call her, isn't going to settle for just $25 million and vanish."

"No, she has her prepaids you said."

"So?"

"So the twenty-five mil is for whoever did the killin'. Probably mister boy-toy, Lugo Rossi. They funneled it through another investment company to make it look legit. And I know just who to talk to about that."

"God you're sexy when you're hot on a case. Have you christened this thing yet? Is that why I smell sex?" Althea looked into the back of the luxury SUV.

"No."

"Good. You can repay my largesse."

"You're not that big, Al. Full-figured maybe but not large."

"Largesse, not large you dumb shit. It's a good thing you're pretty."

"I've never been called pretty before."

Ebb

"And I've got twenty minutes left of my lunch hour. Get in the back and put your pretty cock inside me."

34

THE CIG BUILDING IS BUT ONE PEAK IN THE skyline of Boston's Financial District. The area of the city is bounded by Boston Harbor, Atlantic Avenue, State Street, and Devonshire Street. While the tourists march like ants in Faneuil Hall and Long Wharf, the powerful and money-hungry mastermind economies in the modern skyscrapers that tower above them. Fidelity, Putnam, State Street Bank, Eastern Bank, Bank of America, PriceWaterhouseCoopers, and countless others like CIG all have prime real estate within the financial hub.

Craig Investment Group is located in the second tallest building in that section of Boston and has the appearance that it is made of granite. When one is looking to invest their hard-earned money, fragile glass doesn't inspire the same confidence as granite.

Deni parked in the structure under One State Street and walked the six blocks to CIG, wading through both the after-lunch worker bees and tourists the entire way. He didn't have a security badge but rode the wave of financial gurus through the lobby and up in the elevator to Cecil Brand's office. Again, he didn't knock.

"Excuse me. This is a private office. Who are you?" The money manager was slight and weaselly looking. His frail, thin body held up his bulbous head like a lollipop. His beady eyes looked down his aquiline nose in an effort to stare-down the intruder. His voice was as irksome as his appearance.

"Don't get up. I'm Warren Dennihan. We've met but clearly you don't remember me."

"I don't. And I certainly don't remember having an appointment with you. I don't handle individual finances, one of the consultants can help you down on the — "

" — Oh but you do handle personal finances, Mr. Brand. The Craigs for starters," Deni said.

"Uh, uh, well …. Yes, that's true but, eh, well …. Norman and Olivia Craig have both passed on." Cecil Brand had bravely run away from every fight in his life.

"I'm aware. And it looks like you still handle money for the Destriers."

"Who are you again, sir?"

"Warren Dennihan." Deni produced one of the files that Althea had printed out and organized, a file that he had retrieved from the file-box that was still in his backseat. He handed Cecil a piece of paper highlighting a $25 million dollar transfer out of Roman Destrier's account with CIG, then sat down in a chair in the office.

Cecil quickly scanned it. "What is this regarding?"

"I thought you did this for a livin'? It's regarding twenty-five million dollars. Says so right there."

"I think I'm going to have to ask you to leave now," Cecil said. That was about the extent of his fight.

Deni wasn't sure if there was a silent alarm or if Cecil would call security from the phone on his desk, nor the number of security personnel that would come through the office door. But he didn't want to find out. He was not in the good-graces of the police at the moment. Deni was breathing free air on borrowed time. Trespassing and one or more charges of assault would bring the lenders for that time demanding payment in full. Nor would waving a gun around. He was walking a thin line.

"If I leave now, I'll just come back with the police who will go to the DA who will then turn this place upside down with subpoenas and search warrants."

"For what? It's not illegal to transfer money from account to account. People do it all the time, millions of times daily in fact."

"Not to launder money. Money laundering is illegal. A white-collar crime, sure, but you'd still have to go to prison. I wonder how well you would do in prison?"

"Who is laundering money? Some people want to put money away in higher-interest establishments that are safe, others want to — "

" — Pay off illegal hits that they don't want traced."

"I, I, I have no idea what you're talking about, Mr. Dennihan. I just do what I'm told."

"I'm glad you're such a good listener. So tell me where she is."

"Uh …. Who?"

"Chamille Destrier and her boyfriend."

"To my knowledge, Mrs. Destrier is still married to Roman Destrier and living more than comfortably in New Hampshire."

"And we both know that she and her husband are rarely if ever in the same building. She sleeps around probably as much as he does. Her current

Ebb

cocksman is Lugo Rossi. Is the account with the $25 million in his name?"

"I don't know that and I'm afraid I cannot give you that information even if I did," Cecil said.

Deni pulled his phone out from his pocket as he stood up. He dialed Sheed, who answered but for Deni's purposes it wasn't really necessary. In truth, with his current legal predicament he didn't really want to speak with her.

"It's me. Can you get a warrant to search through all CIG files here on State Street? Let the DA know that we are goin' after Roman Destrier, Monarch, and CIG for money laundering. It might take a week or two of shutting everything down to uncover it, but we can have the all assets frozen until we go through it all. Millions if not billions on lock-down. I'll contact the press, they're gonna love this. We need to let them know that Cecil Brand was the one that blew the whistle on the whole thing."

"Wait, wait, wait, wait, wait. Just wait a gosh-darn minute," Brand said as he stood and came around his desk.

"Hold on a sec, She," Deni said into his phone and then covered the microphone.

"This is Blackmail. Coercion."

Ebb

"Call it what you want. I call it 'not fuckin' around'. I'm tired and people are dead. You could be next if you don't choose very carefully."

"Please hang up your phone."

"Sheed. I'll call you back in a bit." She was yelling about being used when Deni hung up.

Cecil went back behind his desk, taking a few deep breaths before continuing. He typed a few things into his computer.

"The trail to the Caymans account is where the money trail ends," he finally said.

"Cammy is in the Cayman Islands?"

"That's not what I said, Mr. Dennihan."

"Then what the fuck are you sayin'?"

"I'm saying that the funds were transferred into CIG from the Monarch Bank & Trust in Cyprus, where it originated from the Monarch Bank in Dubai. We transferred the money from CIG to their bank in the Caymans."

"Monarch is Roman Destrier's company."

"Which means nothing," Cecil said. "Monarch has more sub-companies and divisions that at some point virtually all money goes through one Monarch product or another."

"How nice for him. Is it also just a coincidence that he is in Dubai?"

334

"Yes. He could be on the moon and transfer money with the touch of a button."

"But why go through all that trouble to hopscotch money? He has his own conglomerate where he basically prints money. Why go through a subdivision in Cypress Hill or whatever?"

"Cyprus, not Cypress Hill. And he obviously didn't want the money tracked by UCC filings. According to the IMF, $600 billion to $1.5 trillion are moved to international banks every year for just that reason. It's technically not illegal."

"Then you just shipped it off to another account in the Caymans from CIG?"

"Correct. As per the request in writing three months ago. All perfectly legal. However, the account in which the money was deposited was again transferred out and closed yesterday."

"Yeah, I know. By whom?"

"It's the Caymans. If it is even still in the Caymans, I would have no idea nor will they tell me. I can only see amounts and bank authorization codes. Once the money left CIG, that is the last transaction I can see."

"So you can't just call someone to tell you who is on the account?"

"No. I would need someone to authorize me to look into other accounts. I would also need bank codes for specific account numbers. But I can tell you that in order to close the account by withdrawal a bank official and a notary would have to be involved. If the paperwork was completed in advance, however, the money could then be sent via check or redeposited into yet another account the moment the initial transfer was complete. The recipient chose to wait three months to transfer it out or withdraw it."

"This is fuckin' frustrating. So at some point the person who's name is on that Cayman account would have to be physically at the bank in the Cayman Islands in order to have the account closed."

"I understand your frustration and I believe that I have already explained that. He or she would only have to be physically at the bank if they chose to withdraw the funds with either cash or a cashier's check. They can transfer the funds out of the account from anywhere in the world," Cecil explained again.

"He must have set this up for his wife in Dubai. You can get the information from the bank there."

"No, Mr. Dennihan, I cannot. Dubai is like the Caymans. Untouchable."

"We are the United fucking States, we can touch whatever country we want. We just gotta get the right people involved."

"Clearly you don't know anything about United Arab Emirates."

"I thought we were talkin' about Dubai?"

"Which is one of the seven Emirs," Brand said. Deni looked confused at the word 'Emirs' so Cecil backtracked. "Basically in the early 70's a group of wealthy sheiks, seven of them, decided to form their own country bordering Oman and Saudi Arabia. Dubai is the largest of the cities and has a $400 billion dollar economy within 1500 square miles. To put it in perspective; the State of California has the world's sixth largest economy because of Hollywood and Silicon Valley, which is about a third of the state's economy — $1.5 trillion in 425,000 square miles. Dubai has the same economy as both Hollywood and Silicon Valley and produces nothing. It's a transport and financial hub the size of San Diego if we are keeping with the California comparison. There is no extradition and those who reside there live like kings. It is the wealthiest place on the planet."

"So if Cammy, her boyfriend, and Roman are there, she's in the wind?"

"Yes. And if her money is either there or in the Caymans, you won't see or touch it. For a $1,000 and a $300,000 minimum balance, you could do it too."

"Fantastic. I'll go cut up my mattress."

35

DENI CALLED SHEED WHILE WALKING back to the parking structure at One State Street. He had gone into the CIG building energized and ready to knock down the string of dominoes. He left CIG feeling deflated and useless. Lisa's call to him early that morning had produced the 'fight or flight' mechanism that all humans possess. Fight had gone into the CIG building, flight was walking out of it.

He walked past the Monarch building which taunted him, further pushing him down into the emotional dumps. The thought of going into the building and creating a stir left his mind as quickly as it had entered it. Deni was one breath away from being arrested, no sense adding insult to injury.

Tracking down Chamille Destrier was only possible by tracking her money, Deni thought. She made Oprah look indigent by comparison; could go anywhere in the world and do anything she wanted. It seemed clear that her travel money wasn't traceable because she was using her own credit card. Literally. Chamille was on permanent vacation with or without Ludo Rossi, who was $25 million dollars richer for having known her.

The twenty-five million was untouchable because it was laundered through two countries before the United States, and at least one more since. The money clearly coming from Roman Destrier's empire, the man himself was in Dubai and therefore also untouchable.

Deni needed to tell Sheed just how fucked the investigation was. If she was looking to him for answers, she wasn't going to be happy. The answers were somewhere in the middle-east which meant that there was nothing that could be done about it.

"I don't appreciate being used as leverage for whatever it is that you're doing, Deni," Sheed said when Deni called her back.

"Sorry about that. I was hoping the guy would tell me where Cammy and Ludo went. I thought I was on their trail through their finances."

"Whatever. You're in no position to be playing games, my dude. Who is Ludo again?"

"Ludo Rossi. Tall, muscular, handsome, and probably on top of Chamille Destrier. Not your type. Why?"

"Oh yeah. I wonder what her husband has to say about that?"

"I don't think he gives a shit since he paid the guy. I'll be sure to ask him if he comes back from Dubai," Deni said.

Sheed was silent or he couldn't hear her with the crowd and street noise of the financial district.

"She? You still there?"

"I'm here. Is he dark and Italian-looking?"

"His name is Ludo Rossi. Take a stab at it."

"Don't be a wise-ass. I was looking to see if he had any yellows. Assault last year, dropped from attempted. He got two years probation. Did you say he was hanging out with Chamille Destrier? In New Hampshire?"

"I don't think they're in New Hampshire or somebody would have seen them. She wouldn't be in the Clearinghouse, that's for sure."

"No, Deni. I mean before that. He was with her? At the event that you crashed? That's the same guy, right?"

"Yeah. I met him at the country club where I was supposedly the last person to see her," he said.

"You can't leave the state without permission if you're on probation. If he was in New Hampshire he either had permission or we can yank his leash. Gimme a sec, I'll call his PO," she said.

"Wait. He's not gonna be in …. " It was too late. Sheed had already put him on hold. Ludo Rossi still being in New England was not likely. Deni felt that he probably had a better chance of seeing God than Ludo Rossi ever again. But it was also just as unlikely that the Italian would be in Dubai. He had served his purpose and neither Chamille nor Roman had any plausible use for him in Dubai.

Deni waited outside the entrance to the underground parking structure. If he went in, he would lose a signal, service, and the call. It seemed to take forever and he was forced to people-watch in the outdoor marketplace in Faneuil Hall.

A mid-day drunk tripping on the cobblestone sidewalk; two pickpockets; and a drug deal later, she came back on the line.

"Deni?"

"Yeah, still here waitin'."

"Nope, no permission and he missed his last check-in. His last known employer was Back Bay Restaurants. He's a bartender at Atlantic Fish Company. He's not supposed to be near alcohol either as part of his probation agreement. His Probation Officer was about to pull his card."

"Wrong. His last known employer was Chamille Destrier. You think that he's still tendin' bar?"

"Who knows? But officially that is where he works and officially he needs to go to prison for violating probation. We can work out more charges down the line if need be," Sheed said. "We can send a couple of local unies or we can go have a crack at him ourselves."

"He's been a very bad boy. I'll bet they would love to learn that their Italian Stallion bartender is a felon. There is no way that he's gonna be there after a $25 million pay-day, but I'm thirsty all of a sudden."

"Yeah me too," she said.

"You're not gonna bring your ball and chain are ya?"

"Ricky isn't here. It's friday at quitting time. I'm pretty sure that's the only time that he moves fast."

"You mean out the door? Probably true," Deni said.

"So you headed there now?"

Ebb

"Yeah, I'll meet ya there."

Atlantic Seafood Company is a popular fine-casual restaurant on Boylston Street near the Boston Marathon finish line. The interior is designed to look like a dining hall on a cruise vessel. It was a nice evening so the outdoor patio was as full as the dining room and bar were on any given day. Deni sat at the bar which ran to the right along the length of the large dining room. He had to finagle two seats by bribing the host to page a party of two that were occupying barstools waiting for a table.

It took forty dollars to learn what he already knew. Deni was told that Ludo wasn't working that night.

Sheed arrived and walked up to where Deni was seated a short time later. "Hey. Place is packed."

"Yeah always. Did you change clothes?"

"Maybe. Why?"

"You never wear a skirt, first off."

"I didn't know if we were going to play a part or what."

"You look good, She."

"Don't get any ideas. What are you drinking?" She took her seat to Deni's right and looked around the room.

"Whiskey. The ushe. They have a big wine list, you wanna look at it?"

"No. I'll have what you're having. Rocks though." She popped another button on her silk blouse. Deni was flagging one of the female bartenders to his left. He held up two fingers like the peace sign.

"You can relax with the buttons, he's not here," Deni said when he turned back around. "I never knew you had a rack, She."

"I'm meeting someone afterwards. Let's just find out if Ludo's been seen or heard from lately."

"I already asked one of the guys that was walkin' around in a suit. Manager. Ludo doesn't work here anymore. No-show a week or so ago," Deni said.

"And this manager didn't report it to his PO I'm guessing."

"He didn't know he needed to. Surprise surprise. They never check 'yes' for the felony question on the application and nobody ever checks it."

"I've got an idea," Lisa said. The drinks arrived and Deni asked for a couple of cubes in one of the glasses.

Sheed thanked the female bartender and asked her to come closer to her. Lisa whispered sweet nothings into the young woman's ear, received a positive response and gave the bartender a wink as she walked away.

"Is that your date later?"

"Nope. But I know where he lives," she said.

"Didn't you know that from his PO?"

"He's a felon who has been two-timing his Probation Officer. You don't think he's in the same apartment that he gave his probation officer do you?"

"No. My guess is that he was living up in that palace in New Hampshire. Or was," Deni said.

"He no-showed a week ago, you said?"

"Roughly. That's what the suit told me," Deni said.

"He was still getting laid by girls here on the side. That girl in particular." Lisa pointed to the bartender who had given them their drinks.

"She's AC/DC?"

"Why put a label on it?"

"Hmm."

"What?"

"Why would he keep workin' here when he had Cammy waitin' up in Wayland?" Deni pondered his own question while he sipped his second whiskey.

"How long did she have him under her wing?"

"Good question. But he seemed comfortable with her. I think he loves her."

"Well, then he must have been a part-timer," Lisa said before taking her own sip. "Besides, what if hubby came home? Can't have tall and good-looking around if he came home unexpectedly."

"That place is big enough where she could have thirty studs in waiting and Roman wouldn't know the difference."

"So what are you saying, Deni?"

"I'm sayin' that I'm gonna take another trip up to the Destrier Estate. I'm gonna have a chat with Nige."

"Nigel Singh? The personal assistant that reported her missing according to the Clearinghouse?"

"One and the same," Deni said. "I would have gone sooner but he would just say that he doesn't know anything and if he called the cops I'd be fucked. But it's clear that she's missing on purpose and he knows more about this Ludo angle than we do. We need to fix that."

"Is that where you're going now?"

"Nope. I'm going to Ludo's apartment as soon as you tell me where it is."

Ebb

"I'm going with you," she said and finished her drink.

"I thought you had a date?"

She began to refasten the button that she had popped. "I *did.* Pay the check and let's get out of here."

36

LUDO ROSSI'S UNOFFICIAL APARTMENT was on the North End of Boston. Which wasn't surprising since the North End is the Italian section of the city. Restaurants and bakeries are congested on narrow cobblestone sidewalks near the Paul Revere House. The apartment was above one such bakery off of Hanover Street which insisted that it made the best cannoli in the city.

Deni knocked on Ludo's door several times but there wasn't an answer. He went for his wallet but Lisa stopped him.

"Don't even think about it."

"What?"

"You were gonna pick the lock and I can't let you do that," she said.

"You take all the fun outta this line of work, ya know that?"

"I'm still a cop, Deni. Although if I keep investigating these murders with you, I have a feeling I'll be hitting you up for a job."

"What makes you think I'd hire you?"

"I'm smart and there is absolutely no sexual tension."

"Okay smarty, how do you suppose we get inside?"

"I'll call is PO and get some uniforms down here," Lisa said.

"See, that's why I wouldn't hire you. You're no fun. I say we go another route."

"No breaking in."

"Fine, no breakin' in."

"If it's illegal in any way, I don't even want you to say it."

"Relax." Deni walked down the hall to the next apartment. He had heard the cover slide off of the peephole when he had knocked on Ludo's door, so he knew they were being watched. He knocked on the door but the person inside didn't open it or answer. He repeated the process of knocking and waiting several more times before his Irish was officially up.

Ebb

"I know you're home, I heard you peepin' out at us. We're cops," Deni said with a nonchalant wink to Sheed. "It ain't illegal to be nosy, we just need your help."

The chain on the other side of the door rattled and the door opened just wide enough for the occupant to look out. The chain was still attached but not yet strained to the end of its tether. The unkempt young woman inside asked to see a badge. Deni made for his wallet but purposely took longer than Sheed who brandished her badge quickly.

"Detective Sheed with the Mass State Police. This is Dennihan. May we ask you a few questions about the man who lives in that apartment?" Lisa pointed her thumb behind her toward Ludo's apartment.

"I don't know nothin' about nothin'," the young woman said.

"You sound proud of it," Deni said. "Ignorance ain't a virtue, hun."

"I don't wanna get involved. I got my own problems."

"And one of 'em is gonna be me. Just open the door all the way so we can talk."

"What are you harassing me for? I didn't do nothin'." She unlatched the chain and opened the door the rest of the way but blocked the entrance. Her arms folded in front of her indicating that she wasn't going to offer them inside of her apartment.

"No, but you're nosy. I normally can't stand nosy people, but as it happens we need that right about now," Deni said.

"I think what he means is that you seem to take interest in those that live around you, which is a good thing. A smart thing," Lisa said. She gave Deni a look that indicated that she was not happy with his approach. "We need to know if Ludo Rossi has been around lately?"

"Ludo owes rent. I was lookin' to see if it was him. He's been ducking me."

"You're the landlord, Ms……"

"I'm kinda the super. I get a lousy twenty-five percent off to collect rent checks and call a plumber when some asshole puts too much shit-paper down the drain."

"So you have keys to the other apartments?" Deni looked down the hall in both directions. He noticed three other doors other than Ludo and the super's.

"Yeah but the owner says that I need to give notice before goin' into any of them. Unless they give me permission."

Deni smiled and stared through her. "But that hasn't stopped you, has it?"

"What are you accusing me of?"

"He's not accusing you of anything. He was just making conversation, Ms……"

"Quit itching at my name. I told you that I don't wanna get involved."

"I'm a detective with the State Police," Sheed said. "You don't think that I can find out your name and everything else about you with one phone call? I'm not interested in anything that you might have to hide. At least not right now. But if you keep giving me the runaround, I might get very interested."

"Listen, I haven't seen him. Loverboy Ludo always has some girl on his arm. He must have found one that took him in because he hasn't been around much lately. I'm not sure what more I can tell ya. If you want to get inside his apartment you're gonna have to call him or the owner of the building. For the last time, I'm not getting involved."

"Unless there's an emergency," Deni said.

"What are you selling me?"

"As 'kinda the super' you have an obligation to keep the other tenants safe. If there was flooding or a gas leak, you would have to go inside the apartment to make sure that the building didn't have to be evacuated. It's the law."

Sheed looked at Deni and then back at the would-be super. Her mind was racing a mile a minute. What Deni said was not true in the strictest sense. She didn't want to sell him out, but she didn't want to face sanctions with the department either. The young woman was the quickest way inside save for letting Deni pick the locks, which was definitely illegal and not an option for her. What she should have been doing was calling the judge on after-hours rotation to get an arrest warrant, that would gain her legal entrance into the apartment. She hoped that she wouldn't have to defend her decision of letting the investigator, who was circumventing the law in her presence by lying to the pseudo-superintendent, to a disciplinary board or Internal Affairs.

Detective Sheed nodded reluctantly. "I think I smell gas, you?"

"If I let you inside the apartment will you leave me alone?"

"Yes," she said.

"Gimme a sec." The door to the apartment closed. The young woman took almost a minute inside her apartment before returning to the hallway. She sorted through the various keys on a ring, each key was marked with a number on it. The key to Ludo's apartment was number three.

She put the key into the deadbolt, unlocked it and then did the same with the lock in the knob. "It's open," she said and went back toward her apartment without physically opening Ludo's door.

"Care to do the honors? You are the police," Deni said to Sheed.

Lisa opened the door and was accosted by a familiar and foul odor. "Oh shit." She backed away from the door and covered her nose. "We aren't gonna like what's in there."

Deni smelled it. How could he not? He also recognized what the smell was from and knew what it meant. It is a smell that cannot be forgotten no matter how much time passes. He nodded to Sheed and buried his nose into the pit of his right arm.

The two walked into the apartment. A small kitchen was to their immediate left. Deni grabbed two paper towel sections off of the roll on the end of the counter closest to the entrance to the kitchen. He gave Sheed one sheet. To the right of the main door was a closet. Deni used the paper towel to open the door. Coats hung neatly on hangers, shoes awaited feet in them on the floor.

A short hallway led to the living room. Blood spatter on the laminate flooring guided them there.

Both were careful not to contaminate potential evidence by stepping in the congealed fluid.

The living room was an homage to Jackson Pollock. Crimson covered the walls and furniture and carpet. Pieces of congealed blood and flesh stuck to virtually every surface. Both took in the scene, both knew the implications. The space was as visually assaulting as the aroma.

"Fuck that's a lotta blood," Deni said into his arm. He touched a wall close to him with a corner of the paper towel. The blood that was splashed everywhere was thickened to a paste. "It's been there a while."

"Agreed. Jesus it's everywhere. We can't go in any further. We gotta call this in."

"What if Ludo is still alive in here. If we wait it could mean the difference between alive or dead, She."

"Look at this place. Like you said, this has been like this for a while. I don't think alive is an option."

37

THE NORTH-END APARTMENT AND THE surrounding neighborhood became a three-ring circus within the hour. Police had locked down a three block radius, no unauthorized cars or pedestrians were allowed inside the perimeter. Or out. Every uniform with an excuse to be in the area was inside the cordoned area if not in the building. Doors were knocked on for potential witnesses, though the officers didn't know what to ask specifically. Forensic teams had staked their claim. Spatter experts wanted a piece of the action. Every detective from Troop H was called to the scene. Even Lieutenant Titanitaukis was present to bark orders. CSU reminded him that it was their show.

Ebb

The owners of the bakery on the bottom floor of the building were allowed to stay open as the authorities needed a makeshift headquarters. The bakery happily served coffee and cannoli for the rest of friday night and into saturday morning. How anyone could eat pastries after having experienced the sights and smells of death was anyone's guess. But the owners made a fortune.

The reasons for having every flatfooted cop in the boroughs at the scene were many, but the common denominator was to cover asses. Boston has murderers and victims just like any major city; however, they had officially declared a serial killer on the loose in Massachusetts, and would-be royalty was somehow connected. Fear of liable kept Chamille Destrier's name out of the papers as a possible suspect. She was sought after to answer some questions and sought after because her name was in the Clearinghouse as a missing person as well. Personnel was called upon to ensure that nobody could accuse the department of dereliction of duty, which would expose them to lawsuits. The common goal was to come up with evidence that could lead them to what had happened in the apartment, because they didn't have a body.

Blood was everywhere. Pieces of tissue and bone were everywhere. The walls were spackled with it. So much so that the original paint color of the interior

Ebb

was in question. The carpet inside the living room was saturated with vital fluids. The hall leading to the bedroom and bathroom was smeared with blood and bile. The bedroom was a horror scene. The bathtub contained blood, tissue, and bone fragments. Someone had been murdered, but who was the question. Ludo? probably, but there wasn't a body.

Ludo Rossi had a felony record, therefore his DNA and blood type were on file with the state. Massachusetts requires that all felons submit blood for the record. The founding fathers of the United States prohibited unlawful search and seizures in the fourth amendment to the constitution in the bill of rights. Federally, a person has a right to refuse any invasion of their person; however, both the state and the federal government get around the 'limitations in scope and purpose' by adding prison time to those who refuse to agree to blood samples. It is considered a contempt charge and any suspect or convicted felon who refuses to allow a sample of their blood to be taken is imprisoned until they relent. While someone has a choice to refuse the violation, there really isn't a choice.

Testing for blood type is quick and can be done at the scene. Which it was. Ludo's blood type matched one of the types found inside his apartment. But his was not the only type, and blood types aren't conclusive enough to determine a victim anyway. It stands to reason that Ludo was likely hurt and bled profusely. It was his apartment and his blood type was present.

CSU initially determined that with the amount of blood present, there had to be more than one person who lost a perilous amount of blood. What that meant was anyone's guess, and nobody dared to offer one. The victim may have fought back and drew a significant amount of blood from the aggressor. There could be more than one victim. It was possible that more than one victim had succumb to one or more aggressors. Was all of the blood from one incident or many? The only indisputable fact was that more than one person bled.

Humans under 200 pounds have approximately 5 liters of blood, or about 1.5 gallons pulsing through their body. It was impossible for the teams to determine how much was on the walls and furnishings, but there was enough blood soaked into the carpet alone to total more than 1.5 gallons.

Tests for DNA take time and a laboratory. This case would get a priority-one designation and it would still likely take forensics until the end of the day on saturday to attain the results. At the earliest. Overtime would be paid to facilitate the speed of the results. Those results would confirm or disconfirm that one of the people who bled a perilous amount of blood in the apartment was Ludo Rossi. If any or all of the other samples aren't in the system, the identity of the remaining victims wouldn't be known until a comparative sample was submitted.

Deni was again persona non grata. When police and CSU personnel began to arrive, he was tossed aside once he was cleared. He tried to leave before Hobbs and Tits saw him, but that was too much to wish for. Getting outside of the perimeter that was set up was a chore, and Deni was on the sidewalk when Hobbs arrived. The two were still arguing when the lieutenant arrived.

Hobbs was angry to the point of violence at the fact that Deni was again involved in what was likely another murder or murders. Even angrier that his partner went behind his back and involved Deni. He did stop just-short of violence as he knew what Deni was capable of and feared that his blood would be added to quantities sent to the lab in Maynard. Also his boss had arrived to break up the would-be fray.

Tits was pissed that Deni was at the scene because he was afraid of contamination. If and when his detectives sorted out what happened and when, he didn't want a defense lawyer to be able to use Deni's presence as reason for doubt. The lieutenant had made a career out of covering his ass, this case would be no different. If heads were going to roll, he would make damn sure that it wasn't his.

Deni was pissed at everyone. Everyone except for Lisa. He felt bad for her. She was going to take a verbal beating from Hobbs and maybe Tits. Maybe even face sanctions. But at least she was alive, which was more than he could say for many of the people who were involved in this case. Lara, gone. Cole, also dead. Gary Rennick. Probably Ludo, and who knows who else? All because of a secret. He would make sure that Chamille Destrier paid for the trail of bodies she had accrued. And she would pay dearly.

It was nearly 10:00 AM saturday before the apartment building was cleared. All tenants were questioned and told to remain in their own apartments until that time. The teams packed up their respective gear and left. Some would go to a lab to continue their work. Others would go back to their beat. Police tape was put up in front of the door to the apartment which was locked; the owner and his sort-of superintendent were under strict rules to not let anyone inside.

For the detectives in Troop H, there would be a massive manhunt. BOLOs were out. For Ludo Rossi. He was considered alive until proven otherwise. For Chamille Destrier. All hands on deck, leave no stone unturned.

Deni's mission had just been escalated. He was hell-bent for justice and on the move to New Hampshire.

Ebb

Part Four

Bloody Hell in Buckets

May

362

38

THE FAST AND ERRATIC DRIVING NORTH ON 93 was fueled by anger and loud heavy metal. Deni cranked Metallica's *Master of Puppets* and other adrenaline-pumping songs from the Octane station on Rdio. The Rover handled the music and needs of the aggressive driver; weaving from lane to lane, on shoulders, around highway construction, in and out of traffic to Wayland. The sixty-eight miles should have taken more than double the thirty-five minutes it took Deni in the congested traffic.

Deni stopped at the front gate and familiar intercom system, the window receding into the driver-side door.

"Good morning. How may I help?"

"Let me in Nige. We need to talk," Deni said.

"I'm afraid that will not be possible at the moment. Shall I schedule another time to meet?" *Shedyule.* Nigel wasn't making any strides in calming Deni. In fact, he was doing the opposite.

"I'm in no fuckin' mood, Nige. Filing a false missing-persons report is a crime. If Cammy is inside or if you know where she is, now is the time to come clean."

"Would later today work for you? One o'clock shall we say?"

"If I come back here at one, I'm coming with the police and search warrants."

"Have you become a member of some layer of police in New Hampshire, Mr. Dennihan? Last I knew you were a mere investigator."

"One with a ton of contacts in this area. Believe me when I tell you that this is gonna get real, and real quick. I bullshit you not. Let me in so we can talk about this before it gets outta hand."

"Mrs. Destrier is not in. Nor has she been. She is missing as you well-know. Frankly there is nothing more to discuss."

"Then let me in so we can discuss it face-to-face," Deni said to the intercom.

Ebb

After a few seconds, the gate opened to reveal the long road lined with tall isosceles trees along both shoulders. Deni drove down the thoroughfare, parking on the circular, front cul-de-sac instead of the parking area off to the side. The fountain in the center of the round valet-style area was pumping water high into the air.

Nigel Singh was waiting for Deni at the fifteen foot tall, double french doors.

"The unexpected visits need to cease and desist, Mr. Dennihan."

"So don't the fuckin' games you people seem to play."

"I don't believe that I care for your tone," Nigel said as he led Deni to the large sitting room. The room was filled with tasteful knick-knacks and appointments, two oversized white-silk sofas toward the middle facing one another. On the left side of the room, a white fireplace that a truck could be driven through.

Deni had been in the room before. The woman of the house had been there to play games then, he would have to tangle with Nigel on this trip unless Chamille unveiled herself.

"Can we both agree that I'm onto your little game? I know it's your job to protect her, you filled out the missing-person report to cover the fact that she fled," Deni said as he took a seat on one of the sofas. Nigel didn't sit.

"I don't agree, nor will I shovel any more coal onto the bonfire of your ego. You know nothing, especially about my duties with regard to the Destriers. I am Chamille's personal assistant, here to help in any task that she deems me worthy of assisting in. Alas, she isn't here for me to assist. She is missing, Mr. Dennihan. And I am deeply concerned about it."

"And I don't believe it for one minute."

"The police have checked the grounds. She isn't here. Would you like to have a look? Would that allay your doubt? Would that keep any further intrusion at bay?"

"Maybe. You told the New Hampshire staties that she never came home from the event at the club, correct?"

"Yes. Not-so coincidentally the very night that you appeared at the front gate looking for her," Nigel said.

"I know what you told the cops, and we both know that I had nothing to do with her quote-unquote disappearance. She took off but not before something terrible happened to Ludo. The last time I saw her she was getting into her Bentley with Ludo. Now it looks like Ludo is dead."

"Mr. Rossi is dead?"

Ebb

"Probably.   I went with the police to his apartment last night and it was like *Slaughterhouse 5* in there. I just left."

"Oh no. Please tell me that this is some sort of sick and cruel trick on your part to get me to speak with you." Nigel sat down slowly on the opposing sofa.

"No bullshit, Nige."

"Do the police have any suspects?"

"Let's see. Cammy has a baby that she gave up for adoption back in '92, which she thinks that she tied up nicely. Only a few months ago the kid practically knocks on the door with an investigator and a big 'ol can of worms.   So Cammy has gotta put Lara and the pest down, and she has Ludo take care of it. I start lifting rocks and she decides that things would be a lot easier if everything pointed to me.   It was public knowledge that I thought Gary Rennick was responsible for Lara's disappearance and murder once her body was found. Bodies are startin' to pile up and killing Rennick made people look at me for the whole sha-bang. Only I didn't do it. Any of it. And no evidence can change that.   But as long as the cases stay open, there is a possibility that she can get jammed up with them. Ludo knows what happened, and he's a loose end. Why take him on permanent vacation when he can just go away forever? Maybe hang me up with that one too?

So to answer your question — yeah. I've got someone in mind."

"I think that maybe you have overestimated Mrs. Destrier's motives, desires and abilities, Mr. Dennihan."

"Really? How do you figure?"

"If everything else that you have said is correct, which I don't concede, how do you suppose that someone of Chamille's stature would be able to handle Ludo Rossi?"

"The bedroom was a blood-bath. She stabs him while fuckin' his brains out. Hacks him up into manageable pieces."

"Seems like quite a set of chores to hide the fact that she gave birth to a child twenty years ago."

"So you're admitting that Lara Myhre was Cammy's kid," Deni said. It was a statement more than a question.

"I'm admitting nothing. I'm merely trying to follow your small-minded logic."

"Have it your way, Nige. Just tell me where she is."

"And I have told you, ad nauseam, that I do not know and that I fear the worst. The news you bring seems to justify that fear, would you not agree?"

"No. I'm gonna need to look around."

"I don't have time at the moment to give you a tour," Nigel said.

"I'll manage. Just stay out of my way."

The one hundred fifteen rooms of the main house took the rest of the day. Deni went from high-ceilinged room to room. Chandeliers mixed with modern appointments. Flatscreen televisions hidden behind works of art. Voice recognition stations and an intercom system masked by bookshelves and antique-looking wall sconces. A library, a kitchen, a formal dining room, a less formal one. Deni searched through solariums and unused bedrooms alike.

Deni took a short break for refreshment offered by the chefs and kitchen crew. He was shown by one of the staff members the wing that was used by Chamille, Nigel, and Roman when he was in. The wing was attached to the enormous mansion but was self-sufficient. It had everything that one would need to live well without a need to venture into the rest of the estate.

The first bedroom looked like it was being packed up. Boxes were mixed with enough Louis Vuitton luggage to open a shop. The second room was the same way. And the third.

"They're leaving," Deni said to the empty suite. The woman who had guided him there was no longer present.

He looked from wall to wall, looking for the intercom system. "Hello? Anyone there?"

"Yes. Do you need something, sir?" The voice was from one of the chefs who had served him a light lunch in the main kitchen.

"There's luggage and packing. Where are they going?"

"I don't know. Nigel hasn't told us, though he wouldn't."

"You haven't noticed that there is less shit on the walls?"

The woman who led him to the suite was back.

"Life at the Destriers is best when you don't ask questions and don't speak unless spoken to. People come and go all the time, we don't ask and they don't tell."

"Ignorance is bliss, huh? Whatever. Where is Nigel? Can you send him up?"

Ebb

"I don't believe that he is still on the grounds, sir. He had a car detailed and brought around shortly after you arrived. He drove away some time ago."

"Where did he go?"

"You can ask around, but I don't think he said. He usually doesn't."

"Great. More games."

39

RYAN WELLS RECEIVED A PHONE CALL FROM
Deni on saturday evening. Ryan was about to sit down
for dinner with his wife when the call came in on his
cell. Angie began to put covers over the platters of food
to keep them warm when she learned who was calling.

"What is it you say, Deni? A friend in need is a
pest? I was just about to sit down for supper."

"Yeah sorry. I need you to call Cromwell."

"It's saturday night. What makes you think the
District Attorney for Wayland County is going to accept
my phone call? It's the weekend and he's probably
sitting down for supper himself."

"She's gonna get away with it, Ry."

"By 'she' you mean Chamille Destrier?"

"Yep. I'm down here in the staff house in back of the mansion. They've cut back on the help and bags are packed."

"Slow down, Deni. You're on the property?"

"Yeah. Place is bein' packed up. Cammy is gone. Nigel is gone …. He never came back."

"Came back from where? You're not making any sense."

"That's because I'm pissed and this case is going tits-up. I came here to see if Cammy was hiding out on her own property. After what happened on the North End, I figured she had to be close. Close enough to dump Ludo. What better place than on her own property?"

"North End? What are you talking about? Take a deep breath, Deni. Calm down and take me through it step by step. Better yet, I'll come to you. Will somebody let me through the gate?"

"Yeah. I'll make sure of it."

Deni met Ryan at the front door to the Destrier mansion fifteen minutes later. Ryan only lived six miles away, but he might as well have lived on the other side of the globe for the two houses were worlds apart. Ryan had been at the Destrier estate before as well, he was just as impressed this visit as he was in the past.

Ebb

"I still can't believe that this place is in Wayland," Ryan said as he walked through the front door.

"Probably get a good deal on it if ya wanna buy it."

"Okay, Deni. Walk me through it. I'm up to speed on Lara Myhre right? She was murdered and dumped into the Atlantic because she was looking into her birth parents. Any new developments there?"

"No. Cammy is Lara's biological mother."

"But that is fact?"

"One hundred percent. I found one of her college sorority sisters, only they don't call 'em that."

"Focus Deni."

"Right. Anyway, how else do you explain Cole Renner's murder?"

"She killed Cole? Is that also a fact?"

"She had him killed. I can't prove it, but I know it."

"If you want me to call Timothy Cromwell, you had better have more than 'how else would you explain' and 'I just know it'. It's not enough. Besides I'm a defense attorney."

"You're an officer of the court, Ry."

"Go on."

"Come with me to the staff house. I was back there pokin' around. I think they're closin' up shop here.   Nigel took off to go to meet up with Cammy, wherever she is."

"Ever the servant, huh? Lead the way."

"Then there was Gary Rennick," Deni continued as he led Ryan through the mansion. "He was crushed in a baler and evidence suggests without a struggle. He was a big boy, he wouldn't have gone into the compactor without one hell of a fight. He was killed after I stalked him for weeks to make it look like I was involved."

"You're right on that.   Between the adoption agency break-in and the Rennick murder, your name is pretty much fucking mud in New England."

"But I'm still free Ry.   So why not ante up? Sweeten the pot?   I go to the Wayland Country Club where Cammy and Ludo are rubbin' elbows with the upper crust.   Again fingers point to me because I was the last to see the two before they go missing."

"So you thought that you would add insult to injury by confronting them here?"

"Yeah.   Well …. Cammy.   I'm pretty sure that Ludo Rossi is dead.   His hideaway in the North End looks like pigs went to slaughter.   Blood on every wall and surface. At least one body was cut up and dragged somewhere else. I've been searching the grounds since Nige took off this afternoon," Deni explained.

"Holy shit, Ludo too? The bodies are piling up."

"If we don't find her, she's going to get away with all of it."

"And you think that Chamille Destrier killed all of these people? No way. The woman doesn't even dress herself, why would she murder all of these people?"

"She didn't do it personally. But she had it done. To hide the fact that she gave up a child for adoption in '92."

"Really? It would be a lot simpler to buy Lara off don't you think? Sign confidentially agreements and give her a small fortune to stay away and quiet? Murder is quite the escalation. Serial murder exponentially more drastic than that."

"Ry - Cammy is rich and bored. Along comes a reminder of what she did back then. Image is everything to her. The college friend I spoke to confirmed what we already knew. Diva through and through."

"Didn't you say that the Myhres are wealthy?"

"Not Destrier wealthy, but yeah."

"So it wouldn't be about money for Lara, would it? You know the family better than I do. I just can't get to Chamille Destrier as a murderer. I've known her for years. We're members at the same club."

"Ry, you are missing the point. Lara wanted to know who her birth parents were, plain and simple.

Money had nothin' to do with it. It was about where she came from."

"And you said that you can prove that Chamille is the mother? For certain?"

"Certain. Plus we have the documents."

"Documents that we cannot show to the District Attorney. I said *prove*."

The two had gone through the main house and were in the back of it, walking down a paved path toward the house for the staff. Ryan looked down toward the man-made body of water that led to the Nashua River. There was another large house down by the water.

"What is that? A boathouse?"

"I think," Deni said. "I haven't been down to it yet."

"There is a rumor that you banged Chamille in every room of this place. I take it the boathouse isn't one of those rooms."

"Very funny. A hundred and fifteen rooms is a lot of fuckin'. You can't believe all the rumors you hear, Ry."

"Maybe we should check it out."

"Why? Nige didn't leave by boat …. Oh shit. Lara. I was so focused on Cammy."

"Let's go have a look."

Ebb

Deni and Ryan headed down to the house on the water. It wasn't just a boathouse. There was a guest cottage attached to it. The entire back of the guest living area, facing west, was glass. Beyond the glass, a deck was attached overlooking the man-made body of water. To the right of the guest living quarters was the warehouse-sized structure that housed two large boats, four Yamaha WaveRunners, and equipment. There were docks between each vessel, each vessel tethered to the large decking. To the far right, a mechanical bay with a gas pump and other machinery.

The guest house was locked, but Deni solved that small hurdle within seconds. Inside, it looked like someone was staying there very recently. Dishes were in the sink, an open bottle of 1997 Silver Oak Cabernet Sauvignon in the sitting room. Whomever was enjoying it was presumably doing so while taking in the scenery through the glass. Remnants of the sunset lingered over the horizon while Ryan and Deni were in the sitting room, the view was breathtaking.

"Don't touch anything Ry."

"What am I new here?"

"Once Cromwell calls the police down here they can dust for prints. I wanna know who was livin' back here," Deni said.

"He's going to want more than a very nice bottle of wine to work with, Deni."

"There's a staff to pick shit up. Whoever was back here, the staff didn't know about it."

Deni walked through the house to the north side of the building, a door beyond the equipment room led him into the boathouse. Ryan followed, his hands in his pockets to ensure that he didn't accidentally touch a wall or surface.

All four of the bay doors were open in the boathouse. To their left was all open-air facing the same view as the sitting room in the guest house. They walked down a small set of wooden stairs onto the indoor docks, the boats floating in their respective berths. Near the first boat, a Bertram 800, were large black bags sitting on the dock as if waiting to be loaded onto it.

"See Ry. I told you they were movin' outta here."

"Duffle bags? Duffles aren't Chamille's style. She wouldn't be caught dead with a bag like that."

Deni opened the first one that he came upon as he walked toward them on the docks. He unzipped it, pulling the duffle open.

"Oh Fuck. Is she gonna be pissed then."

Ebb

Ryan was approaching behind him. "Why?" He looked over Deni's shoulder, eyes growing as large as half-dollars. He turned to his left and vomited into the water.

"Because she's wearing one."

40

"YOU'RE ONE BIG FUCKING CALAMITY aren't you Dennihan? Everywhere you go, there are dead bodies at your feet," Timothy Cromwell said.

The District Attorney for Wayland County was spitting fire. Chamille Destrier's body was discovered to be cut up and shoved into duffle bags. She was a key figure in his community, yes, but she was also the most influential. She had fundraised for him to get him elected into his position as District Attorney for Wayland County. She told the movers and shakers where to donate their money and they complied. With Chamille Destrier dead, he would have a much more difficult time getting the usual wallets to open for his future campaigns.

Her murder would also bring turmoil to the community, further jeopardizing his re-election. If Chamille Destrier wasn't safe under his watch, who was?

State and local police, along with the entire Wayland County Sheriff's Department, were called out to the scene saturday night. Ryan had called 9-1-1, NEESI phone personnel dispatched virtually everyone. The teams were well underway by the time the District Attorney had arrived.

The Massachusetts State Police were on the scene as well, thanks to Deni. Deni had made a call to Sheed, who had Hobbs, a medical examiner, and a CSU team in-tow. The only progress the New Hampshire police had made by the time the Massachusetts team arrived was a canvass of the staff and bright lighting put up inside the boathouse.

The jockeying for ownership and jurisdiction began when Massachusetts personnel arrived, but the fight was short-lived.

Hobbs dramatically shook his head in disgust each time he came near Deni but otherwise left him alone. He took laps around the docks conducting interviews with the staff that had been corralled there.

Sheed rifled-off question after question to both Ryan and Deni, desperate to determine if the body or bodies in the duffle bags were part of the series of murders in her state. Tying the murders together would mean that Massachusetts would take control of the scene, the crimes, the evidence, and subsequent trials if they found the suspect or suspects.

Massachusetts had a serial killer on the loose, with three dead bodies to prove it. New Hampshire had at least one body of their own, the victim was dismembered on her own palatial estate. Territorial pissings were mitigated only by the fact it was an enormous crime scene and many functions were yet to be performed. Each faction did their work efficiently, who owned the corpses and the evidence could be determined later.

'Later' arrived when Timothy Cromwell did. He made his rounds to each faction on the scene. He obtained progress reports from the dive team, the medical examiners, both CSU teams, local police, the sheriff's department, both sets of state police detectives, and finally spoke to Ryan and Deni. He pulled them both aside on the docks not twenty yards away from the duffle bags.

Ebb

"You're one big fucking calamity aren't you Dennihan? Everywhere you go, there are dead bodies at your feet."

Deni stood speechless for the moment as Ryan had instructed him. He wasn't usually adept at following instructions, but he didn't really want to be hauled off to jail to await formal charges either.

"Do you know where I just came from? Your last opus. Regis & Chapman. Do you care to shed any light on the fire over there?"

Deni looked to Ryan who had the same puzzled look that he did. "I have no idea what you are talkin' about," Deni said. "Really."

"No? The fire started at the restaurant and spread throughout the entire building. But it's some coincidence that there was the break-in and now the fire on top of it. NPD was dispatched along with the fire department when the ADT alarm went off. A local uniform called my ADA, who then called me when nobody could get in touch with either Regis or Chapman. Nora Chapman's husband doesn't know where she is either. NPD has since been in contact with the business partner, Regis, but given recent events, I went down to the site personally."

"The tight-ass is missin'? That's not good. Everybody that goes missing in this case ends up dead," Deni said.

"And you just happen to be right there every time. I don't like you Dennihan. I've never liked you. I'm looking for any reason to wrap this entire thing around your neck and hang you with it. Like I said — you are one big calamity."

"I'm tryin' to put an end to all that, Timmy."

"Timmy? My name is Timothy, wise-ass. Or Mr. Cromwell. Or if those are too complicated for you, you can stick with Sir."

Ryan elbowed Deni.

"I'm trying to help here, and I'm feelin' pretty under-appreciated."

"You want *appreciation* for all of this?" Cromwell pointed toward the duffle bags and the CSU teams to his left.

"Maybe we should all just take a breath," Ryan said.

"I'll breath easier when I know for certain that Mr. Dennihan here isn't responsible for these deaths, the disappearance of Nora Chapman, and the fire at her agency. I've ordered copies of your phone records, Dennihan. If your luds show that you were the one that called Mrs. Chapman prior to the fire, your ass is mine."

"Wait. Someone called her prior to the fire? I thought you said that she is missin'?"

"About an hour before the ADT call about the fire, Mr. Chapman said that his wife received a phone call. She left and hasn't been seen since," Cromwell said. "He thought it might be another break-in or something."

"Same thing happened to Cole Renner. Wanna bet that the phone is a burner and it's the same number that called Renner to his demise?"

"An NPD canvas said that one of the patrons at the bar where the fire started was outside smoking a cigarette and saw a white car peeling away just before the craziness."

"What kind of car?"

"He said it was a really nice one but he wasn't specific. He was half in the bag."

"This is unbelievable, " Ryan interjected. He was still shocked at the news about Nora Chapman.

"Well, I can assure you that I had nothin' to do with any of that," Deni said.

"You'll pardon me if I'm not completely satisfied with only your word. I'll need to know your whereabouts — "

" — He was with me," Ryan said. "Tonight correct?"

"You're going to alibi him again? We both know your first alibi was bullshit, Mr. Wells."

"What are you implying? I am an officer of the court. I called everyone here. The staff here can corroborate that Deni has been here almost all day and that I have been here with him since seven-ish."

"Just the same, I think I'm going to pull your card," Cromwell said.

"My license? You wanna pull my investigator's license?"

"I have — "

" — Mr. Cromwell! Can you come down here please?" One of the members of the CSU team called to the District Attorney. The interruption wasn't well-received by Cromwell, but was a welcomed stay of execution for Deni.

The DA walked toward the edge of the dock, both Ryan and Deni followed him the twenty yards. The officer that called Cromwell was standing on the edge of the dock, a diver had his head just above the waterline below him.

"What is it?"

"Sir, we have more than one body. Looks like they were being disposed of."

"That makes sense since they were cut up," The DA said. "Do we have identifications?"

"Chamille Destrier, which we knew going in. We don't know who the other one is. But you need to hear this."

"Hear what?"

Ebb

The officer nodded to the diver who was climbing out of the water up onto the dock.

"Sir, I've never seen anything like it," the diver said.

"Seen anything like what? Tell me."

He hesitated long enough for Cromwell's impatience to rear its ugly head.

"Out with it."

"Sir, they were cut up so they could be eaten."

41

SHEED WALKED ALONG THE DOCK toward the group having a conversation near the far edge where the duffles were found. The boathouse was set up resembling two backwards E's stacked on top of one another. Each leg of the E was decking to each of the vessels; four berths were designed for vessels to fit into the spaces toward the spine of the E, while the open bay doors leading to the pond and the Nashua River were aft of the vessels. The congregation was assembled at the end of the first leg and near the first bay door. Lisa walked past a Bertram 800 nestled into its berth toward the group.

Her partner was barking orders at anyone that would listen to him, which meant only the Massachusetts teams. Hobbs was not making any friends, nor did he seem to be getting anywhere, which is why Lisa decided to seek information elsewhere.

The conversation between the Wayland County DA, Deni, his lawyer, a man wearing a CSU jacket, and a man wearing a dive suit had taken on an awkward pause. Lisa was unsure if the group's pause was because of her arrival or if something awkward had taken place at precisely the moment she approached them. It was the very definition of uncomfortable.

"Did I come at a bad time? Were you guys talking about me?" She spoke to the group but her eyes were focused on Deni.

"No," Deni said but Lisa could tell that his heart wasn't in his answer. The man had the blank stare as though he were off in another world.

"Then what's up boys?"

"Detective Sheed, this is our scene and you are here as a courtesy," Cromwell said.

"With all due respect, nobody has determined who has jurisdiction over this case, your scene or not. So in the spirit of cooperation …. You *do* want me to report back to my superiors that you were cooperative, correct?"

The diver who had been speaking to everyone had worked his way out of the water as Lisa approached and moved toward center-stage of the group on the dock.

"As I was just saying, the contents of the duffle bags were cut up so they could be disposed of, obviously. What isn't so obvious is how," the diver said.

"There are multiple bodies. We have teams working on identifying all victims as we speak," the CSU man interjected.

"Right. Well …. we have the parts remaining in the bags but in the interest of preserving evidence, we need to figure out a way to stop the feeding frenzy that is happening down there," the diver continued as he pointed toward the water.

Cromwell apparently missed him pointing at the water.

"The press is here?" He immediately looked around to get a bead on where the vultures were circling.

"Uh …. Not that I know of, sir. What I meant is that they have a huge lobster tank down there."

Deni spoke up from where he stood to the left of Cromwell, Lisa was behind him. "She was rich. They have a big staff, a couple of chefs …. Maybe they don't wanna make trips up to Maine or order a lobster roll from Kelly's."

Mr. CSU shook his head. "Lobsters live in salt water. They can live outside of water for a while, but they can't live in fresh water. All of these boats are floating in a saltwater tank. This entire bay, the mooring, is one gigantic saltwater pool. They have to open a retaining wall to get the big boats out onto the man-made pond which leads out to the Nashua. Those tanks up there," he said as he pointed to where the gas pump and machinery was located, "full of salt. Whenever the salinity level decreases below 33 parts per thousand because a boat goes in or out, salt is automatically fed into the tank."

"Good for them. What does that have to do with anything?" Sheed felt as though she was falling behind in the conversation as she stood behind Deni. The feeling that she had asked a stupid question was invalidated by the blank looks on the faces of the others on the end of the dock.

The diver continued, "We originally thought they set up the saltwater system because it's easier to maintain the boats. The salinity of salt water makes it more difficult for freshwater algae from the pond or the Nashua to accumulate on the hulls. The advantage is having to use fewer chemicals with the salt. That's why people switch their swimming pools over to saltwater, so they don't have to use so many harsh and expensive chemicals like chlorine."

"Pardon me for my impatience, but so what?" Cromwell looked to Sheed like he was on her side in losing patience with the CSU and dive teams.

"The saltwater is also for the lobsters," Mr. CSU said.

"And? Why is that relevant to the crime scene?"

"Because everybody thinks that lobsters are scavengers but they are opportunists. They eat mussels, oysters, clams, crabs, and are even cannibalistic. Have you ever seen a lobster tank in a restaurant or something and noticed that some of them have antennae eaten off? Well, these lobsters are down there eating the cut-up parts of the victims."

"Oh that is so disgusting," Sheed said behind Deni. She punched Deni repeatedly on the back. "We just ate lobster the other day. Lobsters eat people? Fuckin' gross! Guuuuuuuuuhhhhh!"

"That is pretty fucked. How can they eat people?" Deni wasn't quite as repulsed as Sheed, but he found eating something that could have potentially eaten a human repugnant.

"Maine lobsters are the only crustaceans who could possibly eat a person because they have claws. One claw is a pincher and one claw is a crusher, that is why one is bigger than the other. They get through oyster shells, they can get through bone. And when they are molting they are voracious nocturnal eaters.

Water temp was set below 40 so they are active and tearing into the food."

Mr. CSU took over. "Whomever was feeding the lobsters was either interrupted or was worried about the pH level of the water from an abundance of human tissue. Otherwise he would have just dumped all of the parts into the tank. Since there are still the body parts in the bags, we have to assume one or the other.

Also we only have one recognizable head, belonging to Chamille Destrier. There is another skull in the tank, but it's been torn to shreds. The only thing that we know is that it's a human skull."

"So that's it. It's all tied off. Is Nige down there?" Deni was scratching his head. He was running out of suspects.

"We don't know who is down there other than parts of Mrs. Destrier. Blood and tissue is already being examined like I said. We should know more in a few hours," Mr. CSU said.

"By 'Nige' I assume you mean Nigel Singh?" Cromwell was also scratching his head. Lisa hoped that he wouldn't put too much of a fuss with deferring the case to Massachusetts. Getting it off of his desk would mean less focus on him and less headaches.

Hobbs was approaching the group, very late to party.

"Yeah. Staff said that Nige took off shortly after I arrived to search the house," Deni continued. "He didn't want to let me in. So either he's in a bag or down there," Deni said, pointing to the water, "Or more likely he took off in the car that he had one of the workers detail. The mansion was bein' packed up so this entire estate was gonna be in the rearview."

"So we need to determine if Nigel Singh is alive or dead, and find him if he is still among the living, " Sheed said.

"What's going on over here?" Hobbs was completely in the dust. A uniformed officer was behind him with a notepad in hand.

Deni pointed to the unie. "You. Get a list of all vehicles registered in New Hampshire to either or both of the Destriers. Then take a physical inventory of each of the vehicles on the estate."

Hobbs was incensed. "Who the fuck are you to be barking orders, Deni? You're not a cop. I don't even know why you're not in cuffs right now." To the officer behind him Hobbs said, "Stay right here."

The unie didn't know if he should shit or get off the pot. He seemed content to take orders, he just needed to know which orders he should follow.

Cromwell helped with the decision-making. "Go check those registrations and make it quick. Detective Hobbs — "

" — Detective Sergeant Hobbs."

"Sure.   Neither New Hampshire nor Massachusetts has officially taken jurisdiction, but as of right now it is my house, my rules. Mr. Dennihan is here on a consulting basis for now. The next obvious step is to determine if Nigel Singh is our serial killer. If he is on the loose, both states have a real problem. So put your ego in your pocket and focus on the task at hand."

"But our case supersedes — "

" — Detective *Sergeant* Hobbs, until a judge tells me otherwise, this is my scene. Now in the interest of public safety I want a picture of Nigel Singh in every station house and on every smartphone in New England. Are we clear?"

Hobbs looked at Sheed like he was going to choke the life out of her. She was afraid that she was going to end up in the digestive tract of a lobster and served as tomalley.

She spoke for both of them. "Since the Mass State police have a vested interest in this case, we are happy to help."

"You must be the sensible one," Cromwell said. "Can you boys get those lobsters up? Somebody is going to have to figure out which lobster ate which person, and who those people are."

Ebb

Deni turned to Lisa and whispered, "Sounds like a fun game."

42

IT DIDN'T TAKE LONG FOR CSU TO CONFIRM that Ludo Rossi was another victim of murder. By midsunday morning the techs had found an uneaten finger in a duffle that was then run through the NEC Fingerprint Identification Technology reader, or NEC FIT. That reading was then used to match it to a fingerprint on file with the Massachusetts Department of Probation.

While the fingerprint analysis was being done, CSU determined that the human skull that was at the bottom of the saltwater tank at the Destrier estate belonged to a male. It was the logical conclusion that it had once been the attractive head attached to the body of one Ludo Rossi.

The next in the list of conclusions was that feeding yourself to lobsters was not the preferable way to say goodbye to this world if it was even a possible way for said person to commit suicide. Meaning that Chamille Destrier and Ludo Rossi's killer was still on the loose.

A team was scouring the guest house attached to the to the crime-scene to determine who was enjoying a nice cabernet while the lobsters were dining. They dusted for fingerprints and swabbed the Riedel wine glass for DNA. The fingerprints weren't in the system, the DNA would take some time.

The prime suspect, the only suspect as far as both the NH and MA State police were concerned, in the murders of the two chopped-up victims was Nigel Singh. A BOLO was put into effect by the New Hampshire State Police. Detective Sheed called in the 'Be On the Look-Out' for Massachusetts as well.

The Wayland PD had looked into all vehicle registrations in New Hampshire for the Destriers. All boats and cars were accounted for with the exception of one Bentley Flying Spur. This was the same vehicle that Deni had told police that he had seen both Cammy and Lugo ride away in after the gala event at the country club.

The missing Bentley was also the same vehicle that was detailed for Nigel Singh to drive away in, according to the staffer on the Destrier Estate. While Deni was searching through the Destrier mansion and having a light lunch, Nigel was getting away.

The entire staff was questioned to determine the events leading up to the lady of the house being dropped into the drink and fed to crustaceans piece-by-piece. There were several holes in the timeline as nobody at the mansion had seen Mrs. Destrier since leaving for the gala event.

The DA was busy as were both Detectives Hobbs and Sheed, leaving Deni to move about the estate freely. He eavesdropped where he could, conducted interviews where he could, all to try and piece together what had gone wrong with Nige. What had made him snap?

Nigel Singh was the diligent assistant to Chamille Destrier, had been for at least a decade. He was a live-in and was at the lady's beck and call. No wish refused, no whim denied.

Deni couldn't for the life of him figure out what could have happened for the loyal servant to turn on his master like a rabid dog. He racked his brain to work through the puzzle that was still missing too many pieces to form a picture.

If evidence had pointed to Nigel earlier in the investigation, Deni may have been persuaded to get on board. As it stood now, he was sorry that he hadn't seen it sooner. He imagined that Chamille was frightened about her offspring sprouting up from under the rock from which she crawled, and Cammy would have had her loyal subject get rid of her. If he couldn't bribe away the problem, he would then have done the slaying personally. Deni didn't think that Nige was one to get his hands dirty, but desperate times called for drastic measures. That piece took some rethinking for him, but it fit.

Cole had also been a casualty of war on the Destrier name. Again Nigel would have arranged for the snooping investigator to be put down, but Deni still couldn't see him doing the gruesome chore himself. At any rate, Deni's entrance into the investigation, to his estimation, exacerbated the need to get rid of Cole; he would spend the rest of his life feeling guilty and trying to make it up to Christina Renner.

The realization that Deni was the problem, not Cole Renner, likely occurred to Cammy when it was too late, he thought. Or maybe it was Nige who figured it out. Either way, in for a dime — in for a dollar. Killing Gary Rennick would throw off the police, pointing suspicion toward the ex-cop turned investigator. Deni didn't play chess, but he didn't need to in order to realize that he was the expendable pawn.

And so another piece of the puzzle fit into place.

He heard one of the local uniforms convey the details of the report from the Regis & Chapman fire to a New Hampshire State Detective. An expensive-looking white car was seen speeding away from the scene by one of the patrons of the bar out in front of it smoking before the real smoke started. Deni briefly wondered how many Bentleys were in Wayland, New Hampshire, and concluded that there wouldn't be enough for someone to be able to identify one if they saw it speeding away from a crime. A "white car" was all the witness could muster in his nicotine and alcohol infused state. *If Nige is going to lose this game of his — he's gonna go out in a blaze of glory,* Deni thought.

Deni continued to work through the events in his mind as he eavesdropped about the scene, he understood that breaking into Regis & Chapman had

Ebb

further buried himself under a suspicion of guilt. Only there wasn't any evidence, and Ryan had given him an alibi. It was a false alibi, but nobody could definitively prove it to be untrue. The evidence that was once secure at the exclusive adoption agency had been compromised after the breach, so Nige was forced to escalate damage control. Since Deni wasn't behind bars and investigating freely, further action would be necessary.

Had the missing owner died in the fire, or would Nora Chapman and her partner be more victims found in someone's clambake? Deni continued to ponder. Either by fire or in the intestinal tract of a lobster, he assumed that more were dead at the hands of Nigel Singh.

But why did you turn on Cammy? Think Deni, think. The circumstantial evidence had piled up, but still lacked a smoking gun.

Had Nigel been the one to pick up Cammy and her boy-toy from the gala event? He racked his brain and remembered that he hadn't seen a chauffeur, Ludo had opened the door and entered the back with Cammy.

Did Nige then take them to the apartment in the North End of Boston? Why bring them all the way to Boston, just to turn around and bring them back to Wayland, New Hampshire?

There was only one reason that made any sense to him. *To get rid of them.* Dumping Lara's body out at

Ebb

sea hadn't worked, she came floating back to land with
the tide. Waste Chemicals hadn't worked, Cole's body
was found within a day. Nor did recycling. The
garbage man was an over-achiever. Cutting up the
bodies in Ludo's apartment was another misdirection.
Disposal on the Destrier estate would make their bodies
impossible to find. Deni further concluded that Nige
was learning his lessons about successfully disposing of
his victims.

Wrong again Nige.

Things were starting to fall into place for him,
yet too many pieces of the puzzle were still missing.
Important pieces. The serial killer was on the loose,
Nigel Singh was in the wind. "Be On the Look-Out' was
not good enough. Deni was going to search heaven and
earth. He was going to get justice. For Lara. For the
Myhres. For Cole and Christina. For the sea of
devastated lives left in the wake of a sick and cruel
game.

43

"WHERE ARE YOU GOING?" Ryan shouted. Deni had made his way back to his vehicle at the main cul-de-sac on the Destrier estate while he gave his brain a workout. Ryan had run up the hill after him.

"The airport. If Nige is gettin' outta Dodge, he's gonna wanna get far and quick," Deni said. He was about to close his driver-side door but Ryan had closed the distance between them and was blocking it.

"He's got about a twenty-four hour head-start on you. If he's gone, he's gone," Ryan said as he tried to catch his breath.

"And I'm gonna find out where."

"He has access to the Destrier jet, Deni. It's not like he flew Southwest."

"Even private jets have to have a record of takeoff and landing. The cops are gonna get a warrant and hope that they stumble upon him. Not good enough. Five people are dead so far and one more is missing at the very minimum. I'm gonna find him."

"I'll come with you."

"No, Ry. If I find him it's gonna get messy. I've already got Cole on my conscience, I don't need Ang cryin' on my shoulder at your funeral on top of it. Now get outta the way."

Ryan held onto the door to the SUV in defiance. "Not a chance. Everywhere you go there are more dead bodies. I can help, or at least be a witness if more shit hits the fan."

"Hippies don't tend to do well when it comes to violence," Deni said.

"I'm not letting this go. I'm not letting go of this door either, so you'll have to drag me."

"You're pissin' me off, Ry …. Fine. Get in."

Ryan ran around the front of the SUV to make sure that Deni couldn't drive away without him, that he wasn't being tricked. Deni closed the door on his side as Ryan opened the passenger door and got in.

The Rover sped out of the Destrier cul-de-sac, between the decorative trees down the main drive, and out through the main gate. The airport in Manchester was thirteen minutes away, Deni did in eight. Ryan white-knuckled his 'oh shit' handle for the entire eight minutes.

Commercial airlines like Southwest fly out of the terminal on One Airport Road. Private jets leave from the next entrance beyond it, presumably two, though nothing indicated an address.

The security guard let them drive past without having to stop, the luxury SUV must have fit in with the usual clientele. They sped toward the hangar as if there was a race to get there.

The hangar was all but abandoned. Those who needed to fly into or out of Manchester privately must have already done so by that sunday afternoon. Small prop planes and jets were parked along the perimeter, a few were parked inside the hangar.

Deni drove along the perimeter of the hangar, past each bay until he spotted the Bentley. Ryan saw it at virtually the same moment.

"You were right. There it is. Maybe we should call the police," Ryan said.

"See? This is why I didn't wanna bring you."

Deni parked behind the Bentley, blocking it in so there would be no chance of escape. When the two of them exited the SUV, they looked inside the corresponding spot in the hangar to find what they had expected. It was empty. No plane. No person in sight.

They continued back along the massive concrete expanse along the same path that they had driven. The two had discussed and presumed that the planes being worked on or prepped for flight in the other bays had to have somebody attending them. Deni and Ryan searched for such a person. Hopefully that attendant would also know where the Destrier jet was or how they could find out without too much time or red tape.

The hangar was the land version of the place they had just come from, the Destrier boathouse. The inside was brobdingnagian. Instead of a deep saltwater floor, planes and tools were parked on concrete. Finding someone inside the building took some time, more than three times longer than it took to arrive there from the Destrier estate.

When they finally did find someone, the man turned out to be a mechanic with a shrugging problem. His shoulders continually jumped up to his ears and back into their normal position whenever Ryan or Deni would ask a question about the Destrier plane. His head shook without many answers spilling from it. The only information they obtained after several minutes of interrogation and frustration was the type of jet. A Gulfstream 550.

Ebb

" …. For the last time, I don't know where it went. I was here yesterday working on this rig," the frustrated mechanic said, thumbing toward the plane behind him. "I just know that it left in a hurry,"

"What do you mean by hurry?" Deni was to a point of wanting to beat answers out of the mechanic but could tell it wouldn't do any good. Blood from a rock.

"Not much of a preflight is all."

"Pretend I don't know much about jets."

"There is a long checklist to make sure that the flight goes off without a hitch. The planes have regularly scheduled maintenance, or they need an overhaul like this bird, but there is always a thorough walk-around before departure. Flight plan was submitted and they were outta here within minutes."

"How long does it normally take?" Ryan was trying to give Deni a break from the questioning because he could see how frustrated his friend was getting.

"After the plane is checked? Gotta file the plan with the dispatch who checks weather, rule for flight, flight time, yada yada it takes a hot minute. The passenger must have called in the destination ahead of time or it was planned in advance."

"Fuck. They could be anywhere in the world by now," Deni said.

"Not without refueling.   G550s only get about 6500 nautical miles.   Anyway, just check with the air traffic controller in the tower.   They'll know where the plane was going."   The mechanic pointed to the tower off in the distance by the runway.

"What's to stop a plane from saying that they are going one place and actually going to another?"

"The FAA.   Times bein' what they are?   I wouldn't want to be an unidentified plane that's gone off the beaten path."

"BDR."

Deni was Irish on fire.   Time was being wasted and Nigel Singh was getting further away.   A 6500 mile radius was far and with more than enough time to refuel, he could be exponentially further.

They had a difficult time getting over to the tower as security was very tight.   Once they achieved access to someone that could help them, the ATC was

Ebb

reluctant to help without a full summation. She wanted to fully understand why the attorney and the investigator needed to know where the G550 went. Finally the answer came.

"And BDR is …." Ryan asked.

" …. Is I. Sikorsky Memorial airport in Bridgeport, Connecticut."

"Connecticut? Why would they fly there? It's only a few hours to drive," Ryan asked.

"People have their reasons, sir. Eighteen minutes in the air, about forty-five minutes total travel time sure beats the four hours or more it would take to drive. Plus no traffic. Whatever the reason though, that is the flight they filed."

Deni looked like he had seen a ghost. "And how far is that from Fairfield?"

"It's the next town over. Ten minutes maybe. I'm not a hundred percent sure, but BDR is the closest airport to Fairfield, I assure you."

"We need to get to Fairfield and fast," Deni said. "He's gonna kill the Myhres."

"Well, I don't have a plane in my back pocket."

"You could always get a charter, but it will take time to arrange. It would probably take just as long to drive since you don't have anything prearranged," the woman said.

"Not the way I'm about to drive."

Ebb

"Go Deni. I'll call Cromwell. He can have the Fairfield PD there in minutes," Ryan said. But Deni was already gone.

44

THE ACCELERATOR ON THE LUXURY SUV WAS pushed to the floor. Deni was juggling his phone from ear to ear instead of using the Rover's bluetooth technology as he sped south on I-84 at double the legal speed limit.

The first call was to the Myhre home. There wasn't an answer, but he didn't expect one. They hadn't answered or returned his calls in several days. It was both troublesome and annoying to him at the same time.

He tried both of their cell phones. Again no answer on either number. Directly to voicemail. It was dinner time on sunday and Deni feared the worst.

Next he called Sheed. Lisa answered on the second ring.

"Where are you?"

"This shit again? I'm on my way to Connecticut. Nige flew there last night and the Myhres aren't takin' calls. Where are you?"

"That doesn't sound good. I'm back in Boston. I was about to call you. Reports are starting to come back from Maynard. The lab is pushing nights and weekends trying to give us something to work with."

"The labs are done? Willow works fast," Deni said.

"No. Willow is in ballistics, forensics only has the labs on Lara Myhre completed. Remember the shard that they found under her skin?"

"Yeah. Wood or plastic or somethin' right?"

"Sort of, yes. Both actually. The plastic is actually a sliver of gelcoat."

"What's gelcoat?"

"I had to ask the same thing. It's a polymer resin that is mixed with pigment. It's used on fiberglass boats."

"Boat. Makes sense. Lara was found in the water, she got there on a boat. Did you have the Destrier boats impounded?"

"We're working on it. New Hampshire is giving us a hard time, but as it turns out it's not completely necessary. We know it came off the Bertam 800 - that big one. The first one inside the bay."

"Nice. How?"

"Lab said that expensive boats like that use very high-end materials. Let's see …. " The phone was silent as Lisa consulted the lab report. "Maxguard Premium ISO-NPG gelcoat mixed with Bahama Blue and white. It's manufacturer-specific and they mix the resin with the paint to order, the batch is then assigned to a specific HIN. Before you ask, Hull Identification Number. In this case, BER - for Bertram, NE1215, the boat serial number, and C413 which is the date code. Wanna guess what number is stamped on the Destrier starboard transom?"

"B-E-R, N-E, whatever the fuck."

"That would be correct. Add to that the wood sliver under her skin was teak, which is what is on the decking of the boat, that the man-made water goes to the Nashua River and the Atlantic ocean from there means access, and that the freshwater tanks for holding fish — we have ourselves a winner."

"What do you mean freshwater tanks for fish?"

"The freshwater that was in Lara Myhre's lungs was freshwater. A Bertram 800 is luxury yacht meets professional fishing vessel. The fish holding tanks are huge and can easily hold a hundred pound woman. MA CSU swabbed the tanks at the boathouse and there is trace-blood. They'll have to match it, but it's pretty clear that Lara Myhre was held in the tanks, drowned there, and probably dragged across the upper deck before being dumped into the Atlantic. She had to have picked up the gelcoat and a sliver at some point before going into the water. We got a little lucky that she was killed in a boutique boat that's special order."

"Yeah, real lucky."

"You know what I mean. Poor choice of words, but the point is we now have conclusive evidence. We don't need *Ebb* in our possession to give it to the DA to prosecute."

"Ebb?"

"The name of the boat, Deni."

"Swell."

Deni made one more phone call as he sped off of I-84 and onto the Connecticut Turnpike, I-95. Ryan answered his cell phone after the first ring in Deni's ear.

"I was just about to call you."

"What is it today? Everybody was 'just about to call me'. Now you don't have to."

"WOW. I know that tone. I'm glad I'm not in the seat next to you."

"He did it, Ry. No doubt now."

"Add Nora Chapman to the list."

Ebb

"Dammit I knew it." Deni pounded his steering wheel. "Where is she?"

"In the trunk of the Bentley. I'm still at the airport. New Hampshire CSU puts T. O. D. between four and six saturday night. He left you at the mansion and went straight to her."

"Hmm."

"What? What is it?"

"Why not burn her? Why stuff her in the trunk? He was gonna torch the agency anyway to make sure there was no record of Lara's adoption, right? So why risk draggin' the body?"

"He didn't drag the body anywhere, Deni. CSU says that she was beaten in the trunk. Big man, huh? Like fish in a barrel, she had no way to defend herself. Blood everywhere. That poor woman."

"So she gets a call to meet Nige on saturday. She leaves her family to go meet him and he somehow gets her into the trunk. Then he beats the snot out of her and leaves her right there to die where we can find her?"

"According to CSU. The knock on her head smashed her brain. You can barely tell it's her, Deni. Brutal isn't even the word for it."

"Not very subtle. And now he's going after the Myhres."

"Why? What is the point? It makes no sense," Ryan said.

417

Ebb

"Can you think of any other reason to go Connecticut? I mean .... I'm all ears, Ry."

"No. No. You're probably right. But he already killed the woman who set this thing in motion."

"You still think he was doin' all this for Cammy?"

"I take it that you don't?"

"No, I do not," Deni said as he ended the call. He tossed his cell phone onto the passenger seat and turned up his stereo system for the last ten minutes of the drive. A Perfect Circle's *Orestes* was playing.

> *"Gotta cut away, clear away*
> *Snip away and sever this*
> *Umbilical residue*
> *That's keeping me from killing you ...."*

"Fuck that Nige. I'm gonna kill ya."

45

THE FAIRFIELD POLICE HAD ALREADY ARRIVED at the Myhre home on Fairfield Beach Road by the time Deni had reached the right-hand turn off of Reef Road. Nightfall had come for some time and he could see the flashing lights from the police cruisers several blocks away.

District Attorney Cromwell had called his Fairfield County counterpart who had spared no expense or personnel. Deni didn't know how big the police department was in the affluent community, but he guessed that he was looking at the full compliment as he approached the turn in his Rover.

Ebb

A roadblock was set up to keep all traffic from traveling down Fairfield Beach Road. Deni pushed a button, the window on his SUV recessed into the door. The uniformed officer approached him.

"Gonna need you to turn around, sir. We've closed the road. No traffic in or out."

"Yeah I see that. I'm the reason you guys are here. Who's in charge?"

"Chief Nolan. Who are you?"

"Warren Dennihan. The DA from Wayland, New Hampshire called you guys down here for me. We've got murders all over New England. I need to speak with the Chief."

"It's kinda crazy down there, Mr. Den — "

" — Deni. Just call me Deni. I realize that it's probably not very convenient for you, but just call him."

The officer turned his back to Deni and spoke into the receiver that was clipped to his left shoulder. There was a loud response from the radio on his hip but the officer turned it down so Deni couldn't finish hearing what it was. Another few volleys of conversation back and forth occurred before the officer came back to the driver-side door.

"The Chief will be right up. Park over there for the time being."

Ebb

Deni moved onto the shoulder of Reef Road and waited for nearly twenty minutes before a Fairfield police cruiser crept down Fairfield Beach Road from the Myhre house. A uniformed man with salt and pepper hair exited the front passenger seat of the cruiser when it stopped. Salt and pepper nodded to the officer which had spoken with Deni, the officer pointed toward the Land Rover.

"Are you Dennihan?" Salt and pepper asked as he approached Deni who was getting out of his SUV.

"Deni. Yes. You must be Chief Nolan."

"I am. Do you mind telling me what's going on?"

"I was hoping you could tell me. There are dead bodies strewn all over Massachusetts and New Hampshire, I was hopin' that Connecticut hasn't been added to the list."

"The Fairfield County District Attorney is down at the house pissed off to high heaven. We kicked in the front door to find nothing."

"Nothin'? What the hell are you talkin' about?" Deni took a step closer to Nolan, the two men were nearly nose to nose.

"The house is empty. There's no sign of foul-play. No broken windows, no damage inside ....

Nothing. Are you sure that this suspect of yours is here?"

"No. The Wayland DA thought it would be a cool prank to wake up the entire Fairfield police force for no reason. I haven't slept in days and drove all the way down here just for the hell of it."

"Your sarcasm isn't appreciated. Do you have a permit for that weapon?" Deni wasn't wearing a sport jacket, his weapon was in his shoulder holster. "Private investigators in Connecticut need a conceal and carry permit," Nolan pointed to the Taurus. "Do you have a permit?"

"Did you check out the airport?" Deni ignored the Chief's question.

Nolan paused to see if Deni would answer his question. When he didn't, the chief responded to the question posed to him.

"The plane is there but no pilot or passenger. I've got a team over there trying to track both. You didn't answer my question."

"And you really haven't answered any of mine, Chief. Have you been in contact with either Leonard or Sorche Myhre?"

"So I'm working for you now? Who the hell are you that I need to answer all of *your* questions and you don't need to answer any of mine?"

Ebb

"I'm tryin' to save you from havin' to clean up more bodies. Which if we don't find the Myhres - that is sure as shit what you're gonna do. So without gettin' into personalities can we work together to do that?"

"There isn't any evidence of a crime here. They probably took a well-needed vacation. Their daughter *was* just found dead recently," Nolan said.

"You've gotta be the dumbest fuck I've ever met, and I've met my fair-share. Their daughter was killed by the guy who just flew into your town on a plane that is sittin' at the airport next door. Connect the fuckin' dots, guy."

"You'll watch your tone. You're not a police officer here or anywhere else."

"But they are my clients. Need I remind you that legally you have to cooperate with me pursuant to — "

" — I know the law. Apparently you need a lesson, though. There hasn't been a crime as far as we can see. And there is no active case in which you are involved here in Connecticut, so my cooperation is a courtesy. Are we clear?"

Deni took a step away from the chief. He walked a circle away from him, brushed his hair back off of his forehead with his hand in frustration, and returned to Nolan.

"Vehicles. What about vehicles?"

The chief removed a notepad from the breast pocket on his uniform. "They have a Lincoln MKS, a Caddie ELR, and a Harley Sportster Superlow." He looked up from his pad at Deni. "All of them in the garage. Like I said Dennihan, there is no evidence of a crime."

"What do the neighbors say?"

"Sure, why not keep helping you?" The Chief shook his head. "Nobody knows. Neighbors saw them yesterday grabbing the mail."

"So they were here yesterday? Before the plane landed, they were here and now they aren't. Do you see where I'm going with this?"

"Mr. Dennihan, for the last time …. There isn't a crime here. We don't harass our good citizens in Fairfield, especially grieving ones. They probably took a cruise out on their boat or got away from it all. Haven't they been through enough? I've got the entire police force down here for nothing and now I have to replace their front door."

"Boat? They have a boat?"

Nolan went back to his pad. "Yeah. Let's see …. Outremer 5X. They park it down at the Pervot Yacht Club."

"Is it?"

"Is it what, Dennihan?"

"Parked you fucktard. Is the boat parked there?"

"Your mouth is starting to really — "

" — Yes or no? Give me etiquette lessons later. Parked or not?"

"Probably not. Like I said, they probably went out on it."

"If they did, they're not comin' back. Where is it?"

"We haven't been down there. If it's at the club then it's in the slip."

"Not the boat — the club." Deni went to his Rover, got into the driver seat. Since he didn't wait for a response from the chief, he yelled out his open window to anybody who would listen. "I gotta get to the boat club, where is it?"

THE PERVOT YACHT CLUB WAS NOT FAR FROM
the Myhre home, just a bit further down the same road
in point of fact. Many members of the club lived on
Fairfield Beach Road, those who chose not to walk
would drive their golf carts or ride their scooters down
the road to the marina.

Deni raced down the closed street, weaving in
and out of every vehicle and person who had been
called to the supposedly non-existent crime scene. He
was shouted at and given hand gestures; he couldn't see
what those gestures were in the darkness of early
morning, but he could guess.

The yacht club was just as dark, the lights were off as might be expected at zero-dark-thirty on a monday morning. The front door was locked and nobody was answering the knocks and kicks to it.

Deni was about to pick the lock and go into the clubhouse when he noticed the large gate off the right of the building. The gate led to a steep set of stairs and the docks down below. The main dock had many long wooden fingers off of it; cleats lined each, some had boats tethered to them in berths and some did not.

The gate was locked. It would normally have taken someone less time to climb over the fifteen foot high chain-link fence than to breach the lock, but Deni wasn't most people.

He made his way down to the docks, looking for any sign of movement but there was none. The berths were as deserted as the clubhouse up on the oceanfront cliff. Each step on the wooden structure sounded like the loudest noises in the world to Deni. The more he tried to be silent the louder he seemed to be.

Which boat are you? If you're even still here, he thought. Many of the large vessels were sailboats. *What kind of boat is an Outremer 5x?* He wasn't sure what the size difference was between a boat and a yacht, but he was sure that the majority of the vessels at the club qualified as yachts with room to spare.

Ebb

He moved about each of the long planks off of the main dock, each finger holding dozens of large vessels. None of them seemed to have any current activity. If there were people on them they were sound asleep, he presumed. Each of the yachts were zipped up, each sail lowered. Deni studied each in line as he moved from slip to slip. None of them indicated that they might belong to Leonard and Sorche. None of them indicated any recent activity. He continued to move quickly and quietly throughout the early morning darkness.

The sun was about to come up over the horizon, a soft light glowing off in the distance below the waves that were inching their way toward the coast. He had been frantically searching during what was left of the cover of night with no hint or clue, and Deni was about to give up.

Until he heard an engine start off in a distant berth.

Keeping low and running toward the sound as if he was approaching a helicopter, Deni raced. With the soft rumble of the yacht's engine, he was no longer worried about sound. He was worried about time. He needed to make sure that he got to the vessel before it departed. If it was even the yacht that he was searching for.

Ebb

Nige is probably long gone, Deni thought.

He made out a dark silhouette through the darkness. The person tossed a rope off the cleat into the yacht, taking a bumper with him as he got on the large vessel.

The vessel had two hulls as it was a massive, fifty-nine foot catamaran. He watched it as he moved toward it as quickly as possible from behind it. The catamaran was very wide and very long. The back of the yacht was against the dock, but only temporarily as it was about to launch out of the marina. There were two sets of stairs leading up to the elevated cabin, one on each corner of the stern. Between the two sets of stairs, water bubbled like it was boiling as the propellers rotated below. Above the water, the name of the vessel was in decal on the transom.

Lara's Croî.

Croî was Gaelic for heart. Deni didn't know this because he was Irish, he knew it because he had been to Ireland on a case once. Croî is pronounced 'Cry'. *Lara's Heart* or *Lara's Cry;* either way, Deni had found what he was looking for.

The engine revved. The bubbling water erupted. The sail was down and the yacht was moving out of the berth quickly. Deni ran in full sprint toward the back of the vessel. Arms pumped, legs pushing him as fast as possible, knees alternating to his waist, feet alternating to his buttocks.

Lara's Croî was getting further away from the dock, moving toward freedom. Deni knew if he didn't get on that boat, he would never have another opportunity to apprehend Nigel Singh, never have another chance at saving Leonard and Sorche Myhre.

At the edge of the dock, he launched himself toward the back of the yacht like he was an Olympic long-jumper. Deni's feet continued to kick as he left the dock, floating over the salt water. Those feet looking for a solid surface under them, but they would find none. Instead they found water.

Deni didn't make it.

As his body was being devoured by the ocean, his hands reached for the stern. Although happening quickly, Deni was processing the events in slow motion. His feet were wet, then his knees. As he was coming to the realization that he was going under water, his right hand attained purchase on a rung of the ladder hanging just below the surface of the water on the starboard stern.

The propellor to his left was accelerating, pumping more water and moving the boat faster out of the marina. Deni held on with all the strength he could muster from his right hand and arm. He held his breath as he was being dragged behind *Lara's Croî*. His left arm was being forced away from the back of yacht, away from being able to help pull Deni onboard.

His right arm burned. His lungs burned.

With one final attempt before letting go of the ladder and his prey, he tried to pull himself above water. His left arm went above his head, found another rung of the ladder. He pulled, able to get a gasp of air before going back below another wave of water. He pulled his body toward the ladder, pushed himself up with feet on the bottom rung once he was able to raise them there.

Air. Finally air.

Deni took time in regaining his breath, holding onto the ladder and watching the marina get further away.

Once he was able to breath and the burning of his lungs subsided, he pulled himself up onto the teak wood decking on the starboard stern. Deni was still hidden below the aft deck and transom.

It was time to take personal inventory. No bones broken? Thankfully no. Bleeding? Again no, miraculously. Gun? Yes, still snapped into the holster under his arm. Phone? Yes, in his pocket. He reached into his jeans, his phone was present but it was wet and useless.

He was alone and would have to handle the situation accordingly.

Deni ascended the stairs from the starboard aft deck, peering up onto the main deck. He could not see into the cabin or where the driver was.

A door led down into the hull where he assumed the staterooms were located. He took his Taurus PT1911 out of the holster and took the safety off. His index finger at the ready along the barrel of the pistol, pointing ahead of him as he descended into the hull.

The long, narrow passage led to only one door on the starboard side of the starboard hull. Opposite it, port-side, was a stairway leading up to what he thought must be the cabin or galley. Rather than go up the stairs to his left, he quietly opened the door to the stateroom on the right.

As the door opened, Deni swept his gun from left to right. The head was to his left, toward the starboard bow. Directly ahead of him was a small desk with a lamp that was turned on. The bed was to his right, to the back of the vessel. A small window looking aft of the yacht was just above the two occupants of the bed.

Leonard was spooning Sorche Myhre. The two looked to be sleeping comfortably.

47

NIGEL SINGH LOOKED OVER THE MANY
instruments from the captain's chair. He had just been
studying the weather reports and oceanic charts as well,
trying to decide whether to raise sail or continue
motoring past Penfield Reef. It was going to be a long
trip to the Caymans, conserving fuel was but one of the
many factors he needed to keep top-of-mind.

According to his plan, Nigel would easily be out
of Long Island Sound and around Block Island Sound
by mid-morning. By monday's sunset he hoped to be
roughly two hundred nautical miles off the coast of
Virginia Beach and twice that distance off of the western

coast of Bermuda. At seven to nine knots, it would take approximately eighteen days to arrive at Water Cay.

The trip would take him past Miami; around the Bahamas, south of the Turks and Caicos Islands, between Cuba and Haiti, north of Jamaica, and finally into Water Cay on the tiny — albeit largest — island of the Caymans, Grand Cayman.

The fifty-nine foot catamaran was handling the chop nicely and he was confident that it would negotiate the arduous journey without any substantial problems. The Myhre boat had not been his original plan, but he was nothing if not adaptable.

It had taken all day to get *Lara's Croî* ready for sail. Final preparations took time. Fuel. Food. And the bloody Pervot Club.

The yacht club had been a problem. Neighbors are nosy. The Myhres were popular, getting them on board the vessel without raising suspicion was an impossible task. Nearly. The Destriers were popular as well, but they were insulated from close neighbors. They were seen when they wanted to be seen and were in seclusion otherwise. Not so with the Myhres.

The Myhres were currently locked in the starboard stateroom and he would need to check in on them once they were around Long Island, past Montauk. He hoped to be well at-sea and beyond the reach of the Coast Guard, which had a base on Block

Island. The vessel would be approaching the base in the very near future.

The sunrise had just surfaced across the horizon, Nigel was steering into it as he was beginning to make for open Atlantic. This was a critical phase, getting past the Coast Guard installation and out to sea. Once he was beyond Block Island, it would take the Navy to stop him. And once he made it to the Caymans, nothing could.

Nigel decided that he wanted to get as much distance as possible between the vessel and southern New England. He made the decision to run both the main screw and open the main sail once they were beyond Montauk. He needed to go up topdeck, midship to open the main sail. It was time to check on the Myhres and do just that.

He turned to leave the captain's chair and received an unwelcome surprise.

"It's over Nige. Don't do anything stupid."
"Uh …. "
"Catamaran got your tongue, Nige?"
"Uh …. Deni. Stowaways are never welcome."

Deni had his Taurus pointed at Nigel's chest. There was only twelve feet between them, he knew that there was no way to cover that distance and relieve his adversary of the weapon without being shot. A .45

caliber projectile at such a close range was virtually impossible to survive.

"You didn't leave me much choice," Deni said.

"And you've been quiet a bother as usual. There must be a way that we can come to some sort of understanding. Put down the gun, we can discuss this as gentlemen." Nigel slowly moved toward Deni. He was less than eight feet away.

"Just stay where you are."

"As you wish."

"Half a dozen people are dead because of you, Nige. Between the Myhres and me you'd be well on your way to a dozen and I'm not gonna let that happen."

"The Myhres aren't deceased, they're sleeping restfully. Which I need to tend to if you'll let me pass," Nigel said. He made another move toward Deni, this time very quickly. He received a kick to the inside of his knee for the trouble. The strike made an audible snapping sound. Nigel fell to the deck, the pain was excruciating. He screamed at the top of his lungs as he held is damaged leg.

"Don't fuckin' do that again, Nige or I'll fuck you up in the most painful way I can think of. I've got all kinds of ideas."

Nigel took a moment to compose himself.

"May I stand?"

"If you can."

Nigel struggled but was finally able to get to his feet.

"You need to drug them again, don't you? That's your new go-to. Can't take someone on face-to-face like a man, you gotta be a pussy."

"Have me sorted out do you?"

"You mean figured out? Almost. A couple of pieces don't fit — but I'm starting to put it together. Near fatal dose of Special K makes them go nice and easy, huh? That's what you use, right? Ketamine?"

"Americans. Is this the part where I confess to everything I've done? Explain the story as a means of freeing my conscience? That's not the way real-life works, Deni. Clearly you don't need the gun, please put it down, yes? Everyone has a price, name yours."

"So that's it? Money? Twenty-five million is what it took for you to turn?"

"You have no bloody idea what it takes to earn my affection, nor what motivates me. You seem to like nice things, how much will it take to motivate you? Twenty-five million? I can arrange that amount to be put into an untouchable account for you once we reach the Caymans."

"You'd give up all your money? You killed all of those people for free?"

"You don't have it sorted do you? You disappoint, Deni. The twenty-five million was just the beginning. My price is a great deal more."

"You got sloppy," Deni said. "And here I thought Brits were tidy. Nora in a trunk instead of burning her? Cammy and Ludo? We found them all."

"You simply don't quit do you? Once you've set on something …. Very much like my employer."

"You're still just the help, huh?"

"At least I will no longer be forced to clean up the post-coitus towels of sweat and ejaculate," Nigel said.

"Oh yeah. I forgot to thank you. You were always good like that."

A noise came from behind Deni.

Nigel looked behind his aggressor and received another unwelcome surprise.

"Bollocks!"

A gun went off.

The boom was deafening.

Pain shot through Nigel's chest. His hand went to it instinctively and came back crimson.

"Bloody hell in buckets," Nigel said. The words came out in a muffled gurgle. Those words were his last as he fell to deck of the cabin.

DENI READ THE LOOK ON NIGE'S FACE BEFORE he heard the shot. That was the only warning that he received. He hit the deck, turning to see Leonard Myhre behind him with a Kahr P45 pointed at Nige.

The shot was fired. Nigel mumbled something before falling to the floor, likely dead upon impact. The blood began to pool under him on the polished, dark hardwood.

Deni turned back to the shooter.

"I told you to kill him," Leonard said.

"Holy shit. There was no need for that, I had it covered."

"He doesn't get to live." Leonard pointed the gun at Deni who reciprocated. "Would you have taken the money?"

"Put the fuckin' gun down, Leonard. Don't point that at me. I was tryin' to put the rest of the pieces together. Get him to confess."

"And that is now moot. He killed my daughter."

"He killed a lot of other people too, death was too easy. Now put down the gun before you shoot me, or I shoot you."

"Would you have taken the money?"

"No. Of course not. This wasn't about money. This started because you wanted me to find your missing daughter."

"For which I am paying you money."

"And it got way outta control. You wanted me to find out who killed her, which I did."

"I wanted you to kill him, which I did."

"Where'd you get the gun?"

"I had it hidden onboard. This *is* my boat, Deni."

"Well put it down."

"Once you've answered my questions," Leonard said. "Would you have taken the $25 million to look the other way?"

"There is more than $25 million, you heard him. And no, of course not. I was just keepin' him talkin'."

Ebb

"You had a gun pointed at him, Deni. He would have said anything that you wanted him to for as long as you wanted."

"And you're still pointin' one at me which is startin' to piss me off. Put the fuckin' thing down."

He lowered the P45 and Deni rose from the deck.

"Gimme that thing before you hurt yourself."

Leonard handed Deni the gun, who put it in the wet waste-band in the small of his back. He also placed his Taurus in his shoulder holster.

"Quite the mess you've made," Deni said to leonard as he looked at Nigel. "It's gonna be tough to get the puppet-master now, don't ya think?"

"I don't follow."

"Nige was a grunt. A well-spoken English grunt, but hired help just the same. Where do you think your boat was headed?"

"The Caymans."

"Correct. How did you know?"

"I think he said as much."

"Before he drugged you?"

"Right."

"Uh huh. The money is in the Caymans. The money that came from his employer," Deni said.

"Chamille Destrier was his employer."

"Roman Destrier was his employer, Leonard. It took me a while to figure it out. He always worked for

441

Roman. That's how he kept track of his wife since he was never around. She thought Nige was her loyal subject when in fact he was Roman's. It's his money. All of it. Your daughter snoopin' into who her birth parents is what spawned all this. Cammy might not have wanted it dug up, but Roman really didn't. He's worth hundreds of millions if not billions. A long-lost kid? It wasn't about reputation for him. It was about money. He already had one bitch on the tit, he didn't need another."

"That is no way to speak about — "

" — About *his* daughter? It scared you that she could have found them, didn't it?"

Leonard didn't answer. He just stared at Deni. The rumble from the engine filled the void.

"Why did he kill his wife?"

"He didn't. Nige did," Deni said.

"Roman had her killed. You know what I mean."

"Roman didn't have her killed. He might not even know that she's dead."

"I don't follow."

Yes, you do, Leo. *You* had her killed."

"I beg your pardon?"

"Where have you been all week?"

"Grieving."

Ebb

"You didn't answer my calls."

"I didn't answer anyone's calls."

"You didn't return any of my messages."

"Unless you killed my daughter's murderer, there was nothing to say."

"And you knew that Chamille Destrier was Lara's mother all along. But did Sorche know? Where is she by the way?"

"She is sedated. And no, she didn't know."

"And you didn't know that Lara was looking into her birth parents until I told you. Once I told you, you thought you knew who did it."

"Very good, Deni. You were taking too long to figure it out, so I had to take matters into my own hands. Once I found out that it wasn't Ludo Rossi who killed Lara at the behest of Chamille, it was too late. Nigel had taken care of Ludo and Chamille. But he needed me alive to transfer the money over into his offshore accounts. One of the stipulations at my bank was that I execute the transfer in person, which would give me eighteen days to kill him on the journey. How did you figure it out, Deni?"

"You're still alive. Everyone is dead except you and your wife. Your house wasn't broken into, which means that you let him in. Nothing was broken inside, according to the police. Why not kill you? Then the yacht club. How would Nige get two non-willing participants through the club, down to the docks and all the way over to the boat without someone seeing? And why go through the hassle? The money was in the Caymans, why not just fly there if he wasn't going to kill you? He had the plane. Sailing takes time and preparation. People plan sailing trips like that for a year in advance in some cases. Then when I got onboard and saw you both sleeping — only Sorche's breathing was different from yours. She was drugged and you weren't. I saw the vile of Ketamine on the desk and there was only one needle in the wastebasket. I should have made sure that the door was still locked when I left the stateroom."

"Indeed. He got my daughter to her car because he said that he had a lead on her birth mother. Once she went to her car, he drugged her and got her onto he Destrier boat. He beat her and drowned her before dumping her body into the ocean."

"I know. I just found out. *Ebb*."

"Ebb?"

"The name of the boat."

"Oh," Leonard said. *Lara's Croî* was still bearing east in the Atlantic with nobody steering. The two remained standing as they rocked with the boat.

"Then Roman had Cole killed because he thought that he was getting close to figuring it out. Cole had made some calls for birth records which set off bells and alarms that got back to Roman. He put the $25 million into an account for Nige to deal with situation. He calls Cole and lures him out to Gloucester, where he drugs him up and dumps him in waste chemicals."

"Right again. Only it was you who was still snooping around, not Mr. Renner."

"Then Gary Rennick's murder shifted the focus on me. Again he was drugged, only this time Nige crushed him with recycled cardboard."

"And by that time, I had already arranged for Chamille and her boyfriend to be …. "

"Murdered. You can say it Leo. You're no better than Nige."

"I thought they killed my little girl. I went to speak to Chamille and she threw me out like I was garbage."

"So you hired the man that actually did it. He was double-dippin'. Roman was payin' him, you were …."

"I didn't know that until it was too late," Leonard said. His eyes had filled with tears.

"And Nora Chapman was just more collateral damage?"

"I had nothing to do with that. I would assume that Roman wanted the entire matter dealt with once and for all since there were still records, sealed or not. I will spend the rest of my days making sure that Roman pays for what he has done."

"No, Leo. You're gonna spend the rest of your days behind bars. Murder for hire? You might even get the needle, and I don't mean Special K."

49

IT TOOK SEVERAL HOURS TO BRING THE catamaran back to land. Deni didn't have a dry, working phone and Nigel had ensured that neither of the Myhres had one. If the deceased had one, he didn't have it on his person. Certainly Leonard was hoping that none would ever be found. His doom was on the other end of a phone call.

He had believed that Deni would understand, that he would be able to sympathize. But all of Leonard's pleading and explaining fell on deaf ears.

The coast guard was called over the vessel's radio. Deni didn't know the terms he needed for assistance, so he just yelled "May-Day" into the receiver over and over again until someone picked up the signal. The coast guard then sent a boat to the catamaran and Deni eventually followed it back to land.

In the meantime, both of the Myhres were locked in the staterooms. Leonard in one, Sorche in another. As a former detective, he knew that putting them together would allow them to contrive a story, one in both of their best interests.

Leonard continued to plead over the intercom with Deni to reconsider turning both he and his wife into the authorities. He started by insisting that Nigel Singh and Roman Destrier should take the wrap for all of the murders. Deni assured him that Nige had paid, death was the ultimate price. He told Leonard that he would make sure that Roman paid for what he had done as well. But Roman paying for his sins didn't negate Leonard's.

The pleas then went to bribery. How much would it take for Deni to look the other way? There was money in a Cayman account that could easily be transferred to him.

When that didn't work, Leonard begged for his wife to be left out of it. He insisted that she had nothing to do with any of it and should be spared any more grief than what she had already suffered.

Deni told him that he would let someone else make that decision but that he was not opposed to keeping silent. He didn't think that she was involved anyway.

When the coast guard arrived, they took custody of the Myhres and escorted the catamaran back to shore. It was a crime scene and needed to be dealt with as such; however, it also needed to be maneuvered back to shore.

Deni told his story. And then he told it again. And again.

Chief Nolan took a statement. He would pass it on up the food-chain to see about prosecuting Leonard Myhre, since he was the agent who hired a hit-man and then subsequently killed that hit-man.

The Massachusetts State Police took a statement as well. They wanted jurisdiction over the entire case, and they would fight like hell to get it.

The State of New Hampshire had something to say about that. Nora Chapman was allegedly killed at the behest of Roman Destrier, and they still possessed her body. In addition to upping his conviction rate, Cromwell wanted to seize assets as they related to the crimes. Which meant that the entire Destrier New Hampshire estate and all of its contents could be held in escrow by the state until the case was finalized. Then the proceeds would fill New Hampshire State coffers once convicted. At least that was his hope.

Because the string of murders happened over multiple state lines, the federal government wanted to handle the case as well. Deni had dealt with federal prosecutors in the past and to say he wasn't a fan was the understatement of all understatements. Because Roman Destrier was out of country and in a nation without an extradition treaty with the United States, they were likely to win. The federal government has the ability to apply pressure on foreign soil that individual states are not equipped to exert; in this case the United Arab Emirates, Dubai.

Deni knew that the jurisdictional tug-of-war could go on for years. Meanwhile, Leonard and possibly Sorche Myhre would be in custody awaiting an eventual trial. Speedy trials are relative. And Roman Destrier would still be half a world away handling sums of money that equal the total economy of small countries, free to do whatever he wanted.

The last bit was something that Deni couldn't live with. Roman had started this entire nightmare and he would likely ebb away from justice. He was the first and the last piece of the puzzle that Deni needed to finish.

And he knew just the person to see about it.

Ebb

It wasn't until wednesday morning that Deni could escape the retelling of events and get to the CIG building in the financial district.

Boston was abustle with tourists in Faneuil Hall as always from late spring to fall. Trolleys of every color filled with looky-loos moved past Deni along Atlantic Avenue as he walked toward CIG.

He again followed the crowd of people going into the building, and he again went up to Cecil Brands' office. The door was closed, Deni entered without knocking.

"What is this now? Again? Don't we have security in this building?"

"Not very tight apparently, Cecil. You can make this visit short and sweet by helping me out."

"And what is it that you want from me this time? I'm very busy."

"Right now a forensic task force is being put together to trace a money-laundering operation that you were apart of."

"This again? I thought that I explained this to you already? I didn't do anything illegal."

"You did explain it. To me. Unless you cooperate with me, you're gonna have to explain it to a grand jury. I want Roman Destrier's heart on a plate."

"Do you think that you are the first person to utter those words? Many people before you and smarter than you have taken their crack at him and are worse for wear."

"Only I have an edge. You."

"And why would I want to bring down Roman Destrier?"

"Several reasons. Stay out of jail for one. Another is to help your firm scoop up Monarch's business. Last I knew, you were on the board here. Appointed by Norman Craig himself, yes?"

"Yes. And you've peaked my interest. Go on."

"Their accounts in the Caymans. How much is there and in how many accounts?"

"I …. I …. I …. would have to look into it. As I said to you before, I'm not privied to all of the information you need. Is this some sort of trick?"

"No. No trick. I need to know how much money is down there and how much can be funneled through the Caymans?"

"To what end?"

"If there was a way to consolidate that money and move it out of Monarch control and into another account, that would prove to be a significant loss to them. Right?"

"Depending on how much money we are talking about, yes. Monarch moves hundreds of millions if not billions per day. I don't have access to all of their accounts, but I do have another contact at Monarch - Dubai."

"Good. A large amount going missing would make investors think twice about Monarch and think about another company, like CIG," Deni said.

"Are you are asking me to steal money? Because not only is it illegal but also won't instill consumer confidence in CIG. My contact won't — "

" — No. I am asking you to move it into another account that you control. You can move it back later when I tell you to."

"You're more clever than I thought, Mr. Dennihan," Cecil said.

"People make that mistake all of the time."

"You're going to scare him and his investors."

"We're going to play a shell game."

Cecil nodded his head. "And when he uncovers the shell?"

"I'm going to make him come out from hiding to find his money."

50

ROMAN DESTRIER SAT IN HIS OFFICE on the penthouse floor of the Monarch building in downtown Burj Dubai. The windows behind his luxury car-sized desk overlooked Burj Khalifa Lake; a man-made body of water, and the Persian Gulf another two blocks beyond it.

He studied the reports that had just come to him for signature and didn't know what to make of them. It was after 1:00 in the afternoon on thursday, many people in the office had already left for the day which was customary.

Offices close from 1:00 to 4:00 PM due to the heat, then reopen from 4:00 until 7:00 PM once the scorching hot day would cool a mere ten degrees. The work weeks run from sunday to thursday, so most workers don't return on thursdays at 4:00 PM if they can get away with it.

Roman pressed the intercom on his phone to his assistant. She was American and kept the same hours as her boss, which were many.

"Jana, get Najib in here please."

"He may have already left the building, sir."

"Drag him in here by his beard if you have to, I want him in my office yesterday."

"Yes, sir."

Roman was not usually as curt with his subordinates. He was the definition of proper, which is what made him that much more successful in Dubai. He knew that his assistant would handle Najib, the top man at Monarch - Dubai save for him, with more care than he had just handled her. While a progressive city, women speaking to men in Dubai without respect would not go without a demand for punishment no matter to whom the woman reported and was rumored to be sleeping with.

Najib was standing in front of Roman in his office within fifteen minutes, which was fifteen minutes longer than Roman wanted to wait.

"What is the meaning of this, Najib?"

"I do not know as to what you refer, sir." Najib's english was excellent though there was a slight hint of a middle-eastern accent.

Roman motioned for his subordinate to come to his desk, which he did. He gave Najib a folder, who looked inside and realized immediately why his unusually disheveled boss was taking a just as unusual tone with him.

"There must be some mistake, sir."

"A $1.4 Billion mistake. What is this transfer?"

"Our Cayman assets were merged. According to this report, we moved additional funds into that account as well."

"I can see that, Najib. Why? Why on earth would we build one account that large? That is the very definition of risk. And for precisely this reason. Where is the money?"

"In a Cayman account, RBC Royal."

"The account number doesn't exist. I've typed the number into the computer countless times, nothing. So I ask you again, where is the goddamned money?"

"I would have to look into it. This information coming from the Caymans must be a mistake." Najib was very offended by the curse but avoided pointing it out and further confrontation.

"Get them on the phone and straighten this out."

Ebb

"We are eight hours ahead of them, sir. It is not yet six in the morning there. There is nobody at the bank to take my call."

"Then call them at home."

"Is that entirely necessary? The home is sacred."

"We transferred $1.4 Billion in liquid capital into *one* account and now that account has vanished. One .... Point .... Four .... Billion, Najib. It's not like somebody didn't carry the fucking one. This isn't a rounding error. Almost one and a half *billion* dollars is fucking gone. Missing or misplaced. You had better pray to your Allah that the money *is* only misplaced."

"Sir, I ....."

" — Forget your weekend plans. Gas up a plane. I wanna be in Georgetown by the time their front door is unlocked."

The wheels of the large private jet hit the runway of Owen Roberts International Airport in the Caymans fourteen hours later. It was approaching 8:00 PM local time, which was not by the time the bank opened. It wasn't even by the time the bank had closed.

Najib had taken care of phone calls for Roman during the trip, ensuring that the RBC Royal Bank's president would meet them on the tarmac.

Roman had spent the flight trying to sleep. When sleep wouldn't come; he drank, ate, and had sex with his assistant, Jana. Her plans for the weekend were changed to include the trip to the islands as well.

The Dassault Falcon 7x slowly taxied toward the building designated for private flights. Roman was eager to get through customs and get to the bottom of where his company's money had been moved.

The airplane door leading out to the stairs seemed to take forever to open. Roman stood inside the jet next to the door waiting for the exact moment when it did. The humid, tropical air hit him like a slap to the face. He was first off the jet, first to the bottom of the stairs, and first inside the poorly air-conditioned building.

Roman made his way over to the customs desk with his passport when he was surrounded by a dozen men in white short-sleeve shirts, navy-blue pants with a red stripe down each leg, and caps.

"Roman Destrier?"

"Yes. What is the meaning of this?"

"Royal Cayman Island Police, sir. Do place your hands on your head. You are under arrest on behalf of the United States of America, where you are wanted on suspicion of serial murder and numerous other crimes," the lead officer said with British accent.

"What? There must be some mistake. I've been in UAE not the USA."

"You may sort that out with the American authorities. We have orders and a plane waiting for you, sir."

The RCIP officer in charge handcuffed Roman while he was speaking to him.

"United States Marshals will be onboard the aircraft to speak with you further."

Once he was restrained, he was checked for weapons and relieved of his belt. While this was taking place, Roman looked for Jana and found the eyes of Najib.

"Najib. Contact my attorneys please This is a mistake. Besides, there is no extradition from the Caymans."

"It seems that while the Caymans have sold their soul to finance, they will not due with murderers," Najib said with a beard-hidden smirk. "The Yanks carry a big stick."

"You? You did this?"

"Goodbye Roman. I believe I can carry-on just fine without you henceforth."

Roman cried out as he was being led off by the police. "Jana!"

"She can't hear you. She is still on the plane. Oh, hold for one beat gents," Najib said to the RCIP as he withdrew a piece of paper he had been carrying. They halted, moving Roman to face Najib.

"I almost forgot. I have a brief note for you, Roman. From a Warren Dennihan — I believe you know him. He says, and I quote,

'This is for Lara.'"

Roman shook his head as he looked at the floor. Tears of anger welled up in his eyes, spilling onto the linoleum floor.

"Fucking Deni."

Ebb

EPILOGUE

THERE WAS ENOUGH BUSINESS TO KEEP ALL of the interested parties busy. The Feds, New Hampshire, Massachusetts, and Connecticut had all initially fought for jurisdiction over the events that had unfolded over April and May. As it turned out, they each had more than enough to keep them busy.

Connecticut took over the prosecution of Leonard Myhre. The powers that be had decided not to prosecute Sorche, instead focusing all of their energies on Leonard. Even with mitigation he was facing the rest of his life in prison for the murders-for-hire of Chamille Destrier and Ludo Rossi and the slaying of Nigel Singh. The prosecutor offered a deal to throw in the killing of Nigel for free, but even if Leonard took it he wouldn't breath free air ever again. Myhre rejected the offer, deciding to take all three murders to trial. He must have felt that he had nothing to lose.

Timothy Cromwell prosecuted Nigel Singh in absentia for the Regis & Chapman arson and the subsequent murder of Nora Chapman. The reason for the trial was purely for public appearances since Nigel was already dead. A very expensive public service in both Ryan and Deni's opinion.

The Office of the Attorney General assigned a Federal Prosecutor to bring Roman Destrier to Justice. He was facing the death penalty for setting the entire sequence of events into motion. All seven deaths and the thirty-four related charges, according to federal statute, were the fault of Destrier. Because he had allegedly ordered the abduction and murder of Lara Myhre, the subsequent murders to cover it up, all subsequent crimes were the foreseeable result. Only in the American Justice System can two people be convicted in separate courts for the same murder, several times over. No wonder people hate lawyers.

The burden of proof threshold in federal court is much lower than it is in most states. Ryan explained to Deni over dinner one night that the only snag in the process of putting a needle in Roman Destrier's arm was proving he was responsible for Lara's death. Once that was proven, causation for the rest of the lot was a legal walk in the park.

Ryan had also explained that appellate courts recently streamlined the process in death-penalty cases. Once convicted, it was no longer taking a double-digit number of years to get the job done. Death Row was now a Death Expressway. Deni hoped that not only would Roman get sentenced to death, but that it would be a botched job that took a great deal of time.

Ebb

Massachusetts had the easiest time. They wrapped up the murders of Lara Myhre, Cole Renner, and prized son Gary Rennick with a quick hearing. Nigel Singh was the serial killer responsible and he was dead.

Despite the three murders cleared, the quickness in solving them, and doing so without the need for an expensive trial — there was still trouble in the henhouse. Lisa Sheed had involved a private investigator beyond department regulations and what was deemed legally appropriate. Hobbs went on the warpath and Lieutenant Titanitaukis' hands were tied. He brought it to the attention of Superintendent of Detectives, who notified the Commander, who brought in IAB, who along with the civilian review board decided to impose sanctions. Sanctions being that she was terminated without pension.

Once Sheed had gotten over the initial shock of being kicked off the force, she sought employment from the only place that she was interested in working. To the only person that she thought she could tolerate working for. He was a man, a supremely flawed one at that, but one she admired. Sort of. At least his heart was in the right place. His motives were clear. And definitely no sexual tension.

Deni immediately moved on to a new case. This one was for Ryan, an urgent case with a trial scheduled two weeks later. He moved on to a new relationship as well. Ani was keeping him busy.

The Lara Myhre case not only kept the criminal courts in business, but civil courts as well. Sorche Myhre was kicking a dead horse, and right where it hurt. In the wallet. Lara was not only biologically a result of the Destriers, her death was the result as well. Since there was no heir to the Destrier fortune, Sorche was going after it. Birth-right and wrongful death. Nigel wasn't the only one savvy to double-dipping.

Roman's legal team settled with Sorche for $500 million.

A half billion dollars richer, Mrs. Myhre retained the financial services of CIG to manage her even greater fortune.

Without a family, she drifted off to live out the rest of her days in obscurity.

AUTHOR'S NOTES AND ACKNOWLEDGEMENTS

The previous work is one of fiction, any resemblance to specific and true incidents is purely coincidental. Some of the places, laws, crimes, procedures, and experiences are based upon real research, however. The factual information was used to add a legitimate feel to a completely fabricated story. Without the help of the people and entities listed below, this book at worst doesn't get written, at best isn't nearly as rich and believable.

I would first like to thank the Boston Bruins and the National Hockey League. There was no 'Defensive-Defenseman' Gary Rennick playing for the Bruins or their minor league system. Allowing me to insert my fictitious character in with real players was and is truly appreciated. I have long been a fan of both the organization and league, their hospitality has made me an even more avid fan.

The logistics behind my use of the Dartmouth Hitchcock Hospital is not entirely accurate. While they

Ebb

do have excellent facilities spread out over a number of New Hampshire towns, where certain facilities are located was fabricated by me. The maternity ward therein was also a figment of the author's imagination.

I would also like to thank Blue Ginger, Durgin-Park, TORO, and Margarita's Mexican Restaurants for their hospitality. These establishments are real — and really good. They are very different restaurants in style, very different chef/owners, and yet they share the knowledge of how to treat guests. There is not enough adulation for these establishments.

While the financial district in Boston does exist and sits juxtaposed to Faneuil Hall, there are no CIG or Monarch buildings. I have learned that there is a Monarch Bank; however, the one in this story is not related to it in any way.

I would also like to thank Land Rover and Bertram Boats, specifically the Ferretti Group of companies. Both land and sea, these are the very definition of luxury vehicles. I thank them very much for their support, I would highly recommend them even without it. Although I probably shouldn't have just said that.

Ebb

There is a Sarah, owner/operator of Red Carpet Ready in Boston. If Chamille Destrier existed, she would most definitely have utilized RCR's services on a regular basis. You should too.

To my friends, family and acquaintances who are a part of this novel in spirit. I hope that you can see yourselves in some of the characters, as I drew upon the nuance of your character to make mine come alive. Thank you for being a part of my life and therefore in the fabric of my imagination and this work.

The City of Boston. You continue to be my muse and the heartbeat of New England.

I would like to take the time to thank those that took the time to speak with me. If you enjoyed this book, it is largely because of them. A character or two may have been named in lieu of payment.

Finally, thanks to you the reader for your time. I hope you enjoyed the story.

-sw-

467

ABOUT THE AUTHOR

Photo ©2013 WWPGroup

Scott Wellinger is a well-traveled writer and novelist. He has written many articles, scripts, and essays under pseudo-names. His latest novels feature, among others, the fictitious private investigations of Warren Dennihan. A native of New England, he was born in Vermont and was educated in Boston, Massachusetts. He holds a Master's Degree in Applied Economics and when he is not traveling, he is on a golf course.

Ebb

Also by scott wellinger:

CRASH
A Warren Dennihan Novel (first of series)

Venom

A Warren Dennihan Novel (book 2)

Sinn

A Warren Dennihan Prequel (book 3)

A sample of the bestselling novel *Sinn* follows. (unedited). The full novel is available for purchase in ebook and print at amazon.com, iBooks, GooglePlay, www.WWPGroup.webs.com, and wherever you buy books.

Ebb

Thank You for Reading!

If you enjoyed reading this novel, please help others appreciate it as well.

Recommend it. Please help other readers find it by recommending it to friends, reader groups, discussion boards, or wherever you purchased the book.

Review it. You can add your thoughts to Amazon, Google, iBooks, at the publisher website (WWPGroup.webs.com), reader clubs, etc. If you do write a review, please share it with me at scottwellinger@gmail.com so that I can thank you personally.

Follow me on twitter and Instagram.

Best Wishes,

sw

scott wellinger

the author of **CRASH** and Venom

Sinn

a warren dennihan prequel

Sínn

A Warren Dennihan Prequel

by scott wellinger

Ebb

Ebb

Printed in the United States of America

10 9 8 7 6 5 4 3 2 1

PROLOGUE

TRAFFIC WAS A NIGHTMARE ON STORROW DRIVE. The Big Dig project had ensured that the entire city of Boston was a metropolis parking lot. It had been for years before and would continue to be for the foreseeable future. The colossal construction project had begun in 1991, after two decades of planning, to alleviate the very traffic it was causing. The undertaking was supposed to be finished in 1998, but six years after the due-date there was still no end in sight.

The two lanes headed west on Storrow were just as congested as the eastbound lanes. While those that were aimed west, away from the Interstate 93 ramp towards Harvard and MIT had the Charles River and the Esplanade to view on their right, those headed toward it had only the tall buildings of BackBay to study. The luxurious apartment buildings with back terraces overlooking the Charles were admired and fantasized over by everyone including the eastbound traffic, further taunted by the signage stating *'If you lived here you would already be home'*.

Along the Charles River was the jogging path, the Hatch Shell at the Esplanade where the outdoor movie and concert season had recently begun, and the crew teams rowing their way past the onlookers stuck in traffic. The early May weather was in the mid-to-upper sixties, though lightly raining as it had all spring. The joggers were plentiful in the sun-showers as their faith in the activity was rekindled by the annual Marathon that had taken place just a few weeks prior. The Boston Pops had just played the opening weekend for the Hatch Shell, and the U2 cover band *The Joshua Tree* was supposed to play the upcoming Saturday night. The eight-oared sweep racing shells were moving in the water past the four-wheeled deadlock like they were standing still. Because they were.

The pedestrian bridges that passed over the four lanes of halted traffic had graffiti reminding all who were trapped below of the Bambino Curse. While the city did long to reverse the curse, they wanted to reverse the traffic situation more. Little did anyone know that one of those two wishes would be granted later that year.

When traffic is halted to such an extent, virtually any motor vehicle violation is ignored by the Massachusetts State Police which patrol Storrow Drive. It was an unwritten rule for all of the arteries, not just Storrow. Pullovers in heavy traffic are hazardous to all parties involved. One can't speed, nor weave in and out of traffic when snails are moving past you. Derelict vehicles that overheat or cease to run are met with hand gestures and shouting, versus AAA or a tow truck because help simply can't get there.   In truth, most troopers just sit on the side of the road or avoid the congestion all together during peak times. Nothing will make the already unbearable gridlock worse save for the flashing lights of a cruiser pulling over some poor slob.

The Probationary Trooper William LaDue did not receive the unwritten memo or message regarding discretion during traffic jams. He sat in his 2002 Ford *Crown Vic* patrol unit bored out of his mind. His cruiser parked off of the curb under one of the graffitied footbridges, staring ahead at the park and the General George Patton statue that stood in it. There are only so many jog-bras and swinging ponytails one can stare at to pass the time. The occasional flick of the wipers to clear the rivulets off of the windshield in order to see said jog-bras. He couldn't leave, there was no place to go.   The young go-getter had only been out of the academy for slightly more than ten months, had just gotten out on his own in-fact.   He sat there alone wanting more than to babysit traffic.   He decided to punch in the tag numbers of the vehicles that were not passing him. One such license plate caught his fancy.

The red, white and blue MA commercial plate had a DEC 04 expiration date.   That was not the problem, the end of December was about eight months yet to come. What set off bells and whistles was the fact that the tag was registered for a dark, 1999, tourmaline metallic *Econoline E350*, yet it was attached to a brand new, white, 2004 Chevy *Express Cargo* van. Against conventional wisdom, Trooper LaDue decided to ring him up.

William turned on his lights and gave a long yelp from the siren on his cruiser to alert the squatters. Nobody moved, nobody could move. All hoped the new development didn't include them.

The cruiser continued up on the lawn, pulling next to the white van being sought in the right lane. There were two passengers, definitively, one in each of the bucket seats in the front. There were possibly more in the back, though there were no side windows in the utility vehicle to discern for certain. LaDue was alone in his cruiser, which meant he needed to call a backup cruiser. The situation was already a problem and getting worse.

The Trooper pointed to the passenger, then pointed to the lawn in front of his patrol vehicle. He then reversed his Crown Vic, allowing the van to jump the curb ahead of him. Only it didn't. The van didn't move. William engaged his loudspeaker.

"Pull up onto the curb and turn off your vehicle."

Ebb

The hesitation was notable, but the request was eventually adhered to. The van slowly rode up the curb and onto the newly green park lawn from the combination of wet spring rain and sporadic sun. The gap the van created in the traffic was absorbed by vehicles who were all too eager to move the few short feet forward. The pullover was garnering attention from the pedestrians on the overpasses as well as the runners along the path. Something to occupy those who were stuck in traffic. But not too much. Just another day in the city.

Dispatch was giving the young trooper grief about the backup he was requesting, reminding him of the hour and traffic. As if he was unaware. LaDue was informed that a two-man cruiser was on route but to hang tight. In the meantime, he called out the tag number over the radio to dispatch in an effort to learn more information than what he could obtain from the screen in his vehicle.

"Dispatch, this is Romeo-two again. I've got a Mass tag November-7-8 4-5-Echo. Reads here as belonging to a dark blue 99 Ford, but I got it on a brand new white Chevy. What have you got?"

"Romeo-two, that tag is coming back stolen, along with the vehicle. Take caution, hold off. Backup is on route. Over."

"Roger-that."

Probationary Trooper LaDue was officially excited. Not only did he now have something to do for the remainder of his shift, a large portion of it at least, he now had a situation that was likely to be more involved than a mere traffic citation. He was told to wait for backup but he couldn't. Excitement got the better of him.

He exited his patrol vehicle and walked up the driver side of the van. He did so cautiously, looking into the large side mirror to get a visual on the driver while unsnapping the flap over his service weapon. LaDue was sure to stay tight to the van, making it that much more difficult for the driver to fire a shot of his own at a six o'clock angle versus a seven or eight. The Trooper would have told him to roll down his window, but it was already down. He called out to the driver from just behind his driver-side door.

"Reach both hands out of your window, and open your door from the outside. Slowly. Then step out of the vehicle."

"What is this about Officer? I couldn't have been speeding, we were at a stand-still," said the driver. He stuck out his hands but did not as yet pull on the black handle to his door.

"Just step out of your vehicle and we will get to that. How many passengers are in there with you?"

"One. And me." He pulled the outer handle and the door began to open slowly as instructed. "Don't you have to have a reason to pull me over?"

"And I do. Just tell your passenger to stay calm, you do as your instructed, and we will all get through this as calmly as possible."

The driver was about the same age as Trooper Ladue. Maybe not quite as old, which is to say that they were both barely old enough to rent a car. They weren't still using acne cream but they were still about half a decade from thirty. Once out of the van, the driver was pushed against it; his right cheek pressed into the white, metal side.

The trooper then quickly dodged to his left, looked into the van and came back out of view of the passenger. LaDue was right-handed so using his weapon would not be a possibility without exposing his torso, opening himself up for taking a bullet. He again called into the vehicle while putting handcuffs on the driver.

"Inside …. I need you to put your hands forward so I can see them and slowly climb over to the driver side toward me. Do just like your friend here did and this will go nice and smooth."

"Eat a dick!" The passenger then called out to his friend, "Hey Danny. I think this pig is alone. No backup."

The cuffed driver called back, "Little late for that now. We're smoked. Backup just pulled up." Another two-toned blue cruiser pulled up behind Ladue's. This one contained two State Troopers.

"Fuck!" The shout came from inside the van.

"Listen to your friend here and just come out nice and easy."

"Why'd you pull us over?" The passenger was still not over onto the driver's side, and LaDue was in the process of getting the driver to move to the back of van and sat down on the lawn by the road. He was not yet there when he heard it.

LaDue heard the passenger door to the van open and the word "GUN!" shouted. One of his backups had tried to apprehended the other occupant. Before the passenger could be pulled from the vehicle, he fired at the backup trooper. The return fire hit the passenger. Twice. The passenger fell out of the vehicle, his weapon kicked away, relieving him of it and sending him face-down onto the lawn in the process. Then, "Clear." An ambulance needed to called. The passenger was alive but bleeding badly. The process happened in the time it took for LaDue to get to the back of the van.

Ebb

Once the situation was completely under police control and a short debriefing had occurred, LaDue then moved the driver next to his accomplice and were both told that they were pulled over because the tags did not match the vehicle. The passenger while bleeding and in pain had already been read his Miranda rights as he was picking up a weapons charge along with an attempt on an Officer. For now. That gave them probable cause to search each of them and their vehicle. The troopers started with the suspect's pockets, asking if they stuck their hands in their pockets were they going to get stuck with anything? Knife? Syringe? The driver was the only one who responded, answering 'no', so both of their pockets were emptied. The writhing passenger had no ID. He was pulled further away and was trying to be stabilized by one of the backup troopers. The Driver had a license that identified him as Daniel McKennie.

"What are we gonna find in the van, Daniel?" The protocol was that LaDue would handle this suspect. His stop, his collar, his show. Rookie or not, this was his bust.

"Nothin'. I wanna talk to Warren Dennihan. He is one-ah-you. Statie. Goes by Deni. You know him?"

"Mr. McKennie, are you calling in a get-outta-jail-free-card already? What are you afraid of? You can talk to me. You *should* talk to me. What's in the van?"

"I ain't sayin' nothin' else unless it's to Deni. Nothin'."

"Have it your way, son." Nobody pointed out the fact that the man-child trooper had just called his like-aged suspect 'son'.

The second backup trooper stood watch over Daniel and helped LaDue. The other backup was still questioning the as-yet unidentified passenger, while he tried to get the bleeding under control. His only responses were the repeated insults to the trooper on top of him. "Cocksucka" being the theme while he spit up blood. LaDue opened the back double-doors to the van. It was filled from the back doors up to the front seats with crates.

"I'm willing to bet that whatever is in these crates is not good for you Daniel."

LaDue used the lever end of a tire-iron from the back of the van, after getting help pulling one of the large crates out of it. When he opened it, he was both elated and astonished. The crate was filled with shredded paper as packing and modified Heckler &

Koch *G3 Assault-4* rifles. The second backup was over his shoulder, just as stunned.

"Holy shit boys! It's redneck Christmas. Mother-load."

Ebb

Part One

Metro Trailer Park
May 2004

1

I WAS RELATIVELY NEW TO THE TROOP H
Detective Unit of the Massachusetts State Police
Department. It had been almost ten months, ten months
exactly May 15th, when I was promoted from patrol. I
was still responsible for Boston and Metrowest, but
instead of sitting on the Mass Pike ticketing people
trying to get to and from work I was doing something
important. I conducted investigations for serious crimes
against persons within a certain area of greater Boston.
Those areas were well-defined, though sometimes in the
course of an investigation there were pissing contests
with either the Springfield or Worcester units.

Ebb

Within the various troops, there were ranks that everyone sought to climb. The writing was on the wall for me, I was not going to climb any ladder. I was a Detective Junior Grade, purely by attrition, and that is how I would retire. The politics were obscene, the bullsh more than I could stomach. To be honest, rules aren't really my thing to begin with. Odd, I know, but sometimes what stands between me and the objective is a rule. I like to look at the big picture, the pencil pushers like to scrutinize over whether that picture is on Polaroid or Kodak paper.

So you could say that while I liked my work, I absolutely hated my job. You could say that because it was absolutely true.

I hated my boss, I hated my partner, and I hated the back-stabbing assholes that wanted my job. One would think that in law enforcement the job should be about justice. Justice for the people who were wronged, for the people of the City of Boston. But if you think that, you would be absolutely wrong.

What it was actually about, was politics. Who owed whom what favor, who knew which of their colleagues was dirty and what that damage could do if anyone were to find out. Those little tidbits of information won you chips in a big game that I wanted no part of.

Ebb

So it was customary for cops to consult with other cops on cases. Information traded in exchange for get-out-of-jail-free cards. A collar wasn't a collar until someone from the DA's office was involved. Then other deals were made. Somehow the prisons and county lock-ups were full, but don't ask me how.

What wasn't customary was for me to be called in on one of these deals, which is exactly what happened on Tuesday May11th, 2004. I remember the exact day because the Tribe was at Fenway, and Pedro was scheduled on the mound. I had tickets, but of course I didn't get to go because of this nonsense that I am about to tell you.

It was 6:15 PM and I was at The House, ready to check out for the day and get over to Fenway for the seven-oh-five start-time. That's when the kid called my name, Warren Dennihan. Only everyone calls me Deni, so I could tell right off the jump that I probably didn't know who was calling me.

"Dennihan!" The Trooper calling me looked like he was fifteen years old.

"That's Detective Dennihan, who are you?"

"William LaDue. Trooper LaDue. I got a situation from a routine stop that went sideways, guys callin' for you."

"Oooooooh, you're Billy. The new kid. Billy the Kid, I heard about you. Real go-getter that went to Brown."

Normally I would never have heard of a new trooper, even in my own building which this kid was not. But LaDue was the talk of the Staties. He was from Rhode Island, really smart, and had gone to Brown University. You don't get too many smart guys who want to be a glorified meter-maid for the Commonwealth of Massachusetts State Police. So people talked. The rumor was that he was one of those do-gooder action junkies that thought this was a noble career and he would make a difference. I gave him a year, two at the most before he figured it out. Meanwhile his mom was probably real proud to pay top-dollar for an Ivy League education for a job that pays $35k a year if he is lucky enough to get overtime. But the Massachusetts State Police is the largest police force in New England, so if he had to be a cop at least he was in the Ivy League of shit jobs.

The kid tried to fit in because he was different. Most of the guys in the department were either ex-military or ex-crooks. Either way, none of us had gone to Brown so our options were far more limited than his. This kid could be anything he wanted to be, yet he took the job away from guys and girls who needed the opportunity. Nobody liked him because he was supposedly a silver-spooner, so he tried all the harder. He even put on the fake Boston accent, which was invented to be a strong as mine. He dropped his R's, making them sound like ah's, like 'ah' instead of 'are'. He added them when they didn't exist, like 'sar' instead of 'saw'. My accent, unfortunately, is real.

"Uh, yeah. That's me. Anyway, I got one Daniel McKennie that is in a real fix and all he wants is you. After we Miranda'd him, he didn't say he wanted a lawyer or nothin'. Fuckin' punk just wants you, guy."

"Enough with the accent before you hurt yourself. Did you say McKennie? As in little Danny Mick?"

"I didn't say 'Danny Mick', but yes. He is down in room six waiting to speak with you." Thankfully LaDue dropped the accent, but now he sounded like a preppy douche.

I knew Danny Mick from the neighborhood. I grew up and still lived in Southie. For those that don't know Boston, Southie is South Boston. It is a rough and tumble Irish neighborhood, full of projects and three-deckers, where you are a criminal or you don't have hair on your nuts yet. I dated his older sister, Roxy for a while. By date, I mean we wrestled naked in bed quite a bit back in the day. She was a hot-mess back then and rumor had it that she still was.

"Do you know why he wants to talk to me? What'd he do?"

"Van full of assault rifles. His partner pulled a piece on us. He died on the way to Mass General. My backup called it in so Detective Hobbs is already in the loop. His case now, so you'll have to get with him." The trooper's accent was back. I could see why he rubbed people the wrong way. He definitely pissed me off.

"Hobbs is already down there?"

"Yeah. He told me to find you, but I was gonna anyway cuz the kid's been askin' for you," LaDue said.

"You wouldn't know shit if it was in yer hand would ya? I thought you were supposed to be smart? Hobbs is already my partner. So my case now."

"Whatever. I told him I would find you, and I did. Good luck. Who lets me know where to show up for the trial? You?"

"Just get outta here, Billy."

"William."

The kid had the balls to stare me down. Standing your ground is something I admire. To a point.

"Hey Billy? Kick rocks will ya?"

Ebb

When I had finally gotten rid of the eager beaver, I made my way to Interview Room Six. Outside the room on the bench was my partner, Detective Sergeant Rick Hobbs, the partner that outranked me that I couldn't stand.

Rick Hobbs was the kind of guy that after being with him for twenty minutes, you would actually be so irritated that choking a baby was deemed a plausible outlet for your anger, though obviously not appropriate. Only I had to spend way more than twenty minutes with the bag o'douche, I had to spend a minimum of five days a week with him attached to my hip. He was the know-it-all, holier-than-thou type that never made a mistake. Arrogance is fine, except that he screwed up all of the time and blamed everyone else for his fuck-ups.

Ebb

He was so self-absorbed that he probably liked the smell of his own shit. Other than that he was okay.

"There he is. Where ya been, Deni?"

"I was gonna file my fives before goin' to the game. Pedro is pitchin' tonight."

"Why bother? The Sox do great every year until the All-star break, then they suck their way out of the division. Yankees will be in the World Series again this year, mark my words. Sox will be lucky to get the Wild Card."

"Yeah well, it's a marathon not a race and it woulda been really nice to catch the game. Whatta we got?"

"Spiv by the name of Daniel McKennie. Only twenty-four and he's got a sheet as long as my fuckin' arm. Got caught with his dick in a pig. Ten cases of assault rifles in a brand new stolen van with stolen plates from yet another stolen van. Address puts him in Southie, probably in a triple-decker. You know that neighborhood, it's a metro trailer park. They infest the area like cockroaches. Anyways, he says he knows you and I assume he wants a walk. I don't see it happen'n partner."

"We've been workin' together, what? Ten months right? How is it you don't know I come from Southie? What am I now? Trailer trash?"

"I remember you live there. I make it that's how you know this mutt."

"I used to date his sister, that's how I know him. And just watch your mouth. If things woulda gone different aways back, maybe I woulda been with him. Maybe drivin' the van."

"Whatever. He could be your kid for all I give a shit. But there's no way he walks on this, no matter who you're bangin'."

"I'm not gonna get into it with ya, Rick. Just gimme some time with tha kid, huh? No microphone, no video, just me and him. We good?"

"Knock yourself out. He's snagged, confession or not."

I went into room six and the kid was sitting in his chair, stoic and handcuffed. I removed my sport-jacket and placed it on top of the microphone in the center of the table and took my seat across from him. I knew what Rick agreed to and I also knew what he was capable of. Not a big trust factor between us.

"Got yourself all jammed up here Danny."

"Are we alone or are they watchin' on tha other side a tha mirror?" His accent was a bad as mine. Maybe worse. You tend to run into that in Southie. Get two of us together with an outsider as a bystander and they will tell you that we are speaking a different language, because what comes out of our mouths doesn't sound like english. I probably didn't have to cover up the microphone in retrospect.

"Yeah, just us. But I'm not sure what I can do for ya, kid. You're pretty fucked."

"What am I gonna do, Deni? Slopes is gonna shit a cow, man."

"Aaaah, Danny. Slopes? What did he get you into? Guns?"

He nodded his head. "G3s."

In the thirty-seconds I had spoken to Danny, I had already sized up what was going on. Everybody from Southie has a nickname. When you live twelve to twenty people in one three-family three-decker, you get a neighborhood with a ton of people with the same name. It's called a three-decker, or triple-decker as the non-locals called it, for the complicated reason that there is an entire community of houses with three ascending decks. The houses are practically attached to each other, side by side, the style exactly the same. A basement with three floors built up on top, each floor a different apartment, all having decks both front and back.

The Irish-Catholic community in Southie isn't devout by any means, but they follow the 'no form of birth control' rule. Nicknames were the only way to tell us all apart. Even if you were the one and only, like Warren Dennihan, you still got a nickname. Sean Teague was the given name to Slopes.

In Southie, there are probably fifty Sean Teagues. Slopes got his name because he is one of the rare cases where the disease Bell's Palsy became permanent. Either it wasn't diagnosed quickly enough or an antibiotic wasn't given soon enough, or he didn't take it. In any case the side of his face drooped like it was sliding off his face. He was very sensitive about it, but that didn't stop the nickname. Slopes was a boss for the Irish mob.

Back in the 70s, former IRA 'Volunteer' Patrick Nee came to the US and became a leader with the Mullen Gang. They then went to war against the Killeen Brothers gang over Boston turf. James J. Bulger was the boss of the KB crew back then, he got a nickname too - Whitey. When it was all said and done, the Mullens and Killeens joined the Howie Winter gang, because their war depleted the two gangs to a point where they couldn't survive. When Howie Winter went to jail in '79 for rigging horse races over at Suffolk Downs, Bulger took over the whole shah-bang. The Winter Hill Gang became the biggest confederation of organized crime in the east after the Irish Gang War. In '94 Whitey Bulger went into hiding because he turned FBI informant, but his crew was still doing business without him. They were still bookmaking and loansharking, which were some of the least horrible things they did. The Winter Hill Gang had made the papers recently because they held a bunch of no-show jobs on the Big Dig. They had formed a dummy corporation called the C. Dáil Corp., which James Kerasiotes of the Mass Turnpike Authority awarded a contract without a bid. They got paid for literally nothing. No wonder the Big Dig project was long over the deadline and over budget.

Danny telling me that he had a cargo van full of Heckler & Koch *G3A4s* meant that they were still smuggling guns for the IRA. Those guns were one of the types of the signature weapons used by the IRA in any cause they engaged in. It also meant Slopes had a come-up and was now Mr. Big in Boston. Bottom line was that those guns were going to be paid for in one way or another, which ultimately meant that Danny Mick was fucked in the permanent sense. Prison was the least of his worries. Danny didn't want me to get him out of the hoosegow, he wanted me to get him square with Slopes.

All of the information came to me in just a few sentences, and it took me almost no time at all to connect the dots. I felt for the kid a little bit. As the gentrification had begun in Southie, yuppies taking over our neighborhoods, increasingly fewer legitimate opportunities were available to make a living. I caught a break when I was kid which allowed me to extricate myself from that life without leaving the neighborhood. I was one of the few lucky ones. Danny was on a different path. With more affluent kids like young Billy buying houses, taking over the neighborhoods, and taking the decent jobs, there would be more like Danny getting classed out.

"Jesus Danny. How many G3s?"
"Two hundred."
"And your boy tried to shoot a cop? Why didn't you just take off? Try and dust the rookie who pulled you over?"
"Ya tellin' me? Gridlock on Storrow. Nowhere to run."
"I hate to add insult, but which of you two geniuses decided to move it all during peak traffic? On Storrow of all fuckin' things?"
"Big Dig redirected us. Slopes told us the pickup and drop times."
"Well then he's the idiot. No reason to move that much hardware during broad daylight in rush hour. What's really going on here?"
"No clue, man. I just did what I was told. We got fucked cuz of tha tags. Cops don't usually do pullovers in traffic. Nobody was more shocked than me to see tha fuckin' cruisa flick his lights."

Ebb

"Fair enough. You were unlucky enough to get the one go-getter with a badge. But still .... "

"So what do I do? I'm a dead man. If I PC, they'll think I ratted. If I don't I'll be on the business end of stabbing. You gotta talk to him for me, Deni. He knows you."

PC meant Protective Custody while he was awaiting trial. And he was right. It would actually be easier to kill him while incarcerated than it would out on the streets.

"I'll see what I can do, but I'm not makin' any promises. If Slopes is runnin' the mob crew here which runs guns for the IRA, I might not even get the chance to talk to him. I'm a cop and everyone within 30 blocks of the neighborhood knows it.   He's gonna be pretty insulated. I don't even know where he is these days."

"He never sits anywhere for more than a minute. Go see my sister. She'll get you to him. Please Deni. You gotta help me."

"No I don't. I told you I would have a chat, but it ends there. How does your sister know where he is?"

"Just you and me talkin' here? She gets her junk direct."

"You know the shit I'm gonna take if my partner or my boss hears that I'm runnin' around trying to save your ass? Where were these guns goin' anyway?"

Ebb

"In the end? I got no idea. I just go from point A to point B when I'm told. Somebody else was gonna move'em later. I'm not exactly high up the food chain ya know."

"My point."

"What's your point, Deni?"

"I shoulda gone to the game, that's the point."

2

GETTING RID OF MY PARTNER, RICK HOBBS, was quite the chore. He was nothing but questions once I was finished chatting with young Danny Mick. I didn't know if he had watched the conversation through the glass in the observation room or not, but he seemed to not know what was said. He was all about if Danny confessed, where the guns were going, where they had come from, and the like.

Everywhere I turned he would be there asking me another question, practically dry-humping me up one hall and down the next one. I didn't like the guy anyway, but at that point I was ready to strangle him. I was already in a bad mood for missing the Sox game.

The situation was made worse by the fact that I had to see a girl I used to sleep with back in the day, in order to find a mobster who was probably going to kill the guy I had just spoken to, because he had lost two hundred assault rifles. I really didn't need my partner nagging at me as a topper.

Hobbs knew that I knew all of these hoods and racketeers. I grew up with them. Hell I still lived near them. The entire department knew that I had a relationship with these hooligans, I had been hired specifically for the intel. When I wouldn't go undercover after completing the academy, for what I thought were obvious reasons, they sent me to watch traffic on the Pike. That was the main reason I would never get any further in the department. The higher-ups had long memories and I didn't play politics, so my fate was sealed.

At the age of thirty-two, I was younger than my partner who was a decade my senior. I was in exponentially better physical condition as well but age had nothing to do with it. The old cliché about cops eating donuts was brought to life with Rick Hobbs. But not just donuts. If the foodstuff involved massive amounts of preservatives and fat, he loved it in mass quantities. It is my personal feeling that clogged arteries also clog up blood-flow to the brain. Does that mean that all fat people are stupid, of course not. What I'm saying is that if you are a guy who is not working with a ton of brain power, lack of blood to the noggin is an added hurdle that is ill-afforded. I'm no genius by any stretch, but I would bet the ranch that I would beat him in anything from arm-wrestling to a spelling bee.

"Hobbs! Enough already. I just want to finish my shit and maybe catch the back end of the game, okay?"

"I'm your goddamned senior partner and you never treat me like we're a team. What did he say? Where were the guns goin'?"

"What are you, a broken record? 'What did he say? …. What did he do? …. Where were the guns goin'? …. Why do I have a small penis?' It gets old. I told you I was going in there alone to talk to tha kid. We talked. Case closed. He wasn't lookin' for a walk, he just wanted to talk about the neighborhood. He knows he is goin' away for a long time, and we didn't need a confession. So for the last time, back …. the …. fuck …. off. Any of this gettin' through?"

"I still outrank you last I checked, but have it your way. We're gonna be boxed out anyway. With that kind of hardware, the ATF will be down here first thing."

"They have all the fun don't they? Alcohol, Tobacco *and* Firearms is like the trifecta. Booze, guns and stogies sounds like a good time to me. So you think they will show up in the morning to haul away the lot?" I played stupid. I didn't care either way, to be honest. But he was right. The ATF would want the case especially because it was a lay-up. Maybe the FBI would want in also.

"Guns and the van are already down at ballistics in Maynard, they will probably let us analyze and run them through the database, but they will take over the investigation."

The crime lab for Massachusetts was located in the western part of the state, about an hour away off of route 62 in the town of Maynard. They investigate; blood work, for DNA and toxicology; hair fibers and skin; weapons and ballistics. It was our CSI lab. In this case they would completely strip down the van for fibers or trace evidence that could lead to other suspects involved in the gun trafficking. They will also examine every weapon to determine its origin, who has used it, and if the weapon had been used in any other documented crime. Fingerprints and ballistics would take some time and since Maynard was the only lab in the state, there was a back-log.

Ebb

"Well good for them. Tie it up with a bow and get it off our case load," I said. Hobbs was following me back to my desk. Our desks.

"They are gonna want to trade him in for a bigger fish, Deni."

"I'm sure."

"Sooooo …. "

"So what?"

"Who is your little friend working for? You want me to put a bow on it? Give me the ribbon."

"Do you ever sing a different tune?" I faked sign language and enunciated extremely slowly in the hopes that he would finally get the fact that I was not going to give him Slopes. "I …. don't …. know …. who …. he …. is …. working …. for. He knows he's going away for a long time and I used to bang his sister. He wanted me to talk to her, say goodbye and that he is sorry. Do you honestly think he would tell a cop who he is working for? Surest way to get clipped is to give up his boss. He's well-trained. He'll do his time like a man and shut his cock-holster."

"You must know who he runs with. He is from your neighborhood. Winter Hill Gang? Gotta be, right?"

Exasperated, I sat on my desk dropping my fives in my to-do pile and focused on the pain in the ass partner standing before me.

"You're not my boss. You're my senior partner and I don't know how to say it any different. You keep askin', I keep tellin', but nothin' sticks to that meat between your ears. I don't know. But let's say that you are right, he is workin' for the Winters. What in the holy fuck are you gonna do about it? They been doin' business in this city for a long-ass time. They survived the gang-wars, Federal RICO Task Force .... but you? You think that you are gonna rid the city of them when you can't understand the simple concept of 'I don't know anything more than you do'. How does that play?"

"Why do you always protect them?"

"What are you talkin' about now, Hobbs?"

"You know that metro trailer park like the back of your hand. You know who is doing what five steps before they do it. You could be a goddamned hero. Just go down there and scoop up the whole crew. But instead you let them do whatever they want and you cover for them."

"Let me ask you somethin'. Is that what you think this is? Me covering for a kid in the neighborhood? Covering for 'my people'? You've got some set on you, Hobbs. There have been probably a million man-hours spent tryin' to bring these guys down, and while they get a couple of the dregs, the mob keeps truckin' along. But let me spell somethin' out for you. Where do all of those nickel and dime crooks go if the overlords go down? Disorganized chaos. You think all of those guys are gonna just go out and get a job? No fuckin' way. They go into business for themselves and crime actually gets worse. Those bodegas that are currently under protection are fair game. Pawn shops sprout up all over to take place of the loan sharking. Drugs are on every corner instead of specific ones through the Winters. Or worse? New York and Rhode Island guinea crews move in and pick up the slack. There is no eliminating them, Hobbs. You just try and control it the best way you can."

"So you cover for the kid?"

"I'm done. I got nothin' more to say to you. It's not our case anymore anyway, you just said. You don't get to be a hero on this one. Just give it to the ATF or FBI or whatever and move on."

"I'm gonna request a new partner."

"I've heard that before too. Let me know how it goes."

Hobbs stormed away from me, away from our desks which unfortunately faced each other. The desk farm that was the Troop H Detective Unit was set up in one large room with desks that were like a Tetris puzzle. There were no partitions or cubicles, that was deemed as counterproductive and obstructed teamwork. All partners had desks that were facing one another, not just

Ebb

Hobbs and me. I was thankful that he had decided to walk away instead of having to face him while I finished the work that should have been completed hours prior.

I removed the fives that I had to finish from my to-do pile. Fives are what detectives call the DD-5 form that must be submitted on active cases. My boss, Lieutenant Manny Titanitaukis (who we call Lieu to his face and Tits behind his back), is little more than a case manager. He has to manage our share of the 2,000 homicide cases, 9,000 rape allegations, 75,000 armed robberies, 125,000 reported assaults, 130,000 auto thefts involving a carjacking, and countless other felonies that get called-in every single year. Troop H handles most of the cases since we are responsible for crimes against persons in greater Boston, but the local stations and other departments handle a good many as well. Tits needs to file his own paperwork to keep his bosses apprised of which cases are solved and which are pending. We have to submit a form, the DD-5, for each development on each case that we handle.

I was behind on my paperwork. I was originally going to just submit the fives that Tits was having a fit over and head to the game, but it was now after 9:00 PM which meant that by the time I got over to Yawkey Way the game would be over. So I decided to hunker down and finish all of my outstanding paperwork. Tickets wasted.

Ebb

The realization that the date that I was supposed to bring to the game, the one that I didn't go to, hit me like a ton of bricks. I pulled out my new Motorola *V3 RAZR* flip-top cell phone and saw what I already knew. Fifteen missed calls and twenty-two unread text messages. My ass was grass.

3

I WOKE UP ON WEDNESDAY MORNING ALONE, which was not what I had been planning when I bought the very hard to come by tickets to Fenway. I had been planning my personal opening day game for the 2004 season for a couple of weeks. I had been seeing this girl, Jill, for a while and had promised her we would go. I say promised because we had been down this road before, just not with tickets to the Red Sox. She made me say over and over again that we would definitely go see Pedro throw filth at the Indians. But in fairness, maybe not in those exact words.

She had not answered any of my phone calls last night when I realized that I was more than two hours late in picking her up. I decided against calling her again that morning. For one, I get up at 5:00 AM to go work out and then to The House and, two, she was likely still really pissed and/or sleeping with someone else. I decided instead to listen to the voicemails from the night before telling me what a shit-bag I am while I made coffee. I would have read the stored texts also but I had no idea how to on the new phone. I don't even know why she sent them because she knows my feelings about them, and I definitely never send texts because I have a bitch of a time using the numbers to type in one of the three letters on each button I want for each and every word.

By the time the Dunkin' Donuts coffee was brewed, I had been thoroughly dressed down as the calls went from concern to tears to vulgarities and anger. Needless to say I deleted them. Maybe there would be a forthcoming conversation, maybe not.

I grabbed The Globe. It said that it was going to be sixty-five and sunny. Finally a nice day. I then pulled out the sports section. The Sox won, 5-3 to an always sold-out stadium and now had a 20-13 record. *Dammit.*

The gun bust didn't make the front page, above or below the fold. Didn't even make the police log buried in the small print. I thought that odd. Instead, the front cover was a follow-up about the US bodies that were hung by Iraqis off the bridge in the Sunni Triangle the previous March. They were apologizing for the controversy surrounding the graphic pictures they had used on a story printed in late April. To be honest, I hate that newspaper. It's a rag owned by the New York Times, and I hate Nuevo York. But the Herald is worse.

After the morning shower and putting on the off-the-rack suit from Filene's Basement in Downtown Crossing, I went out to the street to find what was left of my car. My two-door silver Pontiac *Grand Am* a-la 2001 was, for lack of a better term, fucked up.

I had bought the car new in silver because silver tends to hide scratches. When you live in the city, parking is a nightmare. If you are lucky enough or rich enough to park in a lot, the cars are so tight that you need a can opener to get it out. The doors get dinged super-easily and daily. Mostly, you have to park on the street which means that you get love-tapped on both bumpers pretty much daily as well.

The car that was left for me was not love-tapped or dinged. The tires were slashed, all of them, and the only remaining glass was in shards on the inside of the car. Upon closer inspection, my Blaupunkt car stereo with no-skip CD player was gone. It was supposed to have had an anti-theft system also but that had obviously failed. I knew better when I bought the damned thing. When I was a kid, stealing car stereos was my bread and butter. There was no such thing as anti-theft. The manufacturers use the term to charge more for them.

I didn't realize Jill was *that* pissed. So I missed a few dates, welshed on a few promises. She was a hundred and fifteen pounds soaking wet, there was no way she did that on her own. Maybe my stereo was payment for the job. Maybe she was the payment.

The car was a piece of shit anyway but it meant that I wouldn't be going to spar and I would need to take the train into work. I would also have to rec out an unmarked from the motor pool which was going to be a royal pain in the ass. All in all not a great way to start my day.

After the 'HELLOMOTO' was gone from the screen after flipping open my cellphone, I called my partner to tell him what had happened and that I was going to be late. He actually sounded relieved to not have to deal with me for a couple of extra hours and I can't say that I was distraught about that part of it either. He didn't offer to come pick me up, let's put it that way.

With the extra time to kill before I could catch the Silver line to the Red Line on the Ⓣ MBTA system, I thought it a good time to go see Roxy. Danny Mick's sister. It was early and she was probably still drunk and partying, but why not? Last I knew she didn't work nor did she have any plans to.

Ebb

Roxanne McKennie, or Roxy, still lived in the same three-decker that she grew up in. Only she now lived on a different floor. Like almost everyone in that neighborhood, you either moved out to a different floor of the same building, or you moved in with someone else who was on a different floor of their same building. Roxy had moved out and back in so many times that her parents weren't able to rent out the top floor in the likelihood that she would be back. This was one of those 'she was back' times.

The rickety wooden stairs that went up to the third floor to Roxy's place sounded and felt like I was going to fall through them. It was a good thing she didn't weigh much if she had to negotiate these stairs every day. I was a lot younger when Roxy and I had dated, so I was going in the front door on the first floor back then. The creaking and whining of the stairs must have alerted her to my presence because she was waiting for me at the landing at the top of the third floor.

"Warren Dennihan. To what do I owe the honor of your fuckin' presence?"

It was a bad split and she was obviously still not a fan. But looking at her, I was validated in my decision to break it off because she looked terrible. She was thirty and looked like every single one of those years was hard. She was once very pretty, or at least I thought she was back then.

"Hey Roxy. You look, eh, good?" I said it more like a question, which she registered.

"Go fuck ya self." She said it in a way that only Boston women can say it. A way that strips a man of everything he is, down to his bones. Emasculating just doesn't quite say it.

"C'mon Rox. Take the high road. I gotta talk to you about Danny Mick."

I reached the top of the stairs by then but she wasn't letting me onto the landing where she was standing, which put her waist by my face. I was looking up to her pleading my case.

"Seriously, let me in so we don't have to do this in public."

"What? You afraid that somebody might see you slummin'?"

"I still live down here, Rox. I don't wanna do this the hard way, just let me in. Your brother said that you would talk to me."

"My brother don't know shit about shit. What did he do now? If you're looking to bust him, he don't live here. Try downstairs."

"He's in lock-up, so I'm not lookin' for him. He sent me to talk to you. Are you gonna let me in or what?"

"You're a cop, ya cocksucka. Go get a warrant."

"I don't need a warrant. I'm not backdoorin' ya here, Rox. I'm tryin' to help the poor prick. He's in a lotta shit, hun."

"So whatever you find in here you can't use against me?"

"Are you gonna shoot at me? Stick me with somethin'? No? Then I think we're good."

She let me inside and it was a complete dumpster-fire. To say that she wasn't much of a housekeeper would be the understatement of all understatements. I don't think the place was rentable if she did move out for good. If the lower two floors were in the same condition, the best thing to do would be to watch it burn and collect the insurance.

"I love what you've done with the place. Jesus, what is that smell? Open a window or somethin' would ya?"

"The king has spoken. You gonna pay my heat bill? Open a window he says."

"It's sixty-five degrees outside and not raining for once. It might actually be warmer outside."

"You come up here to give me decorating tips Martha Stewart, or you gonna tell me what my brother did?"

"Enough with the attitude, smart-ass. I mean it. I'm in no fuckin' mood. He got busted yesterday moving half an arsenal for Slopes. ATF is gonna be all over the kid today or tomorrow to give up the goods. If he went over or was plannin' on goin' over state lines the FBI might want to get a foot in. Wherever those guns were going, they ain't gettin' there. Slopes is gonna be none to happy as it is, so he gets word that Danny Mick spoke with cops? It's gonna get a damn-sight worse."

"So what are you gonna do for him mister hot-shit?"

"You're gonna tell me where to find Slopes so I can try and reason with the guy. Maybe keep a shiv outta your brother's belly. He does his time and keeps his trap shut, he lives to be an old man. With a little luck, someday a free old man."

"And what do you get? You doin' this outta the kindness of your heart or do I gotta suck you off or somethin'?"

"You're a real class-act, Rox. Top shelf kinda girl. Tha fuck happened to you?"

"You, ya piece of shit. You chewed me up and spit me out. You don't like what you see? Look in a mirror."

"Don't put your shit on me. We were like a million years ago. I boosted shit, which made you get all hot and bothered. We rolled around and had a few laughs but that was pretty much it. I put that crap behind me, but I never forgot where I came from. I might not have been man of the year with you, Rox, but whatever you became ain't on me. You were never an angel but this goin' the extra mile. Just tell me where to find Slopes and I'll leave you to get junked up or whatever it is you do."

Quips and snappy digs at me were over. She was a sobbing mess. It might have been what I said, but more likely I was a reminder of what could have been for her. She had a choice when I broke it off with her forever ago. That choice was to get out of the life if not the neighborhood, or get sucked down into it. At thirty years old it was not too late. But she thought so, and that realization was painful.

I felt bad, but not bad enough to console her. Not bad enough to give her a hug and lie to her, tell her everything would turn out aces. Not bad enough to even sit down in that mess. I stood in front of her like an idiot waiting for her to get a grip. It seemed to take a while.

"Rox? Where do I find Slopes?"

Her midnight makeup from the night before was running off of her face. She looked through me not at me. "Abandoned warehouse down on Wash. I don't give a shit what happens to you, but don't go down there like a storm troopa. For Danny's sake."

"Yeah sure. I know. Try to take better care of yourself, Rox."

"Don't come back here Deni. Ever."

THE CALL TO DETECTIVE HOBBS INFORMING him that I was going to be later than I had expected went over without much fuss. Which was a shocker because he always wanted to be attached to my hip. If he had an inkling of what I was doing, he didn't say it. I couldn't perceive even the slightest of notes that he cared one way or the other what I was doing. Maybe he was requesting a new partner, but we had been down that road a few times in ten months. I was still his partner so we know how that played out.

I hadn't initially planned on going to see Slopes that morning. I hadn't planned on seeing Roxy that morning either, but there was no time like the present.

If, in fact, the ATF was going to talk to Danny Mick that day or the next, I thought it best to discuss the situation with Slopes before hand. Better to be proactive than reactive, sorta thing. The ball was rolling, so this last errand would hopefully end my to-do list with this project.

The abandoned warehouse on Washington Avenue looked like it was a squatter's paradise. The realtor sign said that it was going to be converted into lofts but it didn't say when. That sign was covered in graffiti so either the development was postponed, out of business, or it was just wishful thinking. The windows were boarded up but there was no door preventing an easy access.

I walked right in like I owned the place. But I was glad I didn't own it. Rats were having their way with the first floor. It was difficult to see with everything being boarded up, but I assumed they were rats given the sounds. The sun outside was shining bright for a change, but not enough to provide light inside the derelict building. The sound of the movement of the critters alluded to the fact that they were many and enormous.

The Big Dig was displacing all of the rats in Boston. Tunnels and bridges were being built to send traffic under or over the city to alleviate surface road traffic. Those tunnels were where the rodents lived and had been forced out among the two legged infestation. It got to a point where restaurants in the city were having to buy cats to roam their establishments at night. Exterminators could not keep up with the number of sightings and were ineffective when they did treat. This Chinese restaurant that I frequent has three enormous cats that they let roam the restaurant at night when the place is closed. They are the biggest domesticated cats that you have ever seen in your life outside of the jungle cats you see at the zoo. The owners never feed them.

Making my way in the dark as my eyes adjusted, I was halted by a man carrying a sawed-off shotgun. He didn't have to pump it for me to know that I was in trouble. I wouldn't be able to get to my holster and retrieve my weapon before being filled with holes.

"Wrong way cop."

I raised my hands in surrender. "No need to get all cranked up. I came alone."

"Maybe yes, maybe no. Either way you need to turn around and be on your merry way, for you get tuned up."

"I need to talk to Slopes. It's urgent."

"He ain't takin' calls at the moment."

"Even if I were to say that it's about the 200 G3s that are about to be turned over to the ATF?"

There was a pause. The only sounds were the rustling of the rats and the gears in the man's brain grinding, working on a thought. I could barely see him but I wanted to get a read. I didn't get one. Nor could I tell if he was the only person in front me.

"I'm listenin'," he finally said.

"I'm sure that I have your attention, but I need to talk to Slopes. He knows me."

"Everyone knows you. Like I said, he ain't takin' calls. You could be Jesus himself and he wouldn't see you right now."

"I'm going to reach into my jacket pocket for a business card, my cell number is on it. Will you give it to him? It's extremely important that I talk with him."

"Wicked slow muthafucka."

I slowly pulled out one of cards that were loosely strewn about the inside pocket of my suit jacket. They were always in there. I sent my suits to the cleaners after every third time I wore them and always forgot to take them out. I have no idea what dry cleaning is, but those cards never get damaged.

The card was extended out in front of me between my index and middle fingers. The armed security man moved through the dark building toward me and took the card. He didn't say another word, nor did I. The awkward silence was palpable and I read the situation like that was the end of the meeting, so I turned and left.

Outside of the building I flipped open my phone, dialing my partner after my eyes adjusted back to the bright sunlight.

"Hobbs, Deni here."

"I know, I can see that it's you on my caller ID. What's up? Are you coming in at all today?"

"Yeah, I'm not too far away. I'm — "

" — you're on Wash, yeah I know. I see you. I'm parked up on the corner."

I was stunned and speechless. I turned to my right and then left to discern where my ambusher was lurking.

He flashed the headlights on the unmarked 2003 Dodge *Intrepid* that he had obviously pulled from the motor pool. We normally use my *Grand Am* to get around as it is less conspicuous. The *Intrepid* was dark blue and although not a Crown Vic, it still screamed police car. I looked behind me to make sure that the thug whom had just received my business card didn't see that I had police company, or Hobbs and I would both be dead men.

I hightailed it down the block toward my partner. Seventy-five yards later I was seated in the passenger seat.

"Were you following me?"

"I thought we were partners. But I guess after your conversation with your buddy last night, you decided to take this case over on your own."

"You're kind of a one-trick-pony aren't ya Hobbs? Same thing all the time. We don't have a case to take over. I told you last night, he wasn't askin' for a walk or for any favors other than to talk with his sister. Did you follow me over to her place this morning?"

"The crack-den? Yeah I saw it. Cozy."

"How long have you been staking me out? Did you see who fucked up my car last night?"

"No. That wasn't a lie to buy time this morning?"

"Forget it. Just get us outta here before we get killed."

"And this morning's conversation with one Roxanne McKennie led you to an abandoned warehouse down here on Wash?" He pulled out from his pseudo-parallel parking job and continued up Washington Street. We were headed toward the Theatre District and Chinatown.

"That conversation produced the concern that whomever her brother was involved with might be just a tad-bit upset that the guns are now under the control of the police. That her brother might be in danger. I wanted to see if I could try and protect him."

"Jesus H. Christ Deni. Who's side are you on? This is textbook interference with an ongoing investigation. The only way to protect him is to keep him quiet. Keeping Daniel McKennie quiet keeps Sean Teague and the mob in business and is completely against what we are trying to do here. You know as well as I do that the only play here is to put your friend into protective custody in exchange for his flippin' Mr. Big."

Hobbs had just slipped up. He already knew that Danny Mick was working for Sean Teague, A.K.A. Slopes. He had just said so. What I didn't know was if he had already known that because he listened in to the conversation I had in room six, or if he knew that the abandoned warehouse on Wash was where Slopes was temporarily headquartered.

"First of all, the suspect is not my friend. Second, how long have you known that this was an Irish thing? "

"How stupid do you think I am? We're in the South End, just on the other side of the Channel from

Ebb

Southie. G3A4s are like the Irish calling-card. Your metro trailer park is to the mob what Pawtucket is to the Red Sox. Nothing happens in Boston involving the Irish without Sean Teague knowing or planning it. The question is what are *you* doing?"

"I'm getting out of the way while, according to you, the ATF takes over. Danny Mick getting stabbed in prison does nobody any good. He's not gonna flip on his crew, whoever it is he works for."

"Don't bullshit me Deni. You and I both know who you just saw in there. Is he 'not your friend' too?"

"As usual I don't know what you're talkin' about and I didn't see anyone in there. Pull a bitch and go see if there's anyone in there if ya don't believe me."

"I'm not turning around, we're almost outta Chinatown."

"Where are we headed?"

"Temple. We caught another case."

I tuned the car stereo into 100.7 WZLX, the classic rock station. Hobbs protested but I turned up the volume so I couldn't hear him. Queen's *Another One Bites the Dust* blared out of the tinny speakers. I hoped Freddie Mercury was wrong.

5

WITH THE THOUSANDS OF CASES THAT COME into Troop H every year, Detectives have dozens of cases going simultaneously. Real life isn't like *Law & Order* where you see cops going from place to place talking with witnesses or tracking down leads on one case at a time. In the real world, Boston anyway, we have to plan our day so we aren't jumping all over the city all day.

Traffic is always bad, with the city-wide construction it's that much worse. The Big Dig will have you re-routed one way on this day, and then you are forced onto a completely different route the next. You could never plan on how long it would take you to get

Ebb

from place to place.   If you were going to be in one borough of Boston, you tended to stay there for the day.

If we were on one side of the city, say Dorchester, we took care of all of our cases and made all of our stops that needed to be made in Dorchester. It saved on time and it saved on gas. With the conflict in the Middle-east that was making the headlines every day, oil prices were always on the rise. Gas was getting to be a concern for everyone, especially the pencil-pushers in the Staties.

The general public gets crazy when they read in the paper or see in the news that an error by the police has led to the release of an accused criminal.   I'm actually surprised it doesn't happen more.   Juggling statements from several different witnesses on several different cases in the same day; investigating leads simultaneously, sometimes we mix stuff up.   Or lose them all together.

It was almost the middle of May and my partner and I had already caught over three hundred cases so far that year.   Some of them were closed, most were not. You have to prioritize.   It sounds horrible but some things just never get investigated.   Murders and rapes are top priority while others just don't ever see the top of the pile.

Take what happened to my car for example. I'm a cop and nobody cares what happened to the *Grand Am*. What do you think happens when Cindy Citizen calls in to her local precinct? That one incident involved multiple crimes. Vandalism 1 and Larceny over. Which meant that the value of the thing that was destroyed, my car, was of a value where if there was a conviction up to ten years could be sentenced. Then the civil case which may or may not be taken up by my insurance company. Then there was Larceny over, which means that the stereo/security system that was stolen was valued at *over* $500. That was yet another punishment of up to five years. Up to fifteen years is a long time and would be a righteous bust for someone. But consider yourself lucky if you get a flat-foot to even go out and take a statement. That's what insurance adjusters are for.

The case that we caught out on Temple Place was a woman who had already complained of being stalked and threatened. She had filed a restraining order and been to court to have the temporary order upheld. But that didn't make her stalker go away.

Her apartment was allegedly broken into and her personal garments had been gone through the night before. That was yet another call that this poor woman had called into the local precinct, another case to add to the thousands. She somehow managed to go to sleep after the violation. I had to give her credit for being strong. Going to sleep would have been difficult for anyone without serious medication. But she managed, medication or no.

She woke up that morning to find her stalker in her apartment staring at her through the slats of a closet door. He had apparently never left the apartment the night before and watched her all night. The police hadn't gone out to look at her apartment yet, so she left things they way she had found them as best she could. When she found the pervert in her apartment masterbating while she showered for work, there was an altercation. She managed to get in a few good licks but took many of her own. Crimes against persons, the Staties were now involved.

The victim was in pretty bad shape but she was a fighter. She was coherent enough to give a statement of what happened before heading off to the hospital. She would live another day but she was going to have permanent scars both physically and emotionally.

This case was easy enough for us to close. Hobbs and I didn't have to wait for the Maynard lab to do the blood work. The victim had drawn blood in her struggle with the attacker, both having two different blood-types. The lab could DNA match the suspect, but the victim had told us who it was and the backlog would take forever. With the previous paper on him, his address known, and the injuries we would see when we found the asshole, this was an easy one.

We didn't have any other business on that end of the city, so we headed back to my neighborhood. The guy that was causing the victim years of therapy was from Southie. You normally stick up for your own, but not this guy. It is embarrassing that the perv lived among the people I grew up with. We might be a lot of things, but we aren't skinners.

The suspect came home after we sat on his house for about an hour and a half. The victim got more than a few good swings on her aggressor. We were twenty yards off his front stoop and we could see his wounds.

The toughest part about how that went down was that I had to go all the way back to The House to process the paperwork on that prick, then come all the way back to my neighborhood because that was the end of my shift. It would have been nicer to just go home after we collared him, I was nine blocks away. He confessed in the car ride on the way in. I wish they were all that easy.

Ebb

I was still thinking about the pervert and how much he bothered me when I got home to my three-decker that night.   Also rattling around my brain was the fact that Danny Mick was no longer in holding. Nobody would tell me where he was either.   I went down to check on him when we got back to The House after dealing with the skinner. Tell him how things were progressing. He was gone and off the books. ATF pick him up?   Shipped over to South Bay awaiting arraignment? Nobody knew.

I grabbed a bottle of cheap Irish Whiskey off of the counter as I walked into my house and turned on the TV to NESN. I wanted to forget about Hobbs, Danny Mick, Roxy, and the perv. The Indians were at Fenway again and my beloved Red Sox were not fairing as well. Kind of a shit day all-around.

But it got worse. I took off my jacket, draped it off the back of my recliner, reacquired my bottle of booze, and made my way to the kitchen for a glass when I saw that someone was already waiting for me in there.

I reached for to my armpit for my service weapon. My hand never made it to the Glock. He had me dead-to-rights. His Smith & Wesson *Model 500* hand cannon was pointed straight at my chest. The revolver didn't hold but six shots, but he wouldn't need that many. A fifty caliber projectile through my chest at that range would leave a big enough hole to stick a hand through, let alone necessitate six rounds. Even if I had my nine millimeter in my hand I was grossly out-gunned.

I could scream. My tenants above me would hear me most likely. But would they do anything? In my neighborhood screaming and gunshots were not uncommon. People only paid attention when it got really quiet.

"You're slipping Deni. Never would have been able to get the drop on you back in the day."

"Age. It's a bitch. Nice to see ya Slopes. Maybe you shoulda called first."

"You were lookin' for me?"

"Yeah but I guess you were wicked busy and couldn't talk. Danny Mick. You seen him lately?"

"I heard he got snagged."

"Doin' your work, Sean."

"What ever do you mean, Officer?"

"If we were playin' cops and bad-guys we could do games, dance for days. But I reached out today as a guy from the neighborhood. That used to mean somethin'."

Whether that six pound cannon that he had trained on me was getting too heavy or if he felt like things were maybe getting more comfortable, I don't know. But he lowered his gun, keeping it at his side in case he needed it. He stared at me with his one sharp eye while mulling over the situation.

"Care for a Whiskey?" I raised the bottle from my hand to show him it wasn't top-shelf.

"One."

"Then be a sweetheart and hand me two glasses out of the cupboard behind you." 'Sweetheart' sounded like 'sweet-hot' from a Bostonian and it's meant to sound sarcastic. I'm not sure if I said it to throw him off or piss him off, but in any event Slopes didn't bite.

"Fuck that. Take a pull from the bottle."

"Fair enough."

I unscrewed the top, took a pull and handed him the bottle. He took it with his left hand, his right still on his gun. I didn't really want to share a bottle with him. His Bell's Palsy made him a drooler. There was always a small pool of saliva on the right side of his mouth that sagged with the entire right side of his face. His eye and cheek sloped downward like it was about to slide off of his skull. Thus his nickname.

He took a generous pull himself on the left side of his mouth, all the while keeping his eye fixed on me.

Ebb

The first sip of the cheap crap that I could afford always made me wince. Not so with Slopes. I don't know what he normally drinks but the burn I felt going down was absent from his chest. Irish boys can drink, but I think that Sean Teague could bury me. He wiped his mouth with his sleeve before he continued.

"So did you come to see me because you have information for me, or did you want some from me?" He kept the bottle.

"Let's cut the bullsh. You and I both know that Danny Mick and his boy were pickin' up and delivering a shit-ton of assault rifles for you. I don't know what you were going to do with them or where they came from, all I know is that he had them. That many guns with everything but a four-leaf clover stamped to the side of 'em means that he is a big-dog now. No state case anymore. They are gonna wanna trade up. I talked to Danny Mick last night off the record. He's scared."

"He fuckin' should be."

"Not of the time. Of you."

"Like I said."

"He says he will do the time like a man, but he wants to maybe get out someday. Whoever you got on him, have them protect him in there not kill him."

"Deni I ain't sayin' that them guns was mine. But *if* they were, they had a purpose." He took another

Ebb

long pull of the bottle. Apparently 'one' meant one bottle, not one drink.

"I think everyone gets that. From what I can tell we had an eager rookie who was bored. You got unlucky. In your business you win some, lose some. No need for the kid to earn a shiv."

"It is what it is. Why do you care, Deni?"

"He asked me. And I knew him since back when he was still on the tit. I used to go out with his sister, Roxy."

"Shit, Deni. Everyone used to go out with Roxy. She been rode more than the nags at Suffolk Downs, man."

"Like I said, we look out for our own."

"Irregardless, big risk for you," he said.

"No shit English professor. This is unofficial. My partner knows that it's probably you who orchestrated this thing. But without Danny Mick, nothing gets back to you. The other guy died on the way to the hospital, but I'm sure you know that. The guns will be gone through at ballistics, but if there is nothing there …. Not our case anymore anyway, like I said. I am curious as to where he is though."

"Who? Danny Mick? Fuck should I know. You got him. You just talked to him."

"Had him. He was pulled out of holding sometime today. But no record and nobody knows

538

where he is. Which is wicked fucked up. I figured you know more about where he is than me."

"And why is that? He's at your house."

"Because you have a much more vested interest in where he is than I do. I am just curious, you should be worried."

"Rumor is that ATF has him. I'll find him. You know I will."

"Yeah I'm sure. Listen, he's a sweet kid deep down. Just let him do his time. But lemme ask you a question. Just between you and me slopes, why did you have the kid go on this one? And why in broad daylight? With stolen tags? Somethin' that big — "

" — what are we friends now or somethin'? You give me a swig of your shit booze and you get to ask me things that are outta left field? Not my guns. How many times I gotta tell you?"

"Okay guy. I guess not."

"As far as your request goes? He keeps quiet, he lives. That's my guess anyways, since it ain't my thing. It's how things work in prison. You snitch, you die. Thanks for the hospitality."

He put the open bottle down on the counter behind him and walked past me, out of my kitchen, out of my house.

The visit from Slopes was a bad way to end my day. If that was how it ended. But it wasn't. I was pondering if Bell's Palsy was contagious and if whatever lived in Sean's spit was killed off by alcohol and whether I needed to go to the liquor store, when I heard the locks on my front door rattling.

I was in no mood for company. My car was totaled, my partner was the same douche-bag he was every day, I risked sanctions by sticking my neck out for the kid brother of the girl I used to bang when I was a hood-rat, I had to deal with a poor woman who had begged for help and didn't get any until she was almost killed by the asshole who was tormenting her from my neighborhood, and I had received an unwelcome visit at gunpoint from none other than Sean Teague himself. I was kinda done for the day.

Ebb

At some drunken point in our brief relationship I had made the mistake of giving Jill a spare key to my place. You had to unlock both deadbolts and the lock in the door knob to get inside, a process that she was having difficulty with.

When she finally did gain entrance, I was standing there with the second to the last glass remaining in the bottle of Whiskey in hand. She had been drinking. I had been drinking. One of us was swaying.

"Come right in. Please."

"I've come to tell you how much I hate you Deni."

"Take a number. Hey, couldn't you have called to tell me that?"

"I wanted to see your face when I told you that you're a piece of shit."

"Ah. How do I look? The same?"

"Why can't you be a good guy, Deni? You always make promises, and you always break'em. I'm a good girl. A catch. Why do I put up with your shit?"

"Good question. Come have a drink and we can talk about it for days."

"I shouldn't drink anymore. Besides I am very mad at you. I don't drink with people I'm mad at."

"I'm pretty pissed at you to, but a drink seems appropriate. Why did you have to trash my car?"

"What are you talking about?"

"Are you going to deny having someone kill my car? You seen it? Go look at it."

"You're drunk," she said as she held herself up with the help from the wall in my parlor.

"No shit, so are you."

"I'm giving you back your keys. I need to date someone more like me."

"Ha. Rich from Connecticut? Good luck finding one of those in this neighborhood."

"Educated with a real job, asshole."

"Yeah that makes sense. A business guy? Somebody with money is more your speed?"

"Fuckin-A. But I'm not shallow. I don't need rich, Deni. I just need the guy to be decent."

"That's nice. Keep in touch."

She left and soon after I blacked out.

THERE AREN'T ANY FEDERAL HOLDING facilities or prisons in Massachusetts. How Governor Mitt Romney or any other before him had managed to keep the Federal Bureau of Prisons out of the state was anyone's guess. Instead, what the US Marshals, FBI, and ATF were forced to do with any of their federal persons of interest, was to incrementally pay through the teeth.

The state of Massachusetts, like any other state, have criminals who's acts elevate them to a federal level. If you could call those acts elevated. Most states have at least one federally funded property for super-max, max, medium or minimum-security work camps to house their felons. But those from the commonwealth state need to either be shipped to another state or federal dollars are spent to house them in county facilities.

The closest federal lock-up to Boston was in Berlin, New Hampshire. Unfortunately that facility was only medium security, with only two rows of chain-link fence topped with razor wire. Most men who were either waiting for such elevated trials or had already been convicted necessitated much more aggressive restraints and protocols. So the state charged the government, and therefore every taxpayer in the country, to house them in with the Massachusetts locals.

The Middlesex County jail in Cambridge sits atop the no longer used Superior Courthouse. It is one of the only high-rise maximum security prisons in the country. The courthouse is no longer used because the building was constructed when lead paint and Asbestos were used. The jail above was used with the same materials but when you get your hand caught in the cookie-jar, a little Mesothelioma is deemed part of the punishment. The jail was supposed to be abandoned as well for the same public health reasons, but with overcrowding there was no place to relocate those that call the jail their temporary home.

The high-rise was originally designed to house 160 inmates, though the building that was certified too great a health risk to hold that many routinely holds between 340-400. The cells therein that once held one inmate, possibly two, now had three and sometimes four.

This facility is where they had moved Daniel McKennie to be detained pre-trial. The ATF and the federal prosecutor wanted to move him away from his possible cohorts and put him into protective federal custody. There were a few very real problems with this design. There was no federal facility for him in the general vicinity, which meant he would need to be moved up to Berlin, NH or out to the Super-Max state facility in Walpole. Also the suspect refused to cooperate in giving up his crew. The federal prosecutor assigned to the case couldn't justify the added expense of protective custody in Walpole, nor move him north to Berlin when the person he wanted to protect wouldn't flip and wouldn't ask to be PC'd. So the prosecutor stuck him close by in Middlesex County.

Danny Mick was housed in gen-pop at Cambridge, where he shared a cell with two other inmates. This was not his first time he had been incarcerated, though it was the first time at Cambridge. Danny Mick had been in a juvenile detention center, police lock-ups, even other county facilities in his young past. Consequently he had run into many of the inmates he was currently housed with from the commission of his past misdeeds or during the punishment he received from doing them.

He seemed to be getting on well with those he had come in contact with, both old acquaintances and new. The block was set up in such a way where he felt cautiously optimistic about his new living arrangement, even if temporary.

General Population on E was a long corridor with a polished-concrete floor and light blue, painted, metal caged doors to the cells on both right and left sides. Some metal picnic style tables were bolted to the floor up the middle of the corridor for when one side or the other was let out for rec or chow. There were very few times, at most once per week, when both sides of E block were let out of their cells at the same time for assembly.

Danny Mick had been in Cambridge for roughly three weeks, was getting fairly comfortable with his situation and surroundings, when all hell broke loose.

Memorial Day assembly on Monday, May 31, 2004, was scheduled to be the same as every Memorial Day of years past. Barbecued burger-like substance and hot dogs on stale white bread were served along with a movie projected onto a white, prison, bedding sheet. The same movie was shown every year, Oliver Stone's *Born on the Fourth of July*. Despite the violence in the movie, none had broken out in the jail since it was first shown in the early 90s. It was, therefore, green-lighted for every year henceforth. The prison population seemed to enjoy mixing company with those whom they were not normally allowed social contact, whether they actually watched the movie or not.

Until 2004.

The festivities were cut short because one of the best and brightest housed there decided to clog the all-in-one sink-toilet. The building was old, the plumbing just as vintage. The miscreant stuffed the toilet and continued to flush repeatedly, flooding just his cell at first then backing up the entire line on E. Others began to join in on the fun, stuffing and continually flushing their cells as well. Though the jail is a twenty-four-seven facility, the jail didn't have a maintenance presence on the holiday weekend. The flooding escalated past the point of no return. The building was already more than double past the intended capacity and therefore there was no place to move the inmates. The water flowing out of the toilets and exploding out of the sinks disallowed use of the cells and bunks for sleep. There was also no longer anyplace for evacuating bladders or bowels.

Emotions and tensions ran high while the COs that had the least tenure and couldn't get out of working Memorial Day tried to figure out what to do. Mini fights broke out, which brought out the lug teams, but there was so much chaos it was impossible to squash every skirmish.

Other floors began to flood as well as the entire plumbing system became clogged. Cracks and holes from E egressed water onto floors below but not so much water as to keep the water from rising rapidly. The same such cracks and crevices were depositing water from floors above, down into E.

The toilet-water had risen to a foot above the concrete floor and was still rising. The entire block was wading around as lockdown was thought to cause more problems than allowing them to find higher ground either in the cells or the rec area.

The opportunity was seized. Danny Mick had been up on a top bunk in a cell that was not his own. He was visiting a new-found friend while he waited out the flood. The friend was pulled out of his own cell by a couple of inmates and in all of an instant, Danny Mick was cornered in a cell with three others that were not his cellmates nor belonged in that one. Two others positioned themselves outside the cell to stand watch. Not that anyone would be looking at what was transpiring, there was too much else going sideways to worry about individual cells.

"What's going on boys?" Danny Mick knew what was happening, nervous jokes not withstanding.

Ebb

The leader smiled, then shrugged his shoulders. "It is what it is, kid."

He was about to ask what his attacker meant, when the three pulled him off the high bunk he was using to stay dry. He didn't have time to scream or call for help. His face was shoved to the floor under the rising water that was geysering out of the toilet. The drowning was not a painful enough way to die, so the plastic cutlery that was given for the makeshift barbecue meal had been fashioned to a very sharp point, and then used to stab him too many times to count.

Danny Mick tried to fight back, but with three men holding him under water and his inability to acquire air, the fight was all but impossible. His lungs burned, desperately trying to tell him that they were in need of oxygen. That burning only being surpassed by the burning from each thrust that was being driven into his body, each stab adding to the agony. The jagged edge of the molded and flimsy plastic tearing his flesh both on the way in and out of his body. The water around him was turning pink from the blood and shredded meat escaping this thrashing body. Danny looked more and more like chum being submerged into shark-infested waters. The more he flailed, the more his heart pumped blood out of the increasing number of holes in his torso.

Ebb

The thrashing and splashing was doing nothing to get him on the other side of the mortal danger he was in. He pulled at prison jumpsuits, dug his fingernails into what ever skin he could find purchase on. To no avail. The walls began to close in on the small room around him. His flailing waned. Only his bleeding increased.

When Danny Mick's body had gone slack, his head was pulled out of the water. As if by miracle he still had a very slight pulse. The lead aggressor dug the utensil into the jugular as far as the makeshift shiv would go and sawed the skin from jaw hinge to jaw hinge. The neck opened and the tongue was pulled out through the new hole to cover his adam's apple.

The grisly body was then pushed back into the crimson water. Hands were rinsed in the water's tide and the weapon was hidden as the attackers left the confines of the cell.

The group of assassins then receded into the crowd and commotion in the corridor. With their mission accomplished, they were free to wade through the water and wreak more havoc with the rest of the inhabitants on E.

MY MEMORIAL DAY WEEKEND THAT YEAR WAS pretty boring. Lonely and boring. I was no longer dating anyone and I didn't have any plans with friends because I don't have many friends. The department was looking for volunteers to work because nobody wanted to work the holiday. Barbecues and such. Whether the detectives requesting the day off had someone to remember was a question I didn't care to ask, but I did volunteer.

What I mean by volunteer is that I agreed to work the holiday. They were going to pay me, and they were going to pay me big-time. The Massachusetts State Police have holidays, floating holidays, sick and personal days besides the vacation days that they give their employees. Memorial Day was a paid holiday for Monday. I worked the weekend and Monday which meant that I got twenty hours of overtime and double-dipped on Monday's pay. Time and a half each weekend day and on Monday, on top of a day that I was already getting paid ten hours for.

I needed the money. I still needed a new car. Three weeks and my insurance still hadn't come through with a check for a new one. I was thinking of upgrading anyway. The two-door sport coupe was way too small for me. Trucks and large vehicles are impractical in the city but they are roomy and good in the snow. I had my eye on the Cadillac *Escalade*.

The weekend was a washout anyway. It rained or was overcast every day. Temperatures never reached sixty. Why not get paid to be wet and miserable?

Saturday the twenty-ninth I spent a good chunk at the MMA gym in Brookline. When you grow up in Southie you learn how to fight early in life. Period. Even the dorks and homos fought. Call it a Darwin thing or whatever you want, but in Southie you either learn how to defend yourself or you don't make it out of puberty. I had picked up Mixed Martial Arts at a fairly young age, added to my street fighting abilities made me a pretty good fighter. I took several amateur bouts, a few semi-pro fights, and two UFC fill-ins as an undercard. That is where I met Kenny Florian.

Kenny was a Dover boy who was a natural athlete. He did the soccer thing and got a scholarship for it, Boston College I think. He had come up to MMA a few years back and made his debut the year prior. He was a black-belt in Brazilian Jiu-Jitsu like myself, so we sparred regularly. He was training for the Drew Ficket fight in July and I was training because I had a lesser known fight coming up as well. We were both light or welterweights, depending on the fight. He was a true lightweight, 5'10" and 145 pounds. He would gain weight to go up to welters. I was a true middleweight, 6' and 170 pounds but cut weight to make the fights. It was a good arrangement. We weren't friends so much as we worked out together.

MMA was just one of the ways that I made extra money on the side. When I got promoted to Detective in Troop H, they gave a lousy $5k bump. That amounts to two bucks more an hour, before taxes. Since I was never going to get promoted again, that meant that I was stuck at that pay scale ad infinitum. The only thing I had to look forward to was my yearly cost of living increase, which everybody knows doesn't cover the rate of inflation. Meaning that over the course of my career, I would progressively make less money. They wonder why cops go dirty.

Ebb

My tenants on the floor above me and on the top floor of my three-decker paid my mortgage, which was kind of another way to supplement my meager income. Though I had to set money aside like I still paid a mortgage for when stuff needed to be fixed. When you live in a building that was built in the early 1900s, things tend to go bump in the night pretty regularly, and my tenants aren't exactly gentle on my stuff.

And yet another way to add a little coin to my pockets was to take on some PI work. Private Investigators sometimes get a bad wrap; but with the caseload that cops have, citizens often have to get someone who is a bit more committed to their cause. I had run into a couple of PI's and lawyers on some of my cases, and had taken on a couple of side jobs through them which paid very well. This was completely against Mass State Police rules and if I was caught, not only would I be sanctioned and probably fired, but I could face criminal charges as well. I never took a side job on one of my own cases so I figured criminal charges were a stretch. Also I knew specifically of many cops who were on the take in one way or another, so my secret was safe as long as I kept theirs. Of course my partner didn't know. I hoped he didn't at least.

I wasn't getting rich by any stretch, but I wasn't struggling like others within the department. I had to piece-meal a living as best I could with whatever talents

554

I have, which made free-time and friends a pipe dream. Living in the city, or any major city I would imagine, isn't inexpensive. In Boston, houses were going to the yuppies. Southie has a ton of old buildings that get bought up because they are run-down. The buyers and flippers sell to those who can pay. Nobody can make it in the city on forty grand unless they are on the government tit.

I took Sunday off from the gym, but only because it was closed. Many things in the city were closed down for the holiday weekend. But not the bars.

Boston has a proud tradition of drinking, be it holiday or no. We are a proud heritage of both social and binge drinking. Add to that culture fifty-eight colleges and universities scattered about the city and you have yourself a time. If you throw something over your shoulder in Boston, it will hit a bar or a liquor store. On holiday weekends, the population as a whole hits the sauce pretty hard.

With alcohol comes drunken fights and nonsense. But otherwise crime is pretty low during long weekends. Major crime. The local cops handle all of the drunk and disorderlies, noise complaints, fake IDs, and the other petty bullsh. So while they are busy filling up their paddy wagons, detectives like me are bored. I had very little to detect.

Ebb

One of the drunken assaults was pretty bad and the college chick who's college boyfriend got beaten-up was encouraging her lover to press charges. That is how I got involved. The city cops aren't allowed to handle major crimes. The guy who was roughed-up was in need of hospitalization. The crime actually fit the guidelines for attempted murder, so I went to the hospital to take statements. The boyfriend was embarrassed that he lost the fray and wanted to just lick his wounds and call it a weekend. Man-up. I kinda respected that. But the girlfriend was having none of the man-code and wanted to press charges. Only she can't, it has to be the person who was assaulted or else the charges won't stick. So around and around we went trying to figure out if I had a case to pick up or not. Technically, the state, meaning me or an Assistant District Attorney, could just make a call to investigate without the victim but let's face it — who adds work when they are already overworked and underpaid?

Investigating other cases that I had ongoing was an exercise in futility. Nobody wants their long weekend ruined by scheduling appointments with cops, so those were on hold. My partner had opted for the holiday off, so that was another hindrance on focusing on our open cases.

So that was my Sunday.

Ebb

Monday was much of the same. Hangovers and late starts meant that even the phone calls into the station were sparse. I putzed around after going to the gym but that was about it. I should have felt a little guilty for taking the equivalent of double-time and a half for doing nothing but I didn't. Even Tits didn't come in on Monday, not that I complained.

I was waiting for the dial-up internet modem to finish connecting and squawking static at me when the call was patched through to my desk. I lifted the receiver to my phone, the receptionist told me I had a call on line 4. I was surprised that there were enough calls coming into the station to extend to the fourth line and thankful for something to do that didn't require the internet. I was no good at it.

"Detective Dennihan speaking."

"Your buddy didn't keep his end." The voice was low and muffled like they were trying to disguise it with something over the phone.

"My buddy huh? Who is this?"

"He wasn't gonna keep his mouth shut. Now it's shut for good."

"Who? What are you talking about?"

"He woulda squealed and begged if he hadn't drowned."

Ebb

"I've got no time for pranks, guy. Either tell me who this is and what this is about or I'm gonna hang up."

"You should have taken better care of him Deni. Hiding him at Cambridge isn't hiding him."

"For the last time, what in the hell are you talking about?"

"Danny Mick didn't leave me a lotta room. Had to be done."

The caller had my attention. I had completely forgotten about Danny Mick, to be honest. Out of sight, out of mind. After my talk with Slopes, the subject never crossed my mind again. I had other cases, other things going on. I didn't even know where he was. I figured the ATF had hidden him somewhere.

"Who is this? What did you do?"
Click.

Thoughts ran through my head at about a million miles an hour. *What happened to Danny Mick? Why didn't the ATF move him out of state? Why wasn't he better protected? Who just called me? Was it Sean Teague that went after him? Why? The caller was right, Cambridge was no place to hide him if that's what the plan was. He shoulda been up in Berlin or Walpole. Why was he in Cambridge? Was he really there? Probably a prank call.*

I got on the phone and called the Middlesex County jail in Cambridge. The phone rang unanswered for what seemed like forever. When someone finally did pick up, I learned that it was absolute pandemonium over there. I had to give my name, rank and badge number several times to several different people before someone was finally allowed to tell me anything at all.

" …. these guys flood the place all the time but never this bad. The plumbing wasn't designed for this many — "

" — I'm not callin' for an architectural lesson, chief. I got an anonymous call that said a possible inmate there, Daniel McKennie, is in danger or has already been killed. First, can you tell me if he *is* there?"

There was some fumbling and rustling of papers that I could hear on my end of the phone.

"C'mon guy. Yes or no? Simple question, simple answer."

"It's very chaotic here right now. Give me a min …. uh, yeah. Here he is. Daniel McKennie. E block."

" 'Uh, yeah here he is' like you see him or 'uh, yeah here he is' on some piece of paper or on a computer screen?"

"Screen."

"Get him out of E block."

"You don't have any authority to demand that we move an inmate."

"Do you want the death of an inmate under your care tied to you? I am officially notifying you that there has been a threat against an inmate that you just confirmed is incarcerated there. If something happens to him because you didn't respond to that threat, both you and the Middlesex County are in for some serious shit."

"If we moved an inmate every time someone was threatened, we — "

" — I'm on my way down there. So help me if anything has happened to him, I will make it my mission in life to make you pay for it." I might have broken the phone when I hung up.

WHEN I ARRIVED AT THE MIDDLESEX COUNTY jail in Cambridge, the place was on total lock-down. Mine was not the only Memorial Day that was ruined. Higher ups had been called to come in as there had been massive flooding and riots were beginning to form on some of the various floors. Nobody had time for me until things were settled down.

I sat in the visitor's waiting area for hours as I watched modified school buses pull up and get filled with shackled prisoners. They were being moved to other facilities within the counties. Suffolk County at both South Bay and Shattuck, Middlesex County at

Billerica, and even the minimum security at Roslindale were all going to be filled up with the three hundred ninety-four inmates that were housed at Cambridge. These facilities, like Cambridge, were already beyond capacity but the new prisoners would all be put in the hole if necessary. The solitary confinements of those other facilities were not going to be so solitary by the end of the day. Two and three inmates in a tiny cell designed to be just big enough for one. Those facilities would also now go on lock-down as they had to ensure that inmates couldn't commingle.

So I waited. And I sat. Then I waited some more. I scrutinized every inmate that was led onto a bus to see if I could spot Danny Mick. I did not. All of their jumpsuits were saturated and although it was raining I thought it unlikely that the light precipitation was the reason.

Three hours after my arrival, Deputy Sheriff Dominguez finally came to get me from the waiting area. Personally.

"I'm sorry to have kept you waiting Detective Dennihan. As you can imagine we have had quite a time of it."

"I see that. When I called they said there was a flood, everyone and their brother is soaked." Everyone except him. The Deputy was as starched as the ironing board his clothes were pressed on. His tanned skin looked darker in the white uniform. He looked Latin, of course. Puerto Rican maybe. His accent didn't give any hint of Spanish or Boston.

"It has gone beyond that, I'm afraid."

"How so?"

"We will have to investigate, but it seems that the flood was a diversion."

"Was my guy the cause of the diversion?"

"Come into the office over here so we can speak in private." We were already speaking privately but I followed him.

Deputy Dominguez led me to an office that was behind the empty reception window. There was no need to staff it, there was not going to be any visitors today. Once the door was closed I was offered a seat in front of a desk, the Deputy sat behind it. Whether it was his desk or not I didn't know nor do I know now.

"The plumbing is bad here, Detective. The inmates often flood the blocks to mix up the tedium of — "

" — yeah, I don't mean to interrupt but I already got the plumber's guide to the galaxy. What does that have to do with my guy? Where is he, and is he safe?"

"'Your guy' huh?"

Ebb

"Deputy. You've had me waiting for an eternity and I'm sure that you know why. I called to ask about inmate Daniel McKennie, because I received a call sayin' that he was either going to die or already had. He's *my guy* because it was put on my plate. I'm sure you know all of this, so why are we having to go through the charade?"

"Who did you receive the call from?"

"I have no idea. His voice may have been disguised. Definitely unidentified."

"Do you have a guess?"

"No not really. My *guess* would be that Danny Mi .... inmate McKennie, decided to fess up who he was working for to the ATF, and whoever that was decided they didn't want to be implicated."

"You are not the detective working his case? Because you are listed as one of the two arresting detectives on his paperwork."

The pullover was a traffic misdemeanor, so LaDue would get credit for that but didn't for the felony arrest. He gets credit for the ticket issued for driving an unregistered vehicle. He might even share credit for finding a stolen vehicle. When the guns were found, however; the questioning and therefore the case was turned over to detectives. Hobbs and I were still listed as the cops linked to the case. When we turned it over to the ATF, they should have had their own investigators

564

question McKennie and those investigators should have been the people listed. The fact that I was still on his paperwork was confusing.

"Wait. I'm still on his paperwork? So he really is still *my guy*. Didn't the ATF bring him here to hide him for pre-trial? We turned this case over to the ATF like three weeks ago."

"Yes but he refused to speak with anyone but you. The federal prosecutor tried to put him in protective custody but he wouldn't go. He refused to cooperate."

"That's wicked strange. I'm still on his paperwork even though my partner and I turned him over to ATF is odd to say the least, but whatever. Where is he now?"

"He is dead. Brutally attacked and killed."

He let that sink in and I was thankful for the moment of time. My mind raced as to how a suspect this big had fallen through the cracks. Jurisdictional Purgatory.

"Shit. I'm too late. What happened?"

"Either the flood was used as a diversion, like I said, or whoever did it seized the flood as an opportunity. He was stabbed more times than we had time to count so far. We will have to send him out for an autopsy, but at first glance he was drowned while he was being stabbed so nobody would hear him scream. Have you ever heard of a Colombian Necktie?"

"Ah Jesus. Yeah. Slice from ear to ear and pull out his tongue through like a necktie."

"Correct. That is how they treat snitches."

"That is how who treats snitches? I thought they normally get a buck-fifty."

A buck-fifty is referred to a large slice across a rat's face. The ensuing stitches to sew up the person's face requires a minimum of hundred fifty. When another felon sees the facial scar, they know not to trust the person because of the buck-fifty. That is why the slicing is done to the face.

"There are several ways to deal with a rat, Detective. Testifying in open court earns you more than a buck-fifty."

"So he *was* going to testify."

"That's just it. We don't have any record that he was. In fact, that is why he didn't get PC'd. He refused to testify. We still don't have a record of who he was working for. If we had known, at the very least we would have mandated stay-aways."

A stay-away is exactly that. It is a list of inmates and visitors that are to stay away from one another.

Sometimes it is because they just don't get along. Other times it might be that they are witnesses against each other in the same case. There are all sorts of reasons to keep two or more inmates away from one another. Working in the same crew suspected of gun trafficking on an outstanding case definitely qualified. The trouble being that they had no idea from whom to keep Danny Mick away from.

"Then why the necktie? Why kill him? That's what the person on the phone said to me. He 'wasn't gonna keep his mouth shut'. That it 'had to be done'. Why would somebody think that? If he wasn't going to testify, according to you, who thought that he was?"

"We will investigate. But in all probability, with the chaos and rookies that we had on E? We are not hopeful in finding out, let's put it that way."

"So the kid is dead and nobody is ever going to pay for it? Have you questioned the Block? It had to be someone on E. We can look at known associates of everyone on his floor. Probably won't be long before we make a connection."

" You aren't listening. We've had a massive flood. Mini riots. We had all we could do to lock down the place, we certainly haven't questioned anyone yet."

"So the guy gets away with it?"

"I didn't say that. What I am saying is that it will be difficult if not impossible. We will do our best. We'll start questioning inmates in the morning, look at all the camera footage. But the hard truth?" He didn't finish his question. He didn't have to.

"I'm sure his sister will thank you," I mumbled.

"What was that Detective?"

"Nothing. Which Morgue is he going to?"

Three hundred ninety-four were being transferred out of Cambridge that night. Three hundred ninety-three to other cells, one was headed for the slab at Shattuck.

9

OUR CASE INVOLVING DANIEL McKENNIE had
been over for weeks. I had forgotten about it, truthfully,
and there wasn't any outstanding paperwork for me to
sign that reminded me of it. Three weeks had gone by
and neither my partner nor I had mentioned it or, as far
as I'm concerned, gave it another thought. We were
busy with other cases and he was the ATF's problem,
supposedly. I never transferred him, but I assumed that
Hobbs did. He was my senior after all.

Only Danny Mick, the poor prick, had never
made it that far. I desperately wanted to go down to the
Boston office of the Bureau of Alcohol Tobacco and
Firearms and find out what in the hell was going on

down there.   How had they botched up a witness so badly that he was slaughtered in prison?

That is what I wanted to do. I had already stuck my neck out for the kid, beyond what was reasonable in the eyes of the law and my police department. I wasn't in any trouble, yet.   But if I made a huge fuss over a dead witness from my neighborhood, that could very well change. What good would it do anyway? Danny Mick got himself involved with the Irish mob, Sean Teague A.K.A Slopes, and was now dead. My getting more involved was not going to change that situation. So what I actually did was nothing. I ain't proud of it, but the truth is the truth.

So I let it go with the exception of going to see his sister, Roxy.   The County lock-ups don't send a Correctional Officer or anybody else to the homes of those that are survived by the deceased inmate. They send a kite, a form letter, to those that are on the inmate's contact sheet.   They will also reach out by telephone to those on said sheet. If those provide no response, they may go so far as to look up the phone numbers of those that visited the inmate at the prison from the visitor sign-in sheets.

They do this not for humanity reasons, not because they want to notify next of kin. Not at all. They do this for budgetary reasons. They want somebody to claim the body so that the funeral costs could be deferred to the families that created the societal rejects. The hope was that the family member or loved ones would want better arrangements than what the county would provide. Cemetery space, or any land near the city, came at a premium. Plots were expensive. So the bodies were unceremoniously thrown into an incinerator. The ashes were then disposed of along with the other biohazardous material from the medical wing. More often than not, the bodies were not claimed, either the families couldn't afford better or they didn't care. So ziplock bags of human ashes were disposed of with used syringes, bandages, and other medical waste.

I know what Roxanne said the last time we spoke. I know she didn't want to see me. I didn't want to see her either. But I knew what would happen to Danny Mick if she was not properly notified. If the state could get through to her on a phone, which was a big if, it was a tough way to learn of his death. If she opened her mail, another big if as I had seen Roxy's apartment, it would be an even tougher way to find out. 'We regret to inform you' …. and 'hey by the way come pick you your corpse so we don't incur any further expenses for the taxpayer'.

Boston can be a hard city, with hard citizens. None more so than those who reside in Southie. But nobody deserves to hear that their brother was a human pincushion by form letter, no matter what the guy did. So I took it upon myself to go see her.

Tuesday, June first, I took some personal time and headed over to Roxy's place. I waited until later in the morning because I knew that she was not an early riser. Actually that's bullsh. The real reason was that starting off your day with that kind of news is almost as bad as reading it in a letter. But what time of the day is the best time to learn of a sibling's death? I was just avoiding it for as long as possible. In any case, I went to the gym, beat the shit out of some kid that wanted to spar with me, and headed over.

I was still without a car, so I was forced to use a Dodge *Intrepid* from the motor pool. It was unmarked but a five year old could have told you it was a cop car. Traffic parted for me like I was Moses, and those that were contemplating something illegal waited until I was out of view. There were some people in my neighborhood that worked, because there were plenty of places to park on the street.

The stairs leading up to Roxy's dump creaked and groaned as they had the last time, as I'm sure they did every time someone used them. But unlike the last time, she was not waiting for me on the landing at the top of the stairs.

I don't remember how many times I knocked on the door. Nor do I remember how many sets of knocks.

Ebb

I know that it was a lot. I know I waited for a long time in between, waiting for her to wake up out of her hangover or drug-induced coma or whatever. I remember that the inside of the windows to her front door were so dirty that she could have been on the other side of it and I wouldn't have been able to see her.

Through all of it, there was no answer. I was trying to decide whether I should wait out in the car for her to come home, or if I should just come back later. Those two choices were oscillating back and forth in my head long enough for me to take out the pins that I always keep in my wallet.

I might have mentioned that I used to do some shady things when I was a kid. Steal car radios, the occasional car. A few B and E's. When it comes to picking locks, I have a gift.

For those that have called a locksmith in the past, you know that they have a wrench and some specialized pins for lifting the tumblers inside the lock. I don't need those. I have titanium pins that easily fit into my wallet. I have a few in there as backups but I only use two of them at a time. One to turn the bottom of the lock, the other to lift each tumbler one-by-one. This is what takes most people the longest amount of time. There are a minimum of five tumblers inside the key hole, which is what the high points of a key hit to lift them. Each one has to be lifted and stay disengaged in order for the lock to turn. Getting each one to lift before being able to turn the lock open can be exasperating. You then have to do this for each lock on the door. In Southie, the front doors always have a minimum of two and a deadbolt can have as many as ten tumblers.

I was inside of Roxy's apartment in under forty-seconds. She had two deadbolts plus her door handle. The stink that wafted at me when the door opened was nauseating. It was the olfactory equivalent to a punch to the face. I guess that is what you deserve when you break into someone's home.

The kitchen was to my right as I entered the front door. Against every signal by body was sending to my brain, every signal that my brain was communicating back to my muscles, I continued inside. I was forced to bury my nose into the outside of my right elbow, my eyes were watering like I had been sprayed by a skunk.

It was unlikely that she had any dishes or glassware in her cupboards. They were all in her sink. Food had been left out on the counter. What it was would require a biology degree and a microscope. She wasn't in the kitchen, which is all I needed to know for the moment so I didn't enter any further than that into the doorway.

I turned around, heading into the apartment. The TV was on in the parlor but it was static. She either didn't have cable or it was shut off. The mess was the same as the day that I had gone there. The same exact piles of detritus that prevented me from taking a seat on my visit three weeks prior, had I had a notion to, were still where they had been at that time.

I moved my way down the hall toward what I assumed would be a bedroom. The first doorway I came upon to my left was the bathroom. I am unsure how one would call that a bathroom, except that there was a toilet and bathtub. I wondered how one could get clean in a place that was dirtier than the human that needed cleansing. Mold was growing in the grout between the tiles. Mold that was at a point of taking on a life of its own. There was no decorative shower curtain, just the liner that hung open as if to invite one into the sad excuse for a shower. That liner was also covered in mold. The toilet paper roll contained none, and every cosmetic belonging in a cupboard or medicine cabinet was strewn about.

Completely repulsed, and not wanting to touch anything, I continued down the hallway. My eyes burned like they had bleach in them. Bleach that the apartment desperately needed. Or a fire. I was going to need a shot of antibiotics when I got out of there. I made a mental note of it.

The bedroom door was open. The small bedroom was dark, the shades drawn to close out the already dark and rainy fifty-one degree day outside.

Ebb

The room was situated in such a way where you entered on the left side of the room, the bed and furnishings would have been feng shui'd to the right if the person occupying it cared about such things. The only furnishing in the room was a mattress without a box spring set onto the floor.

Roxy was on her back, on the bed, naked on top of the covers. It was cold outside and just as cold in the apartment. She was as pale blue-gray as the blanket that she laid on top of. The color of steamed bluefish. Her face turned away from the arm that had a needle sticking out of it.

I knew the answer before I had confirmed it, but I felt for a pulse on her neck anyway. She was dead and coming out of full rigor.

It had been in the fifties for more than a week, cold for this time of year but no freezing temperatures. Temperature affects rigor mortis, I didn't need the M.E. to tell me that. I also didn't need a Medical Examiner to tell me that she had been dead for at least twenty-four hours. Before her brother.

I didn't know if that was a blessing or not. But I mulled it over.

By the time the Medical Examiner and his team arrived, I had already gotten used to the smell. The team wrestled with the detectives who were assigned to the case about opening windows, spraying anything that would make the noxious smells more tolerable for the people who had to work in the apartment. The argument was based on whether the opening of windows or the addition of a fragrance or both would contaminate the crime scene. It should give you some idea of just how bad the smell in that place was. People who were accustomed to the smells of death were overpowered by that particular fetor.

Case assignments for Troop H are based upon case load and who is available. For lack of a better term, it is a macabre lottery. The fact that I knew the victim or that Hobbs and I had been originally assigned to the case involving her brother didn't even come up. If I was eliminated from investigating crimes involving people that I knew in the city, I wouldn't be investigating much.

Hobbs and I were full, so our names were not up on the board. When I called it in, two other detectives from Troop H were assigned.

It was a case worthy of assignment only because of my insistence. By all accounts, it looked like a junky-whore overdose. She had track marks old and new, she lived in squalor, had a history of prostitution and drug use. Everyone was busy, why investigate something that doesn't need investigating?

I didn't need a gut feeling to know that she wasn't likely to have overdosed prior to learning of her brother's murder. And there were a number of signs that I looked for, that were lacking. For example, where was her stash? Junkies have a stash-box with all of their paraphernalia and their drugs. None. So where did the needle and the drugs come from? Another thing that bothered me was why she was naked. It was very cold for this time of year and her heat had been turned off or shut off from what I could tell. Why get naked before juicing up?

Once the team started doing a prelim on Roxy, taking pictures and getting her ready for the move to the slab, the M.E. was starting to see things my way. Mark Bowman was the examiner who had been called out on the case.

Ebb

"Deni I thought you were crazy on this one. Another junkie death, why waste time and resources? But I think you might be right."

"Ain't I usually? What brought you over to my side of things?"

"First, experienced heroine users know how much to juice up. When you are completely addicted, you don't want to use it all up in one dose. You want enough to get high, but there is always the next fix. Where ODs tend to happen is when they are forced to quit then start back up, or take time off for some reason and then start back up at the dosage they used prior to quitting. The point is that there is almost always a downtime prior to an OD. They do a short bid in jail, rehab or they try to quit …. so they go back to the same dosage that they were using before they stopped using. The other explanation for an overdose is if they get a bad batch."

"So assuming she uses the same dealer, you're sayin' she was probably clean for a while and went back to it?"

"I didn't say that. I won't know for certain until we do a tox screen, but judging from the track marks and needle holes I would say that it is unlikely that she had a recent break. What makes it strange is that she used enough to kill a horse."

"Suicide? How can you tell?"

Ebb

"I can tell how much she used by the stains inside the syringe where the plunger drew in the fluid. Unless you can afford very good heroine, it usually leaves a coloration on the inside of the syringe."

"So suicide? You just said — "

" — unlikely. I know what I said. Again, experienced drug users know how to hit a vein. This one missed. She wasn't even close. There was enough in the syringe, I'm guessing, to do the trick without hitting one. If you wanted to off yourself you would make sure to hit a vein so you didn't wake up."

"Cry for help?"

"Possibly Deni. But added to the fact that you said her brother was killed in prison yesterday, and that he was possibly involved with the Winter Hills …. I tend to take your side in that she was murdered. At least helped along. I'll do a tox screen of course, but I'm guessing that what she was injected with was pretty horrible shit. Between the amount and the color of the juice …. "

"How long has she been dead, Mark? She's not stiff as a board anymore. I guessed at a day."

"Oh at least. I'll let you know for sure once she is on the table but I would say a day at a minimum. It takes three to four hours to start the chemical process, full rigor at twelve hours. The body gradually comes out of it, dissipating in another twenty-four hours. Give or take. Add it all up? I'd estimate it at about forty hours."

"So she was dead, probably killed, before her brother. Like I thought."

"I would say that it is a fact that she died before Memorial Day Weekend went into full swing. Saturday evening at the latest. When did her brother get killed?"

"Yesterday. Tough weekend for the McKennie clan," I said.

"I would say so."

"But why?"

"Not my department, Detective."

"Not mine either, I guess."

Ebb

Sinn, and other novels in the Warren Dennihan series by Scott Wellinger can be purchased wherever books are sold.

www.ingramcontent.com/pod-product-compliance
Lightning Source LLC
Chambersburg PA
CBHW071331020726
47502CB00001B/56